I've felt him.  Mendev, we feel him. He ha but all will reve are nothing to him. Those under his mantle pass through them like water through a grate. Mendev falls, you fool. Mendev falls. If I come back as a thousand demons, all one thousand of us shall rend your soul!"

Gad signals to the villagers. They unwrap the prisoner's ropes and tie his hands behind his back. They pull him onto a cart, beside his allies.

Gad and Tiberio walk away.

"You want me for a job?" says Tiberio.

"I wouldn't ask," says Gad, "except it's about this."

"Hmm," says Tiberio.

"So you're in, yes?"

"Where are you going?"

"Nerosyan. To find Calliard."

"I'll go with you that far. It's not safe for you to travel alone."

"I'll need you for longer than that."

"You remember why I stopped, Gad."

Behind them, Dobreliel shrieks incoherently. His voice is suddenly muffled. Tiberio glances back to see that a rag has been stuffed into his neighbor's mouth.

"You told him you were going to fool him into talking, and then he talked."

"That's how it works," says Gad.

"I don't understand. Why did he talk?"

"Because he wanted to. Because it's all he had left."

Behind them, the fletchers of Dubrov pull the cart away from the tree. The three cultists thrash in the air and then are still.

The Pathfinder Tales Library

The Worldwound Gambit

Robin D. Laws

paizo
PUBLISHING

Cover art by Daren Bader.
Cover design by Sarah Robinson.
Map by Robert Lazzaretti.

Paizo Publishing, LLC
7120 185th Ave NE, Ste 120
Redmond, WA 98052
paizo.com

ISBN 978-1-60125-327-9

Publisher's Cataloging-In-Publication Data
(Prepared by The Donohue Group, Inc.)

Laws, Robin D.
  Pathfinder tales. The Worldwound Gambit / Robin D. Laws.

  p. ; cm.

  Set in the world of the role-playing game, Pathfinder.
  ISBN: 978-1-60125-327-9

  1. Imaginary places--Fiction. 2. Imaginary wars and battles--Fiction. 3. Fantasy fiction. 4. Adventure stories. I. Title. II. Title: Worldwound Gambit III. Title: Pathfinder adventure path.

PS3612.A87 P38 2011
813/.6

First printing May 2011.

Printed in the United States of America.

To the Thursday nighters, past and present.

Chapter One
The Rip

I'll tell you the whole truth," Gad lies.

He chooses to ignore the distant sound of drums and fire. Distractions must be pushed to the periphery. His mark is too close to taking the hook. Soon Gad will have the tapestry.

He edges back calmly in the velvet-cushioned chair. A perfect ease settles upon him. When he was young, he practiced this attitude before a mirror, for hours uncountable. Now he assumes this confident repose without thought or effort. It is his natural state.

His hands rest comfortably on the table's polished oaken surface. The palms angle upward, signaling openness, inviting trust. Gad's head cocks slightly. The gesture builds imperceptible excitement. It allows Dalemir to share his anticipation. The two of them are not adversaries in a negotiation, but partners, each prospering from engagement with the other.

Gad is the sort of man who is always described by the same phrase, whether the speaker is an associate, a rival, or a sworn enemy. That phrase: *damnably handsome.*

Dark eyes shine beneath firm, expressive brows. His dark hair, severely cropped, is these days peppered with gray. A dusting of stubble, on the precipice of becoming a beard, softens his jawline's intimidating precision. The face is a marvel of geometry: grave in profile, welcoming when seen head-on. Simply by changing its position, he can make nearly anyone stop in mid-sentence, forgetting what they were about to say.

He always knows when to use this trick, and when it would cut against him.

Now, for example. His negotiating partner, Dalemir, teeters on the brink of persuasion. He wants to believe, but is afraid to. Gad must draw him toward his greed, and away from his fear.

Gad chose their meeting place to serve this purpose. Fresh varnish gleams from dark-stained walls. Thick ornamental pillars section the room, proclaiming its solidity. In the corner sits a delicate writing desk, its locks and pulls filigreed with golden wire. A cast-iron furnace, stacked with burning pinewood, heats the chill air. Its feet are clawed and scaled in imitation of a cockatrice. Beneath the woodsmoke lurks a whiff of sweet perfume.

A richly decorated room leads a man to think of money, and the benefits of its acquisition.

The luxurious objects of this room, like the tapestry the two men dicker over, all originate in some other place. Its wood panels, depicting brave, banner-waving knights in pitched battle against demons, were carved to order by woodworkers of Druma. Ceramic plates, bearing the bird and rose of the love goddess, Shelyn, show the unmistakable curvatures of Taldan potters. The velvet curtains, Gad reckons, were shipped in from Cheliax. A gossamer statue of stained glass held together by adamantine coils seems dug from the ruins of an ancient city, perhaps in the wild Mwangi lands.

This is not a country where fine things are made. Artisans thrive in safer places.

Gad rests his gaze on the precious objects, each in their turn. On cue, Dalemir does the same. Gad sees him mentally calculate the asking price and resale value of each. The important number is the spread between the two. Dalemir is already planning what he might do with the price of the tapestry. The merchant's bony fingers work an imaginary abacus.

Dalemir's skeletal frame contradicts his jowled, beefy head. He wears dark garb, cut in the bulky local style. Voluminous folds of cloak and tunic lend his shoulders an artificial breadth. The fur rim of his hard leather hat soaks up the sweat of his brow. Dyed patches in his carefully sculpted beard stand out in the room's waffling lantern light.

Gad's voice is clear and soft. "Fine pieces, aren't they?"

"You can see where the money flows in Krega," Dalemir jokes.

His insecurities must now be plucked, like the strings of a harp. Gad denies him the chuckle he seeks.

The merchant turns to his bodyguard. The massive figure stands at the doorway, a discreet distance from the negotiating men. His expression remains impassive, until he realizes that he is meant to smile. He obliges his master. His teeth are yellow and sharp.

Like the art objects, the bodyguard has been imported to Mendev from somewhere else. A turquoise turban encircles his square, bald head. Enormous muscles bulge beneath a loose silk tunic. At his hips swing twin scimitars, encased in scabbards of embroidered red leather. Tattooed on the back of his hand are nearly a dozen tiny skulls, each standing for a man slain single-handed.

Gad rises, moving to a dressing table. "This jade bowl, for example." He picks up a delicate piece of green stone. Held up to the light, it is nearly transparent. "Authentic Xa Hoi, would you say?"

Dalemir scuttles over to examine it. "I am far from expert in the works of the far lands. If forced to guess, I'd say Guo dynasty?"

Gad smashes the bowl against the wall. It flies to pieces. Plaster shards thunk across the carpeted floor. He stoops, picks up a fragment, and hands it to the merchant. "Not even jade. Cheap beglamered junk."

Dalemir turns the fragment over in his gnarled hand. "It looked like jade. It felt like jade."

"But it didn't ring like jade when struck. It's low magic, likely woven by a Sczarni charlatan or traveling gnome. It fools the eye and the hand, but not the ear."

The merchant lets the fragment drop suddenly to the table. "Fraud or not, surely the mistress of the house will not take kindly to your destroying her property."

A groan of passion echoes from elsewhere in the house. The town of Krega is a rude and shambolic place. This, its most splendid room, serves as office to a brothel-keeper. To rent it for the afternoon, Gad paid her, the operator of Krega's finest such establishment, three gold pieces and a mass of saffron as large as a thumb.

Gad smiles, tightly. "She's scarcely in a position to complain. She tried to sell it to me as authentic. Of course, she had no idea she'd been deceived."

"She should protest to the seller."

"He was a mercenary passing through on the way to the demon wars. He offered it up for services rendered. She doesn't expect to see him again."

Dalemir nods; the detail rings true. Krega acts as a way station for warriors on their way to battle. The Fourth Crusade grinds on. It brings men and women of fortune from all around the Inner Sea to demon-plagued Mendev. Those who arrive from the east stop at Chesed, in Numeria; or in the lawless port city of Egede. On their way to the front, they tramp west, through or around the Estrovian Forest. When they emerge from the forest, they find Krega waiting for them. It sells blades and shields and arrows. It feeds them, shelters them, and in places like this, pleasures them.

"A pity," says Dalemir, "that neither the mercenary nor the bawd thought to consult an expert in such goods, such as you or I. Though I admit to being momentarily fooled, I would not have been for long."

"Doubtlessly so, Dalemir."

"And obviously, if she had gone to you, Ellano, you'd certainly have caught it, as you did today."

Gad takes a deep breath. "Which leads us to an awkward subject."

"I do not like the sound of this. I slogged all the way from Nerosyan, and as my bodyguard here can attest, it is a journey that grows more perilous by the day. Why, last week alone, two convoys were set upon by demons. Creatures that were part horse, part scorpion. Bat-winged monstrosities descending from the sky. Things of shadow. Skeletal warriors cloaked in red and burning flesh."

"Let us dwell on more pleasant—"

"Those who fought and those who ran were slaughtered in equal measure. Never have the demon hordes penetrated so far past the wardstones, which are supposed to keep them in the Worldwound! Your letter assured me that you were ready to purchase. I would not have risked such a valuable item if I thought you a vacillator! To hear now of awkwardness, Ellano . . ."

"Rest assured, I am as willing to pay as ever," Gad says. "But I need not tell you that this latest crusade has summoned more than paladins, heroes, and holy men."

Dalemir removes his furred hat and wipes sweat from his brow. "Too true. Nerosyan is awash in seekers after blood and loot. Mercenaries, mountebanks, and main-chancers. To gain admittance to the fortress, they need do no more than swear they're here to fight demons. An honest merchant is as likely to be accosted by mortal malefactors as by the spawn of the Abyss."

A metallic clamor arises from somewhere to the west of the brothel. It is early in the day for a drunken street fight, but Gad decides that this is what he must be hearing.

He has allowed a pause to linger. Gad covers the lapse with a brooding nod, as if moved to deep contemplation by the merchant's wisdom. "A lamentable state of affairs. And with them, these scoundrels have brought a wave of fake antiquities. I can't tell you how many of these plaster jades I've seen in the last year. And if I had a silver for every supposed Azlanti brooch I've been offered . . ."

"Lice-ridden adventure-seekers think every corroded coil of copper they find in a goblin warren must be the legacy of lost Azlant."

"I'm glad you understand, then," says Gad.

"Understand what?"

"My client's need for assurances of authenticity."

"Assurances? My name is my assurance!"

"Yet we all slip." Gad crunches a piece of the fake jade beneath his heel. "You thought this bowl was Guo dynasty. Last month I mistook a replica for a forty-first-century Ulfen helmet."

"Let me know the name of your client and I'll personally . . ."

"We mustn't insult each other, Dalemir."

"This is most outrageous!"

"Yes, and I'm prepared to pay an inconvenience fee. I must preserve my client's trust in me."

"How significant a fee?"

"Three percent."

"Six."

"Four."

"Five."

"Four."

"I must know the nature of the inconvenience before we fix a price on it."

"The sage Hieron has returned to Egede."

"That pedant?"

"A pedant indeed, and the closest we come to an expert in Kibwean tapestries."

"I heard he was dead."

Shouts chorus from perhaps half a mile off. Puzzlement registers on the merchant's face. The bodyguard grows still.

Gad plunges on: "I am reliably informed to the contrary. We take the tapestry to him, I pay his expenses, and the price of your journey—"

"My journey? I think not. With demons running amok, I'm going back to the fortress and staying put."

"Then I'll take on the risk and go myself."

"With my tapestry? Not without payment in full!"

"A ten percent deposit."

"Not without payment in full!"

Gad shakes his head. "This is awkward. I suppose you have another buyer."

"You know I've been sitting on this for six years, ever since I was foolish enough to . . . How can I be assured of its safety?"

A shrug. "I'll hire guards."

"Guards? Who these days is reduced to guard work in Mendev? Anyone the fortresses won't take! The ones you can afford are either infirm or congenitally criminal. I won't have it."

"You mean you don't trust me."

"To be frank, Ellano, no."

"You wound me, Dalemir."

"We haven't done business before. You talk convincingly—perhaps too much so. How can I know you're not one of the mountebanks you decry?"

"I bleed, Dalemir. Wait, this bodyguard of yours . . ."

"Abotur?"

The turbaned man brings himself to attention.

"Do you trust him?"

Dalemir regards his hireling with uncertainty, as if reluctant to offend him. "He's worked for me for a year. Saved me from fire demons, and from some buzzing insect things. Of course I trust him."

"Then send him to guard me as I take the tapestry to the sage in Egede. This fellow of yours looks like he'll chop my head off if I so much as look at the merchandise wrong."

Abotur curls his lip. The prospect seems appealing to him.

"I am loath to return to Nerosyan without him."

"Then wait here in Krega."

Girlish laughter titters through brothel walls.

"The mistress owes me, Dalemir," Gad continues. "Your stay could be . . . revivifying."

"I do owe myself a rest," Dalemir muses.

"Then our awkwardness is at an end." Gad removes a pair of goblets from a shelf and takes the stopper from a brandy decanter. "Soon we'll all heft full purses."

"Wait, the inconvenience fee—five percent."

"The word on you is correct, Dalemir. You bargain tenaciously." Gad places a goblet in Dalemir's hand.

"As do you, Ellano." Dalemir toasts him. "To mutual enrichment."

The room shakes. Its wooden walls bow inward. They vibrate.

Something has hit the side of the building.

Sandy dust sifts down from the rafters. Ceramic plates fall from the walls and shatter. A buzzing whine pierces the room's inhabitants. It feels like it's coming from inside their heads.

Dalemir wobbles backward. He trips over a chair and bumps his head on a pillar. The sound makes him bleed. Red rivulets seep from his ears and both sides of his mouth. A second thump rocks the building, this time from the roof.

Gad drops to his knees. He crawls toward a closed window. The room heats up.

The bodyguard has pressed himself against the wall, next to the doorway. He grips his scimitar.

Dalemir drops to the quaking floorboards. "Help me!" he cries.

The bodyguard stays where he is.

Gad reaches the window, throws open its shutters. He edges his head up, just past the sill.

Demons attack the town. They fly on wings of shadow, of batlike skin and muscle, of veiny film. They swoop and grab and gnaw. There are dozens of them. Gad has seen demons before, but never so many, or so many types at once.

A red-fleshed demon hovers over the stables. Its horned dragon wings buffet down fleeing townsfolk. Its whip of flame tongues down at them, burning through clothing, searing muscle, severing bone.

A batlike creature, its furred body shaped like a man's, descends on an armored, sword-swinging warrior. It twists the man's head around. A cacophony of screams drowns out the crack of the snapping neck, but Gad thinks he hears it all the same. The dead man's head stares out between chainmailed shoulders. The bat-demon seizes it in long, clawed fingers. Jerking, pulsing animation returns to the murdered warrior's body. He is instantly transfigured. His eyes shrink to red, glowing dots. A gray-blue coloration suffuses his flesh, as if he's been stained by ink from the inside out. He throws off his helmet to make room for sharpened, elongated ears. Hands become claws. With shocking power, the dead man bounds into a blacksmith's shop. He grabs a young blond apprentice, pulling his neck to his mouth. The gums sprout rows of sharpened teeth. They rake into the boy's throat, ripping it into a red, coursing pulp. Blood gouts across the dead man's once-glittering chainmail. His ghoulish corpse keens with primal joy.

A demon with the body of a maggot, the wings of a fly, and the face of a hag spits green bile onto a wagon where half a dozen townsmen tremble. Their flesh liquefies and drains from their bones.

Mantis demons land in the market square, impaling trapped vendors with hooked appendages.

A tornado of shadow beheads a servant girl as she dashes from a tavern. More of the shadow things are inside the mead hall already.

A bald, tattooed wizard hurls projectiles of arcane force at a fly-demon. A beetle-demon lands behind him and wreathes him in devouring flame.

Gad tears himself from the window, involuntary tears rushing down his cheeks. He's thinking. Does the brothel have a cellar? Would a cellar be safe?

A third thump. Flaming shards of wood spray down into the room. A burning beetle-creature with innumerable eyes pokes its head through a gaping hole in the roof. It clicks its mandibles at them.

Deeper in the brothel, the girls sob and wail. Drawn by their fear, the beetle-thing hops down into the room. The bodyguard, Abotur, tries to bar its way. With a segmented, insectoid leg the demon reaches for a smoking chunk of rafter, splintered to a sharp point. Abotur brings a scimitar fruitlessly down on its bubbling carapace.

The demon widens its mandibles. An unlikely voice gurgles from deep in its throat. "Yath!" it exults. "Yath is!" It aims the tip of the rafter shard at Abotur's breastbone. Abotur turns and ducks forward. The demon misses his heart. The shard punctures his abdomen instead. Ribs crack. Viscera spills. The demon leaves Abotur pinned to the wall and tears the doorway open as if parting a curtain. In a blink, the hole is large enough to drag its bulk through. The demon plunges on, attracted by the terror of the defenseless prostitutes.

Abotur's skin pales as blood gushes from his wound. "Help me," he says.

Gad bolts from his crouch to Abotur's side. He helplessly regards the impaling chunk of rafter.

"Gad," Abotur says, "I'm sorry. I never thought—"

Dalemir squirms on the floor. Damp patches on his crotch and an acrid smell show that he has soiled himself. He reddens with indignation. Anger revives him. "Gad? Why do you call him Gad?"

"Shut up," hisses Gad. "Before you bring it back."

A wet crunching sound issues from the brothel's front parlor.

Dalemir shakes. He speaks in a whispering hiss. "Your name is Ellano. Why does he call you Gad?"

Gad gives Dalemir his back. He turns to Abotur. "Hang on, now. We'll get you healed."

Abotur pats his hand. "Thank you for lying to me, Gad."

Gad wrenches away. "That wasn't a lie." He seizes his pack.

Dalemir stands at the shattered doorway, perched ridiculously on one foot, looking for the demon. Crunching has given way to silence.

From his pack, Gad seizes a clay bottle. He pops off the cork that stoppers it shut. "Healing potion," he tells Abotur.

The bodyguard's skin is now nearly white as salt. "Not enough," he gasps.

Gad pours the liquid into the man's mouth. It is amber-colored, the consistency of molasses. Gad holds his lips open. Abotur chokes as the potion goes in.

The potion's magic courses through Abotur's frame. It finds the wound. The torn flesh around the impaling chunk of rafter sizzles.

Mortal voices explode into the parlor. Spells singe the air. Swords clatter against demonic hides and carapaces. The town's crusaders have rallied to mount a rescue.

"Hear that?" Gad tells Abotur. "Just hang on."

Abotur's skin tries to heal itself around the charcoaled wood. A fresh spatter of blood slicks the floor.

"I hope you both die," Dalemir hisses. "You were trying to cheat me."

"Shut up," says Gad.

Dalemir's resentment overcomes his caution. He jabs a pointy digit at his bodyguard. "And you, Abotur, if that's the name your mother gave you."

Abotur's eyes flutter shut. Gad hits his cheek with a series of rapid taps. Abotur blinks.

"You spent a year at my side," Dalemir exclaims. "A year to win my trust. All so this man could steal my tapestry!"

"It is a very valuable tapestry," says Gad.

A smile flickers on Abotur's lips. His head slumps down. Gad tests his carotid for a pulse. Abotur is dead.

Dalemir draws a dagger from his belt. "Scoundrel! Mountebank!" He advances on Gad.

"Bad idea," Gad says.

The merchant stops to think.

The interior wall vanishes in a cloud of flame. Gad tumbles back into the room. The building teeters. On the other side of the hole, bloodied knights and clerics square off against the beetle-demon. Gad can't tell whether the wall was destroyed by the Abyss-spawn or by the crusaders. It doesn't matter. It was a load-bearing wall. The remaining rafters creak and shift.

The roof implodes. Gad dives through tumbling timbers. Struck on the shoulder, he falls. He gets up. Not hurting yet, but he will soon. Dust obscures his vision. Blindly, he stumbles on. He stops short; the flooring has come to an end.

He's standing on the street outside the ruined pleasure house. Smoke and dust rise from its remains. Crusaders struggle out from beneath shingles and boards. The beetle-demon is either slain or playing dead.

Gad sees without seeing: a retreating bat-demon carrying a lithe, elven arm in its talons. An old man's face, lying in the road, torn from the skull. Crusaders dispatching a pink-skinned demon, entirely human-seeming save for its translucent wings and compound eyes. Eggs hatching from the corpse of a centipede-thing, becoming a swarm of baby demons. Rushing for the forest's edge.

Dalemir sprints to his cart. In a stupid and arbitrary miracle, his horse survives. It has escaped the ravaged stables and waits by the cart. From the back of the cart protrudes the tapestry, wrapped in protective muslin.

Even now, Gad thinks of ways to get the tapestry. He hurts too much to simply overpower Dalemir. There's no talking him out of the tapestry, not now. He could claim that they already switched it for a fake, but there's no logic to back it up.

The value of the tapestry, if taken and sold in Cheliax, rattles through Gad's mind as the merchant climbs into his cart to ride away.

He can still get it. Dalemir will return to Nerosyan. Gad is blown, but he can recruit help. Dalemir won't trust anyone who wants the tapestry. That can be the key to it: Use that against him. A double game. Have one team transparently trying to steal the tapestry . . . yes, yes, let Dalemir discover that Gad is in Nerosyan and still wants it. Then send in a second team to offer to protect it from him. A fictitious group with a fictitious grudge. Then the protectors steal the tapestry.

Gad flashes through the entire rip. Whom he'll recruit. The equipment they'll need. The timetable. He can still have the tapestry. To move on to another scheme would be to dishonor Abotur's memory. Yes. He'll do it for Abotur.

Smoke, black as crow feathers, plumes from the burning stable. The dragon-winged demon bearing a whip of flame emerges from it. The monstrosity hurtles through the sky, lashing at a formation of victorious crusaders gathered in the market square. They scatter. A knight in scorched plate armor collapses to her knees, her backplate sliced and smoking. The demon turns, dragging its flamewhip across the remaining unscathed structures. Wood shingles spark and ignite. As it dives up into the sky, it makes one last fillip with the whip. The weapon burns through the cart, the tapestry, the horse, and Dalemir. Flames consume the cart and tapestry. Dalemir's bisected gut sputters. His fat is cooking.

Gad zigzags backward, looking for cover. There is none; Krega burns. He does not expect a renewed attack but leaves town anyway. His horse is dead, and so is Abotur's.

So he walks.

Chapter Two
The Muscle

Gad wanders alone through muddy scrubland. His shoulder throbs. Soon he'll need water. And food. For the moment, he has to think. He will assemble a different team. Not the team he'd have needed to separate Dalemir from his tapestry. This will be for a bigger gambit.

He is two miles from Krega when it occurs to him that he should have done something about Abotur's body. He stops and sits on a rock for a while. In the end he convinces himself not to head back. When his own corpse breathes its last, Gad expects no fuss made. Life is for living. The body is meat. Many in his line of work feel this way. He never talked about it with Abotur. It is not a fit subject of conversation. All thieves court death; to dwell on it is to invite it.

Abotur wouldn't want him to tarry over his corpse, Gad decides. He would want him to act. To take something from the demons they'll always miss.

Gad gets up off the rock and resumes his walk. His first stop will be Dubrov. He has already revised his list. Each rip demands its own roster.

Nothing matters now except these demons. They're bad for business. Gad loves Mendev—it is, as Dalemir said, a haven for scoundrels. As a scoundrel, Gad values this. Demons can't be allowed to overrun the place. They're worse even than lawmen. A lawman you can talk to, trick, inveigle. All demons want is to corrupt and destroy. They place no value on money, on wit or style or pleasure itself, except for the sadistic thrills of torture and killing. They don't deserve a place in this honeyed land.

Gad is no expert on demons. As day turns to night and the night turns colder, he struggles to recall the history of the Worldwound. In history you find the rules. Before a man can break them properly, he has to learn what they are.

Like everything these days, it all goes back to that one moment a hundred years ago. In a distant land, a god named Aroden died. Aroden was once a man, and then became immortal, but that's a story for preachers and saints, and of no import to the gaffle.

When Aroden died, a wound in the world opened. The earth suppurated, and a piece of the Abyss seeped in. That happened in the nation next door to Mendev, a nation that doesn't exist anymore, because the demonlands came through and ate it. (Gad doesn't remember the name of the nation, but he'll find someone who does, in case it matters. Iobaria, maybe? No, that's not quite it.) A black crack in the earth became a crevice, became a sinkhole, became a canyon. Not just a canyon, but a gateway to the Abyss. A portal giving demons free rein to pour into this world. They reduced the kingdom of Whatever to ruins, then came for the lands it bordered. They came for Mendev.

Crusaders signed up from all over to fight them. So many great heroes flocked here that the rest of the world suffered a shortage of them. In their absence, empires fell. It doesn't matter, because if the demons get a foothold the whole world is lost.

At some point the crusaders figured out how to keep the demons out. Gad can't recall when that happened. Should it become relevant, he'll find someone who can tell him the dates of all four crusades. He has a name already in mind.

Gad shivers. Night has fully fallen, but the stars are bright, so he keeps walking and running through the facts as he knows them. A few flakes of snow filter from the sky. They sting his cheeks and remind him he's thirsty. He hears a stream and heads toward it.

At the stream the sounds change, introducing a clanking noise he doesn't like. He melts behind a rocky outcrop and waits. The clanking draws closer. There's a softer sound, of whimpering. An inhuman voice chills his marrow, and Gad freezes.

Down where he filled his waterskin, he sees a spindly figure dragging a prisoner on a chain. He guesses that the former is six feet tall, but so thin that it's hard to see when it stands sideways. It's difficult to tell by starlight, but its flesh seems to be red, like it's coated in blood. On a closer look, the liquid covering its body is a slime of some sort. Droplets of it fall onto the rocks of the shoreline, where they steam and hiss. The creature's head is disproportionately large, a detail emphasized by its pointed ears. Its left hand holds the chain. The right carries a polearm, topped by a massive, serrated blade.

Its voice sounds like bones breaking. "You want to drink?" it asks its prisoner.

The woman shakes her head. She is perhaps thirty years old. Her face is bruised, hair tangled. Her dirtied peasant gown falls in shreds from her battered body. Mucus trails from her nostrils.

"You want to live, don't you?" asks the demon. It caresses her cheek with the backs of its clawed fingers. The corrosive slime burns a welt into her face.

Gad considers his short sword. He's a talker first and a fighter second. He's exhausted and sore. On his best day, he wouldn't tackle this thing alone.

The woman shakes her head.

"You don't want to live?" the demon asks.

Again, she shakes her head.

Gad sees that three of her fingers are missing. He wonders what else the demon has done to her.

The demon stoops to place its eyes inches from hers. "All you mortals want to live. Hurting you reminds you how badly you want to survive. Doesn't it?"

Gad recognizes the technique. When you're running a game on someone, you make a statement and button a question on the end of it. You keep asking until they agree to something. Get them to agree to something, and soon they'll be agreeing to everything.

Ashamed, the woman tightly nods.

"Are you saying yes?" the demon asks. "Are you saying you want to survive?" It lets its acid slime drip onto the bare skin beneath her torn garment. The pain sends her reeling back. With a clattering yank the demon tightens the leash.

"Yes," the woman gasps.

"Say it louder."

"Yes."

Gad can't stand to watch. He surveys the terrain, judges his chance of slinking away without the demon catching his scent. It is distracted. He calculates his odds at seventy-thirty, in his favor.

He can't do it. Lacking power to interfere, he must at least bear witness.

"Then you will serve us," the demon says. "You will prostrate yourself before the demon gods. Through the power of Yath, the gateway and the tower, you grant your soul to our lords, as fair exchange for your survival."

"Don't hurt me any more."

"Agree to serve."

It's useless to think it, but Gad can't help imagining what he'd do if he had a team here. A pair of snipers, one at his position, one prone in that stand of dead weeds opposite. Closer in, heavily armored muscle to intercept the demon when he tries to close. Two would be better, but one would do. A runner, to grab the hostage and sweep her away. If needed, he'd stick his own neck out, distract the demon with a counterproposal while they assume their positions.

The demon thrusts out its crimson, slimy paw. "Kiss it," it demands.

The woman falters. Slime droplets scar the rocks below the demon's feet.

"Kiss it!" repeats the demon.

She brushes her lips against the back of the demon's hand. Her skin becomes momentarily translucent as inky darkness rushes through her briefly visible veins and arteries. A cicatrix rises on her forehead: within a ragged circle appears the image of an undulating, segmented tower. It fumes and roasts, then fades. Along with it go the other symptoms of the demon kiss: the transparent skin, the inky blood vessels. The burn on her face melts away. New skin crawls across the raw, infected stumps of her severed fingers, sealing itself tight. The prisoner clutches her stomach and curls into a ball.

"You will be ill at first," the demon says. "You'll puke out your love, your fear of disapproval, your concern for others. All that makes you weak. Let the writhing truth of chaos enter you fully. Draw strength from it." Using a blackened fingernail as a key, it unlocks the metal collar. It wraps the chain around its chest and shoulders, like a bandolier. With a sudden lunge it leaps across the stream.

The woman convulses. "That's it? You're letting me go?"

A laugh oozes from the demon's cadaverous lips. "Hardly. A tighter chain now binds you. Return to your village. Wait until Yath requires you."

"Requires me? For what?"

"You will know Yath's voice as a buzzing in your head."

The demon bounds away and within instants is out of sight. Vomit sprays from the woman's mouth.

Gad could, as she shudders helplessly a few yards away from him, draw his dagger, step quietly behind her, and slit her throat.

He moves toward her. "I saw what happened," he says.

"Who are you?" she asks, eyes still panicked.

"A traveler."

"Are you going to help me?"

"All I can do is tell you something you need to know. The demon conned you."

She throws up.

He waits until it stops. "The demon conned you," he repeats. "The agreement is not enforceable."

"What? Who are you?"

"Someone who knows a little about contracts. And trickery. He told you he's taken your soul, but he hasn't yet. Do you understand?"

"No."

"It's cosmic law. I'm neither priest nor magician, but I know that much. Your soul isn't his until you make a choice."

"A choice?"

"To do something for them. Until you do evil."

"If I don't do what they want, they'll come for me."

"Maybe they will, maybe they won't."

"And if they come for me . . ." She stops to retch. "They'll destroy me."

"They're demons. Your choice might be between being destroyed, and destroying others. Many others."

She waits for him to say more. "Is that all you have to say?"

"What's your name?"

"Vasilissa."

"Vasilissa, I'm Gad. I don't know you. I've only seen you for a few moments. The worst of your life, is that safe to say?" He is using the technique.

"Yes."

"Yet still I see strength in you," he says. It could be true. She might be strong; she might be weak. He has no idea. "When you hear that voice in your head, use your strength. You can do it. You can still choose rightly."

She spits out a glob of puke and phlegm. "Is that all you're going to do?"

The words catch in his throat. "I have urgent business elsewhere."

"Words. All you have for me are words."

"Words are everything, Vasilissa."

He leaves her, trying not to hear as she calls after him. Dawn throws a diffuse and tentative light along the eastern horizon. His head races from lack of sleep. He tries to remember where he was in his thinking, before the demon and Vasilissa.

Oh yes: the wardstones. The crusaders erected wardstones. Magical obelisks that stand along the borders. Priests must maintain them, and paladins must defend them from demon attack. But the wardstones repel the worst of the demons, or did until recently.

Gad can't stop the demons entirely. He can't seal up the wound in the earth from which they issue. But demons shouldn't be able to get as far as Krega. They should be stuck at the western border, sealed in by the wardstones.

They've found a way to break the rules. They're running a rip. They're gaffling the whole of Mendev, and possibly the cosmos itself. And if it's a con, maybe Gad can stop it.

Whatever they've found that lets them do it, Gad will take it away from them.

One day and about ten leagues later, Gad stumbles toward the village of Dubrov. He has slept and eaten. His food and shelter he has earned almost honestly. The shoulder hurts less, but he favors his right leg now. The left ankle is twisted. It happened when he scuttled for cover as a loathsome dragonfly-thing winged overhead.

Dubrov, like Krega to the south, hugs the western edge of the Estrovian Forest. It is home to the people who make what Mendev uses up. They fletch arrows, carve bows, spin bowstrings. It is a place for half-breeds. Legend says it was founded by warrior half-brothers who shared a human mother. One was half orc, the other half elf. Gad considers the legend improbable but likes it all the same.

He moves through the stubble of a hemp field. When spring comes, it will be planted again. Gad watches the sky for more flying demons. As the cottages of Dubrov come into view, part of him expects to see them ablaze. They stand undisturbed, their thatched roofs touched by stray flakes of snow, their plaster walls straight and true.

Ahead, a perturbed crowd murmurs, gathered outside a cottage near the heart of the village. Nearby towers an ancient oak, like a legate from the nearby forest. Its long arm reaches over the village. A rope hangs from it. At its end swings a noose.

Gad hastens his step.

He guesses the crowd at fifty people strong, give or take. More are coming, drifting from cottages and the woodlands' edge. Soon all the adults in Dubrov will be here. The village mongrels pant and huff, pressing between legs for a better view. Its cats circle warily around.

"Beneath the most patient exterior," declaims a grating voice, "the worst corruption can lie!"

"This is nonsense!" booms another.

The grating voice wavers as it fights to deepen its tone: "And one who argues for a cultist might also be one."

Gad approaches the crowd's outer ring. He scans in search of a half-lovely young thing. His choice is blonde, buxom, and flat-nosed. Her orc blood shows only a little, in the depth of her brow and a greenish undertone in her complexion. Gad graces her with his full smile. When she blushes, the last vestiges of green disappear. She turns aside, letting him shoulder past her into the middle of the crowd.

Eight men have taken a prisoner. All nine wear the rustic garb of village peasants: linen tunics and dyed black trousers. Piped up each leg is Dubrov's distinctive white embroidery pattern, a series of stylized arrowheads. From these markings Gad sees that accused and accusers are all locals.

The prisoner stands two heads taller than anyone else. He is wide of shoulder and thick of neck. Knob-knuckled fists hang like twin boulders at his side. He favors his orc parent, with leathery skin the color of a drying oak leaf. Two canine tusks protrude from his lower row of teeth. The face is bottom-heavy, leading from a massive jaw to an almost conical cranium. A coarse topknot, held in place by a ropy band of hemp, emphasizes his skull's triangularity. He would seem fearsome, were it not for his placid eyes. The men around him hold pitchforks, spades, and a rusty short sword. The prisoner shrinks from them, though not out of fear. It is the captors, or some of them, who betray their fear. The captive's heavy shoulders slump in sorrow.

"Tiberio," Gad says.

The prisoner turns, his posture straightening. "Gad!"

The men who have captured him are mostly part elf. The shortest of them, a balding man whose pointed ears do not quite match, turns his pitchfork toward the new arrival. "Hold it," he says. "Who might you be?" The grating voice is his.

Gad grins. "Let's not point sharp things at one another."

"Identify yourself!"

"Name's Gad. An old friend of Tiberio's. Merely passing through. And you might be . . . ?"

"I am a native son of this village and need not give my name to strangers."

Gad bows. "In the past, I have known Dubrov as a hospitable place. What hardens your heart, my friend?"

"Corruption besets us. We are gnawed from within, by demonic influence."

"It looks tranquil enough." Gad pulls down his cloak and tunic to show off his purpled shoulder. "I got this in Krega. Demons boiled from the sky. Swarmed everywhere. I was lucky. Many lives were cruelly ended."

The inquisitorial villager loses the crowd's attention as the news passes through the crowd. A woman taps Gad's clothed shoulder.

"Krega, you say?"

Gad nods.

The woman is gray and worn, her face wrinkled like a chestnut. "I have a son there. Richza the barrel maker. He wasn't . . ."

"I hope not. I don't know your son, but saw no harm come to a cooper." From a sidelong glance, Gad sees Grating Voice's anger grow. "What is your name?" he asks the old mother.

"Izmaragd," she answers.

He manages to pronounce it: "Izmaragd, introduce me to this gentleman here." He indicates Grating Voice.

"Why, this is Dobreliel." Wrinkles appear over her wrinkles. "He is throwing accusations around, again."

"And he is your priest?"

"No, he is our finest fletcher."

Dobreliel steps forward to seize the attention of his neighbors. "Are you all such mooncalves that you cannot acknowledge the danger we face? As this stranger says, demonkind grows ever closer to our door!"

"It's true," says Gad.

Dobreliel, thrown off, turns his way.

"I saw a winged demon with a whip of flame fell an entire squad of crusaders." Gad adopts the rising cadences of a preacher. "Half of Krega he consigned to flames. Yet we must also be alert to subtler forms of demonic attack. Isn't that so, Dobreliel?"

"Ah," says Dobreliel. "Y-yes. We must."

"And you say my friend Tiberio has turned to demon worship?"

"Yes! He was seen taking instructions from a night-black cat!"

Gad plucks the pitchfork from Dobreliel's startled grasp and rounds on Tiberio. "Tiberio! How could you?"

"I didn't!" Tiberio protests.

The tines of Gad's newly acquired pitchfork jab at Tiberio's wide chest. The half-orc's face crumples. "When I knew you, Tiberio, you were the bravest, most selfless fellow I could name!"

A white-braided half-orc matron protests from the crowd. "He still is!"

Gad ignores her. "You retired from the freebooter's life because you could stand to do no man injury!"

Another voice, from the back: "So he did!"

"And if demons came to Dubrov, I would expect you to be the first to fight them! Yet Dobreliel here says you're now in league with them."

Tiberio drops his voice. "You can't believe him," he pleads.

"This is Mendev," Gad barks. "There is no charge more serious than demon worship. Would Dobreliel dare make it with only a third-hand rumor that you spoke to a cat?"

Dobreliel makes a futile reach for his pitchfork. "It is no third-hand rumor. Spiridion saw and heard it himself." He indicates the oldest of his half-elf confederates.

"Anyone who owns a pet speaks to it from time to time. Surely you amassed more evidence before hoisting the noose."

"Milk curdles when he passes. He was the last to speak to young Miakusha before her baby died inside of her. From the woods, dark things cry his name."

"And which of you has seen these dark things?"

Dobreliel's head swivels as he regards his allies. "Among others, I have."

"Now this is evidence!" Gad thumps the pitchfork's haft against the ground. "Seal this wretched traitor's fate. Tell us what the dark things said."

Dobreliel stops short. "Wait . . ."

"Tell us what they said, Dobreliel. I'll be the first to pitch stones at his swinging corpse."

"Who are you again?"

"You heard the dark things speak."

"You're trying to fool these people."

"Tell us what the dark things said, Dobreliel."

He swallows. "Of course I will! I am not afraid to damn a demon worshiper. They cried in a strange tongue."

"What did they look like?"

"They were creatures of shadow, swirls within swirls, darkness made manifest."

"And what did they say?"

"They said, *Tiberio, come hither, I command you in the name of Yath!*"

"Yath?" says Gad. He lets his jaw drop. "Oh, Dobreliel." He takes a step backward. "I don't think you were supposed to utter that name. The mark of Yath has appeared on you."

Dobreliel's hand flies to his forehead, patting it for the raised mark, for the circle and the writhing tower.

"You're the cultist, Dobreliel," says Gad.

Dobreliel continues to pat his forehead. "There's nothing there. There's no mark!"

"Oh, I was lying about that part. But you gave yourself away, because you know where the mark of Yath appears."

He points to Tiberio. "I know it because I saw it on him!"

"No, you didn't," says Gad, hefting the pitchfork. "Because that would have been your best accusation, and you would have used it first if you'd thought of it. Which leaves us with the question of how an ordinary fletcher knows exactly where the mark of Yath appears."

Sensing a brewing fight, the ringing villagers back up. Their movement creates a break in the crowd, behind Dobreliel. He turns and runs for the gap.

Gad clucks his tongue. "Amateur."

A pair of Dobreliel's allies, including Spiridion, the accuser with the cat story, dash to follow him. The others turn on the accuser and his self-revealed confederates. The fletchers of Dubrov close ranks. Fists and feet fly. Soon the cultists lie on the ground, their heads tucked under their bodies. They whimper for mercy.

Near the oak tree, village women tie two more nooses.

"Before he dangles," says Gad, "I need to interrogate him."

The villagers manhandle Dobreliel. He squirms and bucks. With effort they tie him to the trunk of the hanging oak.

Gad claps Tiberio on the shoulder. To do it, he has to reach up.

The half-orc clears his throat. "You didn't truly think me a demon-kisser, did you, Gad?"

"You have to ask?"

"Well . . ."

"You've been out of the game too long."

"Was it also untrue that you're here by chance?"

"I refer you to my previous statement."

A villager has climbed into the oak. His fellows toss him the additional nooses.

Tiberio frowns. "They don't deserve to die, do they?"

"They were planning to betray your whole village. Starting with you."

"We caught them before they did anything."

Gad shrugs. "This is war. You should have seen Krega. What happened to the girl who miscarried?"

"She sickened and died."

"You understand that they might have done that to her, so they could frame you?"

Sorrow sinks into Tiberio's brutish face.

Gad strolls over to Dobreliel. "It's cruel to give advice to a man who'll get no chance to use it," he begins, "but you shouldn't have run, you idiot. I didn't have you yet. I would have gotten you, but I hadn't yet."

The prisoner spits. Gad sees it coming and ducks. The wind catches the sputum and blows it back onto Spiridion.

"Why are we talking?" says Dobreliel. "If you're going to hang me, hang me."

"I'm not going to hang you, you country moron. Your neighbors are. The neighbors you were going to feed to the demons. What did they offer you? Your miserable life?"

"I won't help you. I won't let you bait me."

"Yes, you will, you squawking gull, because you low-rung cultists are all the same. What did you think you were going to get out of this? You thought you'd get to lick the toes of some six-teated demon bitch for all eternity? Do you know what happens to dead souls once they reach the Abyss? They get mulched up like grass in the gut of a cow. Divided into a thousand squirming larvae, each one a building block for a separate demon. Not a jot of your selfhood survives. You become even more insignificant than you are now."

"Not me!" Dobreliel proclaims.

"You're different than all the rest," says Gad.

"Yes. Yes. When you kill me, you realize my destiny! I become a demon lord!"

Gad snorts. "You believe that?"

"I know it! From the source! From the very voice of Yath!"

"Trust me, I know a lie when I hear it. There is no Yath."

Dobreliel lets out a high-pitched half-giggle. "There is, there is. I heard him in my head."

"Mere insanity on your part."

"No, no, the Shimmering Putrescence, I've felt him. The Gate and the Tower. All across Mendev, we who are destined for Abyssal majesty feel him. He has come. None knew his name before, but all will reverberate to it ere long. The wardstones are nothing to him. Those under his mantle pass through them like water through a grate. Mendev falls, you fool. Mendev falls. If I come back as a thousand demons, all one thousand of us shall rend your soul!"

Gad signals to the villagers. They unwrap the prisoner's ropes and tie his hands behind his back. They pull him onto a cart, beside his allies.

Gad and Tiberio walk away.

"You want me for a job?" says Tiberio.

"I wouldn't ask," says Gad, "except it's about this."

"Hmm," says Tiberio.

"So you're in, yes?"

"Where are you going?"

"Nerosyan. To find Calliard."

"I'll go with you that far. It's not safe for you to travel alone."

"I'll need you for longer than that."

"You remember why I stopped, Gad."

Behind them, Dobreliel shrieks incoherently. His voice is suddenly muffled. Tiberio glances back to see that a rag has been stuffed into his neighbor's mouth.

"You told him you were going to fool him into talking, and then he talked."

"That's how it works," says Gad.

"I don't understand. Why did he talk?"

"Because he wanted to. Because it's all he had left."

Behind them, the fletchers of Dubrov pull the cart away from the tree. The three cultists thrash in the air and then are still.

Chapter Three
The Bard

They travel on foot to the fortress-city. On the journey's second day, they compare the meager contents of their purses and consider buying a worn-out draft horse for Tiberio and a mule for Gad. Then along a distant ridge they see flying demons swarm to attack a pair of riders. They'll be harder to spot if they stick to boot power, they decide.

On the last day of their journey they reach the Egelsee River. Charred planks, the remains of a ruined barge, drift across its cold blue surface. A barge-poler's bloated corpse bumps against the river bank. The current finds it and carries it off again toward the west. Below the waterline, pikefish nibble whitened nuggets of flesh from a second body, trapped in the submerged branches of a fallen tree.

"This is what we face, Tiberio."

"I don't hurt people anymore, Gad." The half-orc breaks his gaze from the gruesome sight, loping ahead on long, trunk-thick legs.

Gad struggles to match his pace. "We'll be up against demons, not people."

"There are always people, too."

"Sure. The ones who've thrown in with the Abyss."

"Maybe they deserve to be hurt. But I'm not the one to do it."

"Many more people—innocent people—will be hurt if this new onslaught keeps up."

Tiberio grunts.

Gad presses onward. "Isn't it selfish, when you think about it?"

"What?"

"Letting others die, for your clean conscience?"

"It isn't up to me."

"What if it is?"

Tiberio curls his upper lip over his tusks. "It's not about conscience."

"Then what is it?"

"I can't do it anymore."

Vast and stony, Nerosyan heaves into view. Dark clouds shine shafts of hard, late-afternoon light on its bastions and battlements. As always, it percusses: hammer on nail, chisel on stone. Its construction is constant. When there is nothing in need of repair, the Queen's restless workmen add another new defense. Since Gad last saw it, new telescopes of glinting brass have appeared on the city's turrets. Soldiers scan the sky for aerial threats. Where before the looking glasses would point only west, to the Worldwound itself, now they are turned in all directions.

Pine scaffolds, their joints bound together with resined rope, scale the fortress walls. Masons beetle across them, mortaring blocks of freshly quarried white granite into place. Pulleyed chains hoist the stones from groaning carts below. Members of martial orders, holding competing pennants aloft, raise pikes and halberds to protect the straining laborers.

The fortress watches over a meeting of rivers: the cold Egelsee, flowing from east to west, and the colder Sellen, running north to south. The Sellen forms the border between Mendev and the demonlands. Many times the chaos-spawn have pushed the border back, seizing its eastern banks, only to be eventually rebuffed by the crusaders. Nerosyan occupies a diamond-shaped oasis of stone and brick between the rivers. White towers, numbering in the dozens, jostle for space along its upper reaches. Green coppery screens angle from the top of each tower, slit to let the snow slide through, and to offer archers unobstructed shots at demons screeching down from above.

"Ah," says Gad, "the Diamond of the North."

"Aren't you still wanted here?" Tiberio asks.

"Who among us can truly say we're not wanted in Nerosyan?"

"I can."

"And you're wondering why I brought you?"

The slap's impact throbs across Calliard's cheek. A red, hand-shaped smudge forms on the right side of his angular face. He works his pointed jaw. With the tip of his tongue he checks to make sure that his small, delicate teeth are still firmly lodged in their sockets. The contents of an upended slop pail soak his flowing linen shirt to his wiry chest. Droplets of stinking water fall from his dark, curly hair. As the moisture sinks into them, the loops of leather cord securing his arms to the rests of his wooden chair tighten.

His captor's voice pitches itself at the junction of silk and gravel. "Shall I repeat the question?"

Mucus, and perhaps blood, runs down the back of Calliard's throat. "Shall I repeat the answer?"

"Where is Gad?" asks the paladin.

"I still honestly don't know," Calliard breathes. "Thus saving me the effort of lying to you."

Fraton rubs his hand. He straightens himself to his full six feet and four inches. His hair sweeps down over his forehead and flows luxuriantly to cover his ears. Fraton's high, flat forehead wrinkles peevishly. A bow-shaped mustache, one shade lighter than his chestnut hair and upturned at each end, spasms.

The paladin has removed the vambraces and gauntlets of his polished plate armor. His pail-shaped helmet lies beside them on a round beechwood table on the other side of the spacious armory room. The rest of the suit scrapes and clanks as he paces a tight circle around his prisoner. A richly dyed tabard surmounts his breastplate. Sewn to its front is a quilted coat of arms. Divided into quarters, the crest encompasses a watchful hawk, a fortress, and the sunburst and longsword of the warrior goddess, Iomedae.

It is the emblem of a knightly order, the Everbright Crusaders. Five like-armored warriors, each proudly wearing the same crest, array themselves around Fraton. Only his crest appears in the frame of golden thread that befits an order's commander.

At a respectful remove, motionless against the armory's stuccoed walls, stand four fighters of lowlier status. These men-at-arms, kitted in chain and leather armor, hold hook-headed glaives.

"You are unaware of his present, exact location," says Fraton, "but you can predict where he is headed."

"I haven't seen him in months."

"But you will soon," Fraton ventures.

"Unlikely," says Calliard.

Fraton steps back to evaluate his prisoner's demeanor. After a pause he says, "You are certain of this." It is half question, half statement.

"We parted on uncertain terms," says Calliard.

"Tell me about it."

"Go to hell."

Fraton lashes out with closed fist, striking Calliard on the other side of the face.

"When you do that," Calliard chokes, "you clearly show yourself to have the upper hand."

Fraton hits him again. "It was foolish of you to return to Nerosyan."

"I agree. In my defense, I was dragooned. Apparently the Order of the Flaming Lance sees the wisdom in having a demonfinder at their beck and call."

"In falling for your claims, the Flaming Lance erred greatly."

"You say it as if I sought their company, when in fact I did my best to avoid it."

"They were misinformed, Calliard, by the web of lies that is your reputation."

"Believe me, I'd be happy not to have one."

"That is your first true statement. As the men of my own order were, when by Iomedae's grace I rose to its generalship, the Flaming Lance shall be redirected to the path of virtue. By turning you over to me, they have taken their first step upon it."

"It's lucky then, that Mendev is not presently in the grip of an ever-fiercer demonic assault. Because, if it were, the ability to sense demonic activity might prove advantageous."

The crusader's chiseled visage contorts. "Sarcasm is the mark of a polluted mind. To sense demonic presence is to invite it to take up residence in one's soul."

"At least get your accusation straight, Fraton. Decide whether I'm a fake or a consorter with chaos. I can't be both." Calliard braces himself for another blow.

Instead, Fraton reaches for his holy symbol, a silver sword over a golden sunburst. He jabs its point at Calliard's face. "That is where you're wrong, you crawling worm. Demons besiege us because we have fallen into sin. When the first crusaders came here, more than eighty years ago, they were warriors of unimpeachable virtue. They fought with sword and spell, but won by purity of character. Then the others came. Freebooters. Adventurers. Pirates, panderers, coffer-fillers. Rogues. They came not for hatred of evil, but for love of gold. They brought with them their whores, their rum, their gambling dice. Their kind could not defeat chaos, because it was already in their hearts. So long as vice weakens the souls of Mendev, the demons shall overrun it, inch by inch. The only way to fight them is to first eradicate you—the degenerates, the blackguards, the silvertongues. And in Mendev, there is no greater incarnation of turpitude, no more egregious flaunter of righteousness, than your confederate, Gad. So tell me where he is, and earn yourself a greater mercy than your case would warrant. By this redemptive act, you'll earn the chance to shrive your purulent soul."

A wintry gust spends itself against the chapel's street-facing wall. Stained-glass windows rattle in iron frames.

The harsh wind adjusts its attack, slicing through the narrow cobbled lane below. Bright sky shines above, shorn of any scrap of cloud.

A multitude of flags and pennons crack. They peacock for glory, mounted on the tight row of war-chapels lining the street's northeast side. Each chapel houses a warrior order dedicated to the extinction of demons, the accrual of renown, and the massing of loot. In some few orders, the three goals are upheld in that order. The chapels stand shoulder to shoulder, each one taking up where the other leaves off. As is the style in Nerosyan, dark timbers proudly expose themselves, stained in rich browns and varnished blacks. Between them the panels are stuccoed white. The freshness of the white and the darkness of the timbers vary from chapel to chapel, a symptom of shifting fortunes.

Across the lane stands a complementing phalanx of taverns and rum houses. Wordless wooden signs, painted as brightly as the flapping flags, hang above each doorway. Their images, carved with grotesque humor, proclaim the establishments' names: the Rusted Hawk, the Frozen Rat, the Shattered Crown, the Crooked Road, the Pony Rampant, the Skull and Snake. A few ascetic orders shun the drink-halls at their doorsteps. Most do the opposite. That's why they cluster here: The demon fighter's calling is a thirsty one. But it is early yet and now only a few crippled ex-heroes and sozzled caretakers bend the elbow in shadowed rum house corners.

Gad drinks watered ale. Red wine stains Tiberio's tusks.

They wait in the tavern kitty-corner to the war-chapel of the Everbright Crusaders. A carved wooden hawk perches atop the chapel's main steeple, the Everbright crest clutched in its oaken talons. The crest flies also on a freshly laundered banner.

"I won't do that either," Tiberio says.

"It's easy," Gad says.

"For you, maybe."

"He's never seen you."

"I'm not the talker you are, Gad."

"It's not about talking. It's about listening. With anyone, but especially with Fraton. Give him the slightest opening and he'll talk until your pointed ears fall off."

"How do I . . . no, I won't do it."

"Fraton may be a sadistic, strutting, self-loving blowhard and a vexation to honest thieves everywhere. But no one has more informants than he does, not even the queen's men."

"So he'll see through me."

"Okay, you're afraid of him. Let that show. Nothing he'd like better. To believe a hulking pile of muscle such as yourself is intimidated by him."

Tiberio crosses his thick arms. "I can't do it."

"You can. He craves that kind of flattery. Let him talk. Then—all right, here's the story. Tell him you want to join the order."

"Join the Everbright Crusaders?"

"Don't worry, he'll refuse. Then tell him you're plagued by terrible dreams, and keep hearing the name of Yath. Even if he keeps his trap closed, his expression will tell us something. Then when he's out of sight, head around to the back alley and do the other thing."

"I told you, I won't do the other thing."

"Everything will be fine."

"I won't hurt anyone."

Gad leans back behind a pillar so he can't be seen from the street. The arch-shaped door of the Everbright War-Chapel, chased in brass with an image of Iomedae, her sunburst sword held aloft like a lantern, swings open. Out step Fraton and his armored holy knights. Gad counts them, to be certain. "That's all of them," he says. "You won't have to fight anyone. I promise. Go."

But Tiberio is already gone, marching straight for Fraton. The mustached paladin holds up his gilt-thread half-cape to shield his face from the cutting air.

Tiberio raises his tree-trunk arm in greeting. Gad sees him square his shoulders. He leans back, basking in the familiar, unconscious marshalling of determination.

"Are you Fraton?" Tiberio asks.

The mustache forms a hard line atop the tall man's lip. "Of course I am." He sweeps on, trailing his knights behind him.

Tiberio's long legs easily close the distance between them. Then he has to slow himself so as not to outpace him. "A word with you, please."

"You come to me reeking of wine, orc-whelp?"

"I wish to join your crew."

Fraton snorts. "My crew, you'd have it?" His knights trade haughty smirks.

Tiberio knots up his heavy brow. It seemed half-plausible when Gad explained it. He's no smooth-tongue. How did he let himself get talked into this? "Your order. I wish to kill demons, your excellency."

Fraton is not entitled to this honorific. Guilty satisfaction tugs the corners of his mouth. "So you have at least one decent impulse?"

"Too many will be hurt if the demons aren't stopped."

"Why the Everbright Crusaders, half-man?"

"You're the fiercest. Everyone says so."

Fraton claps Tiberio's shoulder with a leather-gloved hand. "Fighting demons, my friend, requires more than simple brawn." He says the word *friend* as if he means *dog.* "Steel not only your sinews, but your soul." He pivots and comes to a halt, blocking Tiberio's path, poking at his breastbone. "Before a man may enter my service, he must retrain his heart. He must abstain from personal impurity, for that is what the demon seeks. The hordes of the Abyss hunger for tainted souls. As they destroy the luckless bodies of their victims, they hope to also consign their ineffable essences to the chaos planes. The souls of the righteous are shriven free, to seek celestial reward. But the righteous are few in number, my tusked friend. Sinners, they are many. Like worms, they crawl. Like ants, they multiply.

"You are no good to the Everbright till you purge yourself of every baseness. Cease your drinking. Your whoring. Your lying, your greed. Become holy, and then perhaps—only perhaps—you'll possess the rectitude needed to subscribe to our irrevocable oaths."

A knight behind him snickers. Tiberio wants to see which one, but stays fixed on Fraton. "But what about Yath?"

"Yath?" says Fraton.

"The final battle nears," Tiberio says. *What am I talking about?* he thinks. "Against Yath. This new demon lord."

"New demon lord? What rot! Clearly you have never peered your flatted nose across so much as a single page of a demonological treatise."

"But I keep hearing that—"

Fraton resumes his march. The others follow. Tiberio keeps up.

"You keep hearing rumors and claptrap. Yath does not exist. Yath is a trick, a mirage, an imagining."

"But many have spoken of it. It appears in dreams—"

"There is only one question concerning Yath. It is either a diversion cooked up by the demons to send us scurrying in circles as the true threat grows worse by the day, or it is the name we give to our fear and weakness. Whatever the answer, no crusader worthy of the title should allow such foolishness to dribble from his lips."

"But—"

"Your insistence on continuing this discussion merely proves your unsuitability for the Everbright Crusaders, man-orc. There is no Yath. Those who seek Yath will find only futility and ruin. Now please, step aside, and disturb no more our rightful peace and dignity."

Tiberio steps aside. He waits until Fraton and retinue have rounded a corner. He pivots, striding briskly in the other direction. When he passes Gad's position in front of the tavern, he discreetly scratches his nose. His speed increases until he reaches the next laneway and disappears into it.

He finds the back alley, counting buildings until he reaches the chapel he seeks. He needn't have bothered. The freshness of the stucco and the emblem carved into its timbers make the Everbright Chapel as unmistakable from the back as from the front. Tiberio stands back, judging his route. He is thankful once more for the mannerisms of Nerosyan architecture. To decorate a building in exposed half-timber is to cover it in sturdy handholds. Tiberio uses them to clamber quickly up the chapel's rear face. His bulk is no impediment; heavy muscles propel him ever upward.

Then he is perched on a timber beside a stained-glass window. He wobbles slightly, then corrects. He is a little heavier than the last time he tried this. Retirement has added ten, maybe fifteen flabby pounds, he judges. Road life will melt that away soon enough. In the meantime he feels the heft on his bones, factors it into his balance calculations.

The window's colored-glass design is meant to be seen from the inside. It depicts the warrior goddess Iomedae, her sunlit blade adorned with demon blood. She stands triumphantly astride the ruined carcass of her insectoid foe.

Tiberio peers through her flowing white tabard into the room inside. He sees Calliard, slumped and bloodied, tied to a chair. He sees the ill-equipped, out-of-shape hirelings left to guard him. He understands why Gad said he wouldn't have to hurt them. Why he was silently counting the number of proper warriors who left with Fraton, to make sure that it was the same number they watched going in.

With an elbow he smashes the window, breaking the delicate threads of iron that delineate its separate panels of etched and tinted glass. He pokes his head and hands through. The hirelings stand and stare as, with improbable efficiency, he pulls himself through the constricting frame. He unfolds himself to his full commanding height.

"Hello, Tiberio," says Calliard.

"Hello, Calliard."

The youngest of the hirelings, a slump-shouldered man of thirty-five who relies on one good leg, shuffles a step toward him, polearm outstretched.

"You don't want to do that," Calliard informs him.

The man hesitates. The others make formation behind their friend.

A snow-bearded guardsman shoves the point man from behind. He takes a reluctant step.

"Fraton doesn't pay you enough for this," Calliard says.

Tiberio lowers his lip so that his tusks look bigger.

The guardsman waves his weapon, as if on purpose, to disguise his trembling.

"Yes, Fraton will discharge you if you let me go," says Calliard. "But Fraton will also discharge you after Tiberio beats you to a pulp and then spirits me away regardless. Either the first result will pertain, or the second. There are only the two outcomes."

Tiberio cracks his knuckles.

"If you get sacked without suffering a savage battering," Calliard says, "you can find other jobs right away. You know it isn't hard, in Nerosyan. It's a seller's market for sword-arms, strong or feeble. If you let Tiberio crush your bones and snap your tendons, you'll be recuperating for months. Months of pain and idleness you can't afford." A drop of blood chooses this moment to gather at the bridge of Calliard's nose, then travel down its length and jump from its tip onto his tunic.

The guardsmen imagine themselves looking like Calliard.

"Let's all be smart for once," Calliard says.

The elderly guard gets an idea. He points the blade of his polearm at Calliard's throat.

Tiberio balls up his fists.

"You don't want to do that either," Calliard says.

The man withdraws his glaive.

"Instead," Calliard says, "you want to drop the weaponry at my feet."

With a clatter, they comply.

"Then all of you except for . . ." He looks at the slump-shouldered man. "You. What's your name again?" Calliard has never known his name.

"Zaiko," the man stutters.

"Zaiko, you're going to free me from my bonds, while Tiberio watches you very, very carefully."

Zaiko does this. Tiberio watches him very, very carefully.

He also notices that a dagger hilt pokes from the top of the old man's boot, and that the old man is looking at it.

Tiberio growls at him.

With outstretched palms, the old man shows his surrender.

Zaiko removes the last blood-soaked strap from Calliard's chair. Calliard wobbles to his feet. Tiberio moves to catch him.

"I can do it," Calliard manages.

Tiberio backs off. He turns to watch the huddling men. They press themselves back into the corner.

Calliard drops an arm down to steady himself on the back of the chair. With aching, halting steps, he starts his journey to the door. When he is out of sight, Tiberio picks up the chair. His back to his destination, he takes slow, defiant steps, toe-to-heel, toe-to-heel. Once through the threshold he closes the door, tips the chair back against the handle, and wedges it into place until it's tight.

Calliard slumps against the stairwell wall. Now that the guards are unable to see him, he lets Tiberio help. He falls into Tiberio's side. The big man takes part of his weight for a while, until they reach a landing. Then he picks up the rail-thin prisoner and, cradling him in his arms, carries him the rest of the way.

Calliard flinches as Tiberio presses a damp cloth against his lacerated forehead. They're with Gad, in a rented room above the Skull and Snake. Sharp slivers of daylight, filtered by a shuttered window, stripe across the brown-gray walls. The room reeks of ale and musty bedclothes. If they wanted, they could open the window and crane to see the Everbright chapel across the lane. They are here for two reasons:

One, they all trust the proprietor, a leathery oldster who these days goes by the name of Vladul.

Two, directly across the street is the last place Fraton will think to hunt for them.

Tiberio surveys his handiwork. He has soaked his cloth with honey and a tincture of healing potion. The swelling subsides already. The face will be torn and bruised for a while. "Only the one on your cheek will need stitching."

Calliard nods his silent assent.

"So," says Gad. "This Yath business."

"Mm," says Calliard, watching as Tiberio pokes the end of a thick black thread through the eye of a distressingly large needle.

"I've heard a demon and a cultist say it's real. Whatever it is. And Fraton thinks it's a fake."

"He thinks it's fake because I told him it was real."

Tiberio sterilizes the needle in candle flame.

"Elaborate," says Gad.

"I'm a degenerate, so my knowledge of demonkind can't possibly eclipse his. If I'd told him Yath was just another crazed rumor, he'd be tromping into the Worldwound right now to lay it low."

"No, I meant elaborate about Yath. What is it?"

"Yath is a paradox. It is several things at once, yet none of them. It is neither creature nor matter, not of the Abyss nor of the true world, neither gate nor tower, neither new nor old."

"Thanks for explaining."

Tiberio advances with the needle. "Quiet for a moment, both of you." He plunges the needle into the torn flesh surrounding the slash on Calliard's cheekbone.

Gad takes care not to look away.

Tiberio steps back, turns Calliard into the light, and snips the thread with the sharpened nail of his baby finger.

"Yath," says Calliard, "is a gigantic tower, recently manifested in the Worldwound."

"Recently, as in, at the time the attacks got suddenly worse. When the demonhorde found a way past the wardstone line."

"Right."

"So if we dispose of Yath, we go back to the usual degree of war and trouble?"

Pain cuts Calliard's laughter short. "Dispose of Yath? Why don't you pick an easy task, like disposing of fear and greed?"

"I'm rather fond of greed. I wouldn't touch a hair on its head." Gad paces. "It's a tower, yes? So let's knock it down."

"'Let's knock it down'? Yath is a living stronghold, yes, but at the same time it's also an entity, or a consciousness. The physical tower is merely the central axis of its influence. Demons and cultists feel its presence. They draw power from it, and in turn are pulled to its service. At first they perceived it only dimly, and drank tentatively from it. As every day passes, it grows stronger, as do those who accept its power, who thus make it stronger, and are made stronger . . ."

"And so on . . ."

" . . . and so forth."

Tiberio leans in to tie off his stitch. His efforts leave an ugly knot.

"So," says Gad, "as the aura expands, it envelops more of Mendev, and the demons can operate freely there. Today it's reached as far as the Estrovian Forest. Soon it will be the entire territory, then Numeria, and maybe eventually the world. Is that the idea?"

"As conjectures go, I've heard crazier."

"So how do we kill it?"

"Kill it? You'd be lucky to banish it."

"So how do we banish it?"

Calliard raises his aching body from the bed. He picks up a hand mirror and frowns into it. "I'd have to learn more."

Gad stands over his shoulder, appearing in the mirrored surface behind him. "I'd like to have you do that. But are you good?"

"Who have you told about this?" Calliard asks.

"About what?"

"That you're interested in a tower."

"Until you explained it, I didn't know I was interested in a tower."

"Why are you so ablaze for this?"

"Too much chaos, like too little, is bad for business."

"So you're the thieves' benevolent order, now?"

"Someone has to be."

Calliard laughs, then clearly regrets it. "Only you would say that."

"Also, there's the revenge aspect."

"I like revenge. Who are we revenging?"

"You remember Abotur."

"Heard of. Never met."

"He was upright. Not a mastermind, but solid."

"A plugger," says Calliard. "That's what I heard about him."

"Dedicated. Willing to play long. Spent a year of his life on this tapestry gaffle, winning the trust of his mark. He brought me in late, to sink the tap."

"So it wasn't your rip?"

"Assist only. I told him to be safe it should be more than a two-manner."

"But it was his rip, and he called it."

"A year of his life. I was willing to take a fee and not a share, but you go bringing in additional talent, and his year's investment starts dwindling."

"You told him you wanted a team."

"I told him if it was my rip, I'd have a team."

"But it was his rip."

"That it was."

"And he got himself killed."

"Not because the rip was faulty. Because demons came pelting in from nowhere. Right when we were closing. Wreaking havoc, which is what they do. We let them run wild around here, there's no longer such a beast as a reliable scam."

"There never is."

"There is when I'm running."

"Which you weren't."

"Which I stipulated already, and which is neither here nor there, and you're evading the question."

"What question?"

"Are you good?"

Calliard turns. "Don't mistake me—I'm grateful for the rescue. But if you think I'm going with you into the Worldwound—which is where we'd have to go; I'm not sure of much but I'm sure of that—if you think you can blithely assume I'll be pleased to trot along with you into the suppurating heart of evil and insanity . . . then what do you mean, *am I good?*"

"You know exactly what I mean."

Calliard's demeanor changes. He sits back down on the edge of the mildewy mattress. "I think I'm good."

"You think, or you are?"

"I'm better."

"Are you better enough?"

He flares back up. "Wait a moment. How did this change from a discussion of whether I'm fool enough to accompany you into the—"

"Are you better enough?"

Calliard stares down. "I bought my lute back."

"Is that better enough?"

"I mean, I bought it back and then Fraton caught me and his men crushed it to flinders, but I did buy it back. I played it a little, even."

"Calliard?"

"To be honest I can't say. I shouldn't be anywhere near the Worldwound. I shouldn't even be in Mendev, except I can't work up the imagination to leave."

"How about if I tell you you're ready?"

"I'd like that to be true. After what happened the last time."

"Let's not talk about the last time."

"Yes," mutters Tiberio. "Let us not."

Gad's expression warns the big orc to silence.

"I'm telling you you're ready," says Gad. "It's the only way you're going to get ready."

"Give me time to think."

"That's the last thing you need."

A renewed gust sends the shutters slamming.

"Who else are you thinking of?" asks Calliard.

Gad removes his last cache of emergency coin from its hiding place behind Vladul's wine rack. He sends

Tiberio out into the city to buy six horses and a lute. He reminds Tiberio to buy a horse big enough to carry him.

The three travel by day across the scourged plains north of Nerosyan. The horses veer instinctively east, away from the Worldwound border. Tiberio tracks the sun and corrects their course.

Calliard hasn't ridden in nearly a year. His wounds are healing but the bruises still hurt. He has trouble staying in the saddle. Every half a league or so he sways alarmingly to the right or left. Just in time he catches himself and regains his balance. The problem grows worse when he takes the lute from his pack and begins to play it, the reins draped loosely over his arm. He tunes it maddeningly. Plink plank plonk.

Gad can't stand it any more. He lets his mount slow to plod alongside Calliard's. "You sure we'll find her there?"

Calliard shrugs. "It's Mendev. Who's sure of anything?" He plinks his lute.

"And I forgot why I missed you . . ."

"Where else would she be?" The bard waves an arm. "Demons attack a mixed encampment of crusader orders. Their flames and acid and wrenching winds wipe out the warriors. They tear earth from stone, root from trunk, turn boulders to sand and sand to ash. They fly away, leaving exposed the entrance to an underground ruin unexplored for centuries. A ruin said to be stocked top to tail with the ingenious traps of Isano Golemsmith, celebrated in tome and song. Maker of the sevenfold lock and the evershifting key."

"Right," says Gad.

"And also I spoke to both Gashek and Footless Timon, and they said she said she'd be there."

Calliard twists a key on his lute. He strums the strings. Now the magic is back. Gad listens and the colors around him deepen. The fragrance of the season's first tentative wildflowers rises up beneath the hooves of their horses.

Chapter Four
The Lockbreaker and
the Distance Man

A sprinkling of ash covers the scrubland weeds. As the three ride on, the ash grows denser. Soon the vegetation recedes entirely, replaced by barren earth. Overturned boulders lie scattered across slopes and hollows. A starving hawk circles uselessly overhead.

Eventually the remnants of an old civilization appear. Crumbled bricks, some red, some yellow. A long-buried pillar covered in cracked blue tile. A door and a railing, both cast in bronze.

Amid them are strewn new relics of a recent battle: broken swords, sheared lances, melted helmets. Fresh graveyards, their shallow mounds arrayed in neat ranks and rows, attest to an effort to bury the dead. Still, fragments of skull and bone, raked by the teeth of scavengers, salt the land. They belong to man and horse, to elf and dwarf.

An open pit yawns in the distance. Gad speeds his horse; Tiberio and Calliard follow. The earth yields uncertainly beneath them. They hear the whicker of horses. Four scraggly beasts stand glumly, tied to the last branches of a scorched and toppled tree. The three tie their mounts there and walk toward the pit.

Two weary figures clamber from the pit's edge. Seeing Gad, Calliard, and particularly Tiberio, they freeze and reach for their swords. Tiberio holds out his hands in a gesture of peace. The explorers sheathe their weapons and slowly approach. They are human women, lithe and long-tressed. One wears metal; the other, leather. Mystic symbols cover the latter woman's breastplate. The two appear to be twins.

"Too late," the metal-wearer says. "All cleaned out."

"Anyone still down there?" Gad asks.

"Other than our damnfool time-wasting laggard of a lockpick?"

"That's who we're looking for." Gad bows gallantly. Each woman raises an eyebrow, notes a flash of attraction and moves on. The warriors untie their horses, and another besides, and ride away.

Tiberio climbs down the rope ladder first, followed by Calliard and Gad. The ladder extends for more than forty feet, taking them through a sinkhole and then a stone-lined catacomb. They leap down to a mosaic floor. It depicts a muscled warrior crushing prostrate enemies beneath his boot. An ancient war leader, probably, or perhaps a god. The tiled faces of general and victims have been chipped out and hauled away. Stone benches circle the chamber's edges.

The hall serves as a junction; open archways lead from it to the north, east, south, and west. The three stop to listen. They hear a faint sound of metal on metal. They listen further, finally deciding that its faint echo comes from the eastern corridor. Calliard lights a lantern. They move through a vaulted passageway, its walls and floor also covered in pictorial mosaics. Faces and decorative features, as on the floor in the round chamber, have been hacked out and spirited away for resale.

The tap-tap-scrape grows louder. They move toward it, ignoring other doors. The chamber terminates in another archway. Tiberio pauses at its threshold.

A corpse lies across it. It is the body of a man, cut nearly in two. The jagged slice through his body begins at his right shoulder and ends at his left hip. He has been stripped to his bloodied undergarments. Tiberio looms briefly over him. "About a week ago," he says.

His fingers delicately trace a groove recessed inside the archway. A spike juts from the groove, stopping a five-foot blade meant to scythe out from it.

Splayed in a corner around a bend are a pair of burned corpses. On the opposite side of the hallway, the inner cement wall has been exposed. Tiles spill across the floor in heaps, along with clods of crumbled plaster. Disassembled metal spouts, plaster chunks still attached to their coppered sides, lean against the wall. A fire-spitter, taken apart, though not before it claimed at least two lives.

They follow the tapping noises down a curving set of cement steps. The last step has been pulled away. Those above it are spattered brown-red and spackled in gobbets of dried brain matter. Beside the removed step, now set against a stone urn, sit a bronze trip plate and the spring mechanism it once activated. A bloodied boulder has been rolled to the side. Across from the steps stands a larger-than-life stone lion, another boulder readied in its mouth.

The tap-tapping takes them through an octagonal chamber surrounded by marble porticoes. They step over a severed tripwire on the way in. Stacked by type across the chamber floor are hundreds of segmented metal components. These are magical constructs, deconstructed. From the collection of barbed stinger pieces, the automatons appear to have been artificial scorpions.

They continue on through a narrow corridor. It opens into a smallish antechamber, where a hunched halfling figure pokes thin metal wire into an enlarged, multifaceted keyhole. The door is already open. The halfling's lantern, hanging from an ingenious portable pole device, illuminates the bare shelves of an emptied vault.

Strands of white, gray, and ash-blond interweave into a complex construction atop her head. Supported by an intricate copper lattice strategically bedecked with seed pearls and agate shavings, the great mass of hair remains firmly in place and out of her way. Its owner is stout, round of hip and generous of thigh. Skin crinkles around her eyes and at the corners of her mouth. Blocky, jeweled rings adorn her stubby, fast-moving fingers. Ruby powder sparkles on her lips. Beneath her greasy hardened-leather breastplate, frills and ruffs of unaccountably spotless white lace coyly peek, partially obscuring the thin silver chain of a sapphire pendant.

A magnifying eyepiece dangles on a chain from one of the spokes of her hair lattice. She seizes it, planting it firmly in place between brow and cheekbone, and squints deeper into the lock.

"Vitta," says Gad.

"Who's the orc?" says Vitta.

"Half-orc," says Gad.

"That's what they all say." She turns briefly from the lock. "If you're with Gad, and I suppose you are, I'm pleased to make your acquaintance."

"I'm Tiberio."

"Thought you'd sworn off dungeon-hopping," she says, presumably to Gad.

"Never sworn it in. Nice work taking the traps apart."

Vitta snorts. "Had a bit of bother with the fire trap. Not Isano Golemsmith's handiwork, though. Not by a long stretch. The rumors were wrong. As rumors tend to be."

She bangs the lock with the end of a chisel, frowns, and contorts her padded frame to peer into it from below.

"Vitta?" Gad says.

"What?"

"I can't help but notice . . ."

"The door I'm trying to unlock is already open?"

At her knee sits a leather case shaped vaguely like a coffin. Its velvet drawers cosset hundreds of small tools of copper, glass, and wood. She selects a brush and jams it fiercely into the lock. Inside, something clicks into place.

"Yes," says Gad. "That is what I couldn't help but notice."

"It was open when the first looters got here. Probably left that way when the inhabitants fled. During the last days of the Volobri Exodus, would be my guess. The entire complex is a disappointment. Except for this lock."

"Some might point out that the door is already open and the vault empty."

"Immaterial. As you well understand. It's a lock I couldn't get—some sort of a counter-tumbling action." She turns a wheel beside the lock. With a snap, the protruding bolt snaps back into the side of the door. Vitta exhales in satisfaction. She detaches the eyepiece from her hair lattice, placing it back in its designated spot inside her case.

"Got something juicy for me then?" she asks.

Vitta hangs upside down, suspended by cords from a scaffold of her own design and construction. Hollow tubes, through tension produced by interior springs, press tight against the wall above.

"Remind me why this is necessary," says Gad.

"Why what is necessary?"

"Hanging from your heels."

"Angle-sensitive tumbler cuffs," answers Vitta. Only a single twist of blond hair has escaped from its assigned position. "Hand me the expander."

He reaches into her case and withdraws a triangular device with a gear in the middle.

Vitta snorts. "The small expander."

Gad gives her a smaller version of the same tool. He peers down the round, metal-shod passageway, through the six doors Vitta has already opened, past the propped-up portcullis, to the guard room a hundred feet away. In less than an hour, guards he hasn't and can't pay off will appear to relieve the ones he could and has.

They are deep beneath Bogilar Fortress, in a vault designed to house its baronial family after demons burrowed into their souls. Due to the terms of their demonic pact, the first generation of the Bogilar clan could not die, except of old age. The horrified second generation built this vault, to keep them in until they did just that. Two generations later, all that is left of the Bogilars is the name of the fortress. Only one occupant now dwells in its vault.

Vitta drops the small expander. The impact sounds like a dropped pin but the sound reverberates and amplifies as it travels down the corridor. Gad stoops and hands it back to her. She places the tool inside the vault lock.

"Now a wad of gauze."

He hands it to her.

"No, don't hand it to me, keep it for the moment. Now find the green vial with the yellow liquid in it."

"Not the green liquid inside the yellow vial?"

"How cleverly amusing."

"Got it."

"Now pour just a dab on the gauze."

"How big is a dab?"

"Don't tell me you don't know how much a dab is. After all this time."

He pours a dab onto the gauze. It smokes, dispersing a rotting onion scent. She takes the gauze and carefully packs it into the lock. It hisses.

Inside the vault, something else hisses back.

Vitta pauses. "Should we be concerned about that?"

"Let me guess and say no," ventures Gad.

"Am I to treat that as certainty?"

"If you choose to believe in the concept."

"In which case, grab me," the halfling instructs.

Gad wraps his arms around her waist and extends his leg muscles, bearing her weight. She yanks on a knot. The contraption releases her. Gad totters, regains his balance, edges over to the wall. His back pressed against it, he pinions his legs, gently placing Vitta on the vault floor. Unruffled by the graceless move, she squirrels hastily to her feet.

The liquid on the gauze has stopped hissing. The voice inside the vault has not. There is anger and joy in it.

"This is truly the only way?" Vitta says.

"You're asking now?"

With a nod, Vitta concedes the point.

Gad explains anyway. "Too many demons come at you from the air. We need a distance man."

"I don't mean that." She runs respectful fingers lovingly over the lock mechanism. "They've no one to repair this properly now."

"That's what you're worried about? The lock?"

"What should I be worried about?"

"Just open it."

She points to a spot above the mechanism. "Strike this part right here with the heel of your hand."

"Why me?"

Vitta shrugs. "Thought you'd like to be a part of history."

"In what sense?"

"This lock has never been cracked. Sola of Escadar tried. Barles Sablecoat didn't even get as far as the third door. In a moment, no one will ever get the chance to break this lock again."

Gad strikes it with the heel of his hand.

Nothing happens.

Vitta sighs. She hits it.

Smoke billows from the circular seam surrounding the mechanism. It seems to contract. Vitta reaches in and pulls out the entire lock.

Red eyes stare back at her from the window she's just created.

"Fire," says the prisoner.

Vitta curls her fingers around the edge of the opening and pulls. The heavy door swings open. Diffuse lantern light floods the darkened cell.

A naked man jogs back from the door to assume a bestial crouch in the corner. Shaggy black hair cascades from his head. It covers his back like a cape. Dark tattoos stain the natural olive of his skin. Pink, shiny patches of burn scar dot his flesh, interrupting whatever patterns might be discerned in the tattoos. The whites of his eyes glisten through spears of drooping hair.

"Burning," says the prisoner.

"Come on, Hendregan," says Gad.

The prisoner blinks and rubs his eyes. He leaps up and down, making no effort to cover his nakedness. Then he takes note of Vitta. He grabs the frizzy hair running down his back and bundles it over his crotch.

"Oh, please," says Vitta.

Gad opens his pack. He tosses Hendregan a loincloth. The prisoner seems puzzled by it at first. He pulls it on, folds it inexpertly, unfurls it, and starts again.

"Hendregan," says Gad, "the guards."

"Burn them?"

"No, don't burn them. Just get yourself together quickly."

The grimacing inmate fumbles with the loincloth, finally arriving at a half-satisfactory arrangement. Gad throws him deerskin leggings and a silk tunic and cloak. The last two items are crimson, with orange cuffs and trim.

Hendregan wraps it tightly around himself. Clothing emphasizes his improbable proportions. He is barrel-chested and muscular above the waist, spindly and pigeon-toed below. "You are Gad, yes?"

"Yes, Hendregan. Gad. You remember."

His scowl is one of confusion. "Do I?"

"Yes, you do."

"Gad . . ." He brightens. "Then there is someone to burn?"

"Yes, there is someone to burn."

"Who?"

"Demons."

Hendregan smiles. "Demons. Some burn already. Yet they can also be burnt. Others—the insect ones. Wings wisp away into nothing and smoke. Maggot flesh blackens. Beetle shell crisps. Yes, demons, demons. Burning demons."

"Let's discuss this outside."

"But wait, but wait." The man jigs and trembles. "Why me?"

"You have other pressing engagements?"

"Why do I get to do the burning? What about Esikull?"

"Left Mendev two years back. Let's go."

"Ashetak?"

"Missing."

"Pera?"

"Dead. You are ready for this, yes?"

"Ready?" A new demeanor comes over him. His mad quivering ceases. He claps his hands together, moves toward the exit. A mirror, hanging on the back of the vault door, stops him short. He peers into it, confused. Moves his head from side to side. Realizing that the face he sees is his, he grimaces.

His right hand bursts into flame. He seizes his hair by the fistful. The strands turn orange and disintegrate. He pulls his burning hand over his scalp, until he is completely bald. A few blisters rise along the top of his head.

"I knew it would be you," Hendregan says.

The five ride north for a day. The sky blackens. Spring snow straggles through the air.

The dark bulk of Suma Castle looms into view, barely visible against sooty clouds. Ahead, the trail forks.

Travelers may continue on to the monastery of Tala, to other points north, and eventually to Kenabres, the city of witch-hunters. Or they may turn to the west, toward the border, and the domain of Suma.

Gad takes the turn.

Calliard, lagging at the back of the small procession, urges his horse forward. He circles around Gad and his steed.

"You're not . . ." he begins.

"We are."

"Of all people, I'm in no position to—"

"That's right, you aren't."

Gad spurs his horse. The others do likewise, and follow.

Suma Castle sits on the lip of a high crag. Its central tower punches into the heavens. Atop it, a vast box of ebon stone implausibly perches, held in place by four sturdy buttresses. Around its base, eroded barracks cluster. These in turn are ringed by neglected workshops and storehouses, and are themselves protected by a serpentine outer parapet. This wall bows and bends, accommodating itself to the shape of the mountainous hill beneath.

The riders' horses strain to find safe footing as the slope to Suma's gate grows steeper. There is only one gatekeeper, an ill-fed man who leans on a crutch.

"You have come to fight?" he asks.

Before Gad can reply, thunderous drums pound from the tower. Winged creatures sweep through the air from across the Worldwound border.

Hendregan, until now slumped slack-jawed in his saddle, comes to life. "We have come to fight!" He savagely spurs his horse. The keeper rushes to cover as the horse bolts through the gate.

A flood of airborne demons, their body shapes recalling both reptiles and monstrously bloated mosquitoes, whine toward the top of the tower. Hendregan slaps his horse on its haunches, accelerating it toward the crest of a sloping road. Turning backward in his saddle, he faces the formation of oncoming demons. With open throat, he holds clawed hands aloft and screams an incantation. Fire erupts from his arms and shoots toward the oncoming fliers. The formation falls apart. Creatures inside the mass see the fire wizard and attempt to peel away. Filmy wings break and carapaces slam together as demons collide. Then the ball of fire is all around them. They pop and crack and come apart. Flaming chunks of burning demon precipitate down, extinguishing themselves on the surrounding rocks and on the stone roofs of emptied barracks. A sizzling stinger lands near the hooves of Hendregan's steed, spooking it. Laughing and screaming, the wizard leaps from its bucking haunches. He lands on bended knee and chants again.

The others pepper the dispersing demon mob with arrows and crossbow bolts. Soldiers spill from the main tower to join the fray.

A winged clump of curdled flesh dives for Hendregan, acid sputum dribbling from spiraled mandibles. Hendregan finishes his spell-speech, firing a ray of scorching heat at it. In midair, the ray splits in two. One of the rays sizzles through the curdled flesh demon, blowing a discharge of boiling innards from its hind end. Another perforates the ropy wings of a worm-headed creature, sending it into a tailspin. It strikes the stone shingles of an armory roof, exploding in a shower of putrid slop.

Calliard places an arrow in his bow and pulls back the drawstring. His aim shifts from a fleeing mosquito-demon, its wings smoking and twisted, to a figure emerging from the inky clouds. As he first observes it, it seems to Calliard as if the being forms itself from the encompassing clouds. Then he recognizes it: a shadow demon, or as the scholars sometimes call them, an *invidiak*. It flits over to the parapet wall as soldiers from the tower haul themselves up a ladder to defend it. As it moves, its shape flickers, contracts and expands, as a shadow does when it moves between two torches. Though its form alters from one moment to the next, the batlike outline of its wings remains nearly consistent. Each wing converges to a downturned, hooklike projection from its peak. Taloned legs form, vanish, reform and vanish again. Spindly limbs terminate in long, razored fingers. A crown and collar of ever-transforming horns surround an open, toothy maw. Tiny red eyes glow from the top of its flattened head.

They look into Calliard. He feels the demon's awareness moving around inside him. Exploring him. Testing his soul for flaws. Finding them.

He looses his arrow at it, but the demon is out of range, and the attack falls pathetically short.

At the edge of his hearing, a sandpaper laugh intrudes. The demon leaps nimbly from the parapet back into the concealing clouds. The move seems to be a command, or to correspond with one. The remaining demons scatter for the border.

Hendregan takes a succession of marionette leaps as the demons depart. While the castle's defenders lower their bows, he claws his hands together for a final spell. Amid the densest concentration of demons, a second globe of fire materializes. Half a dozen slain demons splatter in smoldering pieces against the tower's southern face. As many more spin in uncontrolled jags through the air as they strive to remain aloft.

In tense silence, the assembled soldiers watch until the rest of the demons are gone. They straighten their backs as the doors at the base of the tower swing open.

A middle-aged man strides out. A coat of gilt brocade, surmounted by a collar of lynx fur, underlines the grandeur of his strut. Gold medallions swing from his neck on matching chains. Atop his head jaunts a felt hat, its upturned peak bordered in silver ribbon. His ginger beard sharpens an otherwise rounded jaw.

Having made his entrance, he halts a few steps outside the doorway, waiting for Gad to come to him.

With unthinking instinct the soldiers form a ragged honor guard for their commander. They array themselves in two wayward lines, one on each side of the pathway. Gad walks their gauntlet, wordlessly greeting each as he passes. Despite broken arms, poisoned skin, sunken cheeks, and layers of scars, the soldiers of Suma proudly return his gaze.

Gad bows to the castle lord. "General Braval," he says.

Braval claps him showily on the shoulders. "Gad. Once more I have cause to thank you. Your men saved mine some trouble." The bravado is manufactured. Small, testing eyes rest uneasily in his face.

"The least we could do," says Gad.

"Passing through, then?"

"You could say that."

Braval's actorly smile fades. "Wherever you're headed, she'll not go with you."

"I can confirm that by asking her."

Braval puts his hand atop Gad's shoulder and squeezes. From a few feet away, the move looks friendly. "Where are you headed?"

Gad tilts his body westward, toward the Worldwound.

Braval's face hardens. "She'll especially not go with you there."

"As I said . . ."

"She won't so much as see you."

Gad clucks his tongue.

The Lord General of Suma Castle flushes. "She's standing right behind me, isn't she?"

Gad nods.

Fists at his side, Braval stands aside.

A young woman hovers in the doorway. Auburn hair and a certain straightness of the brow-line mark her as Braval's daughter. There the resemblance ends. She is paler and more hawkish than he. Lank curls tangle loosely from her head. Her chin is pointed, her crimson lips straight and drawn. A light dusting of freckles reaches from cheek to cheek, extending across the ridge of her noise. The tunic and leggings she wears are cut for a boy. Though it is not the intended effect, they heighten the otherwise modest curves of her rangy body. Calliard counts a dozen blades on her belt and knows that there are at least two more in each boot.

She cocks a hip to lean against the doorway, deceptively slim arms firmly crossed.

"Jerisa," Gad says.

"Gad," she replies.

The others gather at the far end of the undeclared honor guard. Vitta pulls on Calliard's cloak to bring him down to her height.

"That's not . . . ?" she asks.

"It is," says Calliard.

"This is not a good idea, then," Vitta says.

Calliard sighs. "Which of us is?"

Chapter Five
The Knife

It's Braval who breaks under the weight of their silence. "Pah. Perhaps these matters are best discussed over ale and mutton."

Gad waves to his team. They follow him inside the tower. A grizzled castellan assigns them sleeping quarters. As they refresh themselves, a dirty rain falls listlessly. Drips echo through the tower's gloomy halls. Below them lie the barracks. The team hears the scraping of a sword on a whetstone. The intermittent hacks of a tubercular lung.

A half-blind housemaid comes to take them to the feast. Gad takes her arm as she shuffles alongside him. When she has led them halfway to their destination, she breaks into a whisper. "You've come to deliver us from the demons, then?"

"Yes," says Gad. "It's been bad here?"

Foamy saliva collects on her lower lip. "Every day worse. Something's out there. It wears the most on the masters, though they struggle not to show it."

She takes them to the narrow feast-hall and turns around, padding off to another errand. Save for

Jerisa, the Suma clan is already assembled. The family members have arranged themselves in alternating chairs so that the visitors can sit between them.

There is the mother, Aeris, ghost-thin and still, veiled in dusty white.

The eldest son, Simon, who stares at nothing.

The adoptee, Julnes, already refilling his flagon.

Frane, the middle son, whose shakes have worsened.

The uncle, Berkop, his bald head raked by purple scars, as if clawed by some great bird.

The youngest son, Thriton, the one Gad liked, is nowhere to be seen. His family medallion hangs from the back of his usual chair, so that no one else will sit there. A place has been set for him, though without fork or knife.

"He leapt from the battlements," intones Aeris, seeing the question in Gad's gaze. "I told him to leave, but he wouldn't. Suma honor, he said."

Braval emits a warning cough.

Aeris ignores him. "We lack all else, but retain our ancestral honor. Do as his father and grandfather did. Fight the demons. Don't desert your post. The castle is more important than you are. Its stones and mortar. Defend them at every cost."

"Shut up, you mad bitch," Berkop growls.

As Gad passes, Aeris lays a chalky hand on his arm. "Take her with you and never bring her back," she implores. "One of us at least must escape this awful place. This tomb."

"Shut up, mother," says Julnes.

Simon rouses briefly from his wide-eyed daydream. "I've stabbed you before and I'll stab you again," he tells Julnes.

"I'd welcome the attempt," Julnes sneers.

Braval bangs a fist on the table. Plates rattle. "Shut up, the lot of you," he says. "There's only one of you still fit to call himself a Suma, and she's late for supper." He stands up and shouts, "Where, by Iomedae's tapered tits, have you gotten yourself to, Jerisa? I won't have you humiliate me again!"

Jerisa appears, shamefaced, in the doorway. A series of sulky hops takes her to the table. She notes the spot where Gad is standing and sits down across from him. A theatrical scraping of her chair's legs against the cold stone floor rends the feast-hall air.

Gad sits down. The others follow his cue. Tiberio is the last to sit, his shoulders visibly drooping under the tension of the room.

Sallow serving girls bring in the promised mutton, and salt pork besides. There are gray, mounded bread loaves, boiled turnips, and a jar of pickled beets.

"W-we're ss-sseeing it in our d-duh-duh-duh-*dreams* now," says palsied Frane.

"What?" says Gad.

"Y-yuh-yuh-yuh-yuh-yuh-yuh-yuh-yuh-yuh . . ."

"Yath," snaps Simon. "We're seeing Yath. Rising from the earth. Roots of corrupted stone. Hairs and tendrils and pincers. A parasitic worm, come to devour our minds."

The mother giggles. "This handsome man will sweep you away from here," she tells Jerisa. "To safety."

"No, he won't," Jerisa says.

Gad reaches for the bread basket. "We'll talk about it later."

"No," says Jerisa, "Let's dispense with it now. Because there's nothing to talk about."

"It's Yah-Yath t-told p-p-puh-poor Thriton to jump," Frane says.

Gad studies Frane for a moment.

Julnes downs a flagon and belches.

"I shouldn't have done what I did," Gad begins.

"Be more specific," says Jerisa.

"But whatever mistakes I made, whatever hurt I caused you, doesn't matter compared to the threat out there. All of Mendev might be at stake. The world."

"Find someone else," Jerisa says.

"I need you."

"But for m-m-muh-muh-me Yath h-has d-duh-duh-different plans," says Frane.

"Oho," says Hendregan, as if Frane has told a joke.

Vitta sits beside Frane. "Shush now," she says.

Gad stands. "Let's talk elsewhere."

Jerisa slumps in her chair. "You knew how I felt. From the first minute, you knew."

Braval's fist clatters the plates again. "Aroden's bones, child! This is the family table! Take your filth talk away from us."

Arms crossed, head down, Jerisa leads Gad to an antechamber. "You want to talk?" she says. "Then talk. But I'm not going with you."

"We're going to banish Yath."

"So?"

"You can see that it's the force destroying your family."

Her head swivels involuntarily toward them. "They deserve it," she hisses.

"Even your father?"

"Him it won't get. But him most of all."

"I don't believe you when you say that. You don't believe you."

She says nothing.

"You're right," Gad says. "I did know how you felt, from the very first moment."

"You always know that. With all of them."

"I thought it was what you wanted."

"You knew I didn't want it like that."

"I thought it would finally burst the bubble for you."

"Burst the bubble?"

"To let you see that it didn't matter."

"It did matter. And that's not why you did it."

"Then tell me why I did it."

"I caught you in a moment of weakness."

Gad thinks for a moment. It's a trap, but he's not sure how. "That's right. A moment of weakness."

She moves to strike him.

There's no knife in her hand, so he lets her. It hurts. It never stops surprising him, how hard her blows can be. How much power those skinny arms contain.

"That's what I am to you," she says, "Your moment of weakness."

"On the other side of the ledger, you did slit my throat afterward."

She gives him her back. "If I'd really slit your throat, you wouldn't be breathing."

Another gloomy day. They convene in the feast-hall. The half-blind servant brings them cheese and nuts. Gad arrives late, come from a parley with Braval.

"The old man's letting us stay?" Vitta asks.

"To make our plans, yes. As long as we like."

"He's hoping we'll still be here to fight when next the demons come." Calliard adjusts his lute. The damp air has reversed his tuning efforts.

"More demons to burn?" asks Hendregan.

"Of those, there will be no shortage," says Gad.

"Is Jerisa coming?" Tiberio asks.

"I'll turn her around," says Gad.

Vitta shakes her head. "She's not coming."

"I'll get her there," says Gad.

"What that girl wants, you haven't got to give."

"There's got to be an object we can steal," says Gad.

"An object?" Vitta asks.

"There's always an object," Gad explains. "A fetish, a focus, something Yath needs to stay in this world."

"It's possible . . ." Calliard strums the lute, frowns, and tightens a key.

"We can't go in until we know more," Vitta reasons.

"We've heard of Yath. The Sumas have felt it in their dreams. Who's been there and directly beheld it?"

"Seen Yath and come back alive?" says Calliard. "That's easy enough. To my knowledge, there's only one. Sodevina."

Tiberio leans in. "Sodevina, who broke the Metal Legion?"

"Yes. And found the Bridge of Breath."

"Do you know where she is now?" says Gad.

"I have a good guess. If Braval can spare a messenger, I'll find out."

"Maybe she'll be our sixth," says Vitta. "Because the girl won't."

Gad grits his teeth.

"Another question," says Vitta.

"Ask," says Gad.

"The money."

"The money?"

"We're thieves, remember? A rip isn't a rip without money at the end."

Gad barely shrugs. "There's not a copper."

"Those aren't words that inspire me to risk my life."

He fixes his full attention on the halfling. "The bigger risk is to do nothing, and let the land be overrun. Try thieving then, when Mendev's a steaming lake of sulfur."

"We'll move on. Find somewhere else to set up."

"Assuming Yath stops after only eating Mendev. Calculate the costs of moving. Of finding new contacts. Learning which officials are straight and which are crooked. Shouldering aside the local competition who are already well established wherever you choose to poke your nose. Forget heroism, Vitta. I promise you, this is the only selfish thing to do."

Calliard rises. "Shall I ask Braval about a messenger?"

"I'll come with you," Gad says.

They walk together down tower steps. "You're still good?" Gad says.

"You intend to keep asking?"

"Yes," says Gad.

"I'm still good. I haven't touched a drop in a year. I'm not about to start now."

"Good."

"We might need to work a banishment. What good is a demon hunter who can't banish?"

"If you have the stuff in your veins, you can't banish?"

"I can sense them better, but affect them less."

"An important fact," Gad says.

"Not relevant to the current situation. I've sworn off. I'm clear of it."

"Any bad dreams last night?"

"No. You?"

"No."

They reach the ground floor and head from the castle toward the parade ground, where Braval inspects his fraying troop.

"During the fight yesterday," Gad says. "That demon. The shadowy one on the parapet."

"The invidiak," says Calliard.

"It seemed to shake you."

"You don't trust me yet."

"You had that expression," says Gad.

"It was a larger specimen than I've seen before," says Calliard.

Jeweled slippers whispering across stone tiles, Lord Braval paces the floor of his daughter's bedchamber. He pinches a cold chicken leg between greasy fingers. He has taken one tiny bite from it. "Never has our need been greater," he says. "You cannot desert us now."

Jerisa sits on her bed, atop a bearskin blanket, knees tucked up under her chin. She won't look at him. "I already said I'm not going with him."

"We are Suma. This is Suma Castle. That is all there is to be said."

"Good." She points to the doorway.

Braval grimaces. "You say you aren't going, but I see into you."

"You don't see me at all."

"No more may you go into the world. There is nothing for you there but ruination. Every time you come back to us, you are weaker than the time before."

"Harder to command, you mean."

"Others may give in to wanderlust, but it is not for you. The walls of Suma are all the world any of our clan require."

"How exciting."

He points the chicken leg at her. "That mocking tone. You weren't like that, until you went out there. Mockery is the mark not of the leader, but of the led. It is for wretches and insubordinates. You must expunge it from your manner."

"Yes, father. Right away, father," she says.

"You mean to anger me so that I'll storm through that door and leave you in peace. I am forced to admit that you know me all too well. It is because we are the same, Jerisa."

She laughs.

"No longer," her father says, "will I fall for your devious games. It's far too late for that. Tomorrow our enemies might swarm at us again. If not, then the day after that, or the day after that. Any day a demon might take me. Whether my time comes this week or years from now, you will see me torn apart by an Abyssal foe, as I saw my father die and as he saw his. Then it will be you who must command. And you are not within a mile of being ready for that."

"Simon is the eldest son."

"He'll inherit the title. If he survives me, a prospect which I would not dare to predict. But it is you who is fit to wage war, and therefore must. I have been slow in accepting this necessity. He was the respectful one. The careful one. The one who obeyed. And now he is dead inside, shattered by the horror of our fate."

He kneels at her bedside. "You fought me from the moment you could speak, as you fought your way from your mother's womb. I was blinkered not to see it—your wilfulness, your rebellion, your ambition. These are the qualities of a warrior."

"They are your qualities."

"And my father's, and his father's, too."

She reaches for his hand.

"You must be toughened," Braval says, as he stands and moves away. "As I said, assume Simon survives my death. My titles are split. He becomes Lord; you become General. Consorts shall be found for the both of you. For him, so that the lineage may continue. For you, that your girlish flightiness may be stamped out and replaced with womanly fortitude. Also as a contingency should Simon fall without issue. I'll send a delegation to Kenabres, where presently resides a certain count. If he is as I have heard, he'll fight ably beside you, but is not so glorious or clever as to eclipse your authority. Should he prove unwilling or unsuitable, we'll find another. Until then, I must grant you greater authority over the men, so that you might become more accustomed to wielding it. In time they'll fix themselves as loyally to you as they have to me. But, as I said, you must alter your demeanor to achieve this. This Gad fellow . . ."

"What about him?"

"Seeing you together, I understand."

"Understand what?"

Finally Braval gnaws a chunk of meat from the chicken leg. "You have been poisoned by his example. You think of him as a leader."

"Not anymore."

"You affect to despise him now, but still you see his ease and his impertinence as traits to be admired. Now, this attitude doubtless wins the fickle affections of outlaws and layabouts—"

"I am an outlaw, father."

"Impossible. A noble does not steal; she exercises her right to plunder." Braval stops himself short. He smiles a bearish smile. "Again you seek to distract me from my intent." He sucks a chunk of chicken into his mouth and heartily chews. "Understand this, my precious daughter. Gad is no leader. A leader must be stern, distant, unwavering. Soldiers live in fear; your certitude serves as antidote against that constant condition. Tomorrow I shall . . . are you listening to me?"

She finds Gad on the outer parapet, facing the border, studying the distant, broken landscape of the Worldwound.

"I'll go with you," Jerisa says.

"Good," says Gad.

"But I want one thing from you."

"What would that be?"

"A kiss."

"A kiss," he says.

"A single kiss, and I'll go with you."

In the bleak distance, miles into demon country, a range of hilltops writhes. It segments itself into a half-dozen pieces; they shamble off in separate directions. A spearing shaft of sudden light reveals them as enormous, lacteal worms.

"I'll go there for you," she says.

"One kiss is all you want?"

"One kiss."

"And only a kiss?"

"If that's difficult for you—"

"I'm not sure what your—"

"No. No arguments. No negotiation. One kiss."

"Now?"

"It can be now. Or any time before you leave."

He squints. "So long as you understand—"

"No, no, I don't have to understand. I don't want to understand. That's not part of the deal. The deal is, you kiss me. Once."

"Then that's the deal," Gad says.

"It has to be real," she adds.

"Real in what sense?"

Her hands are on her hips. "Not like you'd kiss your sister."

"On the mouth," he says.

"A real kiss," she says.

"Very well," he says.

"Good, then."

"Calliard's messenger should be back soon," he says. "We might have to leave as soon as tomorrow."

"Well, then you have until as soon as tomorrow."

He moves in and brushes his lips against hers. Placing cool, thin hands on his face, she pulls him in tight. She holds his face to hers, prolonging the contact.

He tries gently to pull away. She presses herself harder to him. He resists, firmly disengaging himself.

She comes toward him. He pulls back.

"You have to understand," he says.

"I told you," she says, "I don't want to understand."

Her eyes glisten.

Chapter Six
The Ring

The granite barricades that once protected Zharech lie in blocky ruins. Like suffocating guardians, bushes and briars close in on them. Throughout the ruined and rebuilt town, a few stone walls remain. From them grow newer structures thrown together from ragged timber. Mud laneways curve to avoid piles of old rubble. Scrawny dogs sniff at them, pursuing scrawnier rats.

Makeshift corrals encircle scruffy nags, malnourished mules, and sleek, muscular warhorses. Grim armored men stand guard at their fences. Vendors hawk from canvas tents, announcing bargain prices on the implements of battle: blades, bows, shields, potions, arcane scrolls. An albino dwarf waves an engraved stick, claiming that it's a rod of might. Gray-robed healers offer to melt away bruises and fuse sheared bone, at exorbitant rates. Lay clerics stand on boxes, proclaiming the superior efficacy of their gods.

The loudest din comes from a half-repaired keep: roars of delight alternate with disappointed groans. Torchlight escapes its arrow slits.

The six ride along Zharech's central laneway.

"You know this place?" Vitta asks Jerisa.

"My father comes here sometimes to recruit," she says.

"Anyone we can trust with the horses?"

Jerisa scans the competing corrals until she spots a familiar face. A gristly old woman, her head a scrawl of white, witchy hair, sits on a high chair beside a corral gate, a longspear balanced on her knee. Jerisa dismounts, exchanges words with her, and drops a few coppers into a sack tied to the chair. Their horses squared away, the six lope together to the keep.

Leather-masked doorkeepers, jeweled in the manner of distant, decadent Taldor, bear scimitars at the gateway to the keep. They brace for resistance as Gad approaches. He trades a few hushed words with them; they ease themselves and beckon in the travelers.

They step into what was once the keep's interior courtyard. The air is choked with sweat and the sour musk of unwashed armpits. Spectators throng around a fighting ring, demarcated by chains strung along a series of iron posts. Coins clank, held aloft in threadbare purses. With open throats, the watchers scream. They curse in the common tongue, vituperate in Elven, and utter vile profanities in Dwarven. Most are ostentatiously armed. Their faces boast the scars of violent struggle. Madness tinges their wild cries, testimony to long months spent in the Worldwound's shadow.

Jerisa's head swivels. She surveys the crowd. "Be careful," she tells Gad.

"Of what?"

"Not sure yet."

In the ring, a blocky woman with traces of orc in her features stalks a wearied, sinewy warrior half again her size. A few strips of cloth preserve the fighters' modesty; otherwise they are naked. Each wears a pair of spiked gauntlets.

The woman's metaled fists run red with her opponent's blood. Her face shines in feral anticipation.

Gad shouts into Calliard's ear. "That's Sodevina?"

Calliard nods.

The opponent totters back on his heels. Sodevina rushes at him, hitting him with her shoulder, knocking him into the chains. Shrieking inarticulately, she grinds the spiked gauntlet into his ribs. The sinewy brawler tries to free himself. She steps aside, letting him go. As he stumbles away, she inserts a leg behind his, tripping him. The crowd yowls its appreciation. She dives on top of him, driving a flurry of punches into the back of his shorn skull.

Calliard remains fixed in place as his comrades press through the crowd. A familiar sensation rises at the back of his throat, raw and acidic. He pales. A chill rises through his bones. Scanning the crowd, he hears the whisper—demonblood—and sees the transaction. A weighty purse switches owners. In return, a glass vial, filled to the cork stopper with a red-black liquid, passes from one man's hand to another's pocket.

Images steal unbidden into Calliard's mind. He imagines himself bumping the purchaser in the crowd, slipping his hand into the pocket, grabbing the vial. Or waylaying him outside the keep, coshing him on the head, and relieving him of his prize as he sprawls unconscious in the mud.

Calliard shakes himself alert. He reminds himself of his promise to Gad. Immerses himself in the shame he would feel, were he to give in. The bard wills away his desire, redirects his attention to the fight.

Sodevina springs from her enemy's back to circuit the chains, clawed hands egging the crowd to greater heights of frenzy. They chant for his destruction. Sodevina tears at the laces fastening her gauntlets in place. She removes one, then the other. Crimson spatter dots her face. The spectators' yowled fury spirals to a crescendo.

Blinking stupidly, the opponent reaches out his arms and pushes himself to his feet. Sodevina hops up and down on the other side of the ring. Her mocking dance dares him to charge. With an enraged grunt, he barrels at her. He slips on his own perspiration, slides across the canvas surface of the ring, and lands throat-first on the chains. Sodevina, who has neatly sidestepped his charge, slips behind him to grab his right arm. She twists the captured limb. The screams of the watchers abruptly cease. A wrenching snap reverberates through the silenced room. The ruined arm juts out at a terrible angle. The defeated man slides to the mat.

She grabs his other arm, pulls that behind him, and breaks it, too.

The crowd screams its hoarse approval. Even the losing bettors cheer their cruel delight. A shower of coins drops onto the mat. Rings, bracelets and semiprecious gems skitter across its surface. Sodevina struts across it, scooping up choice items. A trio of dirt-crusted adolescents ducks through the chains to gather the rest for her. An excited young warrior holds out a hand for Sodevina to shake. She bounds over, grabs it, and pulls him into the ring. He stiffens with fear, as if worried that she's drafted him as her next opponent. Instead she bends him over and plants a ferocious kiss on his callow mouth. He gamely tries to play the part, but freezes again when she bites into his lip. To the hoots of the crowd, she releases the blushing swordsman. Checking the damage she's done to his mouth, he melts back into them. Sodevina moves to the back of the courtyard, a gang of leather-clad handlers swarming in to protect her from the riff-raff.

Gad works his way around the ring to Sodevina and her guardians. The crowd chants for another match. A fur-hatted man in Sodevina's entourage enters a colloquy with his underlings. Two spindle-legged juveniles are fitted with gauntlets and shoved into the ring, where they inconclusively circle one another.

Gad holds up a hand, seeking Sodevina's attention. Slumped on a stool, panting, she takes notice instead of a jug of water handed to her by a follower. She gurgles from it, then upends the rest over her head.

The fur-capped man puts himself in Gad's way. "You're new in Zharech," he says.

"Just arrived," Gad replies. "They call me Gad."

"No one talks to her. They talk to me instead." A trio of burly lackeys drifts to his side.

"And how do I address you, my friend?"

"I am Umir," the man eventually says. "Any permission you seek in this town, you must seek from me."

"And a fine town you have going here, Umir. May you continue to run it for as long as it remains profitable. A moment of Sodevina's time, and we'll be off."

"As I said, I conduct her business."

Gad smiles. "Perfectly understandable. Were this a deal, naturally I'd cut you in."

"Everything is a deal."

"I need merely to ask her questions about a past exploit."

Boos follow the inept, wary ring fighters as they fail to strike one another.

"How much might a brief conversation cost?" Gad asks.

"Her past deeds are not for sale."

"In a higher sense, what you say is unmistakably correct. In a practical sense, what price do you ask?"

Umir gives Tiberio an appraising up-and-down. "This one is with you?"

"This one is," Gad says.

"You want to talk to her? This one gets into the ring with her first."

Gad looks to Tiberio. "He's not that kind of fighter."

"He is if you want to talk to her."

"How about coin instead?"

"Coin I have. What I lack are combatants willing to engage my champion."

"Surely there's some other—"

"Evidently you hear poorly because I'm telling you there isn't," Umir says. "Talking about her old ways upsets her."

"It's good that you care. I promise you—"

"She's my investment. I protect my investments. The big one fights her, or she doesn't talk. The challenger wins by staying in for three rounds. Sodevina wins by . . . well, by winning."

Umir heads back to his warrior's side.

Vitta moves to follow his progress past an ornate wooden door and then stops, held fast by sight of its ancient lock.

Gad turns to Tiberio.

"Find some other way," Tiberio says.

"Do you have any suggestions?"

"I won't do it. I won't hurt her."

"I don't think it's you who has to worry about hurting her."

"You see her. She is crazy. Wounded inside. I won't harm her."

"You heard what Umir said. You don't have to put her down. You only have to last three rounds."

Tiberio thinks. "I don't like it."

"Nor do I," says Gad.

A watery voice insinuates itself into Calliard's ear. "You're of the blood, aren't you?"

Calliard turns. The seller of the blood vial has sidled up next to him. His teeth are skewed in their sockets. Gray stubble pokes from his protruding jaw.

"No, I'm not."

"Brother, I saw you looking. And I can smell the thirst, because I've felt it myself. Zharech is the best place. There're always demons infiltrating in. Some will let you bleed them, in exchange for favors."

Calliard tries to move away. The man grabs him by the elbow. "I do the brewing myself. Right alchemy, every batch guaranteed." His pack bulges open. Calliard can smell the other vials inside. "How long has it been?"

"Let me go or I'll kill you right here," Calliard says.

The blood vendor releases him. "Betweening, are you? Don't think I don't respect that, brother."

"There's nothing that makes us brothers."

"You'll be able to find me," he says. "Just let yourself feel the pull."

Calliard pushes away from him, staggering into a red-bearded dwarf. The dwarf bares his teeth, then lets him pass.

Jerisa watches a man watching Gad. She melts into the crowd.

Tiberio steps over the chains to enter the ring. Umir's men scuttle up to supply him with his spiked gauntlets. The crowd murmurs restlessly as they try to tie him into them. They're too small; long minutes pass fruitlessly by. Beery spectators stomp their feet. Sodevina shrugs. She takes off her gauntlets, ready to fight bare-handed. Umir, face fussily crinkling, appears at ringside. He confers with his investment. Sodevina absently nods. The ring boys come back with new weapons: a pair of long boards, each with an array of rusty nails protruding from them. They offer Tiberio first choice. He takes the one with fewer nails. For the first time, Sodevina seems to take stock of her new opponent.

Umir rings a gong.

Tiberio remains in place. Sodevina remains in place.

From her stance, Tiberio guesses that this is her customary tactic. She lets the enemy come to her. Sizes him up. Waits for an error. When it is made, she strikes.

Tiberio waits her out. The crowd jeers.

Without signaling her intent, she runs abruptly at him. He sidesteps. She compensates. Her makeshift club bangs against his. He pushes her back. Waits again for her to come at him. He keeps up the pattern—her lunging at him, him parrying, then pushing her off— all the while determining their movement through the ring, keeping himself from being herded into the chains.

The restive crowd grumbles. It demands a fight. The remains of an apple sail from the back of the throng. It smacks Tiberio in the back of the head. Fragments of fruit spray over the ring and onto Sodevina's face. She rushes for the chains, as if to leap into the crowd and tear into the offender. An instant later, she realizes her mistake, and turns to raise her club against the blow Tiberio ought to be making. She sways in confusion. "What's your game, you bastard?" she spits.

She takes a swing; he deflects it too late, taking a glancing hit to the shoulder. She follows up but flails wide.

He grabs her club from her and tosses it across the ring. She raises her arms, expecting him to strike. He tosses his club after hers.

"What's your game?" she asks.

He says nothing.

"Why won't you fight?"

Epithets in five languages echo through the keep.

Her foot comes up in a perfect arc to kick him in the throat. He doubles over, winded. Her elbow comes down on his neck. He falls to one knee. Another raking kick cuts him above the ribs. He rolls. She leaps onto him. He seizes her arms before she can start to throttle him. He rolls over, trying to pin her. Her legs windmill, sliding her out of position. She knees him in the groin.

Sodevina is up; Tiberio, down. She fumbles for his arm, to pull it behind him and snap it. With a flex of his muscles, he shakes her off. Though a casual ripple of effort, its force sends her sprawling. She lands on her backside. Her lip purses. Traces of a previous self displace her feral look. She jumps up and sprints over to retrieve her club. Tiberio is only halfway to his feet when she arrives to clout him. With a rocky forearm he alters the trajectory of the strike, preventing the nails from entering his skull.

She surrenders herself to frenzy. A whirl of blows thud across his arms, his shoulder, his torso. Red droplets gather on the links of chain. Tiberio falls, rises, falls. Sodevina smashes him on the back of the head. The crowd deafens itself on its own roared approval.

Tiberio's arm shoots out. He clutches the club, twisting it from her grip. She slips and goes down to one knee. He shudders to a standing position. Tiberio raises the club above his head. The house goes silent, waiting for him to deliver the coup de grace.

He takes the club in both hands and holds it above his head. She scoots back, scrambling free of her vulnerable position. Tiberio brings the club into collision with the back of his head. It bends and splinters. He breaks the already-weakened board over his knee and throws the two halves into the audience.

Tiberio checks to make certain that the pieces haven't hit anyone. In his moment of distraction, Sodevina leaps on him. He falls, the chains lashing his face as he topples. Stunned, he lies helpless as she kicks him. After several hard punts to his side, she halts. Spectators moan their disappointment. She returns to kicking him. A scarlet rivulet runs from the side of his mouth.

Chapter Seven
The Story

Gad clenches each time a new kick lands. Rapt, he fails to see the man edging through the crowd toward him. His stalker is tall and rangy, slightly cross-eyed, his hair a sandy tousle. The man reaches striking distance, hesitates for a second, and scrapes a short sword from the scabbard at his hip.

Tiberio endures another hit. Gad's body judders as if he too has been struck.

The swordsman aims his blow, the point of his blade seeking Gad's liver.

A throwing dagger appears in the man's back.

The would-be killer slumps over onto Gad. Gad turns, catches the falling man—a corpse already—and sees Jerisa approaching him. She plucks the dagger from the attacker's spinal column. In a single fluid motion she wipes it off on her victim's woolly tunic.

"Friend of yours?" she asks.

Gad adjusts the body slightly, to identify its face. "Property dispute," he explains.

"He had property, and you disputed that?"

"Essentially," he says.

She follows his gaze to a crew of roughnecks pushing their way toward them, weapons drawn. They count six certain foes, and as many more who might or might not be with them.

"He had friends," says Jerisa.

"Without friends, what are we?" says Gad.

Spectators scatter as the armed men converge on them.

Gad draws his sword. Hendregan takes advantage of the parting crowd to dash to join Gad and Jerisa. Farther away, Calliard is hemmed in between spectators still transfixed by Tiberio's endurance and the beating he is taking.

Jerisa's arm blurs. Her dagger lodges in an enemy eye socket.

The crowd becomes a mob. With one consciousness, it agrees that Gad and Jerisa are the interlopers.

A rat-faced gnome rushes at Gad with a short sword. Gad parries it out of his hand. Jerisa stabs a sallow blond woman; her hand-axe drops at her feet as she clutches the wound.

The crowd tightens around them. Individual blows and opponents give way to a crushing scuffle. Gad takes a blow to the head. Jerisa is struck in the ribs.

His head on the mat, Tiberio sees his friends engulfed. Palms flat against its surface, he surges to his feet. Sodevina scuttles back to take a run at him. He leaps from the mat into the crowd.

Tiberio lands on a jowly thug equipped with a rapier, knocking him away from Gad.

Sodevina climbs onto the chains and uses them to propel her body after him.

Aware that Sodevina is among them, the press of combatants fearfully recedes.

A toothless, puffy-cheeked woman swings a hammer at Gad's head. He ducks and pushes her back with the flat of his blade.

Tiberio turns to Sodevina, protecting the others from her.

She dekes around him, springing at the toothless warrior. She snatches the hammer from the woman's grasp, kicking her in the solar plexus for good measure.

Tiberio braces for her assault.

Instead she caroms the hammer off the helmeted head of a bald, stocky mercenary.

She's taken their side.

A piercing whistle comes from the back wall. Vitta is there, still at the door that caught her attention earlier, working its antique lock. With her free hand she beckons them.

Tiberio lurches her way. Appalled by his swelling, ruined face, the crowd takes an involuntary step back. The others follow, Sodevina and Jerisa turning to shield their backs. Calliard changes course, heading by his separate route to Vitta's door.

Jerisa expends a dagger. An attacker crumples, the blade stuck in his upper arm.

Sodevina's commandeered hammer fells a waddling dwarf. His broad frame keels back into the pack of onrushers. Limbs tangle and twist; the knot of attackers resolves into a heap on the floor.

A fur-clad woman, her face an occult swirl of tattoo ink, pokes at a retreating Sodevina with her spear. Sodevina steps her way; the woman pales and fades. The crowd loses its impetus. As many now try to distance themselves from the group—from Sodevina most of all—as attempt to surge their way.

The bard parries blows from a nail-headed club. Its wielder sports a wiry mustache and a dozen studs in his large ears. Calliard reaches the door first. The mustached attacker reasons that Vitta must be with him and directs his next blow at her. This gives Calliard the opening he requires to rake the blade of his sword across the man's weapon hand. He withdraws, furiously cursing.

The others arrive to the sound of Sodevina's hammer impacting with an iron breastplate.

Hendregan ducks as a chair hurtles at them from the back of the crowd. It splinters against the wall behind him. His nostrils quiver.

"That lock doesn't open," Sodevina breathes.

Vitta opens the lock.

For the first time since the scuffle began, Hendregan has the elbow room to gesticulate properly. He utters an incantation. Fire appears around his hands.

Gad, knowing what comes next, jostles the fire wizard during the last of his arcane motions. A diffuse ball of flame appears far from the throng, weakly spreading across the stone ceiling.

"What did you do that for?" Hendregan demands.

"To stop you from killing dozens of people."

"They're attacking us," he says.

"No," says Gad, "they think we're attacking them."

Hendregan mutters unintelligibly. Calliard pulls him through the door. Gad follows. The rest are on the other side already. Vitta slams the door shut and resets its lock.

It rattles as someone on the other side tries to force it open. Fists and weapons pound fruitlessly on the heavy door.

The chamber on the other side is dry and choked with dust. The only light is a tiny line escaping from the gap between door and frame. Hendregan, still grumbling, unfolds a segmented staff. It burns with a false and heatless fire, illuminating their new surroundings. It is the most ordinary of a wizard's spells, but Hendregan has altered it so that it seems to burn. He has done the same with all of them.

The flickering yellow light reveals a set of stone steps leading up. A moldering plank leans against the wall near the doorway. Iron bar sliders affix themselves to the doorframe, and Vitta fits the plank into them, barring the door against attempts to batter it down.

"Where does it lead?" asks Gad, meaning the staircase.

"There's still part of the parapet left," Vitta answers. "It might be blocked, or it might lead all the way up to the top."

"Go look," says Gad.

Vitta complies.

Exhausted and bruised, Tiberio lets himself fall against a wall. Dust and grime sticks to his sweaty, bloody skin. "Why did you help us?" he asks Sodevina.

An incessant tic pulls at the warrior's cheek. "You're a better fighter than that," she says.

"Better than what?"

Her flimsy top has slipped in the fray; she tugs it unceremoniously back into place. "In the ring. Couple of times, you could have hurt me bad. But you weren't really fighting. Only taking it. Couldn't figure why that was. When it's me you're up against, it's either stupid not to fight back, or it's something else. Took me a while to realize it was something else. Then when these ones got in trouble, I saw you see that and, then when you followed . . . I saw you were doing it for them. For some reason. And so let's say I got curious and wanted to know what that was." She turns to Gad. "You're the leader, uh-huh?"

"Somebody has to be," Gad says.

Vitta returns. "We can get up to the parapet from here."

"Do we want to get to the parapet?"

"Tiberio could use some air," Calliard suggests.

Sodevina is first to head for the steps. She asks for names; Gad introduces himself and the others.

Cool air blasts them as they pull themselves through a trap door onto the keep's best remaining wall. They hunch below the crenelations of its battlement so as not to be seen from the ground.

"Which one of you's the healer?" says Sodevina.

"He is," says Vitta, pointing to the injured Tiberio.

Sodevina reaches for Hendregan's heatless flame and holds it up to Tiberio's cut face. The swelling has sealed shut his left eye. "What was worth having him endure this?" she asks, returning the light-stick to Hendregan.

"Word is you can tell us about Yath," says Gad.

Her cheek tics faster. "That's what you want?"

"You did see Yath, yes?"

She wrings her fingers compulsively together. "You went to Umir and said you wanted to talk to me. And he said he'd only let you if one of you fought me first."

"That's the summary."

She turns away from them. "You're going there?"

"We are," says Gad, "and need your help."

"Here is my help." She drops her ground-glass voice to near inaudibility. "Do not. Do not go."

Gad moves to sit down beside her. "Somebody's got to put a stop to all this."

"You'll only destroy yourselves. You can see that I'm not right. Uh-huh?"

"Maybe we can help you, some way, in exchange. Get you out of here."

"Here's the only place I ought to be."

"What hold does Umir have over you?"

"Hold?" She laughs. "He thinks he holds me, maybe. I am here by choice. The last choice that I can see. I keep waiting for the one. The one who will do it." She indicates Tiberio. "When I saw him tower into view, I thought maybe he was it. But he wouldn't. I still don't think I understand the answer. Why he wouldn't do it. I know you wanted information from me, but you could have got that from me by winning . . . unless you thought I wouldn't."

Gad lets silence hang in the air. Finally he says, "So you don't want us to go to Yath. Convince us. Tell us what happened."

"You think me stupid, do you?"

"Not remotely."

"You only want my tale because then you'll go, to march off to your destruction, and then your deaths will be on my head."

"Too?"

Hands on knees, she rocks uneasily forward and back. "My comrades. My beautiful comrades. Brave Geraux. Handsome Danan. Two-Staves, who knew more than any magician. Eleenan, whose song was like water. Isane, who I loved and who might have loved me. All dead, as you will die, if you go to Yath. Their deaths on my head. As the deaths of your comrades will be on yours, Gad."

"No one's going to die," says Gad.

Again she laughs. "That's what I said! They didn't want to! I convinced them. We could cover ourselves in glory. Be celebrated as heroes forever. Drag home from the demon tower more loot than we could carry!"

"Loot?" Vitta asks.

"Oh, there is no loot," Sodevina says. "Unless you've found a willing buyer for pus and bile and a million pulsing insectile demon eggs. Call to mind the most terrible images. Imagine the worst visions in *his* head!"

She means Hendregan, who has taken to rocking in unison with the ring fighter. Startled, he takes control and stills himself.

"Take those terrible thoughts and treble them in intensity. That is still a fraction of what you'll behold if you pass the gates of Yath. Uh-huh? Just to set foot within the tower is to court madness. Do you know it's not a tower, not only?"

"It's also a demon," Calliard prompts.

"Yes, yes, and not. It is too many things at once. And that is part of its madness. And it creates madness in you. As lice lay eggs in your scalp. As worms gnaw your guts. The longer you're there, the worse it gets."

Gad moves to face her. "We want to know if there's an object. Something that ties it to this plane. Something we can steal."

"The orb? You know of the orb?"

"Orb?"

"The Wardstone Orb. We went there not knowing about it, but found it was the key to Yath's power."

"What is it?"

"You know what wardstones are, uh-huh?"

"They're supposed to keep the demons out of Mendev, but now they're being counteracted—we think by Yath."

"Yes, yes, of course by Yath. You know the Monastery of Tala?"

Gad shakes his head.

"Twenty leagues to the northeast," Calliard injects.

"The cloistered brothers there are powerful priests of several faiths, joined in study to pit their combined knowledge and abilities against the Worldwound. Advised by a great abbess of Kenabres, they commenced a great experiment. If the wardstones held power against demonkind, perhaps that power could be concentrated. Refined into a weapon against powerful champions of the Abyss, one you could carry with you, into the Worldwound."

"Like a wand."

"Or a holy relic. Since the last crusade the residents of Tala have worked to this end. One generation after another. They consecrated a wardstone. Let it stand for a decade as a bulwark against the demons. Tended its might. Strengthened it with ritual and prayer. When a decade and a day had passed, they erected a new wardstone and then knocked the old one down."

"You say you didn't know of the orb before you left," says Calliard.

"That's right."

"So you learned this story there."

"From the lips of a cruel priestess, as she mocked our failure."

"So it could be lies."

"It could be." She grants the point with growing resentment.

"What else did she tell you?" Gad prompts.

"The moment had come. For ten years, the brothers of Tala had honed their stonecutting skills, waiting for their material to ripen. The old wardstone, now resonant with anti-Abyssal essence, was turned over to their workshop. They fragmented it and cut it and polished it and magicked it. Until they had a crystal globe. Along the way they suffered many failures, producing globes of near perfection. Each of them in turn cracked or clouded. Uh-huh?"

"Uh-huh."

"Yet after all their tortuous labors, finally they had what they'd sought to create. The spherical shape geometrically precise. The crystal of flawless clarity. The priests celebrated. Their abbot, stricken by a withering disease, clung to life just long enough to behold its splendor, then serenely expired. You may say this is an exaggeration, but it is how the demon priestess told it to me."

"She told it vividly."

"Her words lodge in the mind."

"Continue . . ."

"The brothers then held a tournament. To select the mightiest crusaders of Mendev. For the first time in a decade they opened the doors of their fortress to outsiders. Fierce champions battled for the glorious honor of carrying the Orb of Tala into the Worldwound, and using it to scourge the demon warlords and generals there. By tournament's end they had a war party of three dozen and seven great crusaders. At the last minute they were joined by the abbess herself. With fanfare and spectacle they were heralded as their departing convoy left to cross the border."

"And it was all a trap," says Gad.

"Uh-huh. A demon horde ambushed them in a crevasse. Slew the heroes, save one. The last of them, the abbess, shed her false raiments, and stepped forth to claim her true mantle as priestess of Yath."

"This was the priestess telling you the story?"

"Isilda, she is called. Razors in the soles of her boots. The object she had directed the brothers to make was not a weapon against demonkind, but a seed from which Yath would sprout. She planted it in the roiling earth of the Worldwound. Watered it with the blood of the martyred dead."

"So the orb is buried under the tower?"

"The tower grew up around it. The orb lies in a vault deep in its bowels."

"And you and the others found out about it and tried to get it out of the vault."

"Tried? We never got so far as to try." She stops talking.

It was a mistake, Gad realizes, to mention the others. "What prevented you?"

"Even if we hadn't been caught, we still had no way to get to Yath. We would have had to get the orb somehow to the inner chamber, where Yath's consciousness dwells, and perform the ritual of banishment. The others were doubtful, but I said we could figure that out when the time came. Fact is, no one gets inside the inner chamber. No one except its top few chancellors."

"Wait," says Calliard. "You got inside the tower, though."

"Hah?" The introduction of a new questioner confuses her. "That part was easy. Made us cocky. We posed as cultists. They don't know all who serve them. From all across Mendev and beyond, madmen and demon worshipers feel its pull unbidden. Compulsion takes them to Yath's doorstep, uh-huh? Are you sure you don't feel the compulsion?"

"Not that one."

"They are housed and garrisoned until a task is found, and then they are sent back here to undermine us. It is easy because it is a trap. If you are not mad or a consorter with demonkind when you cross its threshold, you will be soon, as the place wriggles through you. We might have withstood this, but by betraying the Abbot of Tala, Isilda prevented that, too."

"Explain," says Gad.

"Until the champions of Tala were betrayed, it was possible to go to the monastery and purchase a salve of protection against demonic influence."

"A salve?"

"Remember?" says Calliard. "We used it to get the Xanthou Pendant."

"That was from Tala?"

"In a roundabout way," says Calliard.

"We need that salve," says Gad.

"They won't give it to you," Sodevina says. "For a week we camped on the threshold of their now-sealed walls. We heard them within, but they would not answer our entreaties. If only they'd spoken to us, I could have convinced them, but they would not. And with foolish pride I took my people into the Worldwound, into the tower, without it."

Gad frowns. "And so you wound up serving Yath?"

She grabs Gad by the collar. "Do not say that!"

"Forgive me, Sodevina."

She pushes him; he lets himself fall, careful to protect his head. "No, they did not succumb. We didn't last that long. We were caught by Yath's priestess, the false priestess, Isilda."

"I'll need to know about her," says Gad. "How she thinks, what she wants."

Sodevina hasn't heard him. She continues as if speaking only to herself. "It was I who got us caught. I could not disguise my revulsion at the awfulness of that place. A true demon-lover strides through it excitedly, in a thrill of perversity. She saw the nausea on my face and sent spies to listen in on us. We were hauled before her. Tortured. Each of us thrown into a special Abyss. Each prison knew us—our weaknesses, our fears—and ate our souls. Of what befell the others, I will not speak. My torture was to see it happen. To watch. Unable to save them. As their sanity was forever ripped away from them."

Hendregan has wandered away, tunelessly humming. He pops his head above the battlement. Vitta scuttles over to pull him out of sight. The wizard has chewed a layer of skin from his lower lip.

"Your friends," Gad asks Sodevina, "are they still there?"

"I led an escape, but they were all slain on the way out of the tower. I alone survived."

"What more can you tell us about Isilda?"

This time she grabs him by the arm. Jagged fingernails dig into his sleeve. "You've tricked me."

The pain of her grip registers in his voice. "How have I tricked you, Sodevina?"

"As Yath tricked me. As my own vanity tricked me. Before I was broken, I would not have been so easily fooled. I'm not convincing you to stay away. I never have been."

"Please let go of my arm, Sodevina."

She does. "I'm sorry," she weeps.

"There's nothing to be sorry for."

"I'm a coward. I wait for a fighter to come and do what I am too afraid to do for myself."

"Now that's the madness talking, isn't it?" He moves to embrace her.

She swats him aside and leaps onto the edge of the parapet, balancing herself with outstretched arms.

"You consider these people your friends?" she asks Gad.

He steps toward her.

"Stand back!"

He stops.

"Answer my question," she demands. From between the stone blocks beneath her, crumbling mortar drizzles.

"Yes, they are my friends. Come down from there."

"If you value them, do not do what I did."

"I do value them."

"Then don't take them into the Worldwound." She glances behind her, seeing how long the drop is.

Gad edges infinitesimally toward her. "Your friends wouldn't want you to do this."

"Perhaps not," says Sodevina. "But are they here to say so?" She swallows a lump of phlegm. "I am sorry, Isane," she says, tipping back.

Gad tries to catch her. She drops over and away. Gad is only fast enough to see her land. The others hear the thud of impact. Together they peek over the wall. Sodevina lies with arms and legs outstretched. The angle of her broken neck, and the spreading dark pool beneath her head, belie a pose that might otherwise seem serene.

Gad curses.

"Oh no," says Hendregan.

Gad peers down at her.

"Oh no oh no oh no oh no oh no," Hendregan repeats.

Jerisa touches Gad's shoulder with tentative fingertips. "She wasn't giving you the chance."

"No, no, no," says Hendregan.

Vitta peers over the parapet, to check if others have heard the fall. This side of the keep is sheltered from the town. It faces onto encroaching scrub, with a stand of trees behind. No one comes.

"It makes no sense," she says. "She had the willpower to fight and win in that ring every night. To go into the Worldwound in the first place. Why could she not then use that force of will to overcome her regrets?"

"Easily said," says Jerisa.

"Easily said, easily done," Vitta says. "To let yourself be undone by, by . . . *bad memories*? It surpasses understanding."

Hendregan twitches.

"Stop talking now, Vitta," Jerisa says.

"But you see my point."

"We should hasten," says Gad, "before they find her. Or come looking for us."

Jerisa reaches into her pack, withdrawing a grapnel attached to a length of thin Nirmathi rope.

Vitta continues: "There is no strength greater than logic. If she had only the wit to use it, she would not be—"

Hendregan cries out, words mangled in his throat. He rends his robe and clambers halfway over the parapet. Tiberio grabs hold of him.

Sobs well in Hendregan's throat. "She couldn't use logic because she wasn't right anymore."

Gad seizes his shoulder from the other side. "I'm sorry you had to see this, Hendo."

The tattooed wizard grimaces at the sound of his old nickname.

"She said she wasn't right," says Hendregan. "And I saw her and I realized, neither am I."

"First, departure," says Gad. "Then we'll talk about this, all you want."

"I never saw it until I saw it in her. I'm not who I was when we first met. Am I?"

"You do want us to get out of here safely, yes?"

Hendregan nods. "But first answer my question."

"No one's who they used to be."

The wizard loosens his grip on the battlement.

"Down before, you blocked my arm. How many would I have roasted, had you not done that? A dozen men? Two dozen?"

"That was no place to let off a fireball," Gad says.

"And so you stopped me," Hendregan burbles. "As well you should. But all I thought was, *I am fire. Let fire burn!* I am as mad as she!" He gestures to Sodevina's body. "And I think myself ready for a place of even greater madness?" He stops to gasp for breath. "Take me back to my prison."

"You don't belong there," Gad says. "No one does."

"I am no longer the man you knew."

"We'll find that man again."

"In the tower of Yath?"

"What do you fight fire with?"

"Fire," says Hendregan.

"And so what do you fight madness with?"

"Madness?" Hendregan contemplates this for a moment.

"Let's get down from here," Tiberio says.

Jerisa sets and tests her hook.

"That's the stupidest notion ever uttered," Vitta grumbles. "Fighting madness with madness?"

Jerisa elbows the halfling locksmith in the shoulder.

They rappel down the wall, Hendregan first, Tiberio last.

Through arrow slits they see a handful of armed figures still gathered by the locked door, waiting for them to come out. The rest of Zharech appears to have already lost interest in them. In a half-crouch, the six dash through the scrub to the forest beyond. Once in the trees, Hendregan unfolds his light-stick. They find a fallen log to slump behind.

"What do we do about the horses?" Vitta asks.

"I'll go," says Calliard. "I wasn't with you in the mob. I'm least likely to be recognized. If they're still waiting for us."

"We'll wait here for fifteen, then circle around to the main road."

"By the big oak?"

Gad nods.

Calliard goes.

"Can we believe her story?" Jerisa asks.

"The part about the tournament at Tala is true," Vitta says. "I was invited to participate, as a trapsmith and lockbreaker."

"You were there?" Gad says.

The halfling responds with an incredulous snort. "Walk myself undefended into a nest of paladins and lawmen? Hardly."

"The salve against demon madness is real," says Gad. "We've used it before."

"What now then?" Jerisa asks.

"We get that salve."

Chapter Eight
The Thing They Need for the Plan

Approaching the corral, Calliard spies two armored men speaking to its proprietor. A pair of standing torches silhouettes them. Calliard ducks below a rubble pile.

Their voices are familiar. He listens intently, straining to identify them. Their words remain muffled. Calliard makes out only the tenor of their exchange. They are asking questions: hopeful, insistent. The old woman deflects them: casual, disinterested. They persist; she bridles. It takes a few more minutes before they relent and clank away. Their path brings them into town, in the direction of Calliard's hiding place. He scuttles around it as they pass. For an instant, he glimpses them. He sees on their over-tunics the crest of the Everbright Crusaders.

Can he trust the woman? She seemed resistant to the lawkeepers' inquiries. He heard no coins drop into her palm. Jerisa seemed to know and prefer her.

Calliard decides to risk it. To lose the horses would be too great a setback. He straightens and moves toward her.

The woman sees him coming. She shifts in her elevated chair. When he is close, she says, "You saw those two?"

"I did," says Calliard.

"They were asking about you. Not you, troubadour, but your party. They asked about someone called Gad. Is that one of you?"

Calliard hesitates.

"Don't answer," she says, "I don't care. You're with a Suma, and that's enough for me."

With the end of her long spear she unlatches the corral gate. Calliard goes in for the horses.

The corral-keeper looks along the path the crusaders walked. "They'll find few friends in Zharech," she says. "Stinking paladins."

The sand-colored stones of the Monastery of Tala gleam orange in sunset light. Thick pines and twisted spruce range around it, crowding the hill it tops. They obscure all but the upper edge of a stone-and-cement wall surrounding the main structure. Three cloisters compose the monastery structure, each marking a different era of construction. The nearest looks down at the world from a quartet of squared, latticed windows built in the manner of the First Crusade. A second cloister attaches to the first, its windows arched in Second Crusade style. A wrought-iron railing edges its roof, protecting a garden. Early spring shoots climb up a hanging rack built for the cultivation of squashes and cucumbers. Behind the second cloister juts up the third, an imposing cube several stories in height, and from behind that rises a chapel cupola.

Through a miserly gap in the treeline, an arched gate, barred by twin portcullises, can nearly be seen. Warrior brothers stand outside it, halberds ready, the blade of divine Iomedae upon their fraternal robes.

The density of the forest works both ways. The crew has hidden itself and its horses behind a wall of reaching cedars.

Jerisa has been gone for a quarter-hour. They have spoken little since their departure from Zharech. They are not talking about Sodevina's fate, or that of the Tala champions. Gad occupies the others with a dice game. When Calliard catches him at it, he stops letting them beat him.

"I don't suppose you've heard any sinister rumors about the brothers of Tala," he asks the bard.

"You'd prefer it if they deserved to be robbed," Calliard replies.

"We need what they have," says Vitta. "Everyone stands to gain if we have it."

Gad nods his agreement. He rolls a triple and sweeps their coins into his pile.

"Everyone gains except us," Vitta adds.

The cedars rustle. They turn, weapons ready.

It's Jerisa.

"You couldn't get in?" Vitta asks.

"What are you talking about?"

"You're back already?"

"After I finish a job, I leave." She throws the vials of salve to Calliard.

Vitta's eyes widen. She scoops up the dice. Tiberio unties the horses' reins.

Jerisa removes one of the daggers from her belt, wiping blood from it with a soft cloth.

Gad gives her a questioning look.

"Don't worry," she says, moving to his side. "Nothing permanent."

She edges closer.

He smiles, a little, and turns away to address the group. "Now comes the hard part," he says.

Jerisa's expression darkens.

"Oh, wait," says Gad. "First a detour. *Then* the hard part."

Gray fog lies on the hamlet like a layer of batting. A ring of stakes marks its border. Atop each stake is a head, mummified or skeletal. Most belonged to animals: sheep, cows, goats, pigs. One is the bulbous red pate of a demon, like the torturer Gad saw on his way north from Krega. Another head belongs to a gigantic centipede. A third looks like an orc or bugbear; its withered condition eludes precise identification.

Inside the protective ring huddle several dozen leaning, misshapen huts. Fist-sized green spiders patrol the roofs. Scrawny chickens wander the hamlet's crumbled pathways. A horrible cooking smell drifts from the huts and toward the visitors.

Vitta frowns. "You sure you want to go in there?"

"I'm sure I don't," Gad says. "You know anyone else in the vicinity who can produce a scroll of banishment to our unique particulars?"

"I'm sure I don't," Vitta echoes.

He steps through the ring of stakes. Tiberio and Jerisa make to follow him.

"Stay here," Gad says. "I'll be alright."

"I thought you said it was dangerous," Jerisa says.

"Not that kind of danger."

He walks slowly, clearing his throat to announce his presence.

Hovel doors creak open. Rheumy eyes blink out at him. A cackling erupts. Hunched women jig from the cottages and surge to greet him. Heads of snow-white or dull gray hair trail after them as they run. The youngest of them can't be less than six decades old. With liver-spotted hands they paw at Gad. The crones run palsied fingers over the leather of his hauberk, his cloak, his face. They pinch his cheeks and yank at his hair. High-pitched coos loosen themselves from wattled throats.

"Oh, Gad!" they cry.

Their gabblings collide into a single rush of chatter: "So long it's been!" "Finally you've come back to us." "Oh, you're still a fine one, aren't you . . ." "Need to fatten you up . . ." "This time it's my soup you must taste." "You mustn't only visit *her* this time." "She won't want to see you." "You're always welcome at my hearth, you handsome devil." "Every time you leave, you break her heart." "You break all of our hearts." "Oh, but it's her heart you break the most." "You're only saying that because you don't have one; you've locked it in a chest and forgot where you buried it." "You and your nonsense!" "Send a message ahead next time so we can pretty ourselves up." "So we can lay in a feast." "All I have for meat is salt pork, but if you wait, we'll cast a deer-luring, and there will be venison for all." "Why don't you bring your friends in?" "You're not ashamed of your grandmothers, are you?" "Speak for yourself; I'm no grandmother at all and certainly not his . . ."

He breaks gently free from the press of fondling hands. "Sorry, ladies. Now that I'm here I can't leave without seeing her."

"You always say that." "Heartbreaker." "Thoughtless cad." "Gad the cad. "That's what they call him, all right."

He moves hesitantly toward the loneliest of the cottages, one that stands at a remove from the others.

The door swings wide as he hits the front step. He moves inside. It smells like cinnamon and dust.

A tall figure stands in a beam of faded sunlight. In the set of her elevated cheekbones and the curve of her ears, there flickers a hint of elven ancestry. Deep folds crease her face. A head of pallid hair frazzles and tangles its way to her waist. Fraying threads dangle from the cuffs and hems of her green velvet robe.

Gad stands frozen in the doorway.

She comes to him, circuiting around a well-kept wooden loom, and cups her hand around his jawline. "Their clucking woke me," she says. "It could only be you. I slumber more and more these days." She stands back to take him in. "Still the same, I see."

"Maeru," he says.

"You're here for a favor," she says.

"That's right."

She turns from him. "You only come for favors."

"I prefer not to cause you pain . . ."

"What's the rip?"

"You're better off unaware."

"Because whoever it is will knock on my door and break me till I spill?"

"I'm already one unintended casualty in the hole."

"A village of witches has its means of defense."

"I can see that from the stake ornaments, but nonetheless . . ."

"A heavy target, then."

"Let's just say the scroll I need from you is one of demon banishment. Big demon banishment."

"Yath," she says.

"Ahead of me as usual."

"We don't get out, but news comes our way. I've no banishments in my repertoire."

Gad opens his pack. He produces a folio of loose-leaf parchment pages. "The fruit of Calliard's researches."

"Of his library thefts, you mean."

"The terms are of course synonymous. He figures that there must be one among you that can do the trick. I understand less of this business than he does. Should I bring him in to confer?"

She pales. "I won't be seen."

"Sorry to ask. It's just . . . if you're following the war . . ."

Maeru recovers her composure. "The demons have mostly left us alone so far. Once they take the fortresses and cities, they'll scour the villages. They'll get to us last, but they'll get to us, if Yath is allowed to stand."

"So you'll help?"

"When have I disappointed you, Gad?"

"We need it woven, not inscribed."

"A piece of cloth?"

"That's right."

"And so you came to me. I'll need to weave in the sigils with enchanted thread."

"You've done it before, yes?"

"It's difficult, but not impossible. Like so many things." She takes the folio and pages through its contents. "I'll puzzle it out. Choose the most suitable incantation."

"Also if you could sew a drawstring on it . . . you can see from this diagram Calliard's drawn."

She nods.

"How long will it take?"

"You'll have to make camp for a day. Maybe two. Your team is good?"

"I wouldn't go in with a wrong team."

"Foolish of me to ask," she says. She parts a gauzy curtain to look out the window. Gusts have blown the fog away. She appraises the others as they stand uneasy guard on the other side of the stakes. "Does that one love you?"

"The halfling? Be serious."

"You be serious."

Gad's face screws itself into a wince.

"How much encouragement did you give her?"

"Too much. It was a time ago."

"Not long ago enough, from where she stands."

"Is there foraging we can do for you?"

She shakes her head. "So you're gaffling Yath. And you expect to do this, and still observe Rule One?"

"Yes. Rule One: Everybody gets out."

"As always."

"Yes, as always."

"But not necessarily in one piece."

"Well, sometimes you warn someone not to go down a certain corridor and they go ahead and do it anyhow."

Maeru sighs. "To look at the two of us, me and her . . ."

"Maeru, don't."

"You wouldn't think . . ."

He tries to embrace her.

She evades him, pressing closer to the window, staring at Jerisa. "You'd assume I was so, so many years older . . ."

A row of wardstones marks the Worldwound border. They line a ridge of raw earth, angling like bad teeth. The obelisks here are huge, perhaps thirty feet high and carved with holy markings. At each base, a patting of cement holds them in place.

The sky on the Mendev side is a turbulent gray. On the other side, it is a purulent purple, slashed with streaks of red.

As it creeps from Mendev to the Worldwound, the vegetation steadily thins. Ordinary shrubs and grasses give way to dried and twisted weeds. The seed pods of some great sprouting contort themselves to look like shrieking faces. Wind blows through the drier specimens, producing an arrhythmic whistle.

The Worldwound side is a vast depression, as if a gargantuan demonic hand once swept down to claw the earth away. Gravel and dirt line its slope.

The angle of the depression conceals the terrain on the border's other side. Gad and Jerisa dismount and crawl to the edge for a better look.

Everywhere before them the earth is broken. Madly circuiting trenches zig through the ground like insect burrows. Pools of goo bubble from the earth, sometimes spewing over into the trenches. Stunted trees twist around one another, their bark deformed into serpentine scales. Spiny weeds stake out scattered patches of ground, black snot dripping from their sharpened leaves. In the distance, a geyser spouts bile-colored liquid.

Half a mile in the distance, a platoon of armored men works its way through the broken earth. Atop glossy, muscled steeds, they trace a winding trail, moving systematically around the trenches. From a herald's pole flaps a pennant bearing a familiar crest.

Gad mutters his most reliable profanity.

"What?" Jerisa asks.

"They're like a curse. Wherever I go, they're in my way."

"Who?"

"The Everbright Crusaders." He peers through a spyglass handed him by Calliard. "And damned if that isn't Fraton, taking point." He puts down the spyglass. "What are they playing at?"

"They're a crusader order, chockablock with paladins, aren't they? Isn't this what crusaders do—plunge into the Worldwound to fight demons and get themselves killed?"

"Fraton prefers to hunt sinners in Nerosyan. And occasionally, Kenabres."

"We knew members of his order were in Zharech. Looking for you," she adds.

"How does he have any idea we were there?"

"Maybe he asked his god. Paladins can do that, yes?"

"If they can't, their priests can."

"There's your explanation, then."

"Fraton's headed to the tower of Yath to capture me?"

"Does he despise you that much?"

"On full consideration?" says Gad. "Yes."

"This is the best place for miles to cross the border. Unless you want to pick your way through rocky hills or dense forest. Anyone coming from Zharech would cross here now."

"It's bad enough having paladins spying on my doings, without having Iomedae herself peeping over my shoulder."

"So it's true," Jerisa says.

"What?"

"Women find you irresistible."

Gad coughs drily.

A touchy silence follows.

Jerisa breaks it: "He's after you. That we can treat as a given. But if he knew you were coming here, now, he'd be set up over there . . ." She points to an outcrop of damaged rock. ". . . where we couldn't see him, and readying an ambush."

"True," says Gad. "I still don't like it."

"We can detour to another crossing point. Or simply wait a couple of days."

"No waiting," says Gad. "We've seen him and he hasn't seen us. We'll give him time to get out of sight and no more."

They crawl back toward the others. Halfway there, they hear the rattle of sword against shield. Bolting up, they dash onwards.

Plate-armored warriors, the Everbright crest sewn on their tunics, encircle Vitta, Tiberio and Hendregan. Calliard is gone.

Gad hears a flurry of movement to his left.

Jerisa is gone.

He draws his sword and charges.

The nearest paladin menaces Vitta, who has lost her footing and defends from a disadvantage with her short sword. Gad comes on him from behind, rattling a blade on the back of his helmet. His target turns, allowing Vitta to roll to her feet and smack him in the back of his knees with the flat of her blade. He falls, slashing ineffectively with his heavy greatsword.

Tiberio faces two opponents. One wears a bucketlike greathelm. Tiberio, his swords still in their sheaths, shoulders aside the paladin's weapon, slamming his body against his enemy's. He grabs the helm in both hands and gives it a deft one-quarter turn. With massive hands he crimps the bottom of the helm so that it can't be twisted back. His helmet's eyeholes firmly lodged over his right ear, the paladin staggers from the fray, unable to see.

The half-orc seizes him by the arm and swings him into his second opponent. They topple into a ditch. The second paladin's helmet bounces off a jutting boulder. He lies stunned, his blinded comrade caught in his limbs.

Hendregan jockeys around the fight, looking for an angle to loose a fireball. He hisses in frustration as a squire comes up behind him to brain him with a war maul. The young fighter's enthusiasm thwarts his aim; the blow goes wide. A delighted Hendregan rounds on him, arms and hands ablaze. He lays them on the young man's neck and shoulders. The squire's skin roasts and blackens.

"Easy, Hendregan!" Gad calls.

The wizard releases his boyish opponent. The squire drops to his knees, crisped skin sliding from his wounds.

"We have no quarrel with you," Gad says.

An armored knight, features hidden by a bascinet helmet, points his lance in Gad's direction. "It's him! The sin-bearer!"

"Sin-bearer?" repeats Gad, ducking a mace blow as a mounted knight gallops in to clout him.

Arrows pepper the ground before the horse's hooves. The yellow fletching identifies them as the product of Calliard's bow. The steed rears up. Gad avoids its hooves. The rider tumbles from the saddle to land at Gad's feet. Impeded by heavy armor, the attacker works to right himself. Gad takes the opportunity to reach down to his hip and pull the man's sword from its scabbard. He tosses it away. It hums with magical power as it flies through the air, thumping into a stand of bedraggled reeds. The knight reaches for a long dagger and drops into a fighting stance. Calliard's arrows circle his feet, driving him back.

The bascinetted knight aims his lance at Gad's chest. Gad slips under the blow and moves in close, turning his opponent's superior reach against him. He bangs his sword hilt against the lancer's hand, forcing him to drop the weapon. "What do you mean, 'sin-bearer'?"

Meanwhile Vitta holds two squires at bay, while Tiberio tears a helmet from a lithe warrior's breastplate and locks her in a chokehold. Jerisa reappears atop a white steed caparisoned in the solar colors of the Everbright order. Behind her she drags a plate-mailed woman, her right heel still entangled in a stirrup.

A squire tosses a sword to Gad's enemy. Gad tries to bowl him over in his moment of distraction, but the knight checks his move and keeps his footing. He whirs a howling sword in riposte; Gad parries, knees groaning to absorb the impact.

"I promise you," Gad grunts, "your leader nurtures a mistaken opinion about me."

Fury echoes in his opponent's helmet. "Are you not the notorious swindler Gad? Gad the Deceiver?"

"I thought paladins were supposed to be . . ." He parries another wheeling blow. Arcane sparks fly when blade meets blade. " . . . charitable!"

"You cannot be allowed to reach the tower of Yath!"

"And why is that?"

The knight drops his sword, draws a dagger, and stabs it deep into the unprotected space between the front and back plates of Gad's torso armor.

"Because," the knight exults, "if you go there, the world ends!"

Gad clutches instinctively at his wound. The knight kicks him in the head. Gad falls. The knight reaches for his dagger hilt, and twists it.

Calliard rides in, astride his horse, the group's other steeds running behind it. He aims an arrow at the knight beating Gad. It pierces the man's hand. He reels back. Flame wreathes him; another of Hendregan's spells has found its target. His tunic and helmet feathers turning to trailing ash behind him, the knight flees. His comrades regroup, arranging themselves into a defensive square.

Jerisa, on her confiscated horse, pounds toward the knight. Rage distorts her features.

Vitta and the others ring around Gad. He gasps into her ear; she shouts his command to Jerisa. "Let's get out of here!"

Thundering hooves drown out her cry. Jerisa reaches the still-burning knight. She pulls tight on the horse's reins. Panicked by the sudden movement and by the yellow tongues of fire coursing around the knight's body, it proceeds to trample him. Jerisa uses the force of the bucking horse to propel her from its back. Arms outstretched, she lands on her feet with appalling poise. The knight's body, flames finally extinguished, ragdolls to and fro under the hooves of the terrified horse.

Tiberio drapes Gad over the back of his horse. He yanks the knight's dagger from Gad's abdomen.

The trampling horse finally leaps away. The rest of the rearguard crusaders, twelve of them still in fighting shape, dash for their mangled comrade. But Jerisa is there first, to rip off his helmet and put a dagger at his throat.

She sibilates into his ear. "You don't get to do that."

"Enough!" Vitta shouts. "Move it!"

Tiberio uncorks a healing potion and pours it directly onto Gad's wound. The flow of blood ceases. Parted flesh gathers together and is made whole.

Jerisa cuts her man's throat. Then his fellows are upon her. She slashes at them with a pair of curved daggers. Though each opponent is bigger and better protected than she, they instinctively ease back.

Hendregan spurs his horse toward the fight.

"No!" Vitta yells.

"Not you too!" shouts Calliard. He follows Hendregan, the reins of Jerisa's horse in his hand. At full gallop it follows his steed.

The air writhes and ripples around Hendregan as he chants an incantation.

A wall of flame erupts between Jerisa and the knight's would-be avengers. Hendregan rides up, basking in its heat. "We're leaving," he tells her.

Calliard brings her horse alongside. She lifts herself onto the stirrups. The six flee over the border, into the demonlands.

Chapter Nine
The Cages

Gad lies propped up against a trench. Tiberio tips a dribble of water onto his lips. Vitta sits at his side. Jerisa has plopped herself down on the trench's other side. She faces him but will not meet his gaze.

"That was our strongest healing draught, wasn't it?" Gad asks Tiberio.

"None of the others would have done it," he replies.

"And we're how far inside the Worldwound?" says Vitta.

"Less than half a mile," says Tiberio.

"That was a rhetorical," says Vitta.

"Vitta, let me . . ." says Gad. His breathing remains uneven.

"What were you thinking, Jerisa?" Vitta asks. "Wait, sorry—I withdraw the question. It bases itself on a false premise."

"Shut up," Jerisa moans.

"Vitta . . ." says Gad.

"We needed to get out of there, not murder that crusader," Vitta says.

"You saw what he did," says Jerisa.

"Gad was already saved. When the rest of us are ready to run, we can't have you plunging further into a fight."

"I'm a killer," says Jerisa. "I kill."

"In the future, here's a simple test for you. Ask yourself: is this madder than whatever Hendregan is doing?" They look around for the wizard, but he's still off on a scouting ride with Calliard. Vitta continues: "If the answer is yes, then you ought to—"

"He was an enemy and deserved my blade."

Gad coughs. "No."

"No?"

"The crusaders, even the Everbrights, aren't our enemies." Gad gathers the strength to talk. "Yes, they're prigs and fools and men of law and they're bad for business. But they're here to fight demons, just as we are. We might even be able to leverage them to our advantage, if we can penetrate Fraton's thick skull. Which is admittedly difficult. Still. Maybe we can trick them into succeeding despite themselves." He briefly convulses, a residual pulse of healing energy seething through his veins.

Jerisa takes a whetstone from her pack. "Gratitude is too much to expect, but a lecture?"

"I should have explained this more clearly," Gad says. "This will be the worst job you ever worked. The worst place you've ever been. If we're going to execute this rip, we have to trust each other, yes?"

"You think I don't understand that?"

"I know that you do," says Gad. "But when you get angry . . ."

"I'll be good from now on," she mutters.

Vitta snorts. "That doesn't sound like—"

Gad silences the halfling with a gesture. "Jerisa," he says, "never risk yourself on my account. If something happens to me, I don't want you breaking away to avenge me. You want to do right by me? Carry on with the plan."

"Nothing's going to happen to you."

"So I don't have to worry about you, then?"

"You don't," she says.

A night's rest and Gad feels hale—disturbingly so. He can't count the number of magical curatives he's consumed over the years, yet whenever he is healed, he still acutely feels their unnaturalness. His heart races. The landscape around him seems sharper. Far-off crows caw more clearly. The potion has repaired not only the wound in his side and the damaged organs beneath, but a variety of other barely measurable conditions. A throbbing corn on his left baby toe has turned to soft and tender flesh. A spot inside his cheek where he bit himself chewing is as good as new. Since his walk from Krega, his left knee has been slightly out of joint. Now it has realigned itself.

The potion leaves him hungry—hungrier than their rations allow. Gad yearns for a great chunk of roasted boar haunch. He joins the others for an ascetic meal of cheese, nuts, and hardtack. Despite his panging stomach, he's careful to take only his share. Tiberio notices and palms him some of his hazelnuts.

The six mount up. They have to ride around the snaking fissures, as the crusaders did before them. The circuiting elongates their journey. A distance that should take an hour to cross instead costs them three.

Molten, liquid shapes mar the purple sky. They open like sores and burst like blisters. The tortured shapes obscure the sun; its trajectory across the sky can be perceived only dimly. Shadows blur and vanish.

The landscape reeks of bile. Across the plain, pools of ooze bubble and seep. Clouds of discolored vapor rise from them. As the travelers move through it, the mist reddens their skin. It coats their palates with nauseating phlegm.

A dark shape coruscates above. Panicked, Hendregan's steed bolts. The wizard stays on its back at first but leaps for safety as the animal barrels toward a trench. The horse's legs crunch appallingly as the beast hits the trench's side and hurtles in. Tiberio climbs down in to pet its muzzle, to comfort it, and then to mercifully snap its neck.

Before the day is half over, the remaining horses sicken. Vitta's is the first to drop. It falls without warning, nearly crushing her beneath its haunches. She climbs aboard Gad's horse. The other beasts grow weak and skittish. An hour later, Jerisa's steed falters, a jarring, choking noise rising from its throat. Once watered, it seems to recover. An hour later it halts and refuses to go on. She dismounts, talks to it, and watches as it lays down and expires.

Nightfall comes early, preceded by a weird pulsing in the sky. Then a starless blackness abruptly comes. By this time there is only one animal left, Tiberio's stout-hearted warhorse. He dismounts; they lead it along, leaving it only the packs and supplies to carry.

Hendregan's flaming light-stick casts a lonely luminance across the cancerous plain. It makes them a target, they decide. The wizard commands it to dim itself. They seek a trench to shelter for the night.

The first they investigate seems crumbled and unstable.

Acrid goo seeps from the bottom of the second.

In the third are piled eleven corpses, stuck together by filaments of amber webbing. They belong to crusaders, their tunics marked with a family crest of distant Cheliax. The knights are freshly dead, their eyes, lips, and ears eaten away. One seems to move, as if still alive. Jerisa jumps down to find it writhing with locustlike larvae.

The fourth trench seems acceptable.

They take their usual watches. When off-shift, they slumber fitfully. Far-off sounds bounce across the plain: the buzzing of swarming wings; screams of agony; a strange, reversed thunder.

The travelers set out feeling more exhausted than when they bunked down.

Hendregan, who since Sodevina's death has seemed tranquil and lucid, reverts to his old demeanor. He clucks his tongue, scratches rudely at his drying skin, and every now and then barks with inexplicable laughter.

Gad sidles up to him. "Are you good?" he asks.

Calliard hears the words and shivers.

"I am well," Hendregan says, and smiles. "I understand this place."

"How so?"

"You'll see."

"You can't say that. You have to explain."

He laughs. "Fight madness with madness," he says.

A flock of flying demons appears at the horizon line. The team scurries for the cover of a trench. The demons wing overhead toward Mendev. Vitta counts hundreds of them.

"Can you figure where they're going?" Jerisa asks her.

"This place plays havoc with my sense of geography," Vitta says. "I can't see the sun properly. And why it gets dark at an earlier hour than across the border—that I don't even want to understand." She withholds from

Jerisa what Gad has already realized—that the demonic flock heads to Suma Castle.

The trenches recede, giving way to scourged and rocky ground. They gasp and wheeze through yellow fog. The six sojourners and their last horse heave themselves up a slope. A viscous rain comes to clear away the fog. They reach the top of the rise. It leads down another grade to a marshy depression.

At odd intervals across the swampy earth tilt dozens of metal cages. Gad gestures for a general halt.

"What are those?" he asks Vitta.

"Wouldn't hazard a guess," she answers.

"How big would you say they are?"

She calculates. "Fifteen high, fifteen long, ten wide."

Calliard steps up. "I've seen them called demon boxes. Also blade cages."

"You've encountered them before?" Gad asks.

"Only in books. In the tongue of demons, they are called *urannag*." Calliard pronounces the inhuman term with a hissing, glottal fury. "In her famous account of an exploration of the Abyssal realms, Ualia the Sojourner describes an entire layer dotted with urannag, as far as the eye can see."

"What does she do about them?"

"She is carried off by a half-spider, losing the opportunity to examine them closely."

"So," asks Gad, "the Worldwound is becoming more like the Abyss, where the demons come from?"

"Since its first appearance, it has always been a piece of the Abyss," says Calliard, "growing onto our world as a fungus grows on a tree. But if urannag are here, the infection may have accelerated. Become more virulent."

"Because of Yath?"

"I imagine so," says Calliard.

"Do we go around the marsh?" Gad asks.

"We don't know how far it extends," says Vitta. "Whatever's on either side of it might be worse." She pulls a compass from her pack. Its dial spins crazily. "And the further we get from a straight line to your tower, the less confidence I have of staying on track. We could get turned around and wind up all the way down in the Shudderwood." The Shudderwood is a haunt of twisted fey, far from their destination.

"Onward, then," Gad proposes.

"Onward," agrees Vitta.

Calliard coughs. He removes his helmet, pats driblets of sweat from his hair, and replaces it. "Onward," he says.

Tiberio coaxes his balking horse down the graveled slope that will take them to the bog below.

Vitta peers through the obscuring rain. "There's movement."

"Where?" says Gad.

"Inside that first cage."

The halfling speeds up. The others cautiously follow.

A whispered cry for help cuts through the sound of rain. Vitta takes the lead. The rest follow. They wade through a soupy mess of sickly, albino-white vegetation. Tangling marsh weeds claw at their ankles. Hairy projections probe their clothing, seeking bare flesh.

They reach between Tiberio's boot and leggings, their leaves flattening tight against his skin. Their veins swell and turn crimson as they suck blood from his capillaries. Tiberio rips the leaves loose only to see them curl around his hands and start to feed from those as well. The others come to his aid, ripping the hungry vines and leaves to shreds.

Visibility decreases as they close in on the cage. They are a few feet away when its prisoners resolve into view. The figures inside are drenched and muddy. They sit trembling in pooling blood. Their emblems match those worn by the corpses the team found the day before. Around them are arrayed the bodies of their comrades. In the tangle of dismembered limbs and bisected torsos it is hard to make a count, but Vitta reckons there are four dead.

Up close, the cage is a chaos of contradictory lines. Its bars swirl and course across the surface of the cube. They widen and narrow, apparently at random. Some of the bars project into the cage. Gears and sprockets are sometimes visible at the joins. Vitta squints at them. There is something in their illogic that makes them hard to correctly perceive. She can't see how the gears are supposed to work. Are they strictly ornamental?

She blinks again and the arrangement of the bars appears to have altered itself.

"Are you seeing what I'm seeing?" Vitta asks Calliard.

Before he can answer, one of the survivors interrupts. "Free us," she pleads. She is thin-lipped and sharp-chinned.

The other is slim, widow's-peaked, and might under other circumstances be handsome, in a sleek and decadent way. "First tell them—"

"Silence!" the woman screams, her words ringing with the authority of rank.

The other turns to her, his hand wadding into a fist. "It's only fair to—"

Cage gears turn according to some unearthly physics. A hidden spear springs out from one of the bars. Its grimy point plunges through the man's spine to skewer his heart. Gad and team stand, unable to look away, bearing witness as life ebbs from him.

Biting down on her slight line of a lip, the caged aristocrat contains her trembling. "You fool," she hisses at her dying underling.

"You weren't planning to warn us," Vitta says.

"Please help me," says the crusader. She speaks without otherwise moving.

"How were we supposed to help you, without knowing?"

"I am Countess Deueria of the Smelika Bounds. My estates yield ten thousand gold a year. I can pay you in ingots, in gems, in arcane implements. My crusade has ended in ignominy, but in Iomedae's name, I beg you to save me. I'll re-equip, assemble a new platoon, come back and slay the demon. I'll overturn this state of shame, I promise it. Just free me."

"What do you have on you?" Vitta asks.

"I carry no gold, for why would one do so in the demonlands?" Her eyes dart about the cage. "I wield the sword Indomitabilis, but it is a birthright and cannot be relinquished. The others carried a rod of many blows, and a crystal sphere. There are scrolls of arcane force . . ."

Vitta turns back to confer with the others.

"As another so-called noble," mutters Jerisa, "I say let her rot."

"It's worth considering," says Vitta. "This gaffle promises no other loot."

"A leader's soldiers are under her protection," says Jerisa. "You heard how she treated him—like a lackey. Perhaps the next count or countess of the Smelika Bounds will be an improvement over her."

"Harsh words," says Tiberio. "She treated her comrade poorly. But consider her fear."

"Hendregan," says Gad, "What do you say?"

Hendregan starts, as if lost in other thoughts. "Me?"

"Do we try to help her, or move on?"

The wizard shrugs. "I don't care."

"Indifference is a vote for inaction," says Jerisa.

"I'm asking you," Gad says, "but this isn't a vote."

"It's a difficult puzzle," says Vitta. "Perhaps knowing how to solve it would tell us other things about the demons and how they construct their traps. Surely we'll encounter others, on the way or when we get there."

Gad pulls at a vine snaking up his leg. "We move on."

"Truly?" Tiberio says.

"I pity her too, Tiberio, but is it worth the risk? I need all of you for this rip. Intact."

"Let's go then," says Jerisa.

Tiberio plods to the cage as the others regroup.

"Not too close," Vitta warns.

"We are sorry," Tiberio tells Deueria. "We have chosen a difficult path, and do not dare stray from it."

Resignation settles upon her. "What path is that?" Deueria asks.

"We've come to destroy Yath."

Deueria laughs. "Good fortune with that!"

Tiberio turns and trudges away.

"Peasants!" she shouts.

"See?" says Jerisa to Tiberio, when he rejoins the others.

They slog deeper into the marsh. Thickening mists obscure their route. They can see up, into the violet sky, but only a few dozen yards ahead of them in any direction. They can still hear Deueria's shouts, even after she vanishes into the enclosing fog.

Tiberio sighs. "Would we have saved her, if she'd been kinder?"

"This is the right decision," says Gad, "but it would have been harder to make."

"Heroes save even the unpleasant people," says Tiberio.

"We're not heroes," says Gad.

"Thank the stars," Jerisa adds.

Vitta, walking ahead, freezes. She holds out her arms, wordlessly commanding the others to stop. She pulls her pack from her shoulders and removes a copper cylinder about two feet long. Pulling out its telescoping segments, she transforms it into a pole, longer than she is tall. She pokes it into the swampy ground ahead.

An object erupts from the soppy ground in front of her. A shower of dislodged muck sprays the travelers. Twisted, looping arms of metal reach from the swamp. They intertwine, snapping into place in a succession of clattering reports. Gears and cogs open like sinister blossoms from the unidentifiable alloy.

It is another demon cage.

"That was close," says Jerisa.

"I was lucky to spot it," Vitta replies.

"How much farther?" Gad asks.

Fog, momentarily shooed away by the impact of the snapping cage arm, noses its way back around them.

"With no line of sight it's tough to be sure," Vitta answers. "My guess? We're a fifth of the way across."

A hum permeates their bones and the sockets of their teeth. Its intensity increases as they near the cage.

Vitta leads them to skirt around it. Their boots squish. Tiberio's horse whickers angrily at the mud sucking at its hooves.

The halfling continues, stabbing the copper pole into the marshy ground. Whenever she finds a spar of solid ground she leads them onto it, even when it leads them on a slower, twisting route.

They pass another cage. Bones and armor pieces litter its floor.

Twice more Vitta's probings activate a cage before they step into it. Each time she pauses to study its construction and listen to its keening hum.

When they are about two-thirds of the way across the swamp, a fast-moving shape appears in the northern sky. It zigzags wildly toward them. It is nearly on top of them before they can make it out. A pair of airborne demons fights over a squirming, protesting crusader. The first demon is a tumorous humanoid kept aloft by dusty moth wings. The other is batlike, hairy, fanged. The second demon locks the warrior's upper arm in its toothy jaw. The first alters its arc to jerk all three figures into a downward spiral.

Its rival places stubbornness over sense. It stays clamped to the victim. The first tries to disengage but is prevented by the panicked grasping of the victim's other arm. The three plunge into the swamp ahead. The thump of their landing is immediately followed by a now-familiar series of clattering reports.

Dispersed by the impact, the fog parts. The two demons and their warrior prisoner are trapped inside a demon cage. As if by instinct, the warrior, a starved and bearded wretch who scarcely fills out his armor, falls still on the cage floor. The enraged moth demon bangs on the cage bars. Blades and spears and garrotting wires disgorge from the cage's bars, floor and ceiling. They slice through the mothman's grotesque frame. They meet more resistance than they might with human flesh, but in a matter of instants disassemble the demon all the same. Ichor bubbles from its remains, staining the surrounding swamp.

The warrior stirs. His back is broken. He bleeds from a dozen wounds. He reaches out with his remaining good hand and grasps the bat-demon by its warty ankles. He pulls hard, screaming the name of the war goddess Iomedae. The demon tries to steady itself but is suddenly pulled from its position. The movement alerts the cage to its presence. A geared and segmented metal arm detaches itself from the top of the cage. It saws off the demon's head. The head bounces, landing on the warrior's horribly angled back. With the last of its energy, the expiring demon clamps its disembodied jaws around its killer's neck. The man screams a battle prayer as he dies.

"Let's clear," says Gad.

Vitta holds up a hand. The gears and cogs are still moving. She waits until they're finished, then continues.

The marsh occupies a bowl of land about three miles across. The travelers can see the beginnings of the rocky slope that marks its end when Vitta's pole finds another cage. It bursts from the marsh as the others did. This time one of the reaching metal spires strikes a boulder as it knits together with the others to form the cage. The cage breaks, sending a jagged arm hurtling toward Vitta. The crew scatters. Jerisa, Calliard and Hendregan go left. Vitta, Gad, Tiberio, and Tiberio's horse duck back and to the right. They step onto marshland untested by Vitta's instrument.

A cage roars from the muck to envelop them.

"Don't move," calls Vitta.

The warning is unnecessary: Gad and Tiberio have already frozen.

The big steed, suddenly stabled in a box of clashing metal, rears in panic. Sensing its movement, the cage releases its supply of hidden blades. The horse groans as the urannag reduces it to meat. Butchered pieces slide across the cage's floor. Their movement prompts further attacks from the cage's blades. A screw-cut spear jams into the cage bottom less than an inch from Gad's left heel.

"Everyone remain calm," says Vitta.

"We're calm," says Gad.

Vitta sucks at her teeth.

Tiberio suppresses a cough.

Discolored fog drifts in. Condensation appears on the underside of the cage's ceiling. Droplets gather and fall to the floor.

"You have a way out of this, yes?" says Gad.

"No," says Vitta.

"No?"

"Calliard," Vitta calls, "you haven't read anything else about urannags, have you?"

"Urannag," answers Calliard. "The plural is also urannag."

"Very helpful. That's all?"

"Afraid so," says Calliard.

"Vitta, you know a way out of this," says Gad.

"I do?"

"You do."

"I will have a way, but I don't have it yet."

"Each time you were watching how the cage worked," says Gad. "Watching the cogs and gears."

"Looking for a pattern. Every machine has to have a pattern. Even a demon machine, born of chaos on the writhing plains of the Abyss."

"The hum," says Gad. "You were listening to the hum."

They stop talking. This cage hums, too.

"It's hungry," says Vitta.

"Hungry?"

"Calliard," she asks, "from what you know of demons, is it possible that these cages are not simply creations of demons, but are in some way demons themselves?"

The bard edges toward her, and the cage. "Possible," he says. "Demons form from the collected matter of destroyed and reconstituted souls—the souls of evildoers who in life dedicated themselves to anarchy and destruction. Certain scholars postulate that the ectoplasmic refuse from this process—scraps, if you will—are sometimes used to form artifacts, constructs, and other devices."

"And such a device, then, would be a sort of sub-demon?"

"Sages use that term in various ways."

"The cage. Could it be incapable of thought and action, but made of demonstuff?"

"It could be."

"Then an anti-demon spell might work on it? Some sort of banishment or exorcism?"

"It might indeed."

"And, demon hunter, you wouldn't happen to know such a spell?"

"There is a particular abjuration," he admits, pausing as if waiting for someone to comment.

No one does.

"Then work it," says Vitta.

Calliard takes his lute from his pack. He sings. His voice, never a beautiful instrument, is rusty. It quavers and growls but finally resolves itself into a ballad. He sings of Yaniel, demon-slayer of the last crusade. The lyric follows her as she goes into the Worldwound alone and disgraced, and through courage redeems herself.

When he reaches the final verse, in which she returns to Mendev, surrounded by the companions who will fight at her side for the rest of her short and glorious life, the notes rise from his throat and from his lute to gain visible substance around the cage. They form a dome of artificial sunlight.

The hungry humming changes to a disconcerted buzz. The cage rattles, as if something inside it has slowed.

"Now, Jerisa," says Vitta, "I want you to throw a rock into the other side of the cage, as far from Gad, Tiberio and me as you can."

Jerisa finds a hand-sized stone in the mud, dislodges it, and pitches it with expert balance through the bars. A blade fires out to strike it, but with less force and speed than before.

"So we've impeded it but not deactivated it," says Vitta. "Jerisa, I want you to try again. Does anyone have an object that rolls?"

Calliard produces a cylindrical scroll case covered in red leather. He removes the magical parchment it protects and hands the case to Jerisa.

"This time," says Vitta, "I need you to creep up to the cage and roll that case across the floor. As slowly as you can."

Jerisa follows the halfling's instructions. The case rolls across the cage floor, coming to a rest unharmed against the opposite set of bars.

"I'm guessing," Vitta says, "that we've muddled the cage's perceptions. It knows I've moved if I'm quick, but not if I'm slow. So now I'm going to try this out and see if what works for a scroll case also holds true for me."

"Are you certain?" Calliard asks.

"She wouldn't do it if she wasn't certain," Gad says.

Vitta snorts. She takes a slow, slight step.

The blades and wires remain in the mechanism.

She takes another.

And another.

And another.

Inch by inch, she makes her way to the edge of the cage. She hunches down. Lies herself flat. Slides her rounded fingers over to the gears and cogs.

"I'm thinking about the pattern," she says. She is not explaining it to the others. She is talking through it for herself. "Each time the blades come out, these gears whir and click. I'd convinced myself there isn't a pattern, because each time it was a different gear that spun first. But no matter how strange, there is sense in every puzzle—provided you take the time to seek it."

She reaches out and snaps off one of the gears. A blade drops impotently from the cage ceiling to rest against Gad's shoulder. The force of the drop is not enough to nick his armor.

Methodically, she pops off the remaining gears. The cage clunks apart. Its pieces fall into the mud. Arranged there, they resemble the petals of a wilted flower, as rendered by a drunken metalsmith.

Gad steps woozily from the cage flooring. A scythe sproings ineffectually behind him. "And what was it?"

"What was what?" asks Vitta.

"The pattern," he says.

"Oh," she says, already bored. "The gear movement corresponds to the location in the cage where the movement occurs, but the order is mixed up. So you have to watch several cages in action before you see what matches what. And then you have to fill in the gaps with a certain amount of conjecture."

Jerisa hands Gad a waterskin. He takes it and drinks deep. "Conjecture?" he asks. "How much conjecture?"

"Some questions are best unasked."

A hundred paces into their march from the cage, she stops. "Wait," she says. She takes measured steps back to the disassembled cage. Ducking down, she paws through the pieces, hefting some, rejecting others outright. Finally she settles on a section of cage bar to which several of the gears and demonic ornaments still adhere. She lifts it, testing it for weight. A nasty serrated blade attaches to its narrowing end. She places this on the ground and, with her boot heel, snaps it off. Using a pair of shears fished from her kit, she systematically clips off a series of sharp projections. She applies a grinding stone against the snipped edges, smoothing them down. Pushing on the newly broken end, she demonstrates the bar's telescoping action. She continues until she finds its minimum length, about two and a half feet. Vitta reshuffles the contents of her pack to make room for it. The piece juts out from it like a flag bearer's pole.

"Isn't that on the heavy side," asks Jerisa, "for a souvenir?"

"It would be, yes," says the lock breaker, trudging on. "If that's what this was."

Chapter Ten
The Lake

The team walks through a forest of moaning trees, their bark the color of maggots. A field of white rocks reveals itself as the eggs of repellent creatures, combining the features of crab and millipede. Fleeing from the hatching, the six are forced into a canyon. It channels them south, taking them further from their destination, which lies to the northeast.

On stone shelves along canyon walls, ghostly figures sit, translucent legs dangling from ledges. They silently observe the six as they're drawn away from the tower.

"They are the fallen," Calliard says. "Too virtuous to be tempted to demon worship, yet too weak to ascend to the celestial realms when slain."

One of the ghosts says to him, "You'll be joining us here soon, demon hunter."

Finally they reach a set of stairs chiseled into the rock. They ascend it up the canyon face. There they are set upon by a trio of starving mercenaries. Numbed by hunger, the ambushers attack without caution. Jerisa's blades fly to their throats and chests. An hour later they are visible as ghosts, mournfully watching the six from the canyon ledges.

The canyon has taken them a day off their ideal route. They pick their way through stony terrain. Gad stumbles between sharp rocks, his ankle plunging between them. Jerisa bounds to his side. Gingerly, she pulls at one of the stones. He pulls his leg out, working the ankle.

"Thank you," he tells Jerisa.

She starts to speak, stops herself short, and instead says, "Of course."

Tiberio completes a teetering step from rock to rock, a dozen yards away. "Is it twisted?" he calls.

"Only scraped," says Gad.

Heat rolls over them in waves. It radiates from the stones and through the soles of their boots. The air shimmers and bends. It leaches the moisture from their skin. Their mouths dry up. Gad reaches for his waterskin and gulps deep. Minutes later, he is parched again. The others suffer too, except for Hendregan. He has stripped himself to a loincoth. Arms outstretched, he basks in the baking wind. A chuckle of delight resounds from deep within him. His tattoos seem to dance.

They arrive at a promontory. Below bubbles the source of the heat: a molten lake. Hendregan gazes at it as if at a long-lost friend. The others shield their eyes from its brightness. Fingers of fire rise from its surface. They twist and fly, breaking connection with the pooling magma. They spiral into puffs of steam and are gone. More flit up to take their place.

The promontory overlooks a narrowing in the molten lake; here it is less than half a mile across. It extends for miles to the left, and continues to the right until it terminates in the side of a steaming cliff face.

Overhead, a sole, careless raptor circles. It pursues a strange, dark bug which it has mistaken for its proper prey. The unearthly insect dives down to escape its talons. They come too close to the lake and merge into a single vapor.

Hendregan finds a shelflike protrusion of stone over the molten pool. He sits cross-legged on it. A meditative calm settles over him.

Gad waits with the others.

Finally, Hendregan's head bobs down. He has fallen asleep.

Gad moves to the magician's side. He feels his skin burn. His lungs rebel against the effort. The hot air is like a stifling curtain. Against every instinct, he pushes on through it.

He touches Hendregan's shoulder.

The fire-master starts.

"Hendregan," Gad says.

"Hah?"

"What are you doing?"

His tattoos ripple and expand. He does not appear to understand the question.

"Hendregan," Gad repeats.

"Yes?"

"Are you helping us?"

"Am I?" says Hendregan. His words are a mumble. He is drunk on heat and flame.

"You are helping us, yes?"

"What do you need help with?"

"A way around this lake."

"Around?" slurs Hendregan.

"We can't go through it, now, can we?"

"Go through it? Why would we do that?"

"Hendregan, you must listen to me. You'll do that, yes?"

He seems to break from his trance a little. "Yes," he says.

"We can't go through it, "Gad repeats, "so we have to find a way around. You can find us a way around, yes?"

"I disagree," says Hendregan.

"You disagree?"

"Who said we can't go through it?"

"I said that, Hendregan, because it's obvious."

He straightens his back. "We can go through it."

"You have a spell?"

Hendregan stands. "A birthright."

He climbs down from the promontory. His bare hands and feet sizzle and blacken each time they touch the rocks. The skin burns away, heals itself, burns away, and heals itself. The tattoos squirm and distort, reforming themselves when the flesh comes back. Gad wonders if they are truly tattoos at all.

Hendregan reaches the shore of melting stone. Tendrils of flame spurt from the lake, enwrapping him. He seizes them, wrapping them into a mantle. The lake roils.

In an uncanny, crackling voice, Hendregan speaks to it. "I am your son," he proclaims. "I am your brother. I am Hendregan."

Gad retreats from the promontory. Tiberio hands him a waterskin. He drinks its contents down. Hendregan's words burn through the bubbling of the lake and the hissing of the steaming rocks. He talks in bursts, as if conversing with the lake.

"You deny my name?" he booms.

Then: "You cannot deny my mother's name." The next word is not human speech: it is a snapping sound of consuming fire.

Then: "You have tasted my flesh. Seen it renewed by your fire. You know I am her issue."

Then: "I am both man and flame, as you are both demon and flame. And through our mutual lineage of fire, I bid you to recognize your obligations, as I obey mine."

Then: "I was conceived in flesh and born in flame."

Then: "There is no need for that."

Then: "As you know what is born of the spark, you sense that I speak true."

Then: "Very well, on that basis, I will tell it. As one brother tells a tale on his reunion with another."

Then: "Yes, my father sought to keep my truth from me. I was raised only knowing the world of flesh. As if the mother he spoke of was also flesh. Yet always I felt the fire in me. The urge to burn."

Then: "Yes, I consigned those things to flame."

Then: "Yes, and those things too. Though punished, though chastised, I burned them. Until I was cast out, and my father too."

Then: "I'll not hear you condemn him. Man of flesh he was, but also a great master of fire. Yes, he tried to stop me as we wandered. But then came the time of his death, when his bride reclaimed him, and I beheld for the first time the fleeting sight of my mother."

Then: "Not for many years after. Until I learned to fully channel the fire within, to go to the birthplace of fire. Only then did she embrace me. Only then did she give me the words of power. Do not make me invoke her authority over you. Instead, let me pass as a brother."

Then: "No, as you treat me, you must also treat them."

Then: "They are not of flame, but do its bidding."

Then: "We have come to destroy."

Then: "We destroy destruction. That which consumes will be consumed. We thus obey the first imperative of fire."

Then: "The tower of Yath. We will destroy it. That is my oath."

Then: "If we fail, may I be consumed and rejoin the primal flame. May you hunt my friends, and devour them. Braise their meat. Blacken their bones."

Then: "Yes, I undertake this."

The bubbling of the lake gives way to silence.

"I don't like the sound of this," says Vitta.

"Trust him," says Gad.

"*Him?*" She snorts.

"I trust him," Gad says. "So trust me."

Vitta swallows a grumble.

Hendregan returns to them, caked in soot. Smoke curls from his naked skin. When he opens his mouth to speak, his teeth glare their contrasting whiteness. "We can cross the lake now," he says. The booming commandments of the molten shore have given way to his usual quavering timbre.

"Cross the lake?" says Vitta.

"Yes," says Hendregan. "But we must go quickly, before they forget. They are beings of the moment."

"Then they won't remember you promised us to them if we fail to destroy the tower."

"That they'll remember," says Hendregan. "Quickly, now."

He leads them to the top of the promontory.

"Hendregan," Vitta says, "you promised us to them."

"Only if we fail to banish Yath," the magician says, "and if that happens, we'll likely be dead anyway."

"A fair point," Gad says.

"Fair?" Vitta sputters.

They climb down to the shoreline, scorching themselves on the rocks.

"And how exactly are we supposed to cross the lake?" Vitta asks.

"Sssh," says Hendregan. He strides to the shore. He commands the pooling lava: "Now is the time!"

In a sinuous wave, the lava parts, rushing from the narrows to slosh against its distant shores. Stones there tumble in to become one with the yellow-red liquid. The parted magma becomes a pair of walls, creating a temporary corridor across the pool. Steam rises from the exposed, glassy lake bed.

"And withdraw your heat!" Hendregan bellows.

The steam dissipates. Cracks rush across the glassy surface. Hendregan steps out onto it. "Now the rest of you," he whispers.

The others hesitate.

Gad steps out, finds his footing. The sharp cracks cut into his boot soles, but also give purchase against the smooth and slippery surface. The lava walls loom around him.

"Stride with heads held high," Hendregan instructs, "but also with dignity."

Jerisa steps onto the cracked glass, then Tiberio, Calliard, and finally Vitta. They make their way across. Vitta is first to step onto the far shore. Hendregan waits, calmly scrutinizing the parted magma, until the others are safely up its slope. He bows, dropping to one knee. "The trust you have shown in your brother shall be rewarded," he says. Then he hops back up, turns, and sprints up the incline to join his allies.

Before them lies a fresh expanse of jagged rock. They pick their way painstakingly through it. As the air cools, Hendregan pauses to clothe himself.

"Was I mistaken," Vitta asks him, "or did I overhear that your mother is some kind of fire elemental?"

Hendregan replies by indistinctly grunting.

"Leave it alone," says Gad.

Vitta persists. "I thought you were a wizard."

"I am a wizard," says Hendregan.

"No, no, if you're of inhuman heritage, if you're part elemental, that means your magic comes from inside you, and not from books. Which means you're a sorcerer."

Hendregan shrugs. "Then call me a sorcerer."

"Which is it?"

"What does it matter?" says Jerisa.

"It might prove important," Vitta answers. "To solve problems, we must each understand what the rest of the crew can and can't do."

"That's my job," says Gad.

Vitta turns to Hendregan. "You're either one or the other. A wizard or a sorcerer."

"Categories," Hendregan scoffs.

"I've never seen you look at a tome, or recommit its incantations to memory," says Vitta.

"When others ask," says Hendregan, stooping to pick up a sharp-edged chunk of volcanic stone, "tell them I am a wizard."

They shelter for the night alongside a high tumble of rock. Vitta and Tiberio find the remains of a long-abandoned village and from its shattered timbers construct a cursory lean-to.

Calliard dreams.

He stands in a castle courtyard. He wonders which one. It's Suma Fortress, he realizes.

Black shapes dot the sky. Demons. Attacking demons.

Arrows fly up at them.

He has a bow in his hand. He is one of the archers.

He looks around. Arrayed with him are all the people he's disappointed. All who know his shame.

He wants to shoot one of the demons but his hand won't release the arrow. The creature looks like a mosquito. It seems frozen in the air.

Everyone else's arrows hit it. It falls from the sky.

He's looking at the clouds. They're inky. Shadows. No, they're not clouds at all. Nor are they shadows. They're a demon, taking shape.

It's the invidiak, the shadow demon, the one that looked into him when he actually fought at Suma Fortress.

Calliard realizes that this isn't real. That it's a dream.

He realizes that the invidiak is real, even though it's in a dream.

He tries to wake up.

Now all of him is frozen.

Around him, the battle rages. Demons drop from the twisted heavens. They beset the legion of the disappointed.

Calliard is grateful. Grateful that they'll soon be gone from his sight, no longer witness to his shame.

He catches himself having this thought. Burns with deeper shame.

The demons are killing them. Tearing at his old friends and loved ones. Scissoring through necks with ebon mandibles. Pulling open ribcages. Roping out lines of viscera.

The invidiak comes to him.

He points the arrowhead at its horned and shifting face.

You can't hurt me, it says, without speaking.

Its red-coal eyes drill into him. *I saw into you,* it says.

No.

Yes. I saw into you, and you are already mine.

Calliard looks for help.

He sees Gad, on the parapet. He is the only one the demons haven't got.

No wait, there's Jerisa, too. Poor girl. Running to follow him.

Who's that? the demon asks.

Calliard shuts his eyes. *I won't let you see them.*

You think they'll save you?

Go away.

He closes his eyes harder. Now Gad is gone, and Jerisa, and the castle around them. There is only shadow, and the shadow demon, and Calliard.

Whoever that was, the demon says, *he trusts you. I can read that at least.*

I'm waking up.

No, you're not. He trusts you but you know that isn't deserved. You know you'll let him down. Bring ruination to him and all the others.

I won't. Not this time.

You will, Calliard. It is as inevitable as your enslavement. You are tainted. Only fit to serve me. Know your master's name. It is Xaggalm.

Calliard tries to pull the arrow further back. His hand won't budge.

I will find a use for you, Calliard, the demon whispers. *You'll do me good service and advance my cause. And then I'll consign your soul to the Abyss. Only when it is torn to shreds, only when Calliard as a discrete consciousness is eliminated, will you know peace. The peace of utter nonexistence. That is the best you can hope for, Calliard. The best you warrant.*

I realize that.

You do, don't you?

Yes.

You're going to fail.

No, no, he won't let that—

What was his name again?

No, no.

Yes, yes. But never fear. Xaggalm is a kindly master.

Shut your stinking face.

Xaggalm laughs. *After you fail, and before you are shredded into soulstuff, I'll grant you what you crave. You'll drink fully of my essence.*

No. No!

Calliard jolts. Tiberio's hand is on his shoulder, shaking him awake. The night is still ink-dark.

"It's my watch already?" Calliard asks. No, that can't be, he watches after Jerisa. She snoozes, propped up against a rock.

"You were groaning," Tiberio tells him.

"Bad dream," Calliard says.

Tiberio looks up. "This is a place of bad dreams."

"True words, big man."

Tiberio waits a moment. Then: "I'll listen to you tell me your dream, if you want."

Calliard stands. "I don't remember what it was." He steps away from the camp and finds a place to empty his bladder.

The next day brings the uncertain cover of a charred forest. When demons soar overhead the six press themselves to the tree trunks, hoping to be hidden by leafless branches.

They wait until the sky empties. They continue the trek. Gad and Vitta take point.

"Any guess on how close we are to the tower?" Gad asks.

"We should already be there," says Vitta.

Dark underbrush turns to soot beneath their boot heels.

"You're worried," she says.

"Sorry."

"It's all right if I see it," she says. "I require no coddling."

"Unlike some of the others, you mean?"

"I didn't say that; you did."

He smiles. "You maneuvered me into saying it."

"What I mean to say is, you can talk to me."

"I've never liked this part," says Gad. "Traveling to the job. There's never an upside in the journey part of it. Until you get there, all you can do is lose."

"We'll be there soon."

"And also I hate the damn wilderness."

"No problems you can solve by talking?"

"That about says it," he nods.

"You could steal the sorcerer's trick, and learn how to con lava."

"I doubt that's teachable."

They pretend this is funny and share a laugh.

Jerisa watches them, wishing she could be easy with him like that.

The forest uncoils to greasy life. At first a smattering of living trees appears amid the legion of burned trunks. They loop and spiral into twisted shapes. Translucent fluid drips from their tattered leaves. Bulbous insect larvae cling to their trunks, vampirizing their sap. The travelers pretend not to see their staring, man-like faces.

As the six trudge on, the Abyssal trees increase in number. Hooked, parasitic saplings compete for territory with briars and burdocks. Segmented vines, sheathed in a chitinous outer shell, gird the forest floor. When stepped on, they release a noxious orange suppuration.

The woods enclose, growing dense enough for easy ambush. Blood-sucking flies cloud around them. The team tries to slap at them quietly.

They hear thrashing in the nearby underbrush and call a silent halt. They ready spells and weapons. The sound of movement forks away from them. For caution's sake, they prolong their pause.

An hour later, they hear talking and stop once more. The speakers buzz and click in the demonic tongue. The group crouches behind a dense-knit briar.

Two figures sickle their way into a clearing, directing unpracticed blows at the clinging brush. Despite their demonic colloquy, the inexperienced bushmen are human. One is tall, jug-eared, gap-toothed. The second is of nondescript height and build, his flat face a vacant pudding of ill-drawn features. Their skin hangs loose from gnarled bones. They wear soiled and tattered robes, dyed a revolting shade of puce. They lurch ahead, their expressions dulled by hunger. They spot a tree warted with throbbing larvae, each as big as a fist. The tall one rushes to it; the other holds him back. They trade halting arguments, spittle flying, demonic utterances stuttering from peeling lips. The pudding-faced cultist releases his companion. He seizes the fattest of the larvae, tearing at it with his fingers. It bursts, spattering him in a lime-green spew. With pathetic desperation he licks the substance from his hands and arms. The second man trips through the vines and begins to lick at him, too. The first chatters out a curse and pushes him into the brush. The felled cultist gets up, reluctantly plucks his own rounded maggot from the bark, raises it to his mouth, and bites into it.

Tiberio, behind the wall of briar, clutches his chest, suppressing the urge to retch.

The cultists finish off the larvae and lie, nauseated, at the foot of their tree. In a complaining tenor, they drone on. Calliard listens intently.

Jerisa readies twin throwing daggers.

Gad shakes his head. She stands down.

A crow flutters into view. It lands atop the briars, perching on a spiking thorn.

The cultists snap to hungry attention. Slowly advancing, they speak coaxing words to the bird. They've switched to the local tongue, as if crows understand that better. Their hands bunch in anticipation, miming the wringing of the crow's neck.

The five brace themselves for confrontation. Jerisa is gone. The cultists are nearly upon them.

The crow squawks and flaps off.

The cultists see the intruders behind the briar. They reach for locust amulets. The trinkets glow with demonic energy.

Jerisa pops up behind them. The tall one falls, a knife in his back. Pudding-face whirls, his invocation broken. He falls, a knife lodged securely in his breastbone.

Jerisa retrieves and dries her weapons.

"You caught what they were saying?" Gad asks Calliard.

"They were complaining of hunger," says Calliard.

"That much I reckoned."

"They came to the Worldwound by compulsion. Were initiated into demon worship with Yath as their Abyssal intermediary. Found a group here . . . the details are unclear. They were afraid of being caught away from their camp. They feared a fiery whip, but at the same time were on the verge of dropping from starvation. The shorter one wondered why Yath would bring them all here and form them into an army without having proper provisions to keep his forces alive."

"So there are more of them nearby?"

"Many more, from the sound of it."

"Why would Yath bring them here and let them starve?" Vitta asks.

"Demons," says Calliard, "care little for the welfare of their mortal servitors. If they survive to destroy others, that's all to the good. If they expire, then their souls are transmitted to the Abyss to become raw material from which more demons spawn."

"That can't be the entire tale. It makes no sense, not even by demonic standards." Gad runs a hand across his thickening chin stubble. "If there is a mortal army, and Yath hasn't taken measures to provision them, he must be planning to use them soon."

"To invade Mendev?" Vitta asks.

"Where else?"

Gad inspects the corpses, pulling at their robes. "We need six of these, one of them big enough for Tiberio. Without telltale bloodstains."

"We can try reverse-tracking them," says Vitta.

Calliard presses his eyes shut, awakening his demon sense. He trembles. A jolt of awareness runs through him. "No need," he says. "There are demons nearby. A large number of them, at what must be the camp. I can find it."

"Take Jerisa with you," Gad says.

Chapter Eleven
The Camp

Calliard and Jerisa set off through the forest. They walk in silence, stepping over vines and ducking low to avoid prickle-leafed ivy. A trail appears in the trees. Without needing to confer, they veer from it, mirroring its path from the cover of the woods.

Calliard quivers and signals Jerisa to stillness. A flightless grub-demon lurches into view along the trail. In its gargoyle jaws it carries a decaying elven arm. The thing pulses along the trackway; they wait until it's out of sight.

They traipse along, keeping a good distance from the trail. An hour later, it forks. Calliard concentrates. He chooses the fork that leads northeast. Jerisa follows.

"I'm not stupid, you know," she says.

"Pardon?"

"I've seen how you look at me. You and all the others."

Calliard searches for a reply to this. "Did I offend you in some way?"

"Pity. You look at me with pity."

"You are mistaken."

"I don't want you to deny it, I just want it to stop."

"I assure you, my pity is in short supply. I waste none of it on others."

"Don't think I'm blind. I see how this is going to end."

"You don't think we can banish Yath."

"That's not what I'm talking about."

Calliard clears his throat uncomfortably. "Perhaps that's where our thoughts should go. The rip."

"A person can see that her actions are hopeless and still undertake them."

"Half the songs in the world are about that."

"She can act foolishly and not be a fool."

"Perhaps we are all fools."

"I haven't convinced myself that I can make him feel for me as I do for him. He never has and never will. He thinks bringing me along will help me see that. But I already do."

"He thinks we need what you can do."

"I already see it, and nothing will change, and it doesn't matter, and still I'm here. And if he asks again, no matter what it is, I'll go there too. And that's how it is. So spread the word: I have shame enough. I don't need pity."

A twinge of pain brings Calliard up short. He rubs his forehead. "We're close," he says.

They shut up and walk.

Muffled sounds soon confirm the bard's demon sense: the murmur of massed men, axes striking trees, inhuman barks of command. The magnified thwack of sword on shield as countless soldiers drill. The hiss of fresh-cut wood consigned to the fire.

Ahead, the corrupt forest thins. Smoke billows through the wood. Jerisa and Calliard skirt around a palpitating egg mass and creep to the tree line. They find bushes to hunch behind and peer into a wide clearing.

Hundreds, perhaps thousands of cultists and soldiers gather there. Rude tents made from rotting clothes flap against a growing wind.

Armored warriors conduct a mock battle, spurred on by gargantuan, bat-winged demons. Laggards suffer the lash of their fiery whips. Weird adornments have been welded to the soldiers' helmets and shoulder guards. They bristle with spikes, horns, skulls. Certain of the helmets remind Calliard of the shadow demon Xaggalm and the arrangement of curved horns around his toothy face.

Axe-wielding cultists expand the clearing, chopping down trees, breaking them apart, and dragging them to bonfires arbitrarily scattered on the clearing's edge.

Their less energetic brethren lie groaning on the stump-strewn ground. Reduced to skin and bone, they clutch their stomachs and cry out for food. A flaming whip lands in their midst; they barely muster the force to scatter. One stumbles, the whip curling around his legs. It pulls tight, severing them below the knees. He screams and crawls, robbed of locomotion. His plight arouses rippling excitement among the cultists. They leap on him, seizing his still-milling arms, and bear him to a crude stone altar. An impromptu ceremony commences. The drilling soldiers try to join it, but are herded back into battle formation by demonic sergeants.

Cultists swell around the altar. They strike up a chant, a tumble of throttled, warring consonants. A long, curved knife is held aloft, then passed between the worshipers. The chant builds.

Jerisa covers her ears. "What is this? A summoning?"

"A sacrifice," says Calliard. "To the demon lords, who will receive the fruits of slaughter through Yath's intercession."

"These people are starving," Jerisa says. "I don't want to see what they do with the body."

"This is our chance," says Calliard. He points to an empty tent on the camp's periphery. With all heads turned toward the altar, they duck and dash their way to it. Inside, in a stinking heap, lie the puce-dyed robes. He and Jerisa rifle through them, searching for one that might fit Tiberio. They find a sack filled with helmets and armor pieces still wet with blood. Jerisa picks out a few suitable items as Calliard locates the last of the robes. Working quickly, they make a rough sack of the robes and wrap them around the purloined armor. About to slip away, they spot a pole from which a variety of talismans, each on a leather string, dangle. There are mummified fingers, chunks of bone, segments of insect chitin. Rendered in tin or clay are the signs of several demon lords: Deskari's crossed locust wings, Cyth-V'sug's moldering tentacle, Pazuzu's fierce avian visage. Calliard seizes a handful of amulets, all of them depicting a misshapen tower that can only be Yath.

A climactic howl resounds through the camp.

"They've killed him," Jerisa says.

"Time to go."

She peers through the tent mouth. "Yes, it is," she says. Perhaps five in six of the cultists remain around the altar, where they have taken up a shuffling, jerking gambol of celebration. The rest, though, fan out through the camp, murderous intent etched in their faces. "One sacrifice has put them in the mood for more."

A couple of the amulets fall from Calliard's grasp and into the heap of robes. He pulls on them to find what he has dropped.

A vial rolls out from beneath the pile. It stops against the toe of Calliard's boot. The stoppered, clay vial is opaque, but Calliard can smell its contents.

Demonblood.

His hand jitters.

Jerisa's attention remains on the approaching cultists. "Take what you've got and let's go!"

Calliard pockets the vial.

"Wait," he says. He throws her one of the robes. She shimmies into it. He pulls another over his head, and dons a helmet for good measure. From its back rises a piece of flattened metal shaped to approximate a pair of menacing, beetlelike wings.

A robed cultist pokes her head into the tent. Her face is a mass of scabs, her left eye sewn inexpertly shut. "Where is Sibotin?" she demands. "He has not long to live, and thus is due for his transmission to glory."

The woman speaks Hallit, a local language. Calliard responds with a blister of demonic growls: *"Who dares employ such a tone in the presence of Xagros? Make proper obeisance!"*

She shrinks from him. "I d-don't—I cannot yet speak demontongue . . ."

Calliard switches to the vernacular: "Then get out of my sight, wretch, before it is you who is fed to Yath's altar!"

She pales and without further word performs an about-face.

Clad as cultists, Calliard and Jerisa exit the tent. He heads for the trees. She catches him by the sleeve, pulling him further into the camp. "When you don't want to be seen in a crowd," she says, "never go in a straight line. Determined movement attracts the eye."

She leads him on a bouncing, seemingly aimless path, first into the mass of cultists, then away from them, then toward the drilling soldiers, then away.

Ahead, a cultist makes a beeline for one of the larger tents. A flaming whip reaches out to encircle him. His robes char as the whip drags him to face a demonic sergeant. "Where are you going?" bellows the demon, in its native tongue.

With pitiful human words, the cultist pleads for forgiveness.

The sergeant orders him to forage for food and water for his soldiers, but still in its own language. The cultist stutters indecipherably. The demon moves to throttle him.

"I see what you mean," Calliard says to Jerisa.

The two of them fade through the crowd and back into the forest. They crouch on its edge, waiting for the bustle of the camp to die down.

"There's one bit of good news," Calliard says.

"What?"

"Plenty of Yath's human followers don't speak the language of the Abyss. I was worried about that."

"Because otherwise, you'd be the only one of us who could successfully impersonate one of them."

Calliard nods.

They look to the sky. Dusk is on its way.

"We got here because you can sense where demons are," says Jerisa.

"Yes," says Calliard.

"So how do we get back?"

"Well . . ." says Calliard.

A new round of savage cries emanates from the altar area. The cultists have identified their next sacrifice.

"I certainly don't want to bunk anywhere near here," says Calliard.

"If we can find that trail, we can work our way back. Let's make as much distance as we can while there's still light. Once we're away from here, I'll feel safer firing a lantern."

They trek through the forest. The trail eludes them. Gloom gives way to darkness.

"I think we're a good ways to the north of the route we took in," Jerisa says. "You feel any demons around here?"

For the first time since they neared the camp, Calliard consults his sixth sense. "None. We still have to worry about cultists."

She pats her belt of knives. "Cultists are not my concern." She unbundles her pack, assembling and filling a lantern. The Suma crest adorns its copper housing.

Calliard takes the opportunity to redistribute the robes and armor pieces. The vial of demonblood burns at his hip. Its pull is incessant. He considers tossing it into the brush. Somehow it stays where it is.

Jerisa is wrong, he thinks. Knowing that your actions are foolish does not make you less of a fool. No, that means you are the biggest fool of all.

As Jerisa strikes sparks with flint and tinder, the sound of drums rolls in from the north. She snuffs the spark before it hits the oil.

"Demons?" she says.

"No," says Calliard. "I don't feel it. And the rhythm is too regular, too disciplined, for an Abyssal horde. Or its human accomplices."

"Who, then?"

"Light the lantern. We'll douse it if we have to."

They creep toward the sound. It beckons them to an edge of the corrupted wood. It borders on a vast, beaten plain crisscrossed by crevasses. It is like the trench-ridden terrain they encountered when they first entered the Worldwound, though here the slashes in the earth are larger still.

Bonfires light a small army of crusaders. Dozens of pennants, each signifying the presence of a separate warrior order, fly above the columns and rows of armored infantry. Cavalry companies array themselves on the army's forward ranks, and along its flanks.

"That must be half the warriors in Kenabres," says Jerisa.

"At least," replies Calliard, surveying them with Vitta's spyglass.

"Then we can tell Gad we're not needed here after all."

"I'm not sure about that. First, they're attacking the camp, not the tower. As long as the tower stands, that camp, or another like it, will continue to draw maddened, disposable foot soldiers from Mendev and beyond. And second . . ." Calliard hands her the spyglass. He directs her to a knot of leaders conferring on horseback at the formation's apex. "Look who's in charge."

Fraton rides out to address a line of his colleagues. Their arrangement, and the deference the other leaders lend him as he declaims, makes evident his position of command. A herald holds the Everbright pennant behind him as he issues his orders.

"I'll give him this much," says Jerisa. "He's fighting demons for once, instead of rounding up thieves and prostitutes."

"A few days ago, I was one of those thieves," says Calliard. "I'm not prepared to give him anything, save for a swordpoint in the gizzard."

"He cuts quite the splendid figure, you have to grant," says Jerisa. "He'd fill me with confidence, too. If I didn't know him."

"If they're drumming now, they're preparing for a night raid on the cultist camp."

"That's not the wisest scheme," Jerisa observes. "Unless they know something we don't."

"Or Fraton, being who he is, has leapt to some lunatic false conclusion."

"You're speaking as if he's leading them to inevitable doom. They're equal in number to the cultists, better equipped, surely more experienced. The demon-lickers are ill trained, rudely armored, starving, and sick. No matter how reckless their commander, they'll cut through them like scythes through a wheatfield."

Calliard reclaims the spyglass. "As a clever killer of my acquaintance once said, the cultists are not my concern. It's the demons. They'll throw out waves of cultists to bog down the cavalry. Then they'll take wing, devastate the infantry and, once the footmen are all dead, come back to capture the leaders one by one. How much fell magic will Yath absorb when they're bled on his altar?"

"We have to warn them," Jerisa says.

"With Fraton right there?"

"Then what do we do?"

Calliard looked at her levelly.

"Get far away from here. So we don't have to hear the screams."

Chapter Twelve
The Amateurs

A half-prone Vitta leans against her overstuffed pack. Gad snoozes, sprawled on a horse blanket, lightly snoring. Tiberio sits cross-legged, chin to his breastbone, also sleeping. Hendregan is awake but resting, his cloak over his face. They have cleared a patch of ground behind the briars so they needn't lie on a carpet of noxious plants.

Predawn light shines into the forest. A sound snaps Vitta from her state of partial alertness. She leaps up, draws her short sword. Uses it to tap Tiberio's knee. He starts, shakes Gad's shoulder, and heaves himself into a crouch. Gad wakens without a sound, brushing drool from his mouth. He nudges Hendregan. Blinking, he turns toward the source of the noise. People move through the brush, coming their way. It can't be Jerisa and Calliard. They're making too much noise.

Vitta listens to the footfalls. With the fingers of her off-hand, she counts her estimation of the approaching party: two, four, five . . .

Through clawing boughs they shuffle into view. Like the cultists before them, they are dizzy, emaciated.

They're clad not in dyed robes, but in motley rags. A couple wear studded leather breastplates and hard caps, but are otherwise unarmored. Three are human women. One of the men is a gnome. The other appears to have some elf in him. Smears of grime slash across their faces. Each is bandaged somewhere.

One of the women has gauze wrapped around her left hand. Only one finger and her thumb remain.

Gad reveals himself.

Vitta hisses his name.

He steps out to greet the travelers.

They back themselves into a circle, brandishing crudely fashioned weapons—a notched sword, a wooden stake, a rusted pitchfork.

He replaces his sword in its sheath.

"What is he doing?" Vitta whispers to Tiberio.

Gad holds out his hands.

"You," says the woman with the wounded hand.

"Vasilissa," says Gad.

She turns to her companions. "Lower your weapons," she says. "This is the one!" She points at Gad. "I knew we were doing the right thing in coming here. We are guided by Iomedae's hand!"

The others' weapons stay up. They regard her with confusion.

She seizes the end of the pitchfork and pushes it down. "This is Gad. The one who found me in the wilderness. Who told me I was not bound by the demon's words. That my soul was still my own, had I but the courage to resist!"

Reluctantly they withdraw their scavenged weapons.

Gad keeps his hands out. "I have some friends over there. They're going to come out now. And then we'll all have ourselves a talk."

Tiberio approaches first. Vitta hangs back.

"This is Tiberio, Hendregan, and Vitta." Gad pauses, waiting for a response from the disfigured woman.

A dazed perplexity works across her face.

Finally he says, "Why don't you tell me who your friends are, Vasilissa?"

She introduces them. The part-elf carrying the notched blade is Elechan. The gnome who wields the pitchfork is Maleb. The two other women are Prebrana and Krasa.

Deep, raking scratches cross over Elechan's jawline and down his neck.

A filthy bandage wraps around Maleb's right thigh.

Another encircles Krasa's torso.

Part of Prebrana's ear has been torn away.

"What are you doing here?" Gad asks.

"We have come to do as you said," says Vasilissa. "To fight the demon."

"He wouldn't have told you that," Vitta blurts.

Dismay ripples through the motley band.

Vitta bites her lip.

"Why don't you," says Gad, "tell me how you and your friends came to be here?"

"You told me that I didn't have to give in to the demon." Vasilissa proclaims proudly. "That my soul could still be my own. I believed you, and yet I didn't. I didn't think I would be strong enough to resist. Through the woods I fled that night. I ran until exhaustion took me, and then I fell. On the cold ground, I dreamed. I dreamed of a terrible tower. I saw it, and I saw the twisted land of the Worldwound all around it. I felt its call. It wanted me to come here, to join the others as part of its army, and worship at a bloody altar. The weak would be sacrificed. From them I would gain strength. And if I myself weakened, I would lend strength to others so that all who had denied the power of chaos, the exultation of evil, would be punished for their imbecility. All this I knew simply from gazing at the tower, which I saw as if from a great height.

"Then in my dream I wandered through its hallways. Endless and winding they were. Not ordinary passageways as you'd get in a true building, but a maze of slippery, twisting, growing, breathing corridors. Each night since then I have dreamed of it, as have all of my comrades here. It changes its arrangement from night to night. But I feel that when I arrive there, I will remember my way around it, as I do the placement of cottages in my home village."

"You've jumped ahead," says Gad. "Go back to the night after we spoke. You woke up from this dream of yours . . ."

"I woke up from this dream and felt the pull of the tower. You told me to be strong, to fight. And you meant that I should fight within myself, to hold true to virtue and not give in to the demon's false promises. But the pull was great. I searched inside myself for the strength you said I had. Nowhere did I find it. So I listened to the tower instead. Through the Mendevian plains I stumbled. A demon came out of the sky at me, a thing of eggs and feelers and of strangely whirling wings. Down at me with feathered tongue it swooped.

"This is my salvation, I told myself. I haven't done anything bad yet. Yes, I've wandered in the direction the tower wants of me. But wandering is not a sin. I have committed no murders, no betrayals! I haven't even told a lie. Now this demon will kill me, and I'll die in fear and pain. But my soul will remain untainted, will fly free to whatever rest I deserve. It will not go to the Abyss, to become demonstuff."

The woman called Krasa weeps.

Each of them could tell a similar tale, Gad guesses.

"But as the tongue flickered all around me, I heard the demon's voice in my head." Agitation builds in Vasilissa's voice. *"You are already marked*, it said. *You are already ours.* It flew away, and in my heart I knew I was destroyed. I tried to remember your words, but in that moment they flew away from me. That night I fell again into the open plain and dreamed of the tower. And I forgot what you had said. Or rather, I recalled your words, but they scourged me, because I knew I was too weak to make them come true. You had chosen the wrong person to speak them to. I was just a poor woman from a poor village. Not a hero. A weakling. And as a weakling, I would make the trek to the tower, and there I would be sacrificed. I would not even make war for the demons. I would only be a spark of fuel for their Abyssal fire.

"Then later that day, I came upon Krasa here. She had found the body of a warrior, freshly slain—perhaps by the very demon that inspected me the day before. Krasa crouched over the body, searching his pack for food."

"I stole from the dead," Krasa says.

"You did as you needed, to survive," snaps Vasilissa. "He had but little food on him—some nuts, a dried sausage—but she held it out to me, to share. I could tell we were sisters, joined by the same misery. And she told me her story, which was also mine: a demon had imposed itself on her, told her she was his, and demanded her obedience. Once it left, she dreamed, and thought choice had been torn from her. She could only go to the tower, and sacrifice, or be sacrificed.

"It was then that your words returned to me," Vasilissa says. "I found myself repeating them. The resolve I could not find for myself, I found for her. As you told me, I told her. Our souls were our own. The demon's words were tricks. We swore to lend each other courage. But then we asked ourselves, where do we go? We can't risk returning to our homes. Each of us needed the other's shoulder, to lean on. Separated, we were nothing. And if weakness struck us again, it would be best to be far from our loved ones, where we could not hurt them. Or worse, lead them into corruption.

"And then I had a thought, one that in my heart I credited to you. The pull of the tower on us would not yield. To resist it would break us. So we would accept it, but falsely. As the demons sought to ruin us with lies, we would do the same to them. Turn the tower's pull against it, and against whatever demon king dwells within it. We would find others like ourselves. We would lend them bravery, and borrow theirs. We would find the tower, enter its dripping gates, and once inside, find the demon king and stab it through the heart."

"And so along the way to the tower, you met the others," Gad says.

"First Maleb. Then Prebrana and her husband, Obida. These we met before crossing the border. Then another, named Knoroz. And finally, in the Worldwound itself, we came upon Elechan, and another named Lishnii."

From the travelers' expressions when the names are mentioned, Gad can tell that Obida and Knoroz were lost. "Prebrana," he says, "tell us what happened to your husband."

"We were wrong to trust the one called Knoroz," she says, her features hardening. "He seemed less sure than the rest of us. But by the time we met him we wanted to believe. One night as he and my husband stood watch, madness took him. He stabbed Obida in the throat, and tried to murder us as we slept and tossed. The tower told him to do it, he said, when finally we captured him and held him down."

"You slew him?"

"With these hands," Prebrana says. Blue veins dance on her arms as she thrusts them out. "No one else did. I do not think it counts as a sin to kill a killer and a slave to demons. But if it is, only I am damned, and not the others."

"And the other you mentioned?" Gad asks.

"Lishnii?" says Vasilissa. "He starved."

"Just yesterday," Prebana adds. "He knew a great many jokes, and told them to us whenever hope grew dim."

"And from here you plan to go to the tower," says Gad.

"It is very close now," answers Vasilissa. "We travel by night now. The dreams exert a lesser hold on us if we sleep during the day."

"The nearer we get to it," says Prebrana, "the more readily we can see in the darkness."

"And your dreams tell you how to navigate inside it?" Vitta asks.

"Yes," says Vasilissa.

"So if we took you there, you could guide us?"

Gad resists the urge to wince. "Pardon us for a moment," he says to the strangers. "My companions and I have a matter to discuss."

"Of course," says Vasilissa, gazing at Gad with an admiration her friends clearly do not share.

Gad leads his companions behind the briars. "We're not taking them with us," he says.

"You heard them," says Vitta. "They know the inside of the tower."

"From demon-sent dreams," says Gad.

"Unreliable, yes, but better than what we have, which is nothing."

"They can barely stand," says Tiberio. "They're starving and we don't have enough to share."

"Leaving them to fend for themselves won't get them fed."

"They're not up to it," says Gad.

"How can you be sure about that?" Vitta asks.

"You're not seriously asking me that question."

"They don't look like much, but they got this far. Demons breathing down their necks, and they kept themselves right. Maybe they've got more in them than you think."

"They don't," says Gad.

"Maybe they'll surprise you."

"They won't."

"Because you can meet someone and talk to them and know to a certainty exactly what they're capable of."

"That's right," says Gad.

"They're going to die out here anyway," Vitta says. "Let them die for us."

"Good point!" says Hendregan.

"No," says Tiberio.

"This is no time to be ruled by sentiment," says Vitta.

"Let them die for Mendev," says Gad.

"Yes, that's the better way of saying it."

"That's not what we're going to do."

"Why not let them decide?"

"They mean well, but we can't depend on them," says Tiberio.

"Perhaps not," says Vitta.

"I'll put my life in your hands, or Gad's, or Calliard's," says Tiberio. "Jerisa's too. But not theirs."

Hendregan counts on his fingers, as if wondering whom the half-orc has omitted from his list. He opens his mouth as if to object, then reconsiders.

"I concede the point," says Vitta.

"Good," says Tiberio.

Hendregan shuffles off to start a fire. He gathers oily leaves and ignites them by muttering the simple words of a magical cantrip. They burst into smoky flame.

"So the two parties remain separate," says Vitta. "There must still be a way to use them."

"Use them?" says Tiberio.

"As a stalking horse."

"No," says Gad.

"They're going in regardless," says Vitta.

"I'm going to talk them out of it."

"They appear determined."

"I can try, at least."

Vitta shrugs.

Gad returns to Vasilissa and her companions. Vitta and Tiberio stay where they are.

He addresses her. "You might be wondering why we're out here," he begins.

The gnome, Maleb, interrupts. "That we were," he says.

Gad sets his shoulders. A group is ten times harder to sway than an individual. He will have to slowly tease it out. To identify the leaders, pick out the sides, read the unspoken shifts, and lever his way into the differences between them.

He looks past the gnome, testing him to see if this offends him. "We're here for the same reason you are."

And yes, the gnome seizes the group's authority. He steps between Gad and Vasilissa. "So you too have been dreaming of the tower?"

"No," says Gad.

"Then why have you come?"

"Because I saw what the demons did. First in Krega. Then I saw what they did to your friend. And I decided that it had to stop. So I gathered a team. Each one of them greatly skilled, and accustomed to danger. What were you, Maleb, before the demons stole your life from you?"

He shrinks a little. "A potter," he says.

"And the rest of you—farmers and tradesmen, yes?" They reluctantly nod.

"Your courage moves me. You know why?"

None of them wants to answer. Finally Vasilissa says it: "Why?"

The gnome eases away.

"It moves me because it's what you have. My team and I, we don't need to be brave. We're trained. To fight, to find our way, to survive in the wilderness. The wizard over there, he can call into being a fireball big enough to engulf a dozen demons. Of all of our swordsmen, I'm the least. But if you came at me with those weapons—even all at once, none of you would have a chance. Yet still, rather than give up your souls, you're ready to die.

"There's no mistaking how much you've achieved by making it this far. You've tramped through a land of horror and madness, and here you still are. There is no place more terrifying than the tower of Yath, yet you're eager to go there.

"But because you're brave, because you've survived so well until now, it hurts me to think you'll go through with it. I feel responsible. Vasilissa told you how I came upon her when the demon let her go, yes?"

"Yes," they mumble.

This is the hard turn, Gad thinks. He's scared them by praising their valor. Now he must give them a way out that leaves their pride intact.

"When I said you were brave, Vasilissa, I had no idea what I was awakening. I wanted to give you the hope you needed to live, and to preserve your soul."

"You did that," she says.

"I did it too well, because I never meant for you to endanger yourself. I never meant for you to come here."

"Not in so many words did you ask it of me," Vasilissa says. "But as I thought about what you said . . ."

"Don't mistake me. You've saved all these people here."

"I wouldn't have done it without you," she says.

"I don't think that's true," says Gad, "but I'll let myself believe it anyway. Now that I see who I'm dealing with, I have a tougher task for you. One that will take more guts than anything you've done so far."

"What is that?" the gnome asks.

"Go back to Mendev."

"Never!" the gnome cries.

"Hear me out," says Gad. "It's an awful favor to ask, having suffered so much. You're on the tower doorstep, and yearn to go inside. But just as we can disarm its traps and kill its warriors and wrench from it its occult secrets, you have it in you to do what we can't."

"I'm onto you," the gnome says.

"Show some respect," Vasilissa hisses.

"His words, those are the trap," says Maleb. "He leads us down a path so that we can only answer as he commands. He says, *You can do something we can't.* And we're supposed to say, *Oh what, oh what, O glorious stranger, tell us what!*"

"So you don't want to hear it?" says Gad.

The gnome throws up his hands. "Go ahead, honey-tongue."

"More cultists arrive here every day. Some are hardened servants of evil. Others are still like you—frightened. Confused. Haunted. Buckling under the weight of demonic influence. The demons have the tower as their missionary. What do the demon-fighters have? They have you, if you agree to do it. The greatest blow you can strike is to find others like yourself, and lead them back to Mendev. Spread the word. Doom is not foretold. Mortals, no matter how humble, still control their destinies. Come back, if you must, to save more who are lost. But do not waste what you have by going to that tower. Leave that to us. If we fall, we can be replaced. We are thieves, my friends, thieves and troublemakers. We will never be in short supply."

"Eloquent words," says the gnome.

"Hush, Maleb," says Vasilissa.

"Now it is our time to confer amongst ourselves," says Maleb.

"Of course."

Gad moves to Hendregan's fire to warm his hands. The sorcerer stares, mesmerized, into his own flames.

Vitta hands Gad one of their last strips of flatbread. "How much of that speech did you have when you started?" she asks.

"Most of it."

"Most?"

"I knew I had to give them a job other than saving themselves. But I didn't know what it would be until I got there."

"Have they taken the hook?"

"It's not in as far as I'd like."

Vasilissa and the gnome exchange anguished gestures as the other ragged travelers look dumbly on.

"Then we should kill them," Vitta says.

Gad grimaces.

"Think about it," Vitta continues. "What happens if they fail to swallow the gaff?"

"Give them a chance to decide, at least."

"Let's say they seem convinced as we bid them farewell. Then once on the trail they decide otherwise. That's possible, you concede."

"They're not sure what they want. That makes them tough marks."

"And it's not greed that animates them, so they're tougher still. So let's say we part on good terms, then once left alone they rediscover the virtues of their original plan. They go to the tower. Get themselves caught. Of course. Then what happens?"

Gad watches them.

"What happens," says Vitta, "is the demons torture them. Shred their flesh. Burrow into their thoughts. Slide like tapeworms into their dreams. And then they know about us. Either we're in the tower already, and the jig is up, or we arrive after them, and we're gutted at the threshold. One way or the other, it's over before it starts. We die. Or worse. Your entire plan, finished. All you've come here to prevent, proceeds. Mendev burns. The Worldwound devours its charred remains. Keeps on spreading. Tell me, how many die, if that's the way the story ends?"

"I won't let that happen."

"So you say." She points to the arguing newcomers. "How many are they?"

"I can count."

"There are five of them. Measured against thousands. Tens of thousands. Hundreds of thousands who stand to suffer much less merciful demises if we let them blunder on."

"A minute ago you wanted to send them in as decoys."

"If we can control them, perhaps that would still be best. But having had time to weigh the odds . . ."

"You'll do it?" Gad asks.

Vitta shifts her outsized halfling feet. "Jerisa will be back soon."

"She won't do it."

"She'll do whatever you ask of her."

"Let's not get into that."

Hendregan sculpts his campfire. As if attached to marionette strings, the fire swirls and twists, forming an undulating tower.

"Hendregan," calls Vitta, "you'd be willing to drop a ball of fire on those wretched waifs over there. Yes?"

"Yes," says Hendregan. "What for?"

Gad grits his teeth. "We're not going to drop a ball of fire on them."

Hendregan creates a miniature army, each soldier a tongue of flame, around his fiery tower. "Give me the word," he says.

"You know I'm correct," says Vitta.

"Not so."

"This is no time to be wise, Gad. It's time to be smart."

Vasilissa breaks from the others to head their way. Gad and Vitta walk to meet her.

"We'll do as you suggest," says Vasilissa.
"I'm pleased to hear it," says Gad.

Chapter Thirteen
The Hunger

Tiberio opens his pack, pulling the stopper on a clay jug of dry batter mix. He pours it into a heavy iron skillet until he has a heaping mound in the middle. He mixes it with water and drops in slivers of preserved meat and chunks of dried apple. Hendregan guides the fire to hug the skillet's underside. The two parties sit in silence watching the fieldcake cook. When the top has crusted brown, Tiberio slides in the tip of a small knife. It comes out sloppy, so they wait a little longer. The half-orc finally pronounces it done. He places the skillet on a rock and cuts the cake into narrow triangles. From another jar he produces white shards of sauerkraut, dropping them onto the cake. The strangers eat first, hungrily chomping at the slices of fieldcake, then meticulously licking each crumb and flake of pickle from their fingers. The other woman, Krasa, seems ready to sob again.

Gad sees that Tiberio is ready to give her his portion. He sidles up behind the big man. "We need you properly fed," he says. Reluctantly Tiberio pops his piece of fieldcake into his mouth.

"Have you found anything to eat here?" he asks the gnome, Maleb.

"No game bigger than a rat. Carrion birds will sometimes land, but they're hard to catch. Once we got a raven. Its wing was bent already. We found a river full of eels but sickened when we ate their meat. There have been no nuts, no berries . . ."

Tiberio takes Gad aside. "We're running out of food, too. We planned on foraging, but as Maleb says, nothing's looked safe."

Vitta is behind them. "You tell us this after you feed the strangers."

"We all knew this," says Tiberio.

"What do you suggest?"

"We don't want to eat any of those demon bugs. Rats aren't worth the trouble it takes to catch them."

"You're telling me what we don't want to do, Tiberio."

"There are birds still. They haven't been able to catch any for lack of snares. I say we stop long enough to catch some crows or buzzards. I have salt to make jerky. Depending on our luck, we'll bag enough to survive on for a week or more."

"Will there be food in the tower?" Vitta asks.

"The cultists who wandered into our camp . . . no one was feeding them."

"It will be better to be wrong, but we have to assume that we'll have to fend for ourselves," she says.

"Which means we should be prepared going in," agrees Gad. "How much time will it cost us?"

"Hard to reckon," says Tiberio. "A day if fortune smiles on us."

"And if it doesn't?"

"Several days. A week."

"I don't like it," says Gad.

"We'll need our wits about us when we get in there," says Vitta. "Hunger makes you stupid."

"They say we're only a day away."

"What are the three keys to a successful rip?" asks Vitta, prompting him to repeat one of his own favorite sayings.

Gad grimly takes his cue: "Preparation, preparation, preparation."

Vasilissa and her party assemble their few possessions and gather before Gad. "Which way should we go?" she asks.

"To the west lies the cultist camp; you risk capture if you head that way. I'd say reverse course. Find a trail or chokepoint stragglers are most likely to come through. Or maybe a stream with drinkable water. Concentrate on solitary travelers. When you see large groups, hide and let them pass you by. They're hard to persuade: there's always someone who sees himself as the leader, or wants to be. He's always the one who digs in his heels against you and turns the others."

"May Iomedae the Protector grant you luck," says Vasilissa.

"And you as well," says Gad.

They turn and pick their way through the woods. Maleb takes the lead only to stop short when he steps over a fallen log and convulses, clutching his injured leg.

The sun is not much higher in the sky when Calliard and Jerisa appear silently in the trees. They show off their stolen robes and accoutrements, and describe the encampment and the gathering army. Fraton's name is roundly cursed.

"I suppose it's too much to hope," says Vitta, "that he died in that battle."

"Fraton?" Gad scoffs. "He's luckier than we are. If I'd known, I'd have sent Vasilissa and the others to him. Let the paladins look after them."

Vitta tells them about the would-be demon-fighters, omitting the part where she argued for their deaths.

"Fraton might have embraced them," says Calliard. "Or he might have burned them at the stake."

As Tiberio uses the last of the fieldcake mix to fix their breakfast, Gad repeats their deliberations on the matter of the food supply.

"We saw birds in the sky as we came in," Jerisa says. "Over the flatlands, to the northwest."

"A quick detour to hunt," says Gad, "and then the hard part starts."

Birds are all too easy to find. A column of vultures and buzzards whirls lazily in the sky. The creatures dive down to the cracked plain, to be replaced by others flying in from the north, south, east and west. They share the sky with assorted demons who buzz indifferently through their formation, on their way either to or from the Mendevian border.

Walls and pillars of a ruined city litter the plain, providing its only cover. The six make frustrating progress across it. They hide from demons wheeling overhead. For every minute they spend on the move, they lose another nine hunched against a crumbling facade or crouched beneath a marble plinth.

They near the spot that draws the carrion feeders. Dozens of corpses, and the bodies of as many horses, strew a dried-up creek bed. The pennants of warrior orders lie dirtied on the ground. The six flatten themselves to the chalky earth.

Calliard reads their ensigns: the Order of the Emerald Sword, the Guild of Diggers and Sappers, the Knights of the Rampant Dragon.

"You saw these companies under Fraton's command?"

"The Rampants and the Greenswords, yes," says Calliard.

"I saw the banner with the crossed shovels," says Jerisa, referring to the pennant of the Diggers and Sappers.

They do not stop to wonder how the fight was carried so far away from the cultist encampment. It could have happened in a dozen ways.

Buzzards squabble atop the rotting haunches of slaughtered steeds. Ravens step fastidiously through the carnage, tearing flesh from dead faces. Sleek kites dive strategically into the battlefield, snatching meat from the beaks of vultures.

The six lie there, watching and at the same time not.

"We won't need snares, at least," says Gad.

They fire with bows and crossbows. Each missile kills a bird. When one dies, its living comrades immediately start to peck at it. It too has become food.

"Odds and evens?" Vitta asks.

They throw fingers to decide who will go to collect the game. Jerisa and Hendregan scuttle up, carrying the purloined cultist robes. The live birds take to the air. Using the robes as makeshift sacks, they pile up the dead ones and haul them back.

"Later," begins Calliard, "when we're eating these birds, we must make a pact never to—"

"Leave that sentence where it is," says Gad.

Tiberio paws his way through the game heaped before him. Though the creatures' stomachs are distended with food, the birds themselves are scrawny, with little meat on them. "We need more," he says.

It takes only moments for the hungry birds to return to their feeding grounds. The team harvests two more waves of them before stopping. They retreat to the shelter of a shattered temple, its roof nearly intact. There they strip the birds of feathers. Tiberio cleans the carcasses. With Hendregan's help, he quickly cooks them. Sprinkling an alchemical salt on the morsels of meat, he seals them against mold and rot.

Vitta gets up to move from the cookfire's smoke. It follows her to her new position. She waves it away. "If, when we get there, the demons lay on a great feast for us, I'm never going to let you forget this, Tiberio."

"I promise you, Vitta," says the half-orc, "I already won't."

It is deep in the night before the last of the meat is prepared and packed away. Gad rouses the sleepers. "We didn't see much cover beyond these ruins," he says. "Calliard, do demons fly at night?"

"You might find a few but not many. A demon can see in the dark, but only for about twenty yards. So they'll fly by day when they can, to avoid collisions."

Gad pokes his head out of the temple arch. The swollen moon reflects light across the plain. "We'll have enough moonlight to move by, if the sky stays clear."

"If that's so, the demons might take to the air when they otherwise wouldn't," Vitta says.

"Likely so, but we've seen how many there are by day. Moving by night, we'll be accosted by fewer of them."

"We'll have to start dressing like cultists now," says Calliard.

They don their robes, their horned helmets, their spiked and rusted shoulder plates.

"We look ridiculous," says Vitta.

Gad adjusts her grimacing mask of a helmet. "You can't let that thought show."

"How can I not? I can barely see through this thing."

"Put yourself in the mind of a cultist. Not the ones like Vasilissa and Maleb, desperately clinging to sanity. You're one of the ones who's embraced madness. Who's yearned all her life to wreak vengeance on the petty fools who mocked you and held you down. Who thinks, by placing this helm on your head, you're one step closer to becoming a demon lord."

"A prize idiot, in other words."

"The outfits alone will fool no one. The whole game lies in how you carry yourselves. All of you. As if the robes and armor lend you confidence. Take every step as if you expect others to fear you. As if you're crushing the faces of anyone who ever stood in your way."

"I almost feel sorry for them," says Tiberio, "when you put it like that."

"Make sure it's only *almost*. They'd be happy to kill you."

"And then dance draped in your entrails," Vitta adds.

"And that," Gad says. "We must each of us let out the part of us that is a killer, a maniac."

"That part of me is gone, Gad," Tiberio says.

"You know what I mean. Let's go. We've only a few hours of darkness left. I'd hoped to be there by now, but the tower isn't even in sight yet."

They plunge, already exhausted, over the moon-swept plain. As they leave behind the field of corpses, they hear strange animals snuffling and crawling across it. Great serpentine maggot-beasts, their undersides lined with reaching feelers, flow across the bodies of the dead. They snap bones and slurp greedily at the marrow inside.

Sickened, the company accelerates its pace.

As the night drains away, they see the occasional silhouette flitting across the face of the moon. Now and then a flapping resounds overhead. They travel without incident until dawn breaks.

A cold unease billows through them. Calliard is first to feel it. He points to a gap in a far-off ridgeline. Through it, they see the protruding tip of a curious structure. It terminates in a series of feathery appendages, like the floating antennae of an aquatic bug. Below it is a conical turret, its grooved surface resembling the abdomen of a scaled insect. The ridge obscures the rest.

Moonlight washes the tower, but is not its only source of illumination. It glows faintly from within, in a glowworm's greenish tinge. This interior phosphorescence pulses as if in time to the beating of a febrile heart.

Chapter Fourteen
The Site

Calliard pitches to the stony ground. His scalp buzzes. A dull tingling afflicts his jaw and limbs. He feels the vial of demonblood inside his pack. Though he has carefully wrapped it in cloth, the vial has nonetheless traveled to the edge of the bag. Through the rough fabric of the pack, through the backplate of his armor, through the quilted layer of padding below, the drug inside the vial resonates. Calliard feels the vial as if it has become a part of him. It throbs like an aching leg.

Tiberio opens Calliard's pack, in search of his waterskin. Calliard jolts and cries out. "No!"

From somewhere nearby comes a lazy flapping sound. A batlike demon flits across the breach in the ridgeline. It interrupts its flight and circles. The group freezes. Hendregan counts under his breath, picturing it swooping toward them, calculating the outside range of his fireball spell.

With taloned feet the demon pushes away from the ridge and flaps away.

"What happened?" Tiberio asks Calliard.

"I don't know," he says. "That damnable tower . . ."

On each pulse of the tower's inner light, the six feel a weird heat brush their exposed skin. Nausea roils them.

Jerisa looks away. The image of a soldier, beheaded by a demon at Suma Castle, bubbles up from months-old memory. She wills it away—the gore, the dead man's pleading face.

"Do we need the Salve of Tala already?" she asks.

"We must ration it carefully," says Calliard.

"Can we all hold out a while longer?" Gad asks.

The group murmurs collective assent.

"If it gets bad—if you start hearing or seeing things, or are weakened by sickness, tell us," Gad says. "We should dole it out carefully, but we also have to be on our game when we enter that tower."

The turret puffs out, exhaling a green cloud.

"What have you talked us into?" asks Vitta.

"That's why we're here," says Gad.

"I know you said it was alive, but . . . what I had fixed in my mind was more tower, less demon."

"It's too late to go back," says Gad.

She starts walking. "No one wants to go back," she says.

The others follow. For a while, as they tramp closer to the ridge, its angle shields the tower from their sight.

They pass a rift in the earth. Wet, fist-sized eggs bubble up from its unseen depths. A red light shines dimly through them from below. It renders the filmy egg casings translucent. Inside, bat-winged embryos flip and tumble. The eggs number in the thousands. As more are vomited from below, those on the top of the heap tumble down its expanding sides. When the eggs break, the creatures inside either expire, gasping, or shake off a gluey coating and take to the air. One newborn careens at Gad; he ducks from its path. Hendregan seizes it with a faintly blazing hand. Its bent, manlike face spews out a peeping curse. The sorcerer tightens his grip; it crisps into nothingness.

"Shall I burn them all?" Hendregan asks.

"Wait," says Gad. "What is this?"

"One of the many spurs of the Worldwound," says Calliard.

"And that means what I think it does?"

Calliard nods. "Climb down far enough into that fissure and you'll come out in the Abyss. It's extending itself into our world. Slowly turning Golarion into another layer of the demon realms. The tower of Yath will be yet another spur, likely originating in a different layer. This one is part of a spawning ground."

"These are baby demons?"

"Not the term a demonologist would use, but, yes."

"Then I'll burn them," Hendregan announces.

Gad grabs his elbow. "I said wait. Calliard, if we destroy this spawning ground, will the demons sense it?"

"Possibly. It could explode into a blazing column higher than this ridge."

Hendregan tries and fails to contain his jittering excitement.

"Or," Calliard continues, "every being in that tower might instantly hear the shrieks of a thousand dying demonspawn."

Gad moves on. "Then leave it be."

"Hold on," says Jerisa. "We're looking at a thousand demons, waiting to be born. That's enough to overwhelm Suma Castle. To raze Krega, or Egede."

Gad stops. "That's not the mission."

"The mission is to save Mendev, isn't it?"

"Yes, by destroying the tower. Calliard, does bringing Yath down seal up this breach?"

"It could well. Yath is itself a breach, but such a mighty one that it's likely accelerating the rate at which the Abyss claims this land."

"We stick to the plan," says Gad, forging on, forcing the others to keep up. "This isn't the last distraction we'll encounter here. This place wants us to fail. To lose ourselves and forget what the rip is."

Jerisa touches his shoulder. "Right," she says. "Now get back to the middle of the formation and let the killers take point."

"Like the plan says," says Hendregan.

Gad complies.

They spot the first traversable slope in the line of rocky hills and alter course toward its foot. Halfway up, their chosen hill shifts to a deceptively dizzying rake. Hearts hammering, they pull themselves upward.

Ant-demons, their heads red and long-tongued, fly overheard in a tight formation. The six press themselves to the steep ground. The demons wing close enough for the party to hear their buzzing gibber. A probing tongue caresses the rocks, coming within a few inches of Jerisa's ankle. Unaware of the intruder's presence, the demons bank upward and are gone.

"What were those?" Gad whispers.

"I've neither seen nor heard of them," answers Calliard. "The collision between worlds may be spawning new demonic types, never before documented."

"And was that demon-speech?"

"Yes."

"Could you make it out?"

The bard blanches. "Most of what a demon says, you don't want to hear. It's all murder and vicious obscenity.

But I did hear this: now that the soldiers of Mendev have been turned to carrion, the priest will come to claim his priestess."

"What does that mean?"

"I wouldn't hazard a guess. But then the other one said this: the final battle is soon to begin."

"Let's keep moving," Gad says.

They groan their way to the top of the ridge. A vast upended plain reveals itself beneath them. From the center of its chaotic jumble of riven earth, the tower of Yath rises. Its form is a forced union of worm and tree. Great roots plunge firmly into the ruptured ground. At its base pools a moat of rancid blood. It laps at the roots, nourishing them. A winding footbridge spans the pool, leading to a gaping archway in the tower's side. Fresh corpses, held fast by straps and spikes, adorn its posts. Gad takes a closer look through the spyglass, then passes it along to Calliard and Jerisa.

"The crusader commanders we saw near the cultist encampment," Jerisa says.

They survey the rest of the tower. The slowly tapering column reaches high into the sky. A bedlam of revolting adornments covers its outer walls. Cascades of dribbling flesh. Knobbly puckers of muscle. Gargantuan, serrated hairs. Feelers and fins and vestigial wings. Bulging, multifaceted eyes hang over networks of leaflike veins. Iridescent scales arrange themselves in jumbled bands. Frames of cartilage form windows and arrow slits. Together these features seem to shift and flow, exchanging positions as if drifting on a liquid surface.

Vitta separates herself from the others. She finds a flat, shelflike chunk of exposed rock and sits herself on it. Dazed, she shifts her gaze away from Yath. Then looks at it. Then looks away.

Jerisa, scanning the ridge for danger, sees the halfling's glazed distress. She looks to Gad; he and Calliard have stepped aside to confer. Jerisa hesitates. She approaches Vitta. She sits beside her, but not too close, adopting a precarious perch on the side of the rock.

Jerisa allows Vitta time to speak.

Vitta's gaze remains locked on the tower.

Finally Jerisa says, "Do you reckon you might need the salve now?"

"This is not how I thought it would be," says Vitta. "It was described to me, but this is so much worse."

Jerisa wonders what Gad would say to this. Or, for that matter, her father. The first response that comes to mind, that the tower is a demon thing, and horror is what one expects from demons, she rejects as clearly wrong. Both Gad and her father listen for a while and then make their points. They set the person to talking. That is maybe the most important part. "I understand," she says, not understanding. "Usually, when you imagine a terrible sight, the reality is not so bad as what you had in your head. But this, this isn't what I pictured either." The words sound good as they come out of her mouth, although Jerisa isn't sure what she pictured, or if she'd pictured Yath at all.

"There's no sense to it," Vitta says, hushed. "The demon cage, that was from the Abyss, but it had a logic to it that could be found, if you looked and watched long enough. But this . . . I don't want to watch it. I don't want to understand. This is not good. This is madness we're looking at, given solid form. Bricks I understand. Turrets and parapets and watchtowers. If the tower had those things, it would also have proper vaults and locks. Its traps would be governed by weight-plates, tripwires, pulleys and gears. Rational thought could be applied to them. This . . . this is . . . Gad should have chosen someone else."

Jerisa reaches to take her hand.

Vitta pulls it away. "I'm frightening you, aren't I? You didn't think I would be the one to crumble. Neither did I. I'm not crazy. Hendregan's crazy. Maybe you are a little too, I don't know. Yet now I see it's a protection to be mad in this place, because there are no expectations to defeat . . ." Now she reaches for Jerisa's hand. She squeezes tightly. Jerisa's fingers go white.

"Cover for me," Vitta whispers. "The others can't see me falling apart like this. Bad for morale. Give me a moment and I'll collect myself. I'm supposed to be the sensible one. Don't let Gad know. He needs someone to depend on."

Suddenly Jerisa wants to smack her. She mustn't do it, naturally. It is better to be solitary than to try to be a leader, she tells herself. "Gad can depend on all of us," she hears herself saying. "Or we wouldn't have been chosen. And you will gather yourself together, because we require your abilities, and you're not weak, you're strong. Aren't you?"

"Don't tell Gad this happened."

"I'll go get the salve for you." Jerisa heads to Tiberio, who has the jars of stolen ointments in his pack. Vitta's remark, about her maybe being crazy, stings. She feels it burn in her cheeks and at the back of her neck. Jerisa pushes the insult away. She thinks of the next time she'll throw a dagger into a demon-worshiper's back.

"Time for the Talar salve," she tells the half-orc. Without comment he fishes into his bag for one of the tiny jars. To hide Vitta's state, Jerisa daubs it on herself first. She follows the instructions Calliard gave them after the monastery raid: place the tiniest bit of the precious substance on each temple, in the hollow of the throat, in a line down the breastbone. "Need this yet?" she asks Tiberio.

"Once we're inside," he says.

She takes it over to Vitta, administering the salve. The yellow-white grease readily disappears into Vitta's soft halfling skin. The supply seems paltry now that they're here. Even if they restrict themselves to a few dabs a day, the treatment won't last long.

Jerisa waits a few moments before asking: "Feel any better?"

"That's not a place," says Vitta, "it's a creature. And we're about to walk straight into its gullet."

In freakish helmets and fetid robes, the six descend a precarious natural staircase to the ruptured plain. They scuttle around slabs of displaced rock. Hop over its fissures and trenches. Skirt its puddles of acrid blood.

Halfway to the footbridge, a trio of fully grown bat-demons drifts from the air to block their path. Calliard bellows at them in the demon tongue. They hiss back. Further rumblings pass between man and demon. Then, suddenly bored by the exchange, the bat-beasts lift off in search of more interesting prey.

"What did you say to them?" Jerisa asks.

"We traded threats, in anatomical detail."

"Charming."

"Minor demons. They only care if you seem weak. Stand up to them, and they assume you're shielded by a mighty patron."

"And that's if they believe you're on their side," she says.

"That's right."

They edge onto the footbridge. Each step is a mocking creak.

"No more talking from here on out." Gad's helmet is full-faced; it muffles his curt delivery. "It's like we're strolling through the village market. Nothing we see here surprises us."

Nails carved from bone secure the drawbridge's posts. The ropes holding together its planks are woven tight from strands of mortal hair.

The party nears the displayed corpses of the slain crusaders. Pins hold their mouths agape to better emphasize the agony of their defeat. With knives and branding implements, their killers have incised demonic symbols on their exposed flesh. An array of postmortem bruises and cuts attest to their use as targets by idle guards. Gad half-expects to see Fraton among them. One of the dead wears the Everbright blazon, but it isn't him.

Closer to the tower, the moat of blood swells with other bodies. Apparently these are victims of lesser renown: common soldiers still bearing the crests of the great crusader companies. For every slain warrior, there is a body clad in cultist's robes.

Later, Gad decides, when it's safe, he'll ask why Yath has filled his moat with the remains of his worshipers. Did they displease him, or simply starve? Or can they all be disguised interlopers who failed to pass muster?

"Oh no," says Tiberio. Realizing his mistake, he replaces his dismayed expression with an orcish lip snarl. He juts out his tusks as if ready to fight.

With a nudge, he guides Gad to the left of the drawbridge. There float the broken bodies of Vasilissa and Maleb. Bumping against the tower roots is another corpse that might be Krasa's.

"Look who wriggled off the hook," Vitta hisses to Gad. To cover her words, she adopts a drooling, vacant expression and a madwoman's shamble.

Gatekeepers study their movements. There are five of them, four mortals and a blood-red demon. The men, well fed and elaborately muscled, wear a higher grade of grotesquely fashioned armor, where they are armored at all.

"You sure they wouldn't give us up?" Vitta asks.

"Too late to turn back now," says Gad. "Translate for me," he says to Calliard. He takes the bridge's last few planks in a clatter of imperious strides.

"Make way!" he barks. "We arrive by Yath's decree! We seek immediate audience with him!"

Calliard repeats his words in the demon speech.

One of the men makes to speak. The red-skinned demon, of the same bony type that once held Vasilissa prisoner, sinks claws into the guardsman's soldier and shoves him rudely aside. The demon yowls back at Gad.

"He asks," Calliard translates, "by what right you demand audience."

Gad yanks up his visor. "By right of blood!"

Calliard transforms the statement into crunching, spitting demon-tongue.

The demon reaches forward to grab Gad by the breastplate. It pulls him up into its grinning crimson face and spits out demonic abuse. Caustic slime scores the breastplate and burns speckled holes into the ragged robes.

"Clearly, he says," Calliard reports, "we are gross imposters, as any true servant of Yath knows that only his greatest generals may personally enter his putrescent presence."

Gad slavers back: "And clearly, you are an ignorant maggot if you do not know the atrocious Gad and his retinue!"

The demon grins wider and sets him roughly down. "You think me ignorant of your pathetic mortal tongue? By whose authority come you hither? If you are but another pack of dreamers, you must go to the training camp, to be treated as any other foot soldier."

"Foot soldier! Your slithery intestines will be ground to paste! If you are so observant, can you not see that we carry ourselves with the authority of the priestess herself?"

"Isilda sent for you?"

Gad butts his chest into the sharp rib-line above the demon's abdomen. "Yes, we have been summoned in dreams. But not to toil and die as gormless infantry. In these hands rests the fate of Mendev!"

"What makes you so valuable?"

"You are the priestess's confidant, then? A stick-leg red demon, relegated to gate duty?"

The demon seems ready to slap him with a slime-coated hand.

Gad straightens his spine. "Dare you delay our victory? Dare you face our priestess's awful wrath?"

The demon drops its claws. "I merely tested you. Had you been ready to spill our mistress's secrets, you would have proven yourselves liars and fools."

"Then I may report to her, when I see her, that her guardians guard Yath's threshold with penetrating surety!"

"Tell her that there is much else I could do for her," the demon says.

"And what name shall I praise?"

The creature puffs out its meatless chest. "Speak to her of Jebel-Hau, of the screaming emanation. At my command, four paladins and three holy inquisitors committed offenses viler than they knew possible, corrupting other souls before they died. Though I take pleasure in my work—" he gestures grandly to Vasilissa's floating corpse, "—my capacities have been grossly overlooked. So much more could I do, were I freed from this post."

"And these others?" asks Gad, indicating his mortal comrades. "Shall they be accorded accolades as well?"

"No. These are mewling lapdogs, unfit to gaze upon the priestess's shadow."

"Both assessments shall be conveyed." Gad sweeps past him.

The team follows him through the gateway.

Chapter Fifteen
The Get-In

Lined in angry pink tissue, the arch resembles a set of diseased gums. Yellow, daggerlike teeth protrude from it. Viscid saliva drips down from the top teeth, spattering the intruders as they step beneath them. The archway twitches. Calliard shudders in realization: on a command from the gatekeepers, the teeth can jut out and the gums slam shut, impaling those caught between them.

On the mouth's other side they find a narrow foyer, lined by hairy stingers. Beads of steaming venom form on their tips as they probe for patches of exposed skin. Calliard shrinks back from them.

Gad eases in between him and the halfling. He claps his hands together. "I can't speak for the rest of you, but I'm going to like this place."

"You're joking," says Vitta. "Wait, I'm stating the obvious again, aren't I?"

Like the rest of the tower, the chamber burns with an inner phosphorescence. It casts a green pallor onto Gad's jaunty smile.

"He's not joking," says Jerisa.

"Of course I'm not. This place is full of demons!"

Vitta's tiny teeth grit together. "You say that as if it's a desirable state of affairs."

"Indeed I do."

Vitta frowns. "That first demon was stupid, I grant you that."

"No, no," says Gad. "Demons aren't stupid. And that works in our favor."

"It does?"

"Stupid people are impossible! They're used to being fooled, and wary of it. Demons, on the other hand . . . what's the signal quality of the ideal mark?"

"Greed?" Vitta asks.

"Close enough—selfishness, of which greed is a major variety. And what is a demon?"

The corridor ahead fills with pea-colored steam.

Gad stops and turns to face Vitta, visor still upraised. "A demon is a creature of pure selfishness. And that's no metaphor. Come on now, we've heard it now how many times since we started? What are they made of? Bits and pieces of rancid souls, all the mortal individuality systematically pounded out of them until only the nasty desires are left. I don't have to tempt demons—they're born tempted. They're made of temptation." He rubs his hands together. "That makes them mine."

"It sounds convincing when you say it," Vitta allows. "Of course, that's what we want to believe."

"All that damn journeying, that was the hard part. Here's where we go to work."

"You're saying this rip isn't as insane as it feels," says Vitta.

The fog parts. The foyer opens into a cavernous central chamber. A sickly radiance suffuses its shadowed vastness. Its fleshy, vaulted ceiling is domed and ridged, like a distorted top palate. Ropy strings of viscera hang across it. Sacs of organic matter dangle from the strands, contained in translucent epithelial sheaths. Vitta tries to count and mentally catalog the various organ types: there are masses of fibrous meat, bags of ochre liquid, twisted arrangements of tubes and fibers. Side by side with these hang cocoons, egg masses, and inexplicable collections of insect body parts trapped inside balls of webbing. Unnatural bugs scuttle along the visceral pathways, stopping periodically to feed from them. They nip off chunks of tissue with sharp mandibles, or spear proboscises into juicy organs.

Cultists and demons wend across a red, nubbled floor. It sinks yieldingly beneath their feet. Some inhabitants move purposefully through it. Others mill in small groups, or stand alone, dazed and swaying. These last denizens hum snatches of demonic chants, or murmur half-intelligibly. A large knot of cultists has gathered along a length of wall. They sit in bored expectation, passing a jug between them. A scrawny woman, her features hidden by an outlandish, grinning helmet, carves lines into her forearm with a scorched and blackened knife.

Tubular, connective passageways open at irregular intervals throughout the great hall, sloping upward into the tower. From these portals issue more cultists and demons. One, a hunching, asymmetrical glob of winged flesh, slashes at the sitting cultists with a razored whip. A few scatter into the tunnels. Others throw out their arms to ecstatically receive its lashes.

Ill-shaped orifices, no two alike, appear at irregular intervals across the skin of the vaulted hall. Some are raw and purulent, others sprouting jagged arrangements of horn or metal. They shudder, blasting forth hisses of air, which become discordant, blatting notes. Together they produce a harsh, insistent whine. Occasionally the sound threatens to resolve into a mad harmony, then lapses back into unsettling dissonance. Vitta pulls her spiked helmet lower over her ears, trying to block out the noise.

Overpowering stenches come at them in waves: vinegar, ammonia, unspeakable effluvia, rotting flesh. A clammy humidity falls upon them. As they slip across the hall, they pass through pockets of shocking cold and others of intense heat.

High up above the milling cultists, openings appear in the sarcous wall. Rivulets of blood trickle from them. The demon worshipers hop to life. They jostle furiously for access to the dripping blood. A few slap their hands into the substance and then let droplets of it fall into their mouths. Most simply hug the wall, licking it directly. They moan and shiver. Once sated, they fall into a reverie. Still-thirsty cultists grab them, yanking them violently from the wall to take their places. The dazed, displaced blood-drinkers stagger to the chamber's corners. Demons mock and scourge them as they go.

Calliard goes numb. He pitches, falling into Gad, who catches him. Tiberio moves inconspicuously to his other side. Together they prop him up. Calliard rediscovers his footing and pushes himself away from them.

"You're good," Gad tells him, more statement than question.

The bard feebly nods.

He can smell it from here. A heady whiff of copper, of decaying fish, of degradation. The pouring blood from which the cultists feed is laced with mesz, the agent that converts the ordinary blood of a demon into narcotic demonblood. The substance Calliard once consumed was almost always spiked with artificial mesz, produced by a forbidden alchemical process. This mesz is purer. Higher demons sometimes ingested it themselves, letting it infuse their blood, using the resulting ichor to enslave and suborn those mortals foolish enough to quaff it. Calliard scolds himself for his failure to anticipate. Of course there'd be fountains of the stuff here. By instilling its blood with mesz and feeding it to its adherents, Yath tightens the bond that keeps them in its thrall.

The cultists revolt him. He wants to wrench his crossbow from his pack and kill as many of them as he can before the demons and their servitors put him down. It's their servility that enrages him. Their shamelessness. He hates it because he recognizes it as his own.

With effort, he tears himself away from his murderous daydream. Gad is issuing instructions. Calliard has to pay attention. To show that he is good, like he claims.

"We need a place to settle in," Gad says.

A mutter half-escapes the confines of Vitta's helmet.

"Yes?" says Gad.

"Nothing," says Vitta.

"There's only one way to win." Gad drifts to the back of their formation to guide them forward. "By remembering who we are."

An antlike demon swoops down from a high ledge, seizing a flabby cultist clad only in a shredded loincloth and a metal, multi-horned headband. It lifts its prey up to the top of the vault, then drops him on a centipedal demon scuttling below. The aggrieved target seizes the cultist, digs deep into his flesh with gigantic pincers, and dashes him repeatedly against the floor. Bones twist and crack. Legs broken, the corpulent cultist uses his arms to crawl away. The hundred-legged demon surveys him with alien indifference. Above it, the ant-demon lets loose a peeping trill of triumph, or perhaps amusement.

"Calliard," says Gad. "Which way?"

He snaps himself to alertness. His helmet's weevil-nosed visor points in turn to each of the dripping corridor openings. "I'm not sure."

"Trust yourself."

"What am I looking for?"

"The one that scares you most."

Calliard repeats his survey of the entryways. "This one," he says, pointing to a gaping archway. An oily substance gathers on the surrounding walls.

Gad heads toward it, drawing the others in his wake.

The passageway widens and narrows at arbitrary intervals. It draws them up into the tower on a persistent but barely perceptible slope. The oily coating stinks of moldy apples. It soaks into their boot soles and sends the sojourners periodically sliding into one another.

A chorus of screams reverberates through the tower, then cuts itself off, as if a hundred tortured victims have obeyed a master's cue.

A convoy of locust-creatures floods the passageway. The bug-demons compose a single shifting mass as they crawl over one another to fill the corridor. The intruders put their backs to the walls. The demons brush them with legs and antennae as they clamber past. One stops, each of its eight jointed limbs clamped tight to Vitta's robe. Then it senses Calliard beside her. As if stung, it slips back into the surging host. The legion of demonic locusts continues on its way toward the great hall. Behind the procession scramble a few laggard cockroach- and silverfish-things.

The intruders forge wordlessly on. After a time, the circuiting corridor deposits them on the lip of a skeletal catwalk. Below hums a large, wet chamber. Reedlike protrusions emerge from its floor to wave in unpredictable unison. Multicolored liquids drip from its ceiling to be sucked in by root structures bunched at the follicle bases.

Flat slate stepping-stones bisect the strange chamber below. They are laid in the first straight line the six have seen since entering the tower. The stones connect twinned open archways positioned at the chamber's farthest points.

Robed figures emerge from the far threshold. Gad feels an impulse to shrink back into the passageway. To be seen to sneak is to get caught, he tells himself. He forces himself to stride on, leading the others, stealing only sidelong glances at the procession below.

In point position caper a pair of slouching male figures, each pathetically naked save for a grotesque iron mask that vaguely recalls the face of a wasp. Atop each mask is a metal loop to which the last link of a red, flaking chain is fixed. A stooped, uncategorizable being holds both chains in a bifurcated claw. Its swollen, housefly head contradicts a humanoid and mammalian body. Segmented ribs tighten the pink-gray skin of a malnourished torso. Knobbly vertebrae form a ridge along its stooping back. With its other claw it waves a bronze censer shaped like a demonic face. A cloud of chalky smoke wafts from it.

Behind this hideous entity strides the group's obvious leader. She is human, tall and lithe. An open robe trails behind her, an exquisite thing of black and purple silk. A white silk garment sheathes her alabaster torso. Its cut is tauntingly revealing, forcing the gaze to a pair of small, imperiously conical breasts. A filmy skirt of uneven strips likewise confronts the viewer with flashes of long, unblemished thigh. Leather boots reach nearly to her knees. A dozen diamond studs run up the side of each boot, emphasizing its length. A gleam of reflected light flashes from their soles.

Sharp cheekbones cut across her haughty face. Tresses of hair float down from the crown of her head, ending at the small of her back. Their blondness borders on translucence.

With eyes the color of ice, she beholds Gad. Ruby lips rise like curtains to show off a hint of pearly tooth. She holds him in her sights as she passes by, wreath of hair furling slowly in her wake.

Behind her march a half-dozen cultists. Aside from their relatively robust physiques, they are indistinguishable from their comrades, outfitted in rude puce robes and outlandish helmets.

The catwalk ends, terminating in a new link of oil-coated corridor. This passage soon forks in two. Each fork in turn leads to another split.

"Which way?" Gad asks Calliard.

"Still the worst one?"

"Mm. How about the second worst?"

Calliard steps ahead to drink in the corrupting ambiance of the four choices. Just past the first fork, the wall recesses to form an alcove. He checks the others. He slips into the alcove. He can't see them, which means they can't see him.

The vial is already in his hand. He has worked it out of his pack and palmed it. With jittering fingers he twists out its cork. The synthetic mesz tang rises to greet him. It is muddy and vague compared to the stuff he smelled back in the great hall. Still, it will do. It will more than do.

Calliard rushes the vial to his lips. A familiar numbing sensation melts across his lips and tongue. The demonblood burns its way down his esophagus. It blasts through his veins and arteries. He feels it everywhere in him. It blots his fear. Dampens his hunger. Allows him to think.

His hand steadies. Icy calm pervades. His demon sense, until now a faded reflection of its former acuity, sharpens. In a blazing flash, it sorts and correlates the tower's multitude of competing sensations. It instantly achieves a state of hard, diamond perfection. The full return of his sixth sense hones the others. At the same time they immunize him from the tower's relentless perceptual assault. Only those sights, odors, and feelings that aid his purpose will dare to disturb him. The others retreat.

Why, he wonders, did I deprive myself for so long?

You feared becoming those blood-head wretches from the great hall. Pathetic and drooling. But they, the blood reminds him, *are weak inside, where you are strong.*

You are yourself again, says the voice in Calliard's head. Now he is ready.

The entire tower flashes in his fervid mind. He feels the greeds and hates and lusts of each of its demons, flaring like pinpricks. There are dim lights and blinding ones. He steers his thoughts clear of the brighter flares: these are the demons who might sense him sensing them.

Above all, at the tower's mystical center, lies a devouring putrescence. A living oblivion. One he shuts his thoughts to, lest it extinguish them.

It is Yath.

But knowing Yath is there doesn't scare him, now that the blood is in him.

He finds the clarity within the tower's chaos. A clear map forms in his head. He knows which chambers are empty and which ones occupied. Their images career in his head. He makes an instant choice.

Calliard removes himself from the alcove, returning to Gad and the others. "I know where we're headed."

He takes them through the left fork, then the right fork after that. The corridor doubles in size. They close in on the void at the tower's heart. Before their tromping, clawed feet can be heard, Calliard senses a troop of slime demons marching through the enlarged passage. He ducks the others into a small, reeking chamber covered in pustular lumps. They hold their collective breath as the red-skinned demons march skeletally past, glaives hoisted.

"A ground assault on Mendev?" Gad asks, when the last of them are out of sight.

Calliard homes in on their ruling impulses. He receives their cruelty, their lust for slaughter. "It matches what we've seen so far," he answers.

"Time slips away," says Gad.

"It always does," says Calliard.

He guides them through a series of forks and loops, down corridors lined in viscera and tunnels honeycombed in sugary toxin.

Finally he comes to a dead-end passageway, surfaced in the hard, mouthlike material of the great hall. Half-formed teeth emerge throughout. From a distance, their arrangements look like tiles. He blinks. Has the blood misled him? Maybe he should have covertly harvested the purer stuff.

He removes his helmet for a better look. "I feel that there's a door at the end of this," he says.

Vitta takes a length of iron pipe and taps it against the terminal wall. It bruises the wall, speckling the air with the tower's blood.

"Gently," says Gad.

With hesitant fingertips she touches the wall. Growing bolder, she taps it with the flat of her hand. She finds the joins that reveal a hidden door. The halfling kneels.

"There has to be a trigger," she says. Examining the partial teeth, she notes that one is larger than the others, worn smooth where the others are grooved. She stands back, taps it with the end of the pipe, and braces herself for trouble.

A slurping wheeze of discomfort follows. Hairline wounds form an archway pattern in the wall-flesh.

"How about a shoulder, Tiberio?" Vitta asks.

Tiberio pushes his weight against the incipient doorway. It pops open, releasing cooler air into the corridor. Beyond is a ribbed chamber, lit like the passageway with an internal phosphorescence. Sword drawn, Tiberio enters.

"It's safe," says Calliard.

As he says, the room is unoccupied. They scout it for additional exits and find nothing. Vitta satisfies herself that it conceals no hidden doors. They drop their gear and establish a watch rotation.

Vitta squinches her face at the door. They've closed it, but a line of green light announces its presence to passersby. "I wish there were a way to hide that again."

"That woman back there," says Jerisa. "That was the priestess, wasn't it?"

"A priestess, certainly," says Calliard. He removes his bedroll from his pack, folds it into a square, and sits down on it, facing a wall.

"No," says Jerisa, "that was her. The one who drove Sodevina to kill herself, and Sodevina's comrades to madness."

"Could have been," says Calliard.

"I didn't like the looks of her."

"Nor of her pets," says Vitta.

"I should have put a dagger in her eye," says Jerisa.

"Stick to the plan," says Gad.

"Aren't we on a demon-stopping mission? Killing their priestess would help with that."

"The tower is the rip. Any other objective is a distraction."

"A good rip leaves room for improvisation."

"Untrue. If we whip a dagger at whatever horrible procession we happen to pass, we'll soon be fighting every cultist and demon in the place. Until we're killed or captured, which won't take long."

"One quick fireball from the wizard, and it would have been over."

Hendregan perks up. "Yes, I should have." A fiery miniature image of the demonic entourage appears at his feet. He gestures, and they dissipate into smoke.

"Fireballs only when called for, Hendregan," says Gad.

The sorcerer slumps in disappointment.

"So if we're sticking to the rip," Jerisa asks, "what in the name of Aroden's balls is it?"

"We catch our breath," says Gad, "then reconnoiter. We find out where the orb is and how it's secured. Based on what we discover, we draw up the final plan, and execute it. Until then we keep our heads down and the priestess-slaying to a minimum. Yes?"

Jerisa crosses her arms. "I didn't like the looks of her."

The first watch is not yet over when a thumping comes at the door.

Chapter Sixteen
The Gaffle

The intruders spring to positions. Preparatory fire crackles around Hendregan's hands.

"Who's there?" The words slurp and crunch, in the demonic tongue.

"Servants of Yath!" Calliard bellows, in the same language.

"Is that a mortal voice?" the demon grunts.

"What of it?"

"Open that door!"

"By whose authority do you demand it?"

"By whose authority do you refuse?"

"Try invoking the priestess," Gad whispers.

"What if they're from the priestess?" Calliard replies.

The door slams open. Flecks of scab, formed on the sheets of torn skin, take to the air.

The inquiring demons are four in number, each twelve feet high. Frog-fish faces hang in hunched, triangular masses of muscle. Glistening amphibian skin gives way, on their sloped backs, to horny plates of natural armor. Cords of saliva sweep across toothy mouths. They sniff the air as if scenting dinner.

"We requisition your hiding hole, mortals!" the first demon proclaims. "By seizing it, you have committed an offense against our rank."

"You speak in Isilda's name?" Calliard asks.

"Isilda? Another mortal? She serves at the pleasure of demonkind! Now for the matter of penalty."

"It is you who will face penalty," Calliard says, "if you persist in this folly."

"As one of the provisions of your punishment," the demon persists, "your group was to choose which one of you we would devour. By arguing, you forfeit that choice."

Calliard remains unruffled. "You are newly arrived in Golarion," he says.

The demon's amphibian nostrils quiver in consternation. "How do you know that?"

"To serve the priestess is to awaken the senses to Abyssal existence. Clearly you are unschooled in the flow of power here in Yath's bosom."

"Demons are demons! Mortals are meat! This arrangement is eternal!"

"So your claim is that you outrank Isilda?"

The frog-demon hisses. "My claim is that you are mortal, and thus may not challenge me!"

A new voice, buzzing also in the demonic tongue, joins the fray from the door's other side. "Who dares utter the priestess's name?" It is the strange fly-headed herald.

Though each is on its own twice the herald's size, the frog-demons duck their batrachian heads in its presence. "It was the mortals." It points an overmuscled arm at Gad.

The fly-demon surveys the intruders. Its tongue darts in and out. It addresses Gad in the common tongue of Mendev. "You lead this cell?"

"I do," says Gad.

With a backhanded wave and a buzzing stream of imprecations, the fly-thing dismisses the frog-beasts. They slink away, hissing.

The fly-beast addresses itself to Gad. "You received the dream-summons of Yath?"

"We did," says Gad.

"To which intermediary have you sworn allegiance?"

"None, so far."

"Yet you invoked Isilda's name."

"We have heard of her."

"From whom?"

"A crazed wretch we met on the trail. Sodevina was her name."

"Explain."

"A vicious half-orc she was. She fought us furiously. Only by stabbing her from behind could we put her down. As she died, she sputtered warnings and anathemas. Told us what Isilda had done to her. From this we decided that Isilda was the mightiest of all the . . . intermediaries, you call them?"

"That is the term."

"We resolved that, were we given the choice, we would swear allegiance to her, who could break such a tenacious one as Sodevina."

The fly-demon drones to itself for a while. It flits its tongue around Gad's face. "You are the handsome one, then," it finally says.

"I've heard that said," says Gad.

"It is you who has been commanded to attend her," says the fly-demon. "These others. They have committed their soul-fates to you, that you may consign their allegiance, as you would your own?"

"Do I not lead them?"

"Answer directly, Yath-thrall."

"Yes," says Gad.

"Then come with me, that you may prostrate yourself before our pale mistress."

Gad bows and taps his heels together. As he follows the fly-demon from the chamber, he whispers into Jerisa's ear: "Nose around. Take the others."

Jerisa and Calliard peer down into a moist, scaled tunnel leading directly down into the tower. Hendregan and Vitta wait a few feet back, with Tiberio guarding their rear flank.

Around them swarms a cloud of biting gnats. Hendregan snarls a petty incantation. Each gnat becomes a red cinder, then disappears.

The tunnel walls lack the phosphorescence of the steaming corridor they stand in. Its depths extend into utter blackness. Jerisa calls for the sorcerer's fire-staff. Still they can't see how far down it goes.

"Are you sure about this?" she asks Calliard.

"Certain, no," he answers. "But it is the best first place to look."

A belch of grinding metal echoes up from somewhere down there.

"And you know this how?"

"I sense its presence."

"You sense the orb?"

"There are two linked presences. The greater of the two is above. The second—smaller, brighter—lies below. The first a spreading stain, the second a minute dot of light. The former, aware, the latter, an insensate object. I could be wrong but I believe the second to be the orb."

"So you sense orbs now."

"As I said, I might be wrong, but it's a good bet."

"Before you only sensed demons."

"Before when?"

"Before you got here."

"Before now, there were no orbs to sense."

"So there's nothing you want to tell me."

"I've told all, Jerisa."

She leaves it there. She pulls items from her pack: an eye-hooked spike, a hammer, a coil of rope. She searches for a likely spot to plant the spike. "I don't like driving spikes into a living tower," she says.

"Who does?" asks Calliard.

"What if it notices?"

As if in response, the dripping walls breathe in and out.

"You can see a layout of the whole tower in your head?" Jerisa asks Calliard.

"Yes and no," Calliard says. "It appears as impulses and images, moving within grasp, then just as fleetingly fading."

"And this is the only way down to where you think the orb is?"

"No. This is the only route that isn't packed with demons. I think."

"You think," says Vitta.

"Risk is glory's handmaiden," says Jerisa, repeating an old maxim. She chooses a join between wall and floor where the substance of the structure seems more mineral than animal. Still, when she clangs in the spike, black ichor bubbles from the impact point. The corridor ripples.

"You don't think it could . . . *expel* the spike, do you?" Vitta asks.

"What risk do we prefer?" says Calliard. "Sneaking past hundreds of extra demons—and presumably cultists as well? Or falling down the tunnel?"

"Should we fall," says Hendregan, "I can lift us with a fiery hand."

"If Gad were here," says Vitta, "he could make that sound reassuring."

Jerisa weaves the end of the rope through the hook and ties it with a double founder's knot. The rope is only about fifty feet long. That it is magical, and will extend as far as they need, goes without saying.

The biggest man goes first. Tiberio hikes up his cultist robes to tie the rope's other end to his belt. He climbs into the tunnel mouth. The rope goes taut.

"Yell if there's trouble," Vitta says.

"Yell when you hit bottom," Jerisa adds.

The spike wavers in its hole.

Jerisa catches herself holding her breath.

They hear bustling down the passageway and brace for confrontation. The sounds veer away.

Finally the tension falls from the rope.

A forlorn echo attaches itself to Tiberio's call: "It's not nice down here."

Now Vitta disappears into the tunnel. Now Hendregan.

Calliard and Jerisa are left.

"You go," says Calliard.

"No, you," says Jerisa. She has the hammer ready, in case the spike requires another hit.

Calliard ties himself in and climbs over the ledge. It yields coolly to his grasp. He pushes off and dangles in the air.

Hand over hand, he lowers himself on the springy rope. A magically imbued softness protects his skin from abrasion. Occasionally he bounces against the tunnel wall. Below, as the merest pinpoint, he can see the yellow-orange of Hendregan's fire-staff. As he inches downward, the green glow from above gradually diminishes, and then is gone. Darkness envelops him. He keeps going. Calliard expects his vision to adjust, to be able to make out the dim form of the surrounding tunnel wall. Instead his world goes impossibly blacker. His inner sense of his own body departs. When his legs or back brush the wall, he jolts in surprise.

The effort of the climb wears into his arms and shoulders. It feels as if he has been climbing for a very long time. The flame dot seems not much closer.

Calliard comes to perceive that within the darkness is a deeper shadow still. It comes to enfold him. The rope spins, adding to his disorientation. The darkness-within-darkness resolves itself. First it is only a region, then a form, then a distinctive shape. It is a horned face, rimmed with teeth. Within the face, two glowing red eyes open.

"Xaggalm," Calliard says, under his breath. Or perhaps merely thinks.

The demon from the Suma parapet. The demon from his dream.

He speeds his descent. He knows from the rapid movements of his arms, from the sweat that trickles down his spine, that he is traveling, more rapidly than before.

The demon face remains in front of his.

He spins, this time on purpose.

The demon face spins along with him.

He stops climbing. His spin tapers and ends. His head pitches woozily.

"What do you want of me?"

The shadow widens its grin, then fades: shape, form, region, nothing. The lesser of the two blacknesses is all that remains.

Jerisa shouts his name from above. She sees that the rope has stopped moving. Without crying back, Calliard continues down. Suddenly he slides, his grip slicked by sweat. His belt stops him short, constricting painfully around his waist. Recovered, he makes it the rest of the way down, touching down on spongy ground.

An arched passageway extends before them. Its luminescence radiates not only from its walls, but from millions of squirming worms. They form a writhing carpet along its peak and sides. They precipitate from their ceiling perch only to wriggle back to the walls. A sulfurous stench surrounds them. Calliard uses the additional control of his demon sense granted by the blood dose to dismiss the stink from his awareness. It will be difficult on the others, he realizes. He decides to pretend that it affects him as much as they.

He unties the rope and shouts up to Jerisa.

The fly-demon escorts Gad through a labyrinth of ever-narrower passageways. Soon Gad has to walk sideways to pass through them at all. He wonders how the larger demons fit. Maybe they don't. Or perhaps the corridors make way for them. For a moment, he toys with the prospect of engaging the fly-creature in conversation. Unable to find the angle in it, he sets the idea aside.

The passageways widen again. They move through a series of large, connected chambers. Milling demons and cultists step aside as the fly demon approaches. After he passes, they return to their previous activities: fighting for scraps of meat, throwing objects at one another. In one corner, a crowd gathers to witness a duel between an earwig-headed demon and an oiled, weaponless barbarian woman. To Gad's surprise, the human seizes the advantage, ripping off one of the demon's mandibles. Swinging it overhead, she buries its sharp tip deep in the demon's skull. She brays in the demonic tongue as its body is dragged away. Gad wonders if she is another Sodevina—come here to destroy the demons, then reduced to their maddened plaything. The last he sees of her, a frog-demon has stepped from the circle to volunteer as her next opponent.

Finally they reach an empty corridor, at the end of which waits a sapphire door. It groans open when the fly-demon nears.

"Kneel to our lady," it says, pushing Gad inside. The doors slam shut, leaving him alone in a perfumed foyer. He remains upright.

Silk curtains part. A slim, pale, feminine hand juts through them. It beckons him to move through the fabric to the room beyond.

Gad steps through. The woman from the procession stands before him. She has situated herself so that Gad is already uncomfortably close to her as soon as he steps through.

Gad admires the tactic. The forced intimacy establishes her power over him. It sets her up as the aggressor, and him as the weaker party. Strips him of the expected advantages conferred by his masculinity.

He gives her the smile and nothing else. Neither discomfort nor a play for dominance. His impassive passivity will force her to make a second move, to follow up her first.

She smiles, too, but only with her lips. "Did Kaalkur not instruct you to kneel?"

"You mean Fly Head? It seemed more like a recommendation."

"I like impudence," she says, "in a well-chiseled man." She reaches out and with the back of her fingers brushes his cheekbone.

He catches her wrist.

Her body tightens in controlled fury. Her diaphanous gown floats freely from her chest.

"We haven't been introduced yet," says Gad. He releases her.

She adjusts her neckline. Nostrils flare. "You will understand, of course, that I must test you. For untoward loyalties."

Gad keeps himself loose. Drains himself of facial and bodily communication. To resort to charm now would be a tell. "Of course," he says.

He hopes Calliard is right about the Salve of Tala. In addition to slowing the wearer's fall into madness in the presence of demons and other aberrations, it is supposed to mask intention. A detection spell—like the one the priestess now chants—should return the result the caster wants, and not the one she fears. The woman produces a locust-shaped golden amulet, chants in staccato demontongue, and waves it in Gad's direction. Apparently satisfied, she drops the pendant's loop over her head. The locust dangles in her decolletage.

"We must be on guard against infiltrators," she says.

"I imagine so."

"You are wondering why you were summoned here," she tells him.

"That's true."

"I am Isilda. You are . . . ?"

"Gad."

"Tell me of yourself."

"A few months ago, strangeness invaded my dreams. At first I thought they were just the perturbations of sleep, but gradually I realized that an alien consciousness—"

She cuts him off. "I know that part."

"You do?"

"It is the same for all Yath's servants."

"Even for you?"

Impatience flickers across her face. "No, I have served him longer." She glides to a gilt-etched table. Gad dates it to the thirty-eighth century, the high Taldan style, and appraises it, dents and scrapes considered, at ten thousand gold pieces.

For the first time he is able to take in the rest of the small, square chamber. Either the walls are stone, or they have been altered by illusion to make them seem so. It is lit not by a weird luminance but by dozens of candles. They mask the tower's punishing scent with perfumes of vanilla, sandalwood, and rose petal. The suite is richly appointed, albeit in mismatched and mostly damaged items. A fluted Hermean vase rests atop a rosewood side table of the Greims school. An erotic ivory statuette, either carved by Landrit himself or by a skilled imitator, athletically conjoins a pair of lithe figures on an ebony pedestal. On the far wall hangs a wooden panel, its chipping paint depicting a six-armed snake woman. She looms above a marbled city, putting its tiny denizens to flight. Each hand holds a quivering peasant, ready to be popped into her pouty, snake-fanged mouth.

A second set of fluttering curtains conceals an exit into another room. Gad glances again at the sapphire door, mentally testing its weight and wondering how difficult it would be to open, should flight become necessary.

"I want you to tell me what I can't already guess about you," Isilda tells him. "Who you were before you heard the call."

Gad opts for the truth, which is easier to remember later. "I was a swindler. I acquired and sold items like the ones in your collection here. On occasion, when fine objects grew elusive, I resorted to simpler burglary."

"And what drew you to this pursuit?"

"Do you often ask men to explain themselves to you?"

"Yes."

"You do?"

"Regularly."

"And what they tell you, is it ever the truth?"

She considers for a moment. "No," she says, as if surprised by her answer.

"Let's say this, then. A man must follow his talents."

"Until you heard the call, you were content with petty evil."

"With lucrative evil," he says.

She gestures for him to sit across from her. "Yet without power."

He takes his seat, careful not to scrape the legs of the chair on the stone flooring. It is a Druman forgery, hardly worth the cost to cart it. The chair she sits on is from a different place and era and worth eight thousand easily—fifteen to the right buyer.

"Gad," she says, rolling the name around in her mouth. "Have I heard that name before?"

"Hope not," he shrugs. "I strive to be unmemorable."

She drinks him in. "Surely this is a struggle for you."

"We all have our burdens."

"I see you assaying the value of my possessions," Isilda says.

"You've caught me," he says. Let her think she's the one conning him.

"These are trash." She rises, her gown puffing around her. She seizes the vase and dashes it to pieces. Gad jolts as if struck on the face. The reaction is unfeigned. She glides back to the table, swishes her chair next to his, and sits. "The lust for a fine object. Hunger for money. These are petty impulses. They blind us to greater ambitions."

"I feel you are right," Gad ventures. "Or think I have come to feel it, since the dreams started. But I can't put it into words."

A silver dome sits on the table. She lifts it up, revealing a platter, a pair of bowls, and a collection of dinnerware. On the platter lie a pair of thick-cut steaks. From appearance alone, they seem finely cooked: charred on the outside, carved to reveal a thin stratus of rare meat in the center. Juice, speckled with golden dots of fat, pools around them.

Since leaving Castle Suma he has eaten fieldcake, dried sausage, nuts, sauerkraut, and carrion bird. Gad wants to grab the steaks with his hands, tear into them with his teeth. It is the correct tactic, he decides, to make his want transparent to her. She seeks to establish his weakness. He needs her to think she has the upper hand.

"Serve me," Isilda says.

An enlarged silver serving fork, its handle of carved greatdeer antler (Brevic workmanship, approximate value four hundred gold) rests atop a pair of nondescript stoneware plates. Gad spears the larger of the two steaks with the fork, deposits it on the first plate, and rises to place it in front of the priestess.

Two cracked stoneware bowls (valueless dross) contain side dishes: boiled beets and noodles with peas. After Gad ladles a single spoonful of beets onto the priestess's plate, she nods *enough*. She does the same after the first spoon of noodles.

"Now you may take what you want," she says.

Gad spears the steak. He takes one ladle full of beets.

"As much as you want," prompts Isilda.

He takes more beets, and several spoonfuls of noodles. After she seems satisfied with his serving he stops, though his hunger tells him to keep piling.

He waits for her to start.

She prolongs the moment.

Finally she slices the thinnest of slivers from her steak. Slowly opens her mouth. Lets him see her tongue. She places the meat insinuatingly upon it. Closes her mouth. Chews.

It is a display of power and ingenuity, Gad understands, to serve up a pair of fresh steaks in a place like this. He considers asking her about the logistics involved: bringing live cattle to the Worldwound, feeding them, protecting them from demons and hungry cultists. He's sure from the smell and texture that it is in fact beef, and not something horrible. The expense and difficulty entailed is incalculable.

Gad can't find the angle in asking. Instead he responds by precisely mirroring her eating. The thin sliver. The open mouth. The tongue. The distinct closing of the mouth. The slow, slow chewing.

She repeats the tease with a second slice of steak, this time somehow thinner than the one before.

Again he responds in kind.

She rewards him with an appreciative smirk. "I assume you suffered deprivations on the trail," she says.

"We had hoped to forage but were not prepared for the Worldwound's utter barrenness."

"I am used to fine viands," she says. "You'll do me a disservice by leaving your needs unslaked."

"Then I'll tuck in."

Porcelain hands interwoven on her lap, she observes him.

He saws off a large chunk of meat and bites into it with manly gusto.

"Yath's sendings," she resumes, "awaken and direct the potential to power. I see it in you, Gad. A mere glance was all it took. Greatness is within you, but lies dormant. You have squandered it in a life of petty gamesmanship. You think yourself clever, but have swindled yourself of your true destiny."

"When I want to fool someone," Gad says, "I talk to them of their magnificent destiny."

For an instant, she bridles.

She regains her glacial poise. "Distrust is laudable. When correctly directed. There are many who would disrupt our activities. But you must never mistrust me."

"You are one of several generals," chews Gad. "Or is the term intermediaries?"

"The term is demonic, and not precisely translatable. And what of it?"

"Do I trust them also?"

Her hand is on his wrist. It is as cold as a snowdrift. "You must trust only me."

Chapter Seventeen
The Case

Hot, yeasty air buffets the back of Jerisa's neck. She stands in a soft, tubular passageway. Outstretched feelers along its floor brush across her boots. Torchlight streams through the end of the passageway, thirty feet ahead. The opening is circular and bounded by muscle. Though neither engineer nor anatomist, Jerisa guesses that the aperture can close itself tight on command.

The others are around a bend and out of sight while she deals with its guardians. Two cultists, better kitted than the norm, stand at lazy attention on each side of the hole. Their bizarre helmets mimic bulbous insect heads. Fearsome as they may be, Jerisa can tell that they limit their wearer's peripheral vision. She can creep close to them—unless they turn their heads.

A chewing sound emanates from the wall as she presses her back against it. Shuddering, she creeps ahead.

Soon she is near enough to them to hear them converse.

"If you cock your head to the right angle, you can see everything," says the nearer of the guards.

"I wouldn't want to be caught looking," says the farther.

"She's a tigress, I wager."

"A mantis, more like. Rip your head off at the pivotal moment. Then eat it. With pepper and salt."

"Might be worth it," says Nearer. "For that one instant of supreme pleasure. Better than standing here forever, guarding another bunch of guards."

"You wouldn't be able to get it up."

Nearer scoffs.

Farther gestures to his groin. "Mine hasn't worked since the day we arrived."

"Speak for yourself."

"I should have done like Shchoka. Put the dreams out of my head. I was a fool to come here. What did I expect to gain?"

"Don't say that," Nearer says, helmet swiveling.

Jerisa, dagger already drawn, pushes herself into the yielding wall.

"I want to be back home. Back in my shop. Kneading dough."

"Shut up," hisses Nearer. "We can't go back. Not after what we did."

Jerisa lunges. She drags her knife's sharp edge across Nearer's throat. It opens easily, gushing blood. She shoves his dying body into Farther. His arms trapped, the second man is helpless to defend as she surges at him. She stabs her knife deep into his kidney. She keeps stabbing until he collapses and dies.

From below the circular opening, Jerisa peers up to see, as Nearer said, a second complement of guards. At a glance she assesses them as more formidable than Nearer and Farther. They wear a mix of plate and chain armor, as opposed to the robes and helmets of the common cultist. Each of the soldiers is an impressive specimen: none are more than two inches shorter than Tiberio, or concede to him a weight advantage greater than thirty pounds. Their rare expanses of exposed skin show off tight, heavily demarcated muscles. Scars of past battles lay proudly atop them.

There's a wrongness about them that she can't quite specify. It lies in their stance or attitude. They seem drunk, but not. They move as if unused to the construction of their bodies.

She sloshes back around the bend to gather the others.

"I need you to take a look at this," she tells Calliard.

She leads him to the circular opening. Calliard eases his head up along with her.

Five guards stalk listlessly through a squarish waystation. Each of the walls is upholstered in muscle; each has a circular opening in it. Beside the openings, on pegs, rows of weapons hang: swords, glaives, hatchets, clubs, and daggers.

Two guards spar with greatswords while the other three dully observe. They battle jaggedly. Certain of their swings are clumsily thrown, while others land with the certainty only long experience brings. The weaker of the two combatants seems at times to be impeded by an unseen force, and at others to lash out with shocking speed. He brings his sword down against its parrying counterpart. Sparks fling out as the defender's sword breaks in two.

The defender unleashes a torrent of demonic expletives.

One of the observers slurs at him, vowels drawn out and consonants sodden. "Talk only in the mortal tongue!"

The defender dashes erratically for a hanging sword. He jabs it at his scolding comrade, still exclaiming in the demon language.

"Xaggalm decrees it: we must seem to be as they are," shouts another of the soldiers.

The defender relents. "I hate this soft and mewling speech."

"Yet we must speak it, to catch traitors in our midst."

The defender drops his volume. "Those two outside. They are waverers. I say we tear out their livers."

"Only on Xaggalm's command."

Calliard motions for Jerisa to retreat back into the tunnel with him.

"You know what that is, don't you?" she says.

"Demonic possession," he responds.

"Which means?"

He takes her around the bend, where the others wait. "The cultists we've seen until now were influenced by Yath, but still chose in the end to follow him. Those bodies are stolen. They belong to ordinary crusaders— likely brave and good ones, or else they'd have been suborned, rather than dominated outright."

"Taken over by demons?"

"Yes. Their true souls are still in there, but they've been pushed into the deepest slumber. Discarnate demons from the Abyss animate their sleeping bodies."

"So whatever wrong they do," Tiberio interjects, "it's not them, but the demons who control them."

"That's right," says Calliard.

Tiberio sets his brow. "They're not our enemies, then. They're captives."

"No, they're both," says Jerisa. "And if they're in our way, I know which of the two I find relevant."

"We have to save them, not hurt them," Tiberio says.

Jerisa ignores him. "And who might Xaggalm be?" she asks Calliard.

"Xaggalm?"

"It was a name they mentioned. Sounded like a commander or something."

"I don't know."

"No idea?"

"Uh, judging from the name, it might be a shadow demon." Calliard feels the hollow ring in his words. He adds a quick touch of pedantry to cover it up: "Or 'invidiak,' as they are sometimes called."

"Like the one leading the demons during that last attack on Suma."

"Like that, yes, I suppose. An especially powerful one, perhaps, if it's one of Yath's commanders."

An enraged exclamation echoes down the corridor.

"They've discovered your cultists," says Calliard.

"Shit," says Jerisa.

Gad looks longingly at his plate. He still has a third of his steak left. He wants to eat it, but has conceded enough to Isilda already. There are also some beets. He wonders how much he'd be giving up to finish the beets.

Isilda tugs at her neckline, redirecting attention to her cleavage.

"What would you have me do for you?" he asks.

"I'll find many uses for you, I'm sure," she purrs.

"Do you want me here, or back in Mendev?"

"You I'll want to keep close at hand."

"To deploy against your rivals?"

"Among other purposes."

"What should I know about them?"

"I'll tell you," she says, rising. She moves to the inner set of curtains. She gestures for him to follow. "At a time better suited for tedious discussion."

He moves to her. Folds his arms around her waspish waist. "Before we slip entirely from the realm of the tedious, there is one piece of business . . ."

She pushes him away. "What is it?"

"My people," he says. "If we're to stay here, we require a safe place to bivouac, where we won't be bothered by an endless stream of demons and rivals seeking to dislodge us."

"Your lackeys? When the time is right, I'll examine your subordinates, and determine which of them can be of permanent use to us."

"If there is greatness in me, as you say, it's this: I pick my people well."

"It is good that you believe so," Isilda says, gliding his way.

He grabs his chair, turns it around to put its back between them, and sits down on it. "If I'm to serve you, we must understand one another."

"Naturally." The response oozes concealed ire.

"I am nothing without my people. They are my greatness."

She leans against a side table. She considers the erotic statuette, perhaps weighing the effect of throwing it against a wall. "What favor do you seek?"

"First of all, that you attach your seal to the chamber we've seized, so no one here can take it from us."

"Done," she says.

"Second, if I am to be at your beck and call, they must likewise be given no other distracting assignment. If suddenly I need to move against your rivals, I'll need their abilities at my constant disposal."

"You're right," Isilda says. "This is a tedious subject. Very well, I'll grant you what you desire. Let this not be a precedent. You are my retainer, Gad, not a supplicant seeking constant favor."

He grants her a cocky grin. "Understood, my priestess."

She sweeps his way. "And now, the favor I require from you . . ."

Tiberio approaches the possessed crusaders.

The tallest of them, a ragged beard obscuring his jaw, drops into a fighting stance, greatsword held to strike or parry. He jabbers out in demonic syllables.

Tiberio copies their odd, jerking movements. "Speak in the human tongue, as Xaggalm commands!"

The tall one shifts to common speech. "You too are clothed in flesh?"

"You need to ask?" Tiberio bellows.

A bald crusader behind him sniffs the air. "I cannot smell two souls."

The tall one clouts him. "Because you are restricted to the five mingy senses of your borrowed form, you coruscating chunk of quasi-matter."

The bald one attempts a grimace and nearly manages it. "When Xaggalm lets me depart this stinking rack of flesh, I'll break its useless fingers. I'll hurl it from a turret."

"Silence yourself," the tall one orders. He grabs one of the dead guards by the collar and hauls it up to shake at Tiberio. The difficulty of the effort surprises him, and the corpse slips from his grasp to land at his feet. "Is this your handiwork?"

"They were weak. Complainers. Said they wished they were back home and had never heeded the call."

"So you slit their throats?"

Tiberio recalls Jerisa's whispered account of her kills. "That one's throat I cut. The other I stabbed in the side. We are better off without them."

"We did not hear you do it."

"I am trying to train this clumsy form to move silently. It is a useless thing—strong but graceless. It hears well, but compared to the last mortal I possessed, that is its only virtue."

"Why did you not approach us as soon as you slew them?"

"The mortal bodily need. The one that follows food consumption . . ."

Possessed faces wrinkle in disgust. "Speak no more of it, newcomer. What are you called?"

"Has Xaggalm also commanded you to use only mortal names?"

"That he has."

"Then my name is Tiberio."

They tell him their meat-names and lead him to the guardhouse.

"I heard you sparring before," Tiberio says.

The bald one shoves him. "And we will spar again. Wait your turn."

Tiberio bares his tusks. The bald one chokes out a stillborn laugh. The fight resumes.

Tiberio watches it for a while, then exclaims: "Do you hear something?"

The contending warriors pause.

Tiberio concentrates, an ear cocked in the direction of the northward exit. "It is likely nothing."

The tall one twitches its cheeks. "You said your meat-shell hears acutely."

Tiberio shrugs. "Sounds abound here."

The tall one kicks his shins. "We must guard this post against intrusion. Do you wish Xaggalm to consign us to oblivion?"

The possessed mortals plunge through the circular opening. Tiberio follows, marveling. Days ago, he was afraid to speak to Fraton and pretend to be an aspiring crusader. Now he has demons convinced that he is one of them.

Stepping through the opening, he quickly whistles.

Jerisa leads Vitta, Hendregan and Calliard through the guardhouse and down another corridor.

They slide down a damp slope. It leads to a low-ceilinged tunnel. Vitta can still stand normally here, but the others have to stoop. Their boots squish into its earthen, puddled floor. The usual dim green light emerges from the ceiling's cracked tiles. They seem ceramic, but when touched they shrink back as if alive.

Vitta picks up a moist handful of dirt. "We must be at the tower's deepest point now," she says. "Where it ends, and the Worldwound begins."

"Or vice versa," says Calliard.

The tunnel takes them through a series of twists and turns. "Which way are we going?" asks Calliard.

"North," says Vitta.

"No, south," says Jerisa.

"Toward madness," says Hendregan.

"Welcome back to the conversation," says Jerisa.

He giggles.

The ceiling opens up again. They find themselves facing a high wall. It stretches up for at least a hundred feet. Spooling green mist conceals its upper reaches. Like so much else of the tower, it is of a mottled material, alternating patches of stone, metal, skin, and insect skeleton. Innumerable sculpted faces bulge from its surface. Each depicts a slumbering demon. Calliard counts at least one example of every documented Abyssal denizen, and many unfamiliar ones besides.

"I've lost all sense of where we are," says Jerisa.

Vitta adjusts her pack. "I just hope we're still in the Worldwound, and haven't stepped through a gate into the Abyss itself."

"That distinction," Calliard says, "holds no meaning here."

"Hoo hoo hoo," says Hendregan.

"Something strange about these images," Calliard mutters.

"What?" says Vitta.

"I'm thinking," says Calliard.

Hendregan points to one of the nearer heads. It represents a fly-demon, like the herald of Isilda's entourage. "Eyelids," he says.

"What?" repeats Vitta.

"He's right," says Calliard. "In life—"

"Not the correct term," Hendregan interrupts.

"An actual demon," Calliard corrects, "a demon of this type, would not have eyelids. Its eye is a compound eye, eternally open, like that of a fly. A fly does not sleep, not like we do, and neither does a fly-demon." He edges closer to the sculpted head. "Not that any demon sleeps, for that matter. As far as I am aware."

"What does that mean?" Vitta asks.

"Stop that," says Hendregan.

"Stop what?"

"Stop looking for meaning here," the fire sorcerer replies.

A softly breathing tiled material extends from the base of the wall. It ends a few feet away from them, giving way to the wet earth that lines the floor of the low tunnel. To continue onward, they must step onto the purring tiles.

"I'll do it." The words come out in Hendregan's lucid voice, but trail off into a crackling giggle.

With a sliding motion, first his left boot, then his right, he moves onto the tiles.

As one, the demon faces open their shuttered eyes.

Chapter Eighteen
The Guards

Tiberio trudges back toward the station behind the demon-possessed guardsmen. He commits to memory the mortal names they are forced to go by. The tall, bearded one is Aprian. The bald one calls himself Baatyr. The guard whose helmet is cut to expose a pair of notched ears is Ergraf. Pachko grimaces through a face like the head of a mace. The fifth is Matesh; thin-browed and beak-nosed.

The flesh-clad demons twitch and snarl. Tiberio's false report raised, then disappointed, their urge to violence.

Baatyr wheels on him. "I sense weakness in you," he grunts.

Of course you do, Tiberio thinks.

He butts his chest-plate against Baatyr's. "You wish me to slay this rancid rack of stolen flesh?" The absurd bravado of demon-speak is surprisingly easy to fall into after being immersed in it for a few minutes. The hard part, Tiberio realizes, is to speak it as if it is not ridiculous. The demons spout their nonsense with utter belief, with neither wink nor smile. There is no humor in them. They do not step outside of themselves or care how others see them. This must, he concludes, fit what Gad was saying before. They are abstractions. Walking, talking exaggerations. Tiberio must be as they are. He must carry on as if this is his normal way of being, too.

Aprian, at the head of the formation, spins on his heels. He pushes his way through the group to get at Baatyr and Tiberio. He bangs their helmets together. "You wretched dung stacks!" he exclaims. "These bodies must be preserved! Xaggalm has so ordered!"

Fear tightens around Tiberio's heart. He'll hide it, he decides, by pushing his luck.

"Mortals are plentiful! Let me murder Baatyr's meat-form, then let him find another."

Aprian batters his own helmet against Tiberio's. The half-orc judders back. Spots caper across his field of vision.

"Fool! The bodies we might take here are spavined, wormed, depleted by hunger and deprivation! We had to find these in the humanlands! You don't mean to say you came upon this solid specimen—" He jabs Tiberio in the join between shoulder- and breastplate. "—in the tower, or out in what mortals call the Worldwound?"

Tiberio summons an indignant bray. "By no means! This body is adequately conditioned, and therefore taken in Mendev. But Baatyr's barely breathes. Should I deign to take it apart, I'll be performing him a service."

Aprian chews at his lip. Underestimating the strength to put into the gesture, he draws blood. A red stream dribbles unnoticed down his chin. "Something is skewed in you," he finally says.

"I yearn for destruction, yet we are consigned to menial duty!"

"No," says Aprian. "It is not that."

Tiberio increases the intensity of his shrieking. "We should be leading legions! Raiding towns! Not lodged in our commander's bowels!" His throat hurts.

"Carrion!" says Baatyr. "You know not the importance of what we guard."

"Bah!" burbles Tiberio. "What is more important than havoc?"

"No task is more vital than ours," Baatyr presses. "If Xaggalm did not tell you of it, it is because you are unworthy."

With a casual movement, Aprian snakes out his arm, wrapping Baatyr in a headlock, choking off his windpipe. Confused by the effect on his borrowed form, Baatyr gasps and struggles, then finally relents. Aprian releases him. He clutches his neck.

"If our master has not explained," says Aprian, "it is not for us to do so. Yet you helpfully remind us, Baatyr, to return to our post."

With a choking sound, Baatyr signals his acquiescence.

"Walk alongside me, Tiberio," says Aprian, forcing his way back to the group's point position.

Tiberio follows. When he passes Baatyr, his rival's face twists with hatred and issues a garbled threat.

Gelatinous droplets form on the ceiling above. They land, smoking, on Tiberio's armor. He tries not to flinch.

"Tell me, Tiberio," says Aprian, "how you procured this form."

"It was in a village the mortals call Dubrov."

"I know it not."

"An insignificant place, populated by peasants and nobodies." Tiberio can't help picturing the place. He imagines a wheat field, late afternoon sun shining through feathered heads of grain. He recalls the fragrance of fresh-mown hay. Hears the delighted shrieks of the village children rushing between cottages. Wishes he was back there now, hitching a plow or thatching a roof.

"And this body, it was a farmer there?"

"Yes."

"The scars it bears, these were not acquired through a life of petty toil. When did you claim it?"

"A few weeks back."

"Then this body has had another life."

"It could be so," says Tiberio.

"A life of war. Did you not plumb its memories?"

Tiberio does not want to talk about this. "Who cares for mortal thoughts?"

"You do not find them delicious? Their fragilities? Their doubts, their fears, their regrets?"

"To kill them is delicious. To reject their pleas for mercy. The rending of muscle, the breaking of bone. The looks on their faces as life drains from them, as they understand that they're dying."

"So the mortal, Tiberio—he is a mystery to you."

"To put it that way suggests that I care."

"And how did you come upon this place, then?"

Aprian is testing him, but Tiberio can't see how. Wanting him to tell a story, perhaps, so he can sift it for mistakes.

"There was a mortal cultist there," says Tiberio.

"What was his name?"

"Why would I register such an irrelevancy? He was a fletcher, I think."

"And Yath pervaded his dreams," says Aprian.

"He saw this Tiberio, this hulking brute, as an impediment to his plans. So he accused him of witchcraft and congress with a succubus. His idiot fellows believed the fletcher's deception. The fletcher took him to be hanged, but then diverted him to a hidden altar. He summoned me, and I claimed him, and that was that."

"He used the seven invocations?"

"The mechanics of demonology do not interest me."

"And this Tiberio, how did he resist you?"

"Pitifully. I took him easily."

"He must have left a foothold for you, then."

"It was guilt. He regrets his past."

"What he did when he was a warrior?"

"He grew sick of killing. Can you imagine that?"

"Yes, mortals are laughable," says Aprian.

"I hate them."

"As do we all," says Aprian. "And so you turned this body back to its purpose. To slay."

"Yes," says Tiberio.

"And who did you first slaughter?"

"Dobreliel."

"Dobreliel?"

"The fletcher."

"You recall his name after all."

"Yes, now that I think back on it, he told me his name over and over as he begged for his life. Said that Yath would know it. That he was destined to be Yath's chancellor on earth."

"So you slew him for his effrontery?"

"For commanding me. As if by summoning me, I became his chattel."

Aprian manages a half-formed snigger. "They all do that."

"So I sent him to his destiny."

A coating of saliva appears around Aprian's mouth. "Tell me how."

"I throttled him."

Aprian appears to deflate. "That is all?"

"Dead is dead," says Tiberio.

"You did not torture him? What kind of demon are you?"

"One who acts quickly when anger seizes him."

"Did you spawn in the Arid Fields of Tiglah, Tiberio?"

Tiberio tries to remember if he's ever heard Calliard talk of this. His mind remains a blank. "What if I did?" He says it indignantly.

"An ascetic, then, are we?"

"Describe me as you wish. I want only for the world to crumble."

They reach the guardhouse. Aprian slaps him on the back. He calls to the others. "We have another Arid One!"

Baatyr lobs a gob of spit at him. "Let this dampen your desiccated spirit," he mutters.

Aprian seats himself on a bench. "Your kind is no fun at all, Tiberio."

Tiberio recalls one of Gad's mottoes: use what they want to believe. "Fun? You think I'm here for fun?"

"You yourself said you delight in the pleading, in the tearing of flesh."

"Indeed."

"Then you must not deny yourself the torture, first."

"I care only for what hastens Yath's victory."

Aprian leaps up, enraptured. "The screams of the helpless fuel him, Arid One. You must not shirk from them."

"What Xaggalm decrees, I shall accomplish." Tiberio's head spins. He wants to run away from them. He steadies himself against the wall. Under his touch, it undulates. Caressing him.

Aprian draws uncomfortably close. "We'll tutor you, Tiberio."

Matesh cracks his gnarled knuckles. "We can snatch a few strays from the main hall," he says. "For practice."

"Xaggalm says no distractions," says Tiberio.

"Xaggalm told us to stay sharp," says Matesh. "We must guard the orb, but he can't expect us to wither down here."

"Which do you enjoy more, Tiberio?" Aprian asks. "Men, or women?"

"What's the difference?"

"It is a matter of preference. The women are physically weaker. A mighty terror of violation drives them, and that can be powerful in the extreme."

"Yes," hisses Matesh. "We'll start with a woman."

"Yet there is another school," says Aprian, "one that I subscribe to. It holds that a man, who believes himself to be strong, suffers greater degradation when he breaks. Women expect to be destroyed, but to certain men it comes as a shock. The profundity of that moment . . . it must be savored, extended . . ."

"We can take one of each," says Matesh.

Aprian surrenders to contemplation. "They'll be dulled and blunted, these cultists and receivers of the call. They've already endured much. Fresh subjects would be better, but where to find them?"

"Don't stir yourselves for me," Tiberio says.

"Entrust yourself to us, Tiberio," says Aprian. "We'll guide your hands. Expertly."

Hendregan stands before the wall of staring demon faces. The others huddle behind him. "Wait till I have them fully rapt," he says. "Then go quickly. And whatever you do, don't look at them."

He takes another step. He opens wide his eyes. A crazed fire leaps behind them. "Oh, my sweet things," he whispers. "We too are brothers. In madness, if not in flame. Meet my gaze, sweet brothers."

He holds aloft the tips of his fingers. With a puff of devoured air, they ignite. Slowly he weaves them in the air, drawing the attention of the staring demon eyes. As if threading a loom, he gathers their gazes. Their eyes meet his. Reflected gouts of flame whirl in them.

A last few of the demon heads crane their stone necks to see behind them. One by one, he draws their attention.

He has them all now.

"We have much to talk about, my sweet brothers. Tidings to bring you from the lake of magma, where still more of our brothers abide."

Whether they are blinking, purulent, bloodshot, stony, rheumy, drilling, he has them.

"*Go*," he hisses to the others.

Jerisa leads Vitta and Calliard past the wall and into the dark beyond it.

Hendregan speaks without speaking, sings without singing. He communicates only with the conflagration in his irises, with the charcoal behind his pupils. The song is mad and jagged, a flutter of images, and it transports them to the moment they crave. To the burning chaos at the end of the world.

"Sit up straight," Isilda instructs Gad.

His spine is already erect, but he has one leg folded in behind the other. A subtle blocking move to keep her at bay. She stands six paces away from him, facing him head-on. Her already revealing neckline has, as if by its own accord, peeled itself back another step. She angles her body to confront him with a glimpse of ivory breasts, then adjusts herself to deprive him of it.

"We've moved entirely from the realm of the tedious, then," Gad says.

"I said straighten yourself."

"I'm plenty straight," he says, "but before we go further I have a suggestion."

A twitch of annoyance shivers across her perfect clavicles. "You have already been granted your boon," she intones.

"Not a request, not a favor," Gad says. "A suggestion."

The priestess crosses her arms. The gesture deepens her cleavage but for once the effect appears uncalculated.

"When we are conducting business," Gad says, "it goes without saying that you are my mistress, and I your vassal. But when we set aside matters of conquest and worship for sensual diversions, perhaps a . . . an equality of action and reaction might prove mutually pleasurable."

"It," she says, "would not. Now straighten yourself, that I might proceed as planned."

"Yes, my priestess."

She nearly smiles.

He straightens his legs.

She straddles him, slowly lowering herself onto his lap. She places icy hands on the back of his neck.

"You were wrong," she says, "but I can guess what you were thinking."

He turns on his flashingest grin. "And what was that?"

"It is not unheard of," Isilda says, "for persons who exercise authority elsewhere to prefer the opposite in the trysting chamber. While this reasoning may be generally sound, you must understand this, Gad, because I will only explain it once. I am not such a person."

"Understood. In both cases, absolute authority."

Her eyes flutter shut. "Yes."

"In that case, I await your next command."

She adjusts her position, pressing against him.

Gad responds with a tight intake of breath.

She pushes her swannish neck toward his lips.

He grazes it with a kiss.

She slaps him.

"I find that discouraging," he says, feeling the sting reverberate.

"You have been instructed," she says.

"I have?"

"Take no action without permission."

"Thank you," he says, "for making it clearer."

"Very well then." She leans back into him, arranging herself as before: her neck near his lips.

He waits.

"When I tell you," she says, "you will kiss me six times on the neck. You will begin at the base of the neck and work your way up. The last kiss you will situate just below the line of my jaw. Space them evenly."

"When you tell me?"

"Yes, when I tell you," she says, through a ragged breath.

"On this side of your neck, I take it?"

"I don't like sarcasm."

He waits.

"Now," she says.

He follows her instructions.

"Yes," she says.

"Yes?" he asks.

"Do it again."

"Now?"

"Yes, now."

Six kisses, evenly spaced, starting at the base of the neck and ending below the jawline.

She shudders.

After a few moments, he says, "Awaiting further instructions."

"Shut up."

"Yes, ma'am."

Clamping her fingers over his cheeks, she presses her mouth against his. She thrusts her tongue in. Her front teeth click against his. She alters her center of gravity, as if to knock the chair over. Gad counters the move to maintain their balance.

"No," she says.

"No?"

"No."

He shifts his weight back. Braces for the inevitable fall. The chair drops backward, its feet scraping hideously against the stonelike floor. It breaks.

The pain of the impact punches through him. It radiates from his shoulders and down his back. Her dress has opened itself completely. She resumes her assault. The force of her kisses pushes the back of his head against the shattered chair back. She grabs his hands. Plants them on her breasts. Isilda throws her head back. A keening sound rises from deep within her.

The room shifts and buckles as the pain reaches Gad's neck and flows up into his scalp.

In his peripheral vision he sees a pink-white shape emerging from a pinpoint hole in the ceiling. At first he can't make it out, except to perceive it as a shifting blob of matter. It billows itself into the shape of a fat, ribbed worm. For an impossibly long time its emergence continues.

In the meantime, she claws her fingers into the back of his left hand, directing him in a series of mauling caresses, first of her left breast and then of her right.

By the time it has fully separated itself from the hole in the ceiling, the worm is as long as Gad's forearm. It dangles for a painfully extended instant, then drops to the floor with an audible plop. Only a ring of interlocking teeth distinguishes its head from its posterior. The worm oozes toward a corner of the room, where a hairline crack in the tower awaits it.

Another slap crashes across his face.

"Don't look at that, idiot!" Isilda cries. "Look at me!"

Gad raises his head and pretends to be seeing only her as she tears at the laces of his tunic. Only when the worm has completely oozed itself into the fissure in the wall does he stop dividing his concentration between it and the priestess.

Soon she has him against the wall, next to the curtained archway. His shirt lies at his feet. Her sharp teeth sink repeatedly into his hirsute chest.

Her bedchamber, Gad reckons, waits on the other side of the curtain. He weighs his risks and advantages. All else being equal, he decides, he'd sooner not give up the full goods.

Reason one: it's his only power over her.

Reason two: it's going to hurt.

Reason three: that worm thing.

Reason four: oh, yes—he despises her.

How to fob her off without scotching the plan?

He can't mention the worm thing. You can never keep power by seeming weak.

He can't say he's not aroused. Contrary evidence is too close at hand.

Taking the upper hand with her would cool her ardor, but by too much. He has to leave her wanting more. Not wanting his head on a plate.

He's boxed himself in. There's no choice but to follow it through to its squalid conclusion.

She's seizing chest hairs between her teeth and methodically yanking them out. She stops. "You're thinking," she says.

"Pardon?"

"I can hear you thinking."

"What was I thinking?"

"I don't know, but stop it." She pushes him through the curtains and into the gloomy bedchamber. The tower's green glow is stronger here. An iron four-poster dominates the room's cramped confines. Colorless tallow candles, mounted on high, wrought spikes crafted to resemble spear-hafts, cast fitful light across the room. Silk garments lie in bright-hued heaps on the marblelike floor. A jumble of wardrobes and side tables lines the wall.

Gad plants himself. "You want me to put up a wee bit of a fight now, don't you?"

She scratches his pectoral muscle. "Your fight," she says, "has already been put up."

In the room they've just left, the outer door rattles in its hinges. A fist bangs insistently on it.

A flush, barely detectable in the green-tinged candlelight, steals into her cheeks.

She mutters what Gad takes to be a profanity. "Make a sound and I'll slice you to ribbons," she tells him. She points to a battered oaken wardrobe. It sits cornerwise, near the archway. "There. Now." She shoves him toward it.

He steps quickly into the wardrobe.

She closes its doors over him. "Your silence will be absolute," she says.

Inside the wardrobe, darkness reigns.

He hears her slippers shushing across the floor. Then the whispering of the curtains as she parts and steps through them.

The knocking on the door grows in intensity, and is then stilled.

Muffled voices filter through the wardrobe doors: Isilda's, and a man's.

Hoping to hear better, he cracks the doors.

"I did not like that at all," she says. "You will not knock like that again. Perhaps I will withdraw your right to knock at all."

Of the male voice, he can puzzle out only its scoffing tone.

"You knock as if you have the right to enter," she says.

In response, he hears surprise and protestation.

"You forget your place here, Fraton."

Fraton?

The new arrival has, Gad presumes, entered the room. Now Gad can hear him.

"I am sorry, my darling. The rigors of slaughter exhaust me. I have speckled sword and shield with the blood of a hundred champions. So naturally my next thoughts went to you." Now Gad can not only place but make out the voice. There is no mistaking it: it is Fraton. Fraton, cultist and traitor.

"I had to have you right away," he says.

Calliard and Vitta follow Jerisa into the limitless dark. She reaches out with Hendregan's fire-staff. Burning light throws into relief an inky labyrinth of narrow corridors. The walls roil and bend. Within their blackness, there are pools of still deeper darkness. She signals the others to move forward.

And walks into a wall. Staggering back and clutching her face, she bumps into Calliard.

"What the hell?" she whispers.

She motions for stillness as she waves the fire-staff across their path. In a dizzying play of impossible angles, the walls rearrange themselves. Gesturing for Calliard and Vitta to remain in place, she tentatively kicks at the join between wall and floor. The impact does not come. The corner is already somewhere else.

"The maze is moving around us," Vitta says.

"No," says Jerisa. "Wait."

She causes the fire-staff to snuff itself. Utter blackness comes. Calliard can't see the hand in front of his face.

"The wall . . . what it's made of . . ." she says, "We've seen it before. An object should either be dark, or illuminated. You can't get blacker than black. But you saw the way it swirled. A darkness that is absolute, and yet in places more absolute still."

"A contradiction in terms," says Vitta.

"Yes," says Jerisa. "Calliard, you know it."

Calliard allows himself an anxious clearing of the throat.

"The demon that led the attack on my castle," Jerisa says.

"Yes, I recall it," says Calliard.

"It was made of shadow. Same as this maze."

"Chaos shadow, from the depths of the Abyss," Calliard acknowledges.

"It's a demon, then?" Vitta asks.

"Insofar as it is part of the tower, and the tower itself is a demon," says Calliard. "Yes."

"I don't know about that," says Jerisa. "But this is how we navigate a labyrinth of shadow. Vitta, take my hand. You grab Calliard."

Vitta complies. With his free hand, Calliard reaches out, feeling the wall. It remains in place under his touch. They inch along, Jerisa pulling them through the dark.

"Shadows move," Jerisa says, "in harmony with a light source which is also moving. By carrying a moving source, like Hendregan's staff, I was causing the maze to shift. The only way through is without light of any kind. Without the moving light, the walls stay put."

"And how do we travel a maze we can't see?" Calliard asks.

"Vitta can answer that one."

"By memory," Vitta says, "and consistent right turns."

Time stretches forever in the black as Jerisa feels their way through. They see a green glow and head toward it. Finally the shadow walls open and they find themselves in a dripping cavern.

At the end of the cavern stands a sheer, partially translucent wall. Jerisa activates the fire-staff. Alert for traps, they inch their way to the wall. The surface of the wall flows and clicks and rattles. A series of locks and dials swim within it.

"It's a vault door," says Vitta, hushed.

Through its glassy substance, a crystalline orb can be seen. It hovers above a twisted, asymmetric pedestal that sluices forth a milky substance.

"The orb," Calliard says.

"Yes," Jerisa affirms. "That's it."

As they observe the vault door, it undergoes an accelerating metamorphosis. The familiar shapes twist and bend. The door becomes a ball, becomes a strip, becomes an ever-devouring recursion. Geometry devours itself, surrendering to a void of corruption. Perception fails.

Vitta falls to her knees, staring. "I can't open this," she breathes.

Jerisa doubles over, retching.

Calliard tries and fails to tear his gaze from it.

It is a spider a cancer a purulence a shimmering an unknowledge a strangulation a curse a destruction acidic gout fat wrapping encircling eating defecating undoing screaming intertwisting improbable exploding imploding parasitic a rotting a

corpsemetal
painflower
angeldeath
massacrestructure
voidhowl

"I can't even see this," says Vitta. "I'm looking but I can't see it. No, I see both everything and nothing at once. This is—this is—this is . . ."

"Pure irrationality, given solid form?" suggests Calliard.

"It's in my brain," whispers the halfling. "The more I see it, the less I . . ."

Calliard squats beside her. What worries him is that the door, this manifestation of chaos distilled, worries him so little. He feels his blood harmonize to its vibrations. The mesz in his body finds attunement with the vault. If he knew a lock from a hole in the ground, maybe he'd be able to help. "It's just a lock," he says. "Just another puzzle."

"No," she says.

"In its illogic, there must be a hidden logic of its own."

"Those words hold no meaning here," she says.

"They do, they do; it's just different, that's all."

"It's the end of locks, the death of keys . . ."

"No, no, no, remember who you are. Remember how your mind works."

"It doesn't, not here."

"There has to be a way," he tells her.

"I can't," jabbers Vitta. "Can't can't can't can't can't can't can't . . ."

Chapter Nineteen
The Wild Card

Isilda drops her voice. Now Gad can make out neither her words nor Fraton's. He catches only the shifting tenor of their volleying persuasions. The traitor paladin implores, wheedles, charms, jokes, demands. The Yath-priestess deflects, temporizes, warms, chills, commands, dismisses . . .

Gad thinks about his shirt. Which room is it in? She took it off in her receiving room. Did she have the sense and subterfuge to kick it into her bedchamber? If so, it's likely safely concealed among her own messily heaped garments.

Suddenly, he is not sure where his dagger is. Did she take off his belt, and with it, his scabbard? He checks. No, he still has his weapon.

He prepares himself for what will happen if Fraton opens the wardrobe door. He draws the dagger. Envisions the angle of attack. Tries to recall how tall the paladin is. The dagger must be buried in Fraton's neck before he understands what's happening to him. He's too good to face in a head-on fight. Three times they've traded blows, and three times Fraton has triumphed. That gives Gad one strike. If he misses, he's lost. Unless Isilda intervenes on his behalf, and that's not a possibility he's prepared to bank on.

It will grant his blow extra force if he pushes off from the back of the wardrobe at Fraton. Gad leans against it, testing it to see if it will support his weight.

With a wooden thunk, the back of the wardrobe slips. It comes away to reveal an entrance to a hidden chamber.

Jerisa blocks Vitta's view of the vault door, breaking its hold on her. She reaches down, interlaces her slim fingers around the halfling's deftly stubby ones, and pulls her gently to her feet. Calliard follows. Jerisa douses the fire-staff. Taking the lead, with Vitta in the middle, she feels her way back through the shadow labyrinth.

They reach the wall of sculpted heads. Hendregan holds its collective gaze; they are as helpless to break with him as Vitta was from the vault door. Without looking away from the sculpted heads, he mouths the words, *I'll meet you around the way.*

Jerisa nods. They move into the low-ceilinged tunnel and wait. A thwarted chattering rises through the corridor. Frustrated, inhuman bayings reach a crescendo and fall silent.

Hendregan appears. He holds out a hand to reclaim his staff. Jerisa gives it to him.

"They were sad to part with you?" Jerisa asks.

Hendregan puffs out his cheeks and sticks out his tongue.

Jerisa tilts her head in weary disregard. They reach the wet slope. She fights for balance, working her way up it. She finds a horned projection jutting down from the arch above the slope and tests it for strength. Judging it sufficient, she ties a rope around it. She whistles to the others. Hendregan goes first. Calliard urges Vitta on. She takes second position with him behind her.

Hendregan disjointedly hums.

"You're doing that out loud," says Calliard.

"Yes," says the fire magician. He hums a few bars longer, then stops.

Approaching the guard station, Jerisa finds a flat and bony rock. She pours a heavy oil from a flask outfitted with a specially formed lid. It drips loudly onto the rock. The flask's lid allows her to precisely control the rhythm of the falling drops. The flask is the third of the three items Jerisa took from the monastery at Tala, the one she did not expect to find but liberated all the same.

To an unattentive listener, the falling drops join the general wash of sploshing and plopping that sounds constantly through the tower.

Tiberio knows the rhythm. It spells out his name in the old sound code of the southern pirate isles. He turns to the possessed guardsmen.

"This body needs sustenance," he announces.

"What of it?" jeers Baatyr.

"I hunger!" says Tiberio.

"Again, I say, what concern is that of ours?"

"Are there not rations here, to keep this meat alive?" He directs a meaningful gaze at a cask. He has seen them sneaking morsels of dried, discolored jerky from it.

They form a menacing ring around him. "What rations there are, we secured," says Aprian. "For ourselves."

"Xaggalm assigned me here. Surely he meant for me to share your provisions."

Baatyr guffaws.

"To one such as Xaggalm, the state of your gullet is surely of profound disinterest."

"How am I expected then to find food?"

All of them laugh.

"If I go for food, and Xaggalm seeks me, will I not be scourged?"

"Xaggalm never comes here, fool."

"Then I will go and hunt now. And what I find, I will not share."

"Go, dung-wrapper!"

He tromps away through the circular opening he used to come in.

The other demon-ridden men turn instinctively to their cask, turning their backs toward three of the four exits from their station. Jerisa nimbly steps into the room, throwing darts in hand. She urges the others through, then follows them out, unseen.

They reach the well-like vertical tunnel before Hendregan complains: "I could have burned those demon-men."

"You may get your chance yet," says Jerisa.

"The real people are still there, locked in those possessed bodies," says Tiberio.

"Even so," says Jerisa.

They climb up the rope.

The wardrobe door opens.

Gad wheels, stabbing outward, then stays his blow.

Isilda stands before him. He sees no sign of Fraton. She has wrapped herself in a velvet cloak, covering her revealing gown.

"You were prepared to murder him," observes the priestess.

"Obviously," he says.

Her smile is snakelike. "It is flattering when suitors fight."

Gad leaps from the wardrobe. "Where is he? I'll kill him still."

She peers behind him, seeing the dislodged back panel. "You didn't go back there."

"Thought about it," he says. "Didn't have time. Should I have been fleeing him, instead of waiting to stab him?"

She strokes his chest. "Are you asking me which one of you would win in a fight?"

He places his hand on hers, ending her caress. "I'm asking who that is."

"You're not to go after him."

"He's your husband, then?"

Isilda's giggle reminds him of breaking glass. "Husband?"

"If I'm the one hiding in the wardrobe, that makes him the husband."

"Hardly," she says.

He looks for a place to sit. There is only the bed. He stays put. "That was the knock of a man who reckons he has a claim on you."

"That was the knock of a man who has to knock."

With a slip of the shoulder she guides him out of the bedchamber and back into her receiving room. Gad masks his relief over the change of venue.

"Have I the right to knock?" he asks.

She drifts away from him. "You do not."

"He outranks me, then. In your affections, or as a soldier of Yath?"

Isilda turns. She studies his face.

Gad tilts his neck to show it at its most shockingly handsome angle. He sees this take effect on her.

She is pulled toward him.

Her tone falters. "I was about to say that curiosity ill becomes you. But you do have a way about you."

"A man discovers he has a rival. He'd be a fool not to learn as much as he can about him. You don't let many fools in here, I wager."

Suspicion blinks across her face. "There is more than one way to be a fool, Gad."

Now he moves her way. "I shouldn't have asked which one of us you favored more."

She stiffens. "There you are correct."

"That implies that you are a prize to be won. But you are more than that."

"What am I, then?"

"We are not creatures of petty morality. Whom we choose to couple with is no one's affair."

Though she lets his words hang in the air, they seem to mollify her.

"I am a man," Gad continues. "One who seizes what he desires."

"I sense that," she says.

"I am not accustomed to sharing."

"Few here are."

"This is what I understand you to be saying: where you are concerned, Isilda, I must accustom myself."

"You must not think of him at all."

"Because he holds power here? Not only with you."

"His name is Fraton. You think yourself a clever fellow?"

"The word *clever* is always a condescension."

"Nevertheless, be clever. Strive to remain unknown to him."

"It will help me to do that if you tell me who he is."

She pokes the tip of his nose. "You are a clever fellow. Now begone. My moods are quicksilver, and a weariness descends upon me."

"When will I see you next?"

"When you are summoned."

Isilda gives him her back. He heads for the door.

In their absence, the room they've appropriated has exuded a coating of pulpy saliva. Vitta assembles the pieces of a metal shovel from her pack and uses it to sweep the exudation into a corner. Jerisa examines the soft beginnings of an orifice that seems ready to open near the ceiling.

Gad paces. "So, then. Fraton."

"We should have guessed," says Jerisa.

He shakes his head. "There're plenty of priests and paladins who'd like to see us hang," he says. "That doesn't make them servants of Yath."

"That we know of," Jerisa replies.

"We have no idea when they turned him," ventures Vitta. "He could have been honestly persecuting us for years."

"Then he got to like how it felt to interrogate a sinner," says Gad. "First it starts with harsh words. The fiery rhetoric of unswerving virtue."

"Fiery," says Hendregan.

"It starts to excite him," says Gad, "to see the fear he puts in his prisoners. It's for their own good, he tells himself. Terror of sin will lead them to the gods of light. But the pleasure of it grows. Then one day he gets angry. He finds himself in a cell with a hardened prisoner. One who doesn't fear him. Maybe with a smart mouth."

"Someone like you," says Jerisa.

"For example during the Bolchev rip," suggests Vitta.

"It would be before then," says Gad. "He hit me like a man who was used to it. But the first time he lashes out, he doesn't mean to do it. Guilt haunts him afterward. Maybe he prays for guidance. Maybe he tells himself he won't do it again."

"But then he does," says Tiberio.

"But then he does. And he can't escape it this time—he liked it. And the next time he's quicker to remove the gloves. So he has to tell himself it's right. Iomedae needs her warriors to be strong. To be ruthless. To win. And when it's right to slap, or punch . . ."

" . . . it must then also be right to haul out the hot tongs and the thumbscrews," says Jerisa.

"And then one night he calls down Iomedae's powers. He tries to heal a comrade, or to sense the presence of an enemy."

"And nothing comes," says Jerisa.

"And nothing comes."

"She won't answer him any more. He's lost his righteousness."

"But he won't admit it."

"He's too arrogant for that."

"And eventually, one day, something does come in answer to his prayers. Something that is not Iomedae at all."

"A demon."

"A demon," Gad says. "If this happened not so long ago, in the past few months, maybe it's a servant of Yath. If Fraton's been turned for longer, maybe it's a sending from one of the demon lords. We could guess all day and not know which one. And it whispers into his ear: You know, Fraton, all these months, you've already been serving us. You just couldn't see it. Well, now you do see. And Fraton, you have two choices. You can repent your sins, unburden yourself to Iomedae's grace. Throw off all your prestige, your leadership of the Everbright

Crusaders. You can scourge yourself and go off on an arduous quest of atonement. Or you can bow before me, and keep all the power you had before, and more besides. Continue to take the pleasures you've learned to love. The ones that celestial bitch Iomedae would humiliatingly strip you of. She'll humble you. We'll elevate you to a terrible throne. When we win, as we are about to do, you won't have to settle for the fear of a few wretched prisoners. All of Mendev will fear you. And you won't have to hide who you are. All you have to do is carry on as before. Win the trust of the other paladins. And one day, when the wound has opened far enough, we'll ask you to bring them to us, assembled into a single, shining army. And then we'll chew them to pieces. And then, with the defenders of Mendev gone, you'll lead your true army, an army of demons and demon worshipers and the demon-ridden. At its head, you'll ride into Mendev, lay waste to it, and claim your magnificent destiny."

"In other words," says Jerisa, "a con."

"That's right."

"They took what he wanted to believe, and turned it into what they wanted him to do."

"It's a guess," says Gad, "but it fits what we've learned. What happened back on the battlefield. How they'd get him and why they'd want him."

"It fits human nature, is what you mean," says Jerisa.

"And halfling nature, and half-orc nature, and and and . . ."

"Let's assume the conjecture," says Vitta. "What does it mean for the rip?"

"We can't get caught unawares by him," Gad says. "The moment he spots any of us, we're cooked."

"Any of us? What about Tiberio?"

A mournful look crosses the half-orc's face. "I approached him back in Nerosyan. He might not remember me . . ."

"You're memorable, Tiberio."

"Maybe all half-orcs look the same to him," offers Vitta.

"Probably so," says Gad, "but we can't wager the fleet on it."

Vitta addresses Hendregan. "What about you, fire wizard? Or sorcerer, or whatever you are? Does Fraton know you?"

Smoke drifts faintly from the magician's pores. "There was an incident, sadly, on the outskirts of Kenabres."

Gad groans. "So the only one of us he couldn't spot at the outset, he can spot now."

"He seems to have free run of the place?" Jerisa asks.

"If he can swan up and rap on the high priestess's door, it's safe to say he does."

"Have I mentioned," says Jerisa, "that I still don't like the entire high priestess part of this?"

"You have registered that objection, yes." Gad's pacing quickens. "Fraton's a complication, but that's all he is. The job is still the orb. Let's run through the casing again. Jerisa, is the route clear?"

"We're inside a gigantic creature," she says. "In a state of perpetual alteration." She points to the growing orifice. Feathery protrusions have appeared around it. They move as if brushed by a gust of air. "What we find tomorrow may not be what we found today."

"But the route as reconnoitered is clear."

"At present, yes."

"Tiberio, what can go wrong at the guard post?"

"They can figure out that I'm not one of them. Half the time, I want to laugh at their madness. The rest, I want to throw up. Gad, impersonation is not my game."

"You've done all right so far."

He works his tusks anxiously. "The time I have to spend in their company, it goes on so long . . ."

"Believe you can do it, and they'll believe you. That's all it comes down to. And remember, walking abstractions are easy marks."

"You say that like you believe it."

"Tusks up, Tiberio. You can do it. Hendregan, the wall of demon sculptures?"

Hendregan chortles.

"Translation, please."

"Worry not," says Hendregan. "We are brethren, those faces and I."

"How comforting," says Vitta.

"And the vault door?" Gad asks her.

"I don't know," Vitta says.

"You don't know?"

"You didn't see it," she says. "*Vault door* fails as an adequate term of description. If the demons are abstractions, it's an abstraction of a concept that can't be abstracted. A physical paradox. A macrocosmic reflection of the Worldwound itself."

"But can you crack it?"

"I said already. I don't know."

"No door, no orb."

She tosses the metal shovel against the wall. The sound of impact is disconcertingly organic. "This is the part of the plan where all it says is *Vitta figures something out*. And I'm telling you I haven't figured anything out. I can't even see where to start. After staring it down,

I'm surprised I can string words together instead of drooling and giggling like Fire-Master over there."

Hendregan has created a flaming representation of the face wall. He sheepishly dismisses it.

"We don't have much time," says Gad.

"I am well aware of that," the lock-breaker snaps.

"With Fraton prowling around," Gad says, "we'd better plan for a crumble. I'd feel easier if we had a back exit."

"Hold on," says Jerisa, "you went through everyone else's part. What about you and the priestess?"

"What about it?"

"Explain what we're getting out of that, again."

Gad maintains a steady tone. "The right to stay here and have this conversation unmolested, to start with."

"And unmolested is the right word?"

"We all have our sacrifices to make."

"Jerisa," says Vitta, "let's stick to business."

"This is business," Jerisa says. "You asked us what could go wrong. What can go wrong with you and Isilda?"

"If it does go bad?" Gad purses his lips. "Most likely, her slitting my throat mid-coitus."

"I object to both elements of that scenario."

"Ahem," says Vitta.

"A second exit," says Gad. "It would be good to have one. So far we've only seen the front gate. Jerisa, I need a scout-around. There's always a hidden way out, if only for the leaders. Around the roots of the tower, maybe?"

She checks her knives. "Right," she says.

Gad rubs his forehead. "And where did Calliard say he was going, again?"

"To relieve himself," Hendregan volunteers.

"In that case," says Gad, "shouldn't he be back by now?"

Chapter Twenty
The Sidetrack

Calliard stumbles, insensate, through narrow corridors of bone and yellow and red wax. His head lolls. His feet impel him on as if pulled forward by a puppeteer. Rounding a corner, he bumps into a mantis-demon. He stands drunkenly oblivious as it spits digestive fluid onto his chest and arms. The mantis-demon opens its mandibles for feeding, then stops itself short. Barbed antennae dart around, belatedly reading the occult resonance that surrounds its would-be victim. An instinct for survival trembles the demon's stick-thick limbs. This one, it realizes, is protected. Frantically, it wipes its acidic slime from Calliard's tunic. It scampers away as blisters rise on Calliard's neck.

Unfazed, the bard continues on his muddled way through squamous tubes, over a bridge of tar, through a forest of rushlike hairs.

He comes to in a lightless place. He's lying down. The floor around him is scratchy and damp.

He perceives, but does not see, a malignant presence.

Red eyes make themselves visible. It is the big shadow demon again. Xaggalm.

"You are ready to speak to me now," it says.

Calliard can't tell if the words are spoken or drip directly into his mind.

"Where have you taken me?" he asks. His own voice is unfamiliar, pitched and cracking.

"You brought yourself here, Calliard."

"No."

"It's pointless to lie to me, Calliard. I smell your shame."

"You're running a bluff on me," says Calliard.

"I also smell what courses in your veins."

"Let me go."

"You took the demonblood, as was inevitable."

"It was only a moment of weakness."

"It is in your moments of weakness that you mortals show your true selves. This is who you are, Calliard."

"It was once, but I can stop."

"How difficult it is, to constantly deny yourself."

"Maybe so."

"Why would you come here, to the wellspring of blood, if not for this?"

"If you want to kill me, do it."

"You are too valuable for that, Calliard. We have need of you here in the realm of the living."

"I won't serve you."

The air chills. The demon chuckles. "You already do. There are others of my number who would only enslave you. They would not see the entirety of your potential."

"A standard demon line."

"Perhaps, but in this instance entirely accurate. Why have you spent your life learning to sense and fight us? Because you feared what was within your own heart, and sought to expunge it. Every day you spent girding yourself against us made you a stronger servitor of the Abyss."

"Half-baked philosophical nonsense," Calliard sputters.

"Whether you accept it now or later is of little consequence. I have more to offer you than words."

"Riches? Authority? Revenge? I spit on all of those."

"I had in mind a more concrete gift."

Abruptly, Calliard can see within the shadow. Darkness becomes radiant, its own form of illumination. Xaggalm towers over him, the edges of his form curling and twisting. With a dagger-sharp finger, the demon etches a wound in its own bristling forearm. An oil-thick discharge bleeds from it, so red and dark as to be without color.

A blazing euphoria courses through Calliard's body. It ripples under his skin. He feels his organs rearrange themselves in his chest cavity. His bones liquefy and re-harden in a current of electric joy.

It is the sensation that came the first time he tasted the blood, so many years ago, the one he thought he could never recapture. This time, the sensation is a hundred times stronger.

"You think you've tasted the true essence before, child? No, no, no. All you have experienced until now is diluted, adulterated slop. The blood of minor demons. Burnt and muddled in an alchemist's alembic. This is shadowblood, Calliard. As a student of demonology, you have surely heard of it."

"Shadowblood is a legend. A lie."

"Your senses tell another tale."

A fresh wave of shame rolls over him, momentarily blunting the ecstatic rush. "I searched for it and never found it. Every avenue a dead end."

"It was hard to keep you from it, Calliard."

"What are you saying?"

"I'll give you credit. You were dogged in your pursuit of it. But the time was not right. We needed you fresh for the final battle."

"You're lying."

Xaggalm leaves the accusation unanswered.

Calliard asks: "What final battle?"

"Don't be tedious. Open your mouth, and I will feed you."

"In exchange for what?"

"Do not spoil this moment with stupid questions."

"My soul. My allegiance."

"You must go through these gyrations before you convince yourself. Very well. Purge your last vestiges of shame, Calliard."

"I won't give you my soul."

"You want to go?" The demon waves a finger, coated in his blood, under Calliard's nose. "Go. I won't tell the others. They needn't learn about you or your friends or their doomed and cretinous plan. Not until it suits me."

"I don't believe you."

"Then don't. Tell your friends all about me. Tell them you've already betrayed them. Sacrificed them to your thirst. You promised them you wouldn't partake. Didn't you?"

"I . . ."

"You told them you were good."

Now it is Calliard who will not respond.

"This was decided the instant you agreed to come here. Eventually you will concede this. So go." Xaggalm shivers, and the trickle of blood falls upward, rushing back into his opened vein. The cut in his shadowy substance seals tight. The demon widens a toothy smile. "I am as patient as night, child. As patient as night."

Calliard stands at a junction between blood-slicked corridors. The oozing demonblood, heady with mesz as it is, no longer fascinates. Its redolence is nothing, now that he's had a whiff of shadowblood.

He can't remember how he got here or how to get back to the others. He plucks images from his journey to the shadow room as if recalling a dream. In his mind's eye he conjures a vision of the orb. He concentrates on it until it feels real to him. He seeks its presence in the tower. He senses it far below. Comparing its depth to his present position, he estimates the number of levels he must travel to reach his destination.

As he lumbers on, the lingering elation instilled by the shadowblood's proximity painfully ebbs. Calliard's skin prickles. His feet and fingers go numb. In the waxen maze he nearly faints, and must stop to gather his strength. Since coming to the tower, he has lost the knack for distinguishing night and day, or guessing the passing of the hours. His internal compasses have all attuned themselves to the unrealities of the Abyss. All he can tell himself is that time slips, like a key failing to turn in a lock.

He arrives at the hiding place, pale and dried-out. The heads of his comrades swivel as one toward him. His shame must be written on his face.

But all Gad says is: "Where were you?"

"I got lost."

"Lost?"

Calliard throws himself on the chamber floor. It has grown a lush carpet of violet moss. Together the strands feel like the surface of a cow's tongue.

Vitta reaches into a wooden cask, withdrawing white chunks of pickled herring. She passes them to the bard, along with a flask of brandy. Both cask and flask are gifts from the high priestess.

Calliard throws dignity aside to tear greedily into the vinegary morsels of fish. He chews rapidly, mechanically, his chest heaving between gulps. When he is finished, he lets a few abstemious drops fall from the spout of the cask into his open mouth. Vitta gives him more herring; he eats the second portion nearly as quickly as the first.

"Water?"

She hands him a wineskin. "I've boiled it, but be careful."

He ignores the halfling's warning. His larynx bobbles as he half-empties the skin. He wipes water from his lips.

Hendregan plays a game with the purple moss. It has decided he's different from the others. Its strands shrink from him. He crawls on all fours, watching the cilia plaster themselves to the floor as he nears them.

"Where's Tiberio?"

"The guardhouse," says Gad.

"They expect him down there," says Vitta.

Calliard nods his understanding. Tiberio has to keep up the ruse. "And Jerisa?"

"Still hunting for a second way out," says Gad.

"Still?"

"She went out last night, and several times today," says Vitta. "Without result."

Calliard blinks. "What do you mean?"

"By what?" asks Vitta.

"How can she have been out last night and also today?"

Gad ducks down to look into his eyes as a healer might. "Calliard, how long do you think you've been gone?"

"A couple of hours?"

"Calliard, you've been gone for a day."

A few hours pass before Jerisa returns. Tiberio arrives later still. They bunk down for a restless night, trading watches. When morning comes, Tiberio wakes Gad and readies himself to slip out.

"You're holding up, yes?" Gad asks.

"They won't be fooled much longer," Tiberio says.

"They don't need to be," says Gad.

An exhausted nod, and Tiberio is gone.

Gad leans back against a wall, fighting the urge to doze. Perhaps it takes him.

A too-familiar buzzing swells on the other side of their door. It yanks open.

The others stir, hands traveling to their weapons.

The fly-demon, Kaalkur, flanked by a pair of heavily armored sentries, stands in the entrance way.

"Milady requires you," it buzzes at Gad.

Gad follows it.

Jerisa reaches for the waterskin. "I'm going to find that exit," she announces.

Kaalkur takes Gad to the threshold of Isilda's chamber. To alert her to their presence, it increases the pitch of its buzzing wings. The door swings open.

"Come in," she says.

Gad steps inside.

Isilda's blond hair has been severely upswept. The gown she has chosen is layered, dense, surmounted by a shimmering cape. A welter of lace covers her neckline, ending in a ruffed collar rising nearly to her chin.

A new chair replaces the one she broke last time. Wrought in black iron and ornamented by swirling demonic sigils, it is a sturdy piece. It would take great effort to tip it over and immense force to smash. Gad considers the workmanship impressive, though the signs would restrict its sale to a narrow and untrustworthy clientele.

He goes to her. "You had me near madness, waiting for your summons."

She withdraws from him, gestures to the chair. "There are matters on my mind other than you."

Taking a seat, he finds a position of perfect poise. "It grieves me to hear that."

She narrows her eyes. "Somehow this morning I find your humor less pleasing than before."

He leans back. "Why would that be?"

Isilda's slim arms fold together. "The name Fraton . . . was it familiar to you?"

He lets himself seem agitated. "You've been with him, have you?"

"Address my question."

"I've trod a tangled path. Along the way I've heard many names."

She seats herself on a twin of the chair they broke, arranging it so that her table separates them. "Evasion is admission."

Gad returns his demeanor to its unruffled state. "You told him about us?"

She plucks up a silver fork from the table and stabs it distractedly into the tablecloth. "Don't be a fool."

A smile. "You told him about me."

"I merely mentioned your name."

"In what context?"

"I said that it was nagging at me."

"What was?"

"The name *Gad*."

"And he turned red and asked you where you'd heard it, exactly."

"No. He turned white."

"That I consider a compliment. How did you recover?"

"Recover?"

"When you gave yourself away like that."

"Who says I gave myself away?"

"He asked where you'd heard the name. And let me guess. You said *that's what I'm asking you*. Your face shining with gorgeous rage. Just as it is now."

Contradictory emotions chase each other across Isilda's face. "I did say that."

"And you do scare him—though he won't admit it, not even to himself—and so you backed him off. And he told you that Gad was the name of someone he despised."

"Detested."

"Yes, right. Despised gives me too much credit. And you pressed him for details."

"And he confirmed the tale you told of yourself. More or less. That you are a thief and a swindler and an enemy to common morality."

Gad tries another flashing smile. "And you said, he sounds like our kind of people."

She frowns. "No such words crossed my lips."

"And he told you why, even after turning to Yath, he hunted thieves and sinners. Like me."

"If you can guess our conversation so well, what was that explanation?"

Gad runs a hand over his close-cropped hair. "Truth told? That's the one part I can't work out. Eliminating the competition?"

She turns his grin back on him. This time, it reminds him more of a cat's than a snake's. "You're not entirely clever, then."

"No one is entirely clever."

"He said you and your confederates were more dangerous to our aims than all of the paladins and crusaders of Mendev."

"And you told him not to worry, that we are allies after all."

"I did not."

"His belief is insane, of course."

"Is it?"

"Even if I hadn't turned to Yath, what threat could I pose to the assembled hordes of demonkind?"

"Fraton said that the forces of law cannot defeat us. They are blinkered, naive. They think they can stop us by virtue and courage alone. It is those who live by guile and trickery, who have no respect for the law yet still oppose the forces of evil, who stand the greatest chance of halting our victory."

"So that's why he feared and hunted us."

"That was his claim."

"And then you changed the subject, and allayed his suspicions."

Her cheeks color. "Yes."

"Because when you wish to distract a man's thoughts, you cannot be denied."

"And you'll not distract me from my question."

"Which is?"

"Assure me, Gad, that your presence here is not one of guile and trickery."

Jerisa presses herself to the passageway wall, dagger in hand, ready to plunge it into the fly-demon's eye, should it buzz her way. She'll hope for a quick kill—this is unlikely but possible, given the enchantments on her ancestral blade—then launch in on its human bodyguards. If human they are, under all that armor.

She isn't here looking for an exit.

If the fly-demon does come her way, and she gets herself killed as a result, it will be her own idiotic fault.

If it doesn't, and Gad catches her, the mortification will be unbearable. Worse, in many ways, than being killed by a demonic fly-creature.

Death, even torture, would mean only physical pain.

She's been so right until now. Except for the foolish protective moment when the crusaders stabbed Gad, back at the border.

But that wasn't as humiliating as this.

She understands full well that Gad's dalliance with the priestess is a gambit. An essential part of the game.

She's succeeded in keeping her upset over this below the surface. Well, almost succeeded.

Okay, not succeeded at all, but at least kept it securely within the realm of verbal complaint . . . until now. And here she is.

It's all so stupid. She doesn't even know what she'll do if she gets there. What she can do that will possibly help. She's the moth, he's the flame.

This can't be helped. Her heart commands it. Her absurd, self-damaging traitor of a heart.

The buzzing grows fainter. The demon and its retainers are heading the other way after all.

Jerisa steps back and resumes her study of the fissure in the corridor wall. She's never infiltrated a living fortress before, but in her day-and-some of looking for Gad's fabled second exit, she's begun to reach certain conclusions. The creature needs air to breathe. Or something in the air. Later she might ask Calliard for the fine details, if by that point she still cares.

At any rate, this seems true: Yath draws this air not through one set of nostrils, as people do, but from thousands, scattered throughout the structure. They have one such orifice inside their barrack, wheezing in air almost unnoticeably. And here is another one. For air to reach its destination, whatever that might be, it must be drawn along a duct of some variety. Or so she reckons.

Time to put theory into practice, Jerisa decides.

She reaches up to the breathing apparatus, gently separating its feathery air-gills. She pries apart the rubbery lips. Walks herself up the wall. Places her feet in, and, against a wet slurp of resistance, slides herself in.

Chapter Twenty-One
The Discovery

Gad laughs. "You can't ask a man to prove he isn't a liar," he tells Isilda.

"I am doing exactly that."

"Whatever I say will seem like a deception."

"Nonetheless, I demand that you assure me."

"I can't."

"No?"

"I am a liar, Isilda. Absolutely I am. A cheat and a deceiver and a mountebank. In any situation, unequivocally, I pursue the main chance. Which is why I'm here, in your parlor. I live for luxury and pleasure. And power. That's why I burn to have you, because you are all of those. And why you burn for me—the pleasure part, at least. Put me to work for you, and I'll enhance your power and wealth. You are going to win, aren't you?"

"Of course we are."

"I'm not talking about *we*, I mean you and you alone. Yes, the demon hordes are going to win. Anybody can see that. Which is why I'm throwing in with them, as would any cheat, thief, and so on. But you're going to win against your rivals, here in the tower, and become Yath's ranking mortal servant."

"Which rivals would those be?"

"Fraton, for one. And Xaggalm."

"You know of Xaggalm?"

"I've been waiting for you to ask me this. To prove my usefulness. We've been keeping our ears open, my confederates and I."

She stands and comes to him. "What have you learned?"

"The shadow demon runs a sloppy ship. His guards come and go through the tower at will, raiding for food when they should be at their posts."

"We might leverage that against him, but it would be difficult. Demons abhor discipline."

"They hate failure more."

"Yes."

"To get back to Fraton. No doubt you've gleaned much to use against him. As the man he detests more than any other, I can catalog for you his flaws and vulnerabilities. Time and again I've used them to overcome him."

"And what is the secret to that?"

"No secret at all. It is the oldest trick, from which all other tricks spring. Find what your mark already wants to believe, and suggest that is true."

She moves behind him. Lightly, she touches his scalp. "There is more to it than that."

"There is brazenness. That is hard to teach."

Isilda purrs. "You may be of use, but do not worry yourself about him," she says. "Until I decree otherwise."

"Command received and understood."

She climbs onto his lap. "This is where we were before a previous interruption," she says.

Jerisa wriggles on hands and knees through the duct. Rings of muscle rib its pallid inner surface. They constrict around her, resisting her progress. Gobbets of phlegm form wherever she touches it. They flow together to form larger globs. The gobbets scrape at her flesh. They seek her eyes, her mouth, her ears. She kicks, using the increasing moisture lent by the phlegm coating to propel her farther in.

She reaches a branch in the duct. Her sense of space tells her which one will take her into what ought to be Isilda's inner chamber. If she has calculated it right, that is.

Jerisa picks up speed as the tube slopes down. Unable to resist her slide, she pops out head-first. She catches herself on the way out, grabbing onto the orifice's engorged outer rim. It contracts, gathering force to spit her out. If she lets it, she'll fly headfirst into the stony floor, breaking her neck. She squishes around, disrupting its hold. Mustering all her strength, she pulls her legs up under her. She makes herself into a ball. Then she lets go, allowing the duct to spit her out. She lands feet first. The goop coating her soles sends her sliding onto the mattress of Isilda's four-poster bed. She lands on its heap of silk sheets, clipping her elbow on a post as she goes. Biting down hard, she suppresses the urge to cry out.

She rolls over, stands up, and lets herself adjust to the dimmer light of the priestess's bedchamber.

Locked drawers on a row of chests cry out for investigation. Mucus dripping from her sopping body, she slides to them. The coating on her fingers dulls the sound as she jimmies the first of the locks.

She opens the drawer. Gems and jewels jam it to the brim.

A curtained archway beckons. Jerisa flattens herself beside it, ready to hear the worst.

"Wouldn't you like to go in there?" His wrists held fast, Gad has to gesture toward the bedroom with a turn of his head.

"Don't tell me what I'd like." The priestess bites his neck and ears. She kisses him on the lips. He returns it, meeting force with force.

Isilda stands, pulling him up next to her. She tears at his tunic, pulls it up over his head. She pauses to run sharp-nailed hands up and down the tautness of his back. He tries to get the tunic the rest of the way off. She laughs cruelly and yanks on it. It pulls on his throat, choking him. He ducks down, letting the tunic come off in her hands. Surprised by the sudden loss of tension, she falls back. She hits the table, sending an antique plate crashing onto the floor. A wild expression comes upon her. She bounds back to him, seizes his leggings by the waist, and pulls them down. She nips and scratches at his muscular legs. He groans, only partly in pain.

In the bedchamber, Jerisa draws her dagger.

Gad pulls at the knot in Isilda's hair. It falls as a spray of golden silk. She snaps her head back and forth, letting it flow crazily around her head. He yanks the cape from her back. Tears the lace from her throat. He turns her around and bites the back of her neck, as she has bitten his. He seizes her wrists.

"I didn't ask you to do that," she says.

"Yes, you did," he says.

"Well argued," she concedes.

He takes her wrists and places them on the back of the iron chair. As he bites at the flesh between her hard-edged shoulder blades, he slowly unlaces her corset.

"Tell me you worship me," she demands.

"I worship you," he repeats.

"Tell me your life meant nothing till you saw me."

"My life meant nothing till I saw you."

"I am your queen, and you are my worm."

"You are my queen, and I am your worm."

"Tell me what you love about me."

"Your power."

"*Yessss*," she breathes.

He tosses the corset aside and reaches into her skirts.

"Not here," Isilda commands.

"The bedroom now?" he asks.

"No, the wall."

She turns around and directs a punch at his gut. He pivots, deflecting the blow's full force. Even so, he wheezes, stunned. He shakes it off, his hand forming an involuntary fist.

"A worm does not punch a queen," she says.

"Well argued," he says. He picks her up and carries her to the archway. He pushes her against the wall beside it.

Jerisa stops breathing.

"Take me," Isilda orders.

Gad obeys.

He is relieved to discover that one of his fears is unwarranted. No demonic surprises await him between her legs.

He pushes into her with all of his anger.

His contempt.

His loathing.

Isilda gasps, exultant.

Jerisa's knuckles, wrapped around her dagger hilt, whiten and shake. One of the lengths of curtain has parted slightly from the others, caught between the bitch-priestess and the wall. Through the gap, Jerisa can see her throat.

She sees Gad, too—his shoulder, part of his chest—but looks away.

It is only the throat that matters, the snowy, terrible throat. In her mind, she choreographs the blow. She will sweep the curtain aside with her off-hand and, in the same motion, step through it, then stab out in a wide, circular arc. The dagger will punch through into the base of her neck, where the arteries branch. The priestess will pitch over, a hand clasped to her throat, fruitlessly trying to staunch the gouting flow. She'll have no time to call down the magic of her demonic masters. Instead she'll collapse and die at Gad's feet.

Jerisa imagines Gad, doused thickly by the dying woman's blood. On his face, shock, then disapproval. The image is too humiliating to bear. Jerisa banishes it from her consciousness, but too late. The old feelings flood in again. It is shameful enough that she is even here. She must withdraw, slink away, never let Gad discover that she was here. It is a sickness in her that drives her to these lengths. Deep in her heart, the fibers are somehow tangled, and have been since the day she first saw him. If only she could reach into her chest and tear out the diseased bit. Maybe then she could see him as a comrade, like he sees her.

The priestess wails her pleasure. The sound pierces Jerisa, dirty and cruel.

It triggers a thought. Perhaps that is what this is about. If she were to do this, to murder the priestess in the act of coupling with him—perhaps the rashness and extremity of the act would once and for all exorcise this madness in her. Bring it to the surface and release it, as a hot needle lances a boil.

She catches herself in mid-spring. Forces herself to back away. Heedlessly she rushes back until she smacks into a piece of furniture. It responds to her blow with a wooden thunk. Jerisa freezes, ready for the sound to attract the lovers' attention.

Instead the demon-worshiper screams her ecstasy.

Jerisa has bumped into a wardrobe. Jostled, its doors swing open. A frame of green light marks the join where its hidden back panel is loosened.

From the other room, the priestess lets fly a crescendo of animal yelps.

Desperate to escape her exclamations, Jerisa pulls away the panel and steps through into the hidden room beyond.

Calliard wanders through the tower. He weaves across the bridge of tar. A halfling-sized demon scuttles out onto it, sniffing out his confusion. The creature is a demonic parody of a cherub. Matted curls stick to its round, disproportionately lolling head. Scarlet eyes puff out below a ridged, overhanging brow. Dragonfly wings buzz from its pale, fleshy back. Fangs descend from its blackened gums. Needlelike claws bloodily break the surface of its ill-developed fingertips. It launches itself at Calliard, stubby legs pounding below it.

He pulls his sword from his scabbard, hacking at the hissing child-demon as it comes his way. It growls peevishly as the blade opens a red fissure on its back. Its claws rake through Calliard's robe. The bard feels the stinging pain of a superficial wound. The creature hugs his leg, biting through the robe. With the hilt of his sword, Calliard strikes the crown of its head. The pommel sinks deep into a soft part between shifting plates of skull. The Abyssal cherub rears back. Calliard kicks it from the bridge. It plummets out of sight and is swallowed by the black river below.

Mouths open on the walls of the surrounding flesh-cavern, chattering in what might be appreciation.

Calliard drops into a fight-ready stance in case the cherub has allies to avenge him. Aside from the chattering teeth, the cavern remains silent.

He inspects his wounds: mere grazes. He looks for signs of poison at their edges. The cherub-demon, he recalls, is documented in the seventh folio of Praligeus's *Abyssal Synoptic*. He dredges the reference from long-buried memory. The entry lists no toxic after-effects of their attacks.

The bard presses on, focusing on his destination. At the center of the tower, Yath itself blazes like a headache. At its base, there is the orb, the next strongest of the sources of Abyssal presence. Without the experience needed to perceive past them, the bright darkness of these two sources would obscure the locations of other places and entities. Gathering himself inward, he focuses through them, parts their veil, and peers beyond.

He feels where he must go.

A dim green light illuminates nearly a dozen immobile figures, each on a black marble pedestal. Each is a human or half-human male, naked, a dull face staring out in open-jawed rigor. The hideous blankness of their expressions notwithstanding, each is in his own way an appealing specimen. One is a burly mass of muscle, the next possessed of a callow, androgynous beauty. There are blonds, brunettes, redheads. One is definitely half-elven, another possibly so. The tallest of the set is a half-orc, his proud features favoring the human side of his lineage. Their bodies bear the signs of lives lived ruggedly: scars, burns, broken and reknitted bones. Puffs of dust gather in their folds and crannies.

At first glance, Jerisa takes them to be grotesquely rendered statues. On a closer look it's clear that they're neither chipped from stone nor carved from wood. These are corpses, skillfully preserved. Stuffed and mounted like the hunting trophies in Suma Castle's great hall.

Gilded letters affixed to each pedestal proclaim the names of the victims. The definite half-elf was called Urio. The possible was Alatar. There is a Cleaon, a Razi, and an Ignacy. Two of the men are named Gronal. Though separated by a generation, a resemblance can be seen in their weathered faces. Jerisa wonders if they were father and son.

She clicks a fingernail against the closest of the figures, a dark-complected man whose face when alive would have been wide and raffish. The tap reveals a hard coating, sealing in the preserved flesh. It is almost sticky to the touch, like a resin that has nearly but not entirely hardened.

Jerisa suppresses a shudder. She tours through the maze of figures. Those in the back ranks reveal a history of rough transport: chipped lacquer, missing fingers. The row nearest the entrance looks fresher.

She plunges deeper into the room to find a slab of wood outfitted with straps and buckles. A dark brown stain has seeped unevenly into its center. Scores along its surface show the use of various sharp implements to prepare the figures for display.

In a corner sits a clay tub closed shut by a cork stopper. Beside it, a battered pail holds a handful of brushes, from the broad to the fine. Jerisa pops the cork. Inside is a brown, gluey substance. It gives off a heady whiff of naphtha.

She pushes the cork back in and surveys the rest of the room, looking for another way out. She stops short before stumbling over an empty pedestal. Five gold letters announce the identity of its destined occupant: F R A T O N.

Next to it sits another unused pedestal. Its label has only three fresh and gleaming gold letters: G A D.

Chapter Twenty-Two
The Beating

Perception becomes excitation as Calliard rushes through a dead-end corridor covered in gummy skin. He lifts a trap door, enameled like a rotting tooth, and drops down in.

Utter darkness compasses him. Now it is brighter to him than light. He sees the demon form before him from the stuff of blackness. The glowing eyes are last to materialize.

"So soon?" Xaggalm asks.

"Let's get it done with," says Calliard.

"I was certain it would take you two more days to succumb."

"What response do you expect to that?"

Xaggalm wraps a shadow arm around him. "Self-justification. Excuses."

Calliard hardens his stance.

"Nothing to say at all?" says Xaggalm. "Ah, I see. You intend at least to deprive me of my pleasure. The resistant type to the end. I can extend this as long as I please."

"Until I degrade myself before you."

"That is the point of the transaction, Calliard. How long have you devoted yourself to the study of my kind?"

"Too long."

"And you expect to come here, and show defiance, and still win your reward?"

"Your observation is valid," says Calliard.

The demon general laughs. "How scholarly of you! You'll have to do better than that."

The bard takes a deep breath. "Tell me what is required."

"Surely you are conversant with the first steps, at least."

Calliard lowers himself slowly to his knees.

"Very good," says Xaggalm.

"What words must I say?"

"Words? Unnecessary, lute-picker. When you drink of this, the need for it becomes all the oath I need." The demon opens the vein in his wrist. "Open your mouth, baby bird." The shadowy ichor spatters onto Calliard's lips, teeth, and tongue.

Jerisa hastens down the corridor toward their commandeered barrack. She sees Calliard heading toward the door from the opposite direction.

They meet in front of it.

"What are you doing?" he asks her.

"No," she says, "what are you doing?"

He wrenches open the door and slips inside.

Gad arrives, pale and scratched, not long after.

Vitta watches Hendregan as, with flaming hands, he scorches away a field of stingers sprouting from the wall. They loft in the air as threads of cinder before breaking apart.

"Escape unscathed?" Vitta asks Gad.

Gad throws himself onto his bedroll. "Mostly."

Vitta adjusts her increasingly woebegone coiffure, pulling at her metal headpiece to twist it back into shape. "You didn't have to give it up to her, did you?"

"What kind of boy do you think I am?" Gad answers.

Jerisa, sitting in a corner, draws her knees to her chin. Tiberio stares ahead.

"Are you good, Tiberio?" Gad asks.

The half-orc shakes his head. "They're hinting at something. Something bad."

"What do you mean?"

"They mentioned it before and then let it drop. Now they've taken it up again."

"I'm in no state for riddles, Tibe."

"They're suspicious of me, and from the hints they're dropping they're going to test me."

"Test you how?"

"Let's end this, Gad."

Hendregan breathes rings of fire and watches them drift to the ceiling. They leave circular scorch marks. The room rumbles discontentedly.

"Cut that out," Vitta snaps.

"No flame, no light," Hendregan replies.

"What's that supposed to mean?"

"Air on your skin is simply slow fire. Rust is slower fire still. All is flame, and will be returned to flame."

"That clears it up," Vitta says. She turns to Gad. "Tiberio's right. What are we waiting for? There's nothing more to be gained or learned here. Why aren't we going?"

"We were waiting," says Gad, "for all the pieces to come together."

"Were waiting, past tense?"

"Past tense." He produces Isilda's pendant, with the mark of Yath appearing as a flaw in its central gem.

Vitta reaches for it. "Finally something we can sell," she says.

He pulls it away.

"So we're ready?" Vitta asks. "Finally? Before the demon-ridden sentinels force Tiberio to some awful atrocity, or this chamber comes to life and eats us?"

"Calliard," Gad asks. "Are you good?"

Calliard nods.

"He doesn't look good," says Jerisa.

Vitta bounds over to her. "That's enough out of you, you morose little—"

"Enough, Vitta," Gad warns.

Vitta looms over Jerisa. "We need reasons to go, not reasons for fear. We've got enough of those as it is."

A knife has wriggled its way into Jerisa's hand. "You think I want to prolong my stay here, halfling?"

Gad slips between them, steering Vitta away. "We all understand that's the tower talking, yes? It's in our heads. Like we expected. Our supply of the salve is wearing thin. If you were the tower, what would you want to do to us?"

"Pit us against each other," Vitta mutters.

"That's right. So we're not going to let it win, are we?"

"No," says Vitta.

"We're going to tear it down, yes?"

"Yes," says Jerisa.

"We're ready to burn it?" asks Hendregan.

"Metaphorically or otherwise, yes, Hendregan, we're ready to burn it."

The fire sorcerer claps giddy hands together.

"And," says Gad, "we're going to be steely. We're going to find reserves we didn't know we had. Yes?"

"Yes," says Tiberio.

"Because we're going to need them," says Vitta.

"And then the last obvious point I always make," says Gad.

"We're not greenhorns," says Vitta.

"Humor me," says Gad. "Call it a ritual."

"Go ahead and say it, then."

"I say it because someone always forgets."

"I said, say it."

Gad says it: "Getting the thing? That's not the rip."

Jerisa completes his thought, a lesson learned by rote: "The rip is getting out after you've got the thing."

Jerisa returns to the group after one last errand. She leads Gad, Tiberio, Hendregan and Vitta down below. They climb down through the well, edge through the tunnels, and reach the guard post. Tiberio goes ahead. He finds the demon-ridden men waiting for him.

"You'll turn that body into a glob of fat if you're not careful," Baatyr tells him.

"I don't understand," Tiberio says.

"Always off scouring food," Baatyr says. "It's as if you don't love us, Tiberio."

"Looking for food is not finding it. If only you would share . . ."

Baatyr scoffs and stalks over to a rickety chair. Tiberio looks around. Only Aprian is there with him.

"Where have the others gone?" Tiberio asks.

Aprian bares his teeth, in what is meant to be a grin. "They're finding you a present."

"Food?" Tiberio asks.

"You can treat it as such," says Baatyr. "Afterward, if you want."

Tiberio slumps against a wall. Baatyr and Aprian laugh at him.

The sound of an approaching group snaps them to attention. They seize their weapons and clank over, ready to confront the newcomers.

Gad, the others behind him, grunts at them. The most outlandish of the captured helmets obscures his face.

"What did you say?" Aprian demands.

"I said, let us pass, meat-rider," Gad replies.

Aprian places the point of his sword at Gad's throat. "You'll eat those words, cultist. None are permitted here, save by a general's permission."

Gad dangles the sapphire pendant in front of him. "And by this, the emblem of Isilda's favor, I prove to you my right to pass."

Aprian lowers the sword.

Gad moves confidently toward the round opening that will take them on toward the orb; the others follow. Before Gad reaches it, the absent guards step through the opposite door. They bring with them a weeping, starving figure, his head and shoulders covered by a burlap sack.

"Please don't," the prisoner says.

Hendregan closes his fist. Blue flame appears around it.

Gad whacks his shoulder. "Don't steal their fun," he says.

A tense instant flickers by. Hendregan douses the fire. He follows Gad through the opening. Jerisa and Vitta go with him, leaving Tiberio with the possessed guardsmen.

Baatyr produces a roll of soft leather bound by a gut string. Its contents clink together. Baatyr carries it to a crudely assembled wooden table. He unties the string, revealing an assortment of torture implements. Tiberio sees scalpels, pliers, nails, a hammer, and a series of hooks. Except for their well-honed blades, the devices are crusted with rust.

Aprian shoves the sobbing captive into Tiberio. "Your present has arrived."

Jerisa leads the remaining members of the party to the wall of demon heads. As before, Hendregan steps forward; the others hang back. "Once more, my brothers," he intones. He steps up to transfix them. When he has them wholly entranced, Jerisa takes Gad and Vitta past and into the labyrinth of shadow.

When they have reached their destination, and Gad stands for the first time in front of the chaos vault, Vitta says, "It's bad, isn't it?"

Gad puts his helmet back on so he doesn't have to see so much of it. "Worse than I imagined."

"You can't imagine this," says Vitta. "You have to see it."

"But shouldn't," says Jerisa, copying Gad's trick.

"So you figured out how to get through it," Gad says.

"Watch me," says Vitta.

"I'd sooner hear you describe it."

Vitta removes a jagged length of iron from her pack. It is the scrap she took from the trap she disarmed on the plain of cages—the urannag. Its end is scorched and partially melted. "It's a matter of rational principles after all. I feared that I'd finally found the perfect vault. The one I could never crack.

"Locks are mastered through logic. You learn how they think—or, to say it better, how their designers thought—and work to defeat them within the parameters of natural law. The nature of metals, their relative hardness, and how they are shaped in a forge. The mathematics of geometric shape, keys against tumbler. These are the factors that determine a lock-breaker's success. Rational, predictable, reliable factors.

"Chaos is the enemy of logic. It cannot be out-thought because there is no thought in it. A lock of pure chaos, one might theorize, would by its nature resist all effort to break it.

"Yet—and this is the key, the figurative key that allowed me to understand what my literal, physical key would be—a chaotic lock is itself a paradox, a contradiction in terms. An oxymoron."

"An irregular pattern," Gad says, sneaking a look, against his wiser judgment, at the sickening swirl of the chaos vault.

"Precisely," says Vitta. "You can either have a pattern, or an irregularity, but you can't have both. Not in the same object. And that's what a chaos vault is—an irregular pattern. Chaos doesn't contain things, lock them in, control them. That's the job of its eternal opposite, the law principle. Such is the arrangement of the spheres and planes, the core structure of existence. A law beyond law."

Jerisa fidgets, pointedly.

Vitta pays her no mind. "So in order to be a lock at all, a chaos lock must have within it a kernel of its cosmic adversary: order. So all I have to do to impose order on this is to locate the kernel, and seek leverage from there."

She hoists up the chunk of ruined cage. "Every lock or trap devised in the Abyss, or through demonic power, is then to a greater or lesser extent a contradiction of itself. The more sophisticated the device, the more of the law principle it omits. Which means . . ."

"A lesser chaos trap contains more law than a greater one," finishes Gad.

Vitta excitedly approaches the rushing vault. "Exactly. And is therefore, according to the rudiments of occult theory, contagious. This piece of the lesser trap will introduce more order into the chaos vault door. The reaction, once triggered, accelerates and multiplies. Corrupting corruption itself."

"Fighting paradox with paradox."

"Perhaps we should do this now and talk about it later," Jerisa says.

"Indeed," says Vitta. She times the interplay of moving elements in the translucent door, performs a last mental calculation, and with great force jams the piece of demon-cage into the demon-vault. Blinding green sparks ring the point of impact. Pale beryl flames run down the cage bar, flaring around Vitta's gloves. The chamber floor pitches; its walls shudder and groan. Gad and Jerisa brace themselves. Vitta fights the door as a vortex forms around the point of impact. The cage bar wrenches up; she nimbly tucks in her arms and legs, riding with it. An order leeches into the mad scramble of competing shapes centered on the bar. The door tries to absorb the bar, pulling Vitta toward it. She lets go, landing on her buttocks and skidding backward into Gad. A demonic face appears in the door. The impact point has become its mouth. As it tries to suck in the bar, the translucence of the door fades. The demon face melts away, replaced by simpler forms. The unearthly substance transforms, becoming mundane: iron chased with flanges of steel. Recognizable locks and wheels appear in its surface, along with rivets, joins, and lines of solder.

"So now you unlock it," Gad says.

"Don't have to," replies Vitta. "The contamination does all the work."

Wheels spin. Tumblers click. The bar, its end melted and smoking, clatters to the floor.

The vault, now a pair of doors segmented in the middle, swings wide, allowing access to the insectoid pedestal and the orb it contains.

"We could simply work detection magic on you," says Aprian, "and peer into your soul, Tiberio." The possessed warrior jabs a swollen finger into the half-orc's breastplate. The demons have not been taking care of the stolen bodies. They've been sparring with one another to pass the time, and now bear a series of bruises, scrapes, and infected wounds. "But where would be the joy in that?"

Baatyr takes a happy clout at the back of the prisoner's head. "Xaggalm cannot station us here, no matter how important our post, and expect us to succumb to boredom."

"Diversions must be had," says Ergraf. "Don't you agree?"

"Naturally," says Tiberio, striving to match their mocking casualness. "If you must pretend to suspect me, merely to justify laying hands on some cultist, I'll not blame you. Much."

Aprian barges closer to him, their armor pieces banging together. "Oh, this is no pretense, Tiberio. And this equanimity, in the face of such an accusation? You are no demon, Tiberio."

"It is not a demonic obligation to rage stupidly at every provocation. Should I lash out against all of you at once? Or bide my time, pick you off one by one, and exact a vengeance that is cold and certain?"

Tiberio's threat appears to give them a moment's pause.

Aprian recovers first. "No such action will be required. Prove yourself to us now. If you are one of us, the pleasure of the trial will outweigh the sting of any insult."

"Easily said," says Tiberio, "for you."

"Let us acquaint ourselves with the vessel for your trial," lisps Baatyr. He pulls the hood from the quaking cultist. "Who might you be, wretch?"

The prisoner is a gaunt human of Kellid stock. Jaundiced skin and sunken cheeks declare his malnourishment. The effect accentuates the bulbous shape of his skull so that it seems monstrously enlarged in relation to his teetering, bony frame. Grime sits deep in his wrinkled flesh. He smells of blood and urine and the tower's dank organic stench. A few remaining teeth dangle from pus-dotted gums. He tries to speak; terror reduces him to a series of plaintive gasps.

Baatyr smacks him in the face with the back of his mailed hand. Blood trickles tentatively from the prisoner's pitted cheek.

"Tell us who you are!" Baatyr demands.

Aprian scrutinizes Tiberio for any hint of sympathy. Tiberio contains his reaction.

The prisoner's stammering gradually yields intelligible speech. "I am Nenarok. I am Yath's good servant. Do not harm me."

Baatyr gut-punches him. The man doubles over and tries to fall to his knees, but the demon-ridden sentinel grabs him, arresting him in mid-fall.

Tiberio can't help but flinch.

"Good servant?" Baatyr laughs. "Yath has no good servants. But you'll serve him well by surrendering to whatever treatment we deem you worthy of. Understand?"

"I have done all that Yath asks," the prisoner gasps. "I do not deserve this . . ."

Baatyr slams the prisoner's head against the torture table. He allows him to lie on the floor, burbling. "Tell us how you lived, Nenarok."

"Mercy," Nenarok cries.

Baatyr kicks him. "Follow instructions," he says.

"I felt the call," the wretch gurgles. "I saw the tower in my dreams. Until then I was neither good nor evil, but the pull on me was so strong I could not resist. It promised me power, and—"

"Not that part," says Baatyr. "Who were you before?"

"You don't object to this?" Aprian asks Tiberio.

Tiberio tries to shrug. "He is only meat," he says.

"And spoiled meat at that," Aprian laughs.

"Who were you before?" Baatyr repeats.

"A cobbler."

"Where did you live?"

"A village outside Kenabres."

"Did you live alone?"

"No, with my wife and two children. The croup took my wife and daughter. Just before the visions started."

"What did they look like?"

"My wife was stout and solid. My daughter, lovely in her way."

"You were saddened when they died?"

Tears sneak across the man's face. "That was before I embraced Yath. Before I saw that all is chaos and destruction. Now the fate they suffered will be visited upon the entire—"

A kick in the face silences him. "And your son. What of him?"

"The tower told me to bring him here. He was too young to understand. On the trail, there was no food . . ."

"A most satisfying tale," says Aprian. "Don't you agree, Tiberio?"

"Yath permits the strong to prosper, and fuels itself on the wailing of the weak."

"You say it, but without conviction. Show us who you truly are, Tiberio the half-orc."

"What do you want me to do?"

"First, hoist him to the table."

The prisoner's body is limp as Tiberio picks him up. Midway through, Nenarok starts to thrash. He wildly kicks and claws at Tiberio.

"Punch him," Aprian commands.

Tiberio tries to still his flying limbs by hugging him close. He tips back against the torture slab. Nenarok flails free. Tiberio grabs his arm.

"Just hit him," Aprian says.

Tiberio places Nenarok in a hold.

Aprian's lip curls. "You can't do it, can you?"

Baatyr and Ergraf join the struggle, taking control of the prisoner's windmilling limbs. Tiberio steps away as they strap him onto the table.

Aprian places a rusty scalpel in Tiberio's hand. "Carve him up a little. Start with the ribcage, maybe."

Tiberio holds the scalpel.

"No," Nenarok begs.

Aprian whispers up into Tiberio's ear. "What sort of demon are you, Tiberio? That hesitates at a spot of cut-work?"

Tiberio turns the scalpel on him.

Harsh laughter curdles from demon-ridden throats.

"You were right all along, Baatyr," he says.

"He kept us entertained, though," says Baatyr. "All these days. Almost but never quite slipping up."

"Should have dragged it out longer," Ergraf says. "Back to boredom after this."

Aprian bellows cheerily. "Showing patience, are we, Ergraf? We'll have to keep Nenarok, and test you next!"

Ergraf twists the prisoner's neck, breaking it. "No," he says, "He was tedious."

Tiberio points the scalpel at Nenarok's killer. It wavers in the air.

"Now this is stranger still," Aprian says. "We knew you couldn't torture a helpless wretch. But you can't even strike at us, can you?"

"Back off," says Tiberio.

"Is it your concern for the meat we wear?" Aprian asks, to a chorus of guffaws. "Trust me, we'll ride these bodies till they fall dead."

"He's not going to give us a fight at all," Ergraf says.

"Won't stop us from giving him one," Aprian answers.

They advance on him. Tiberio drops the scalpel.

"Let's make this one last," says Aprian.

They strip Tiberio of his armor. They leave theirs on. The beating begins.

Hendregan holds the attention of the demon faces, drawing them deeper into his crazy reverie. Before them ripples an ecstatic vision: the world, burning. They jubilate as the fire spreads from the world called Golarion to a thousand realms unknown. Leaping tongues of fire course from these material realities to the cosmic spheres beyond. The Abyssal eats the celestial and is itself consumed. Distinctions between law and order, between good and evil, singe, ignite, and are turned to ash. The law beyond law blackens, twists, fragments, and is gone. Creation in its entirety is engulfed. The demon faces are demons no longer: they are a purer, higher manifestation. They are destruction, red yellow blue, and the gray smoke that lingers after.

A thudding sound enters Hendregan's consciousness. At first he casts it away. It comes back. Eats at the edges of his fiery vision. It intrudes first as an awareness of pain. The consequences of frail mortal action spill into the perfection of his apocalypse. He tries not to understand what it is. Tries to recapture the utterness of the flame.

He feels the demons' awareness peeling off from his own. Struggles to recapture it.

No good. He hears the smack of metal-shod fist on flesh. Groans of agony suffuse his madness. Empathy dispels it.

He identifies the groans as Tiberio's.

He pictures what the demons are doing to him.

Too late, he dismisses the image from his mind. But now the fires are gone.

The demons see his madness as alien to their own. Not that of a true brother.

They wake from the dream.

Open their eyes.

And scream.

Gad and Vitta reach the twisted pedestal. Behind them lie scattered the remains of disarmed traps: the gears and cogs of a spear trigger. Spore-throwing fungi, melted by alchemical powder. Gas jets stuffed with rags, stiffened by fast-hardening glue.

Gad reaches for the orb.

An unearthly wail assails their ears. It rises to ear-splitting and falls to merely painful, then repeats the cycle again, and again, and again.

"Hendregan's burned," Vitta says.

Gad snatches the orb from the pedestal. He runs for the chamber beyond. Vitta sprints for it, too, an instant behind him.

The vault walls close. In the instant before they touch, he sees Jerisa on the other side, running.

The vault doors smash together. Their closing frees them from Vitta's contagion effect. The process that brought them within the confines of ordinary time and space reverses itself. Its metal components melt and swirl. Translucence returns. Gad averts his gaze as unassimilable chaos crawls across its surface, scrambling the vault's geometry.

His legs crumple beneath him. He hits his head but scarcely notices as new senses flood his awareness. Unwanted perceptions crash over him in waves. He plummets endlessly through a well of unthought. Eternal evil and primal chaos ripple together through his consciousness, competing to destroy it.

He tells himself: I am Gad.

I still have my team.

Chapter Twenty-Three
The Crumble

Time dissolves.

The chaos opens, but is not disrupted or reduced. Through the translucent field steps Fraton, flanked by dull-faced knights. Bright tunics swathe their breastplates. They bear upended versions of the Everbright Crusaders' emblem, its heraldic devices caught and crushed in the buglike tentacles of Yath.

Still addled by his contact with the chaos vault, Gad tries to stand. A false crusader's sword-point appears at his throat.

Gad woozily regards his old enemy. "I believe this is where you say, *So we meet again, Gad.*"

Fraton steps briskly over, so he can loom above him. "Tiresome witticisms. How I have missed them."

"You're not glad to see me, then?"

The fallen paladin yanks Gad to his feet. Vitta is already standing, a sword also at her throat. Fraton snaps manacles on Gad first, and then on the halfling.

"You're wondering whether we got all of your people," Fraton says.

"As long as you're reading my mind, I'm also thinking of a number between one and ten."

Fraton slaps him.

Gad smiles.

Fraton frowns. "You believe it shows weakness to strike you."

"Right again. You don't even need me for this, do you?"

Fraton's tightly waxed mustache vibrates. A mirthless smile cracks his lips. "Oh, I need you, you self-satisfied bag of snot."

"I see you've been attending demon invective class," he says.

Fraton sniggers. Gad has never heard him laugh before.

"I've a revelation for you, Gad. It comes at the cost of some personal discomfort to myself, but will nonetheless be more than worth it. Long have I prayed for the day when that damnable smirk would be rubbed irrevocably from your face."

"Switching deities along the way, no less."

"Our meeting here demonstrates the frailty of fair Iomedae. Despite her virtue, despite her power, despite the depths of my devotion to her, you always slipped through my fingers. But now that I bow, through Yath's intercession, to the Lord of the Locust Host, here I am with you finally in chains."

"This isn't the first time I've had your manacles around my wrist."

"But it will be the last."

"Refresh my memory. Have I heard you say that before?"

Fraton comes close enough for Gad to smell his breath. Wine and nutmeg. "The theme for this discussion is weakness. My purported weakness in wishing to see you suffer. The goddess Iomedae's, for failing to deliver you to my grasp. Despite your litany of gross and flagrant sins."

Gad leans in to whisper to him. "Don't forget. You're on the side of the sinners now."

Fraton slaps him again. He breathes in, recovering his composure. "No, no. I haven't changed. I've seen the true light. Demons punish sin. Only they do it utterly and completely. When a sinner dies, he is tortured. Taken apart. Reduced to cosmic fuel. By demons. Take notes, master of japes, for this is your own imminent fate." He pauses.

"If you've forgotten what you were on about," volunteers Gad, "the subject was weakness."

Fraton makes a fist but refrains from its use. "Yes. Weakness. If invited, you could no doubt pontificate endlessly on what you perceive to be my manifold weaknesses."

"Yes, but that would be rude."

"A true weakness, however, is exposed when a quality a man considers to be his greatest strength is revealed to be a fraud."

"You've been rehearsing this, haven't you?" Gad glances at Vitta, seeing the fear in her stance.

"What would you say is your greatest strength, Gad?"

"How about we skip to the part where you answer your own question?"

"Some might say your wit. The falsely agreeable arrangement of your facial features. Your composure while trapped in a losing position. But these are all to varying degrees peripheral to your success. Wouldn't you agree?"

"I would."

"In the end, your exploits are indirect in nature. You act through others. Make them stronger than they are. Smarter. Greater as members of your team than they could ever be on their own." He strides over to Vitta. "Like this ridiculous creature." He pulls Vitta's hair, crumpling her copper headpiece. Her face convulses in silent pain.

"Stop that."

Fraton pulls harder, bending Vitta's neck back. "Your greatest strength, Gad, is the loyalty you instill in your cat's-paws." He releases Vitta. "And now I must show you that this strength is merely weakness disguised by cocksure arrogance. You find these absurd, these marginal, these broken creatures, and con them into thinking they are whole—provided they do your bidding. Execute your plans. But they've seen through you, Gad. Seen how you manipulate and exploit them. Their loyalty is betrayal." He reaches into his tunic pocket and withdraws a letter. "I suppose you consider the reading of personal correspondence to be another example of rudeness."

"Yes, etiquette is my primary concern here," Gad says.

Fraton flaps the letter at him. "I found this slipped under the door of my quarters here," he says. "I now quote in full, omitting salutations: *I have been betrayed, and so have you. It has come to my attention that you are the betrothed of the priestess Isilda. The man who owns my heart is known to you: his name is Gad. He and the priestess have been dallying behind your back. That means, of course, that he is here in the tower. In exchange for free passage from the tower, for myself and the others he has selfishly lured here, I'll help you capture him. If interested, meet me at the bridge of tar in six hours. Yours, Jerisa of Castle Suma."*

"She met with you?"

The mustache primly rises. "I was considering it, when the demon faces screamed. Now, unfettered by any promise to your jealous little assassin, I can freely consign your confederates to tortures incomprehensible."

"Let them die quickly," Gad says. "With honor."

The paladin's blue eyes twinkle with delight. "Wouldn't dream of it, you bilious rodent! No, no, no, you can be sure they'll expire exquisitely, and by inches."

He nods to the other antipaladins, who take them from the vault. Waiting for them, also manacled, are Jerisa, Hendregan and Tiberio. The first two are bruised and cut. Tiberio weaves on his feet, battered almost beyond recognition. Blood leaks from the sides of his mouth, spattering on his boots. The possessed guards form a protective knot around the prisoners. Scorch marks blot their armor and helmets. Clearly, they took the brunt of one or more of Hendregan's fire spells before overcoming him.

"Can I have a word with her?" Gad asks.

"Provided your words remain audible," Fraton answers, "I might find an exchange between the two of you surpassingly edifying." He nods to Gad's guard, who leads him up to Jerisa.

"You bitch," Gad says.

She flinches. "The letter?"

Fraton holds it up.

"Why?" Gad asks.

Jerisa battles back tears. "Because I love you."

"You're cracked in the head, Jerisa."

She leans forward, brushing his lips with her own. She pulls back. "And because you never loved me."

"You bet I didn't." Gad headbutts her.

She falls. The guards grab his manacled arms and yank him away. Blood gushes from her flattened nose.

Tiberio and Vitta regard Gad in appalled surprise.

"More than I'd hoped for," Fraton clucks.

He nods to his corrupted paladins, and then to the demon-ridden sentinels. They shove their prisoners onward, prodding them into the guard station. On the torture slab, fist-sized demons in larval form feed already on Nenarok's corpse. They sprout mandibles to scissor his cooling flesh, their maggot bodies bloating.

Gad and the others shuffle along in defeated silence. The sentinels lead them into a passageway they haven't ventured into before. Bowel-like strands dotted with black bug eggs dangle from its ceiling, dripping rank fluid. Fraton tics fastidiously as droplets land on his armor and eat at the fabric of his fine half-cape. The corridors double and triple back on one another, weaving the group through a confusing, subtly up-sloping path. Though he pretends at surety, Fraton must periodically consult the demon-ridden sentinels to choose the right route.

In time they arrive in an arched, womblike passageway, lined with wooden doors. Pores in the walls sweat blood and pus.

Isilda waits there with her retinue. Her fly-demon buzzes expectantly. Leashed attendants hunker together, grasping whips woven from the hairs and shells of monstrous beetles. The priestess stands haughtily straight.

"Deliver the captives," Fraton tells his men.

One of them pulls on Gad's shoulder.

"No, not him," corrects Fraton. "The others."

He walks with his men as they lead Vitta, Tiberio, Hendregan, and Jerisa to Isilda's group.

A bored Baatyr dumps the prisoners' captured gear in a corner.

"Fraton," Isilda says.

He performs a perfunctory bow. "Priestess."

Her nostrils flare, as if detecting a change in their relative positions.

Fraton waves Jerisa's letter at her. "We have matters to discuss."

Isilda reaches for it. Fraton snatches it back and puts it in his tunic pocket.

"Mysterious pronouncements ill become you, Fraton." She sneaks an anxious glance at Gad. "What has he told you?"

"There is nothing I need to ask him," Fraton says.

"I can open him up for you," she says.

"Of that I have no doubt," replies Fraton, "but further effort on your part will not be required."

He clicks his heels together, pivots on them, and returns to his entourage, and to Gad. They depart down an oozing side tunnel.

Jerisa leans close enough to whisper into Isilda's ear. "Perhaps it's time you put him permanently on his pedestal."

Isilda freezes. Her white features go paler still. Words of demonic power burn from her throat. She draws her delicate fingers into a claw. A crackling green light wreathes them. She brings her open hand crashing down on the back of Jerisa's skull. Jerisa totters and falls, Abyssal energy coursing through her lithe frame.

Tiberio lunges. With slashing whips, Isilda's eunuchs force him back.

Jerisa falls limp at Isilda's feet.

Fraton and his guardsmen prod Gad up a winding set of muscled stairs. The possessed guards have melted away, presumably to return to their post.

"Aren't you going to ask what she's going to do to them?" Fraton asks him.

"I had that conversation in my head already," says Gad. "It didn't go well."

Fraton beams. "And what did I tell you, when you asked me? In your head?"

"The usual. Wouldn't I like to know. Tortures unimaginable."

"Ah yes," says Fraton.

A pause descends. The cultists and their captive navigate a warren of narrow passages. In the distance, Gad sees the bridge of tar.

Fraton ends the silence. "Still, I would like to see you beg."

"Would you now."

"You asked that I grant your pawns merciful deaths. Would you sink to your knees for that?"

"You're no longer in a position to promise that. Isilda has them."

Perturbation gnaws Fraton's features. "She was toying with you."

"And I with her," says Gad.

"To no effect," Fraton says too quickly.

Gad smiles.

The ex-paladin shudders with rage.

"Some efforts are their own reward," adds Gad.

"She didn't let you . . ." Seeing his men surreptitiously observing him, Fraton cuts himself short.

"A gentleman never tells."

Tension falls from Fraton's shoulders.

"But we're neither of us gentlemen, are we?" Gad continues. "So why not?"

Fraton's gloved fists constrict.

"*Let me* is not the right way to put it," Gad helpfully clarifies. "*Insisted* would be an apter word. Insisted vigorously."

"Shut up."

Gad stops short. "Oh no, Fraton." A guard's sword-point jabs him forward. "I don't believe it. You don't . . . you *feel* for her, don't you?"

"I told you to shut up."

Gad shakes his head. "You poor bastard."

"I'll have you gagged."

"But what if I do decide to beg later? You won't want to miss that, will you?"

One of his ex-paladins chortles.

Fraton punches at Gad's throat. Gad turns, avoiding much of the blow, but still winds up with hands on knees, aching for breath.

"There," Fraton says, peevishly.

"I always think," Gad gasps, "that we're reaching an accord. And then comes the throat punch."

"Your mockery merely sharpens my appetite for what is to come," says Fraton.

"All these years, you'd think I'd learn to anticipate the throat punch." The guards push him on. He does his best to straighten himself.

"You'll be torn apart."

"You always did take too much pleasure in the throat punch," says Gad. "That's how you ended up here. Isn't it?"

Fraton seethes.

"I guessed it," Gad says, "and now I see I'm right."

Fraton grabs him. Spittle flies from his teeth and into Gad's face. "And who was it who first moved me to strike a helpless captive?"

Gad lets the words hang in the air before responding. "Don't tell me I was your first."

This time he's braced for the coming blow.

"The instant of your dissolution will seem to you like an eternity," Fraton says.

Isilda caresses Jerisa's ravaged face. "A great honor awaits you all," she says. "Beyond those doors lies a special cell, one for each of you, from which you can never escape. The tower feeds itself on the distress of its enemies. I tell you this because fear, the anticipation of certain doom, heightens its pleasure in the interchange. Already the tower's awareness reaches into your souls. Determining first if you might be turned to our cause. Though you are thieves, the garbage of mortal society, I somehow doubt that it will so anoint you. Instead it will use what it gleans from you to tailor for you a special pocket of the limitless demon realms. There, alone in your personal Abysses, you will destroy yourselves for Yath's nourishment."

"Sodevina," Vitta blurts. "Sodevina spoke of this."

The priestess turns her attention to the halfling. "Ah, Sodevina. The one who escaped. How does she fare?"

Vitta says nothing.

"Suicide, then?"

Vitta looks away.

Isilda claps her hands together. "Marvelous. Even after escape there is no escape." She turns to her fly-demon. "Throw open the doors," she says.

Fraton's men lead Gad into familiar corridors; he reckons that Isilda's chambers are not far off. He studies the traitor paladins. How Fraton got to this point is clear enough. Gad wonders how he coaxed them to demon worship. He tries to work out which one of them chortled when he needled Fraton. They're all wearing helmets, so it's hard to tell.

"You've done me one favor," he tells Fraton.

"And what is that?" Fraton picks up his cue reluctantly.

"When I get out of here and back to Mendev—"

"You're going nowhere."

"When I get back, I won't have Everbright Crusaders in my way anymore. Are these all that's left of them?"

The ex-paladins veer toward him to listen in.

"Mendev's greatest warriors lie slaughtered in the Worldwound," Fraton says. "Yath's army readies itself for the final assault."

"You could turn only these four, so you killed the rest."

"There is nothing in the matter that will avail you now."

Gad addresses the closest of the ex-crusaders. "So what was it for you there? You also liked the power too much?"

"They won't snap at your bait," Fraton says.

"And were you surprised when you got here," Gad persists, "and found yourself lackeys? Before, you were mighty paladins. Respected. Beloved. Now you're lower than fly-demons. Deferring to possessed men."

"A provocation as obvious as it is desperate," Fraton says.

"Don't worry," says Gad, still addressing Fraton's men. "He's planning to take over. You are planning to take over, yes?"

Fraton speaks loudly, as if to be heard by hidden ears. "By no means," he says.

"I mean, you can't displace Yath, that goes without saying. But you do mean to push aside Isilda, and whoever else, and become Yath's undisputed top man."

"Allow yourself some dignity in your last moments."

"I thought you wanted me begging. Listen, Fraton. When you assemble a team. When you bring it into danger. When you ask them to abandon all else on your behalf, in the end you must adequately reward them. Shouldn't they all be chaos generals, feared and feted? It will require a little treachery, but that's well within your bailiwick now, wouldn't you agree?"

Fraton permits himself a brief, sputtering laugh. "With you as my vizier?"

"You think I'd expect you to fall for that? Please."

"Then what do you stand to gain by this proposal?"

Gad's manacles clank as he shrugs. "It offends me on principle, to see poor leadership."

"Poor leadership?"

"You haven't thought ahead for your fellows at all, have you?"

Fraton halts the procession. "And what would you suggest, wiseacre?"

"Your chief advantage is also your primary danger: Isilda. You must decide whether to dispose of her now, or use her to improve your position, and then kill her. My impression of her—"

This time Fraton's blow is a roundhouse punch. Gad reels.

"That's what you think I'd fall for?"

Gad raises his cuffed hands to rub a forearm against his aching jaw. "As the old saying goes, better a terrible scheme than none at all."

Chapter Twenty-Four
The Abysses

Hendregan awakens on a forest floor. The ground is dry and hard. He pats it. Brown leaves and pine needles stick to his hand, along with pebbles and flecks of dirt. He rises, dizzy, to a sitting position. All around him thrust the trunks of straight, dead trees. A hot wind flows through them, blowing grit into his face.

He looks up. The sky is the dull white of faded vellum. Grabbing a nearby branch, he pulls himself to his feet. The branch snaps in his hand. Shavings of bark fly around him, snatched up by a warm gust. The break point in the branch is brown and dead.

Hendregan spins around. He stands in a forest of firewood. Whichever way he turns, it extends through his entire field of vision.

A dusty chuckle rattles his throat.

At the periphery of his consciousness, a vital fact cries for his attention. Some sort of wrongness he ought to consider. He brushes it off, like the dirt on his robe. Never has he found lined up before him such a tempting target. This is what he was made for.

He has so many fire spells at his disposal. Which one to use? The fireball would be most dramatic, yet perhaps a waste. It would be more delightful, more respectful to the spirit of ignition, to start with the smallest flicker of flame. To let that catch, then grow, roaring on its own power through the parched forest.

Then again . . .

To hell with that, he concludes, rubbing sulfur and the feces of an Iobarian cave bat together between his thumb and forefinger. The incantation rips eagerly from his throat. He chooses the point of central impact for his summoned ball of flame. It will land a hundred yards ahead upon a particularly dense collection of dehydrated trees, their trunks tightly interwoven. If he hits exactly the right spot, he'll transform the dead forest with an explosion of outward-rushing embers. From each small impact a new source of flame will be born. The forest will fall at once, like burning dominoes.

His fireball whooshes into existence. It lands precisely as planned, enveloping the twisted stand of trees. It crackles, consuming the air around it.

The trees, the brown weeds at their roots, the papery leaves that lie upon the forest floor, remain unharmed.

The fireball expends itself. A fizzle of diffident smoke spirals skywards.

Hendregan runs toward his center point. Branches snap at his heels. He trips over a toppled log. Arriving, he looks for scorches, for patches of soot.

Nothing.

He stops to think. The missing fact nags at him.

Was the fireball dispelled? It did not seem so: the flame raged, but failed to feed. Presumably some spoilsport protection spell retarded his own magic. Hendregan performs a simple detection. The entire forest registers as magical, and yet not. He catches a strong whiff of demonic presence.

He remembers: This is the Abyss. His Abyss.

Hendregan wills a blue flame to manifest around his hand. It appears with a puff. He places his blazing palm directly against the crumbling bark of the nearest tree. Nothing happens. He brings his hand near to his face. Waves of heat buffet him. With the flaming hand he plucks up a leaf. It retains its shape and form, refusing to ignite. The same happens when he touches a clump of weeds, a loop of thorny briar, the flattened shell of an old acorn.

The swelling sun beats down on him. He combs through the dead wood for new targets to burn. From an ash tree he rips a sheet of powdery bark. A militia of red ants scurries across the exposed wood. It swarms toward an outnumbered force of larger black ants. The two forces wage furious warfare on one another.

Aiming with his fingertip, Hendregan shoots a jet of flame at them. It shoves them to and fro, but none of them are burned.

He rushes pell-mell from the forest, running until he reaches one of its ragged edges. Bursting from the treeline, he startles a fly-demon. It reminds him of the tower, of the priestess Isilda, of all the demons he's supposed to immolate. He concentrates his scattered embers of a mind. First, this demon, the one in front of him, will fall as a pillar of ash. Then he'll burn his way out of here, and back to his companions. He drops a fireball on the demon. Conflagration surrounds it. Then it emerges, unharmed and unconcerned. Even its filmy wings remain unblemished.

Hendregan aims the simplest of arcane projectiles at it. Like all of his incantations, he has altered this standard of the discipline into an expression of cosmic fire. Comets of occult power arc through the air to strike the fly-creature in its compound eyes. They fuff ineffectually into sooty vapor.

The fly-demon's deformed body agitates as if in laughter, then lifts into the air on iridescent wings. It circuits through the cloudless sky, circling several times, then zips off into the distance.

Hendregan hears himself screaming: "No! I am fire!"

He runs, following the path of a cracked and waterless creek bed. Breath flees his lungs. He keeps on going. Rounding a bend, he comes upon a village. Two dozen huts cluster in close colloquy. Plank construction. Thatched roofs.

Inhuman strength fills him. Hendregan sprints toward the cottages. Peasants, clad in some indistinct style, issue from their doorways. He shouts at them, warning them to stand aside. Their houses must burn. The fate of the universe hangs on it. They dumbly make way for him. In sleepy confusion they seem to consent to what he is about to do. Selecting a cottage as the central point of the blast radius, he speaks the words of combustion.

In its doorway a mottled pup appears, panting. A yellow-haired peasant girl runs to grab it. Somehow the girl understands that Hendregan means to incinerate her house, and with it her dog. She dashes closer to the blast point. Hendregan can still abort the spell.

He chooses not to.

A coursing ball of flame envelops the cottage, the girl, the pup. It spreads out to obscure the surrounding houses.

The peasants watch curiously, as if they have never seen fire before. Or heard of it, for that matter.

The fireball dissipates. All stand unharmed: child, dog, cottages.

Hendregan plants his feet firmly on the sandy ground, ready for the villagers to attack. They shake their heads at him in bemusement. Not knowing what to make of him.

He is used to being regarded as a dangerous madman. It is, more often than not, a fair and fitting description. This reaction is new to him. Yes, these people also see him as a madman—but a harmless one!

Only when he bolts for the girl do the peasants treat him as a threat. He gets to her before they do. She squeals in panic as he clamps his hands around her head. He commands them to alight. The blue flame appears, without effect.

The men of the village seize him, pulling him away from the girl. He winds up in the dirt. The thudding pain of their kicks and punches scarcely distracts him from the greater terror:

The demons have consigned him to a world where nothing burns.

Vitta doesn't like the light in this place. It exists without apparent source. It's green, like the phosphorescence of the tower. It casts faint, unpredictable shadows, as if its point of origin is at once invisible and in constant, random motion.

It shines, if that is the word, on four walls, a ceiling, and a floor, all of iron. The sides fall flush into one another, with no rivets or weld points. She feels the floor: its surface is cold, leaving a prickling sensation that lingers after the hand is withdrawn. The chamber looks to be a cube, ten feet on each side. Surprisingly regular for a chunk of the Abyss.

This must be a trick.

Isilda said that each of them would be cast into a personal Abyss. In her case, it follows that this would be a prison she can't get out of.

Nature of trap: magical.

Type of magic: demonic.

Mode of attack: mental.

Worst outcome: madness, soul corruption, obliteration of distinct identity.

Best counter-measure: awareness, focus.

If the priestess spoke truthfully—a large assumption, but scarcely unwarranted—this is not an illusion. She is in a pocket of the Abyss, a physical place which nonetheless exhibits the mutability of an illusion. Though it may draw its apparent physical properties from her fears, it cannot be dismissed by disbelief. What happens here will be real, though chaotic and inconsistent. That said, willpower remains the key to emotional survival here. At its most illogical, a logic will nonetheless underlie all that unfolds. This place will try to drive her mad. She will remind herself who she is and where she is.

The prison will react to what she does, Vitta postulates. It exists to anticipate and counter her.

An egotist, she thinks, would take ironic pleasure in this. Having a layer of reality, no matter how small, reconfigured for the sole purpose of achieving one's destruction, would to a less practical mind seem a high compliment, if a perverse one. Many would find it preferable to be the center of a universe dedicated to their ruination than to be a footless pawn in the real world.

Vitta, however, does not fit this definition. She'll find her way back to a place that makes sense. To achieve this, she must be other than the person it anticipates. It will expect her to act in accordance with her standard impulses. To thwart it, then, she must do the opposite.

It expects her to attempt escape.

So she sits on her hands and waits.

Vitta has never dealt well with inaction. She becomes conscious of her various minor aches and pains. Of the contents of her bladder, though they ought to be relatively meager. Of the rumbling of her gut. Still, she waits.

After a time that feels to her eternal, but is probably no more than ninety seconds, the chamber rumbles. The walls shift. The floor and ceiling adjust. When they finish, she's in an eight-foot cube.

Of course, she thinks. The trap has anticipated her anticipation. It will, by way of gradual threat, try to force her to action.

Vitta will not be stirred.

The Abyss won't simply kill her. Crushing her bones is too easy. Hardly worth the expenditure of demonic power required to bring this prison into being. It wants to draw out the torment, to break her as it did Sodevina and her allies.

To allow her to commit suicide by inaction would be to let her win.

She calls its bluff. She sits still.

Her pack rests at her side. Her tools remain within it. It might be the real item. More likely, it is an Abyssal duplicate, accurate to the last chisel-head. Its existence here further supports her hypothesis: she's meant to attempt escape, only to see the possibility yanked away from her.

She toys with the cage. Vitta will try driving it crazy, and see how it likes that. She opens her pack, withdraws her kit, and removes a thin file.

She uses it to smooth her dirtied nails.

The walls move in again. Now it's a six-foot cube.

Vitta wonders how close they'll come before they relent. They'll make it uncomfortable for her. She makes a bet with herself: they'll squeeze her into a two-foot cube. She thinks about the least painful position to adopt when this occurs, but resists the temptation to practice it. The cube might see what she's doing and work some unpleasant countermove.

She puts away her file. She warbles an old halfling tune her mother taught her. The sound of her own singing voice has always annoyed her. With luck, it will annoy her jailers more. If jailers there are. She imagines a crew of demons behind the scenes, working gears and pulling cords. The vision is too fanciful, too comical to be correct. Nonetheless she draws amusement from it.

The cube tightens again. Four feet.

Two feet. As predicted.

Vitta pushes her back against the cube. From past experience in confined spaces she knows the neck and spine are the first to give. The longer she can keep her head up, the longer it will take before she succumbs to pain. She pushes her knees up as far as they'll go, pressing them against the opposite wall of the now tiny-cube. To avoid seizing up, she alternates between tensing and relaxing her muscles.

With a grinding scrape, the walls retreat. The cube increases in size beyond its original dimensions. Her well-honed feel for dimension tells her that it is now a fourteen-foot cube, give or take.

She is surprised that it gave up this quickly. Like the demons it spawns, the Abyss is evidently impatient. Vitta allows herself the slightest of smiles.

The walls slam shut, crushing her to paste.

The perspiring tunnel Fraton's party traverses forks in two. Blackness curls from the tunnel opposite. It reveals itself as the preceding tendrils of an unusually tall, red-eyed shadow demon. The shadows dissipate, flow toward Fraton, and reform. The demon blocks his path.

"Xaggalm," says Fraton.

"Fraton," says Xaggalm.

"Step aside," says Fraton. "I seek audience with Yath."

The demon speaks in an insinuating trill. "You may attend him after me."

"My business is most urgent, shadow."

"As is mine."

Gad sees a figure hesitating at the far tunnel's threshold.

"We are infiltrated," says Fraton. "I have brought Yath a prisoner, to show that they are thwarted."

"I have brought him a thrall," says Xaggalm, "to show the same." He turns to the lurking figure. "Come here, slave."

Calliard slinks into view.

Gad steps back, stricken and staring.

Calliard looks down, unable to return his gaze.

"What did you do, Calliard?" Gad stammers.

"Answer him," Xaggalm says.

"I'm sorry," says Calliard.

Xaggalm laughs. "What kind of explanation is that?"

Tiberio is back in the fight ring he left behind in Zharech. He faces Sodevina. Hordes of warriors bunch around the square of chain that separates the ring from the surrounding hall.

Sodevina smashes him in the face with a spiked fist. He spins into the chains.

She comes at him. He grabs her arm before it can punch him.

"You're dead," he says.

"Maybe so," she answers.

She kicks him in the groin. He falls to the mat. She picks him up by the top-knot and bashes him into a metal pole.

White spots distort his vision. He slides across the mat, away from her. He turns to face her, arms held up to block her blows.

"You were sentenced here?" he asks.

"For what?" she says.

She weaves around him. Dizzied, he tries to keep up.

"For killing yourself," he says.

"This is your Abyss, not mine." She drives a fist into his knee. He drops. She kicks him in the throat.

"Some Abyss," he growls. He grabs her leg and pulls her down. Skidding quickly over her sweat-slicked back, he places her in a hold. She bucks against his weight; he compensates, keeping her pinned. "This is no different than the ordinary world."

"In the ordinary world, you never put me down," grins Sodevina. She tries to scrabble out from under him.

He increases the pressure, halting her progress. "What's that supposed to mean?"

"You are stronger here," Sodevina gasps.

"Why should I fear that?"

She rolls underneath him. He catches her. The maneuver places them face-to-face, him on top of her. "Because the part of you that is strong here is the real you." She loosens an arm and uses it to elbow him in the tusk. "The one you tried to hide away." Sodevina grabs his ear and claws at it. A spray of blood spurts into the audience. They roar their approval. "The one that yearns to kill."

Her knee pounds into his crotch. Then she's on top of him, the spikes of her mailed fists ripping into his flesh.

His hands find her throat. "You're wrong," he groans.

"Am I?" she asks.

He tries to release her. His fingers disobey the command. Tiberio's thumbs press into her windpipe. "No," he says.

"Welcome back, Tiberio," she says. Her eyes roll back as he chokes the life from her. He shrieks in dismay as her body goes limp and slumps over. He dives onto her, shaking her, begging her to revive.

The crowd screams his name.

"No," he says.

He leaps up, backing away from Sodevina's corpse. "This isn't real. You aren't real. This place knew the real you. It made a copy to torment me with. You're not real. I didn't kill anyone."

Someone taps his shoulder. "You killed me."

Tiberio pivots.

He recognizes his new opponent. It's Emmel Speargate, the first man he ever slew. The one Tiberio tossed into a pit trap. He'd tried to take more than his fair share of the loot. From a mingy score, at that. Emmel was ready to murder him in turn, over this handful of corroded coins. By the law of the rip, Tiberio had every right to do it.

He remembers, as if it is happening again, the sight of his treacherous partner's impaled body leaking out its last blood. The cruel thrill that crept through him as he stood, coldly observing his slow death. Later, he'd turned the encounter into a funny story he told at the tavern. When recounting it, he'd mimicked the sound of his body hitting the spikes below.

Emmel has a sword.

"I'm sorry," says Tiberio.

"No, you're not," says Emmel.

"Go ahead and kill me," says Tiberio.

"If only," says Emmel.

Tiberio feels his fist fly out. It breaks Emmel's nose. The sword falls into his waiting palm. He tries to drop it, but his fingers curl around the hilt. The blade bounces up to slice through Emmel's neck. The head separates from the body and arcs into the crowd.

Tiberio tells himself it isn't real, that it takes more force than that to remove a man's head. He decapitated someone once. It wasn't that easy.

Then the victim of that attack is upon him, prodding at him with a halberd. Tiberio can't remember the name. It happened on the streets of Egede. There was a dispute. Both of them were drunk. He had it coming, but also didn't. Tiberio could have backed down that day. He chose not to. Back then, he relished any fight. In particular against outmatched opponents who were foolish enough to cross him. He liked being a man's last mistake.

This time, Tiberio decides, he'll let the fellow kill him. He throws his arms wide. The halberd comes jabbing at his chest.

Tiberio's sword arm takes command. It slices improbably through the halberd's oaken haft. It razors across the man's neck. He topples, and another takes his place.

Tiberio gazes into the crowd. There are others there he hastened to their graves, but not so many as to fill a room.

Once he's done murdering the people he's slain once already, the Abyss will throw up still more for him.

A boy, no more than twelve, clambers under the chains. He swings a spiked mace. Matted dark hair falls over his eyes. Hunger marks his skinny frame. "Remember me?" he asks.

Tiberio shakes his head. His sword arm jitters impatiently.

"You killed me and my father," the boy says.

"No," says Tiberio. "Maybe your father, but not you."

"Not by your hands, but I died all the same," he says. "Without him, I starved."

"No," Tiberio sobs, sword rising.

Xaggalm's shadow form flickers angrily at its indistinct edges. "You overstep your bounds, Fraton," the shadow demon says.

Fraton goes straight as a spear-haft. "The same could be said of you, invidiak."

"Breathtaking impudence from one made only of flesh." Xaggalm sends tendrils of shadow to twist around the fallen paladin's face.

Fraton retains his poise. "Shall we take up the matter of precedence with Yath himself?"

"I would be pleased to do so."

"Typical demonic arrogance. Yath will rank us by our accomplishments, not by who is man and who is will-o'-wisp."

"You dare compare your deeds to mine?"

"I led the mortal army to its doom, clearing the way for our certain victory. As we speak, the forces I have organized marshal themselves to, in rapid succession, smash the fortresses of the Mendev line. What have you done, Xaggalm? I do not speak of ancient history, of the past's failed campaigns, but of the here and now."

"I'll devour your soul."

"If you thought it safe, you'd have done it already, shadow-stuff. But to return to my prior thought, what boasts can you make to Yath? That you tried again against Suma Castle, and were repelled? By, if word is to be believed, a fireball-tossing mage and a band of minor criminals."

Xaggalm's dark substance flickers erratically. "You weave the rope I'll use to hang you."

"Incidentally, the very same crew of knaves who thwarted you have been captured. By me. Who have you got? The weakest of the lot. The one ruined by demonblood. Some prize."

Xaggalm wraps his claws around Fraton's throat. The fallen paladins draw their swords.

Jerisa pulls the fur blanket tighter over her head. A chill pervades her bedchamber. Gradually she stirs to life. The frayed edges of an oddly vivid dream rise through her mind. They lose their solidity and are gone. She gets up, makes use of the chamberpot, and dresses herself. Something about the faded dream tugs at her. Frowning, she tries to call it back.

Yes, Gad. It has been so long since she dreamt of him, but last night, the spirits—or whatever they are— wove her a good one. He came back, along with a few of the others: Tiberio and Calliard. Along with them they had a mad fire wizard and an abrasive halfling. They fought demons here at the castle, then went into the Worldwound to fight some more. The dream grew tangled then, as would a real adventure with Gad. As dreams do, it got worse as it went on. She can't remember its conclusion, but dredges up the feeling that it was on the way to a very bad end.

She wonders whom she might tell about the dream. Her father reacts poorly to the mention of Gad's name. Come to think of it, so does the rest of her family. One of the maids, perhaps.

Hungry, Jerisa pads out the door and into the corridor. A damp draft tugs at her. She slips back into her room for the fur blanket and wraps it around her shoulders like a cape. She heads to the kitchen. Through arrow slits pours the white light of dawn.

Jerisa stops short. By this hour, the smell of bread should be wafting from the kitchen. There should at least be heat from its oven. The door to her brothers' room hangs open. She peeks inside. The beds have been made up. No one is there.

Finding the kitchen empty, she calls out for the servants, one name at a time. She gets no reply. She yells for her mother, her father.

It's wrong here, she realizes. She sprints down the main corridor to her parents' chamber. It too is empty. Neatly abandoned, like her brothers' room, as if its departed occupants knew they wouldn't be coming back.

Jerisa hastens to the servant's quarters a level below, but they too are tenantless. She stops at the armory to add a short sword to the dagger she always wears. She straps on a leather hauberk and heads out to the parade grounds. Deserted.

She searches the sky for demonic marauders. Nothing.

The only creature she finds in the barracks is a buzzing fly caught in a web near the doorway. The sight of it pulls at her thoughts. The buried memory refuses to surface.

Blankets lie across the cots, folded with precision. Boxes at the foot of each bed, which would normally house the soldiers' few personal effects, along with their battle gear, contain only a thin coating of dust.

The entire castle, household and garrison, has been evacuated.

How can this have happened without her knowing? Without them taking her with them?

They decided she was a liability. Unfit to be with them.

She goes to the stables for her horse but finds it also bare. So is the chicken coop. Clapping loudly, she calls out for the dogs who come around for scraps. Echoes are her only reply.

The fortress gates stand open. They dwarf her as she walks through them.

Jerisa heads down a dirt trail. When it splits in two, she takes the path that will lead her to the closest village.

It is uninhabited, as is the village after that, and the next, and then the closest town. Long before she reaches the silent, windswept streets of abandoned Nerosyan, Jerisa has concluded that she is alone in the world.

Chapter Twenty-Five
The Audience

Fraton flushes as Xaggalm's sharp fingers tighten around his throat.

"I hate it when demons and cultists fight," says Gad.

The interjection startles the shadow demon enough for Fraton to slip free of his grip.

Xaggalm's shadowy horns sharpen and bend toward Gad.

A furtive gleam lights Fraton's face. As if he is pleased to see someone else bear the brunt of his enemy's effrontery. As quickly as it came, it is replaced by a glower.

"How about I solve the precedence issue for you?" Gad proposes.

The demon jabs its claws into Gad's abdomen. A whirl of shadow energy courses at the point of impact.

Fraton pulls on Xaggalm's arm, ending the contact.

Drained, Gad falls. A traitor paladin catches him.

"We'll go in together," Xaggalm announces.

The moment of Vitta's death spans an agonizing gulf of elongated time. Time slows to heighten her perceptions as she is crushed between the iron walls. Each incremental moment of injury blasts through her nerve endings and into her brain. The crushing of her nose. The shattering of her brow. The explosion of skin as it is pushed from her skull. The smashing of her ribcage into splinters; the trajectory of each splinter as they explode through heart, lungs, liver, and gut. The pain reverberates even after there is nothing left of her to feel it.

Then she is back in the ten-foot iron cube. She gasps, feels her hands, looks at her legs, finds herself intact. Remembered suffering screams through her like a banshee. Vitta throws herself to the iron floor, hoping to lapse into unconsciousness and thus escape the pain. She can't. An appalling alertness grips her.

She throws herself up to a sitting position. Reexamines her assumptions.

Clearly, her personal Abyss can and will kill her. It will raise her from the dead and then, she is sure, kill her again. She must now presume that it will do this over and over until she escapes.

Until she escapes a prison that is undoubtedly rigged to prevent her from ever escaping.

She has two choices, then. One, wait and do nothing and suffer this repeatedly. Two, try to get out, despite the near certainty of failure. Doomed inaction or futile action.

Vitta leaps up. Pulls her toolkit from her pack. Removes a small hammer of shining alloy. She presses herself against one of the walls. Its burning touch reaches through her armor and clothing. She focuses past the hurt. It is nothing compared to her death by crushing. She taps the wall with the hammer, counting out the hits in three-inch intervals. Simultaneously, she counts the minutes, expecting the walls to move in on her every two minutes. This does not occur. The Abyss seems prepared to reward her activity. She has tapped her way along the entirety of one wall and is one-third across another when her ten-minute count elapses.

The walls slam shut. She dies again. This death, impossibly, hurts worse than the one before.

Fraton takes long strides to match the shadow demon's speed as it glides toward the center of the tower. Gad notes the quality of the ex-paladin's front. The physical effort must be considerable, but Fraton keeps his face impassive. No sweating, no puffing, no redness in the face.

As if concerned for their fragile truce, neither general speaks.

Fraton's men concern themselves less with keeping up than with securing their prisoners. Gad tests them by slowing his pace. They shove him onward.

Gad tries to catch Calliard's attention. The bard stares straight ahead, or at his shoes, or to the inflamed and feverish corridor walls—anywhere but at his friend.

"We'll find a way out of this," Gad whispers.

Xaggalm's head turns.

Calliard does not respond.

The sound of dripping liquid builds. They turn a corner. The corridor widens. Before them gapes an oozing mouth of an arch, twenty feet high at its apex. A curtain of energy warps and shimmers across its threshold, concealing whatever lies on its other side.

Viscous, semitranslucent egg sacs grow from the surrounding walls. One bulges out, detaches itself from the surface it clings to, and slops down to the floor. From the egg bursts a quartet of wriggling, transforming fetuses. Gad watches in riveted revulsion as they develop and grow. They become segmented, serpentine things who regard the scene with goggling insect eyes. Within a minute, they are as big as adult humans. They shake, hissing angrily, as layers of egg-slime drip from their newly formed bodies.

The generals step aside as three of the demons, snarling and clawing, rush away from the arch-mouth and around the corridor bend. One of them swipes at Gad as it passes; an ex-crusader guard feints fearfully at it with his sword.

The remaining newborn, confused, turns itself in circles before finally rushing into the curtain of energy. It disintegrates instantly. Not a drop of its green blood survives to spatter the walls.

The two generals take an uneasy pause to survey the rest of the eggs. Seemingly satisfied that the hatching is done for the moment, they bow in unison before the shimmering energy. Fraton signals for his men to bow as well. They poke Gad and Calliard with drawn blades. Gad grabs one of their forearms for balance and grudgingly sinks to his knees. The bard drops down unaided. The guards comply with Fraton's unspoken command and drop as well. They lay their swords on the floor, hands on hilts, ready to use them if Gad or Calliard try anything.

Fraton and Xaggalm prostrate themselves further. Fraton physically flattens himself against the floor. The shadows constituting Xaggalm's demonic form flow from a kneeling to a prone posture. They kiss the rippled, muscular ground.

"O Yath," intones Xaggalm, "it is I, your unquestioning servant Xaggalm, whom you have named general, who seeks direct communion with your ineffable presence."

Fraton repeats the same greeting, substituting his name for the demon's.

"I bring a gift, for your service," Xaggalm says.

"I bring a hated foe," says Fraton, "for your consumption."

The energy gate dissipates. Gad tries to peer beyond the archway. He sees but does not perceive. A blurring occludes his vision. Pain shoots from his scalp into his head, down his neck and into his shoulders. Nonexistent insects skitter across his skin.

Calliard weeps blood-red tears. "Yath," he mumbles. "His blazing awareness. Cutting through me. Harbinger of all ends. His everywhereness. His everywhereness."

Gad reaches for him. "Pull yourself together."

"In my blood in my blood . . ."

The nearest guard shakes his sword at them.

Xaggalm drifts to Calliard's side. "To your feet," he commands.

Calliard stiffly obeys. "Everywhereness, everywhereness . . ." he says.

"Yes, yes," says Xaggalm. "Feel Yath pervade you. You shall be his mortal herald. Eclipsing all others."

Fraton's mustache twinges. He strides to Gad and yanks on his collar, pulling him up.

"Hear that?" Gad says to him. "Sounds like Cal's your competition."

"You understand nothing," Fraton says.

He pulls Gad's arm, leading him to the mouth.

Calliard's feet move as if by their own volition, pulling him toward the archway like iron filings tugged toward a magnet. Xaggalm flows through and around him.

The fallen crusaders bring up the rear.

Seeing them approach the arch, Xaggalm forms his toothy maw into a grinlike shape.

Fraton halts. "What?"

Xaggalm's shadowform ripples smugly.

"What's so amusing?" Fraton demands. He looks to his men. Realization dawns. "We did not seek permission for the entry of my retinue," he says.

Xaggalm makes a trilling noise.

"You meant for them to cross the threshold and be torn apart," Fraton accuses.

"Would it not have been amusing?" Xaggalm asks.

"It would not," says Fraton.

"Matters of precedence, mortal. I can't have you appear before him with an honor guard, while I stand before him unaccompanied."

With visible effort, Fraton suppresses the retort he clearly has in mind.

"You may bow a second time before him," suggests Xaggalm, "and revise your supplication. It would show faith in our master's patience."

"Pranks are beneath you at a time like this," Fraton sniffs. "You four wait here. Should more hatchlings emerge, you are free to defend yourselves."

The ex-paladins unhappily nod.

Fraton steps through the archway, pulling Gad with him.

Vitta has been crushed to death a dozen times now. No longer is there a distinction between the pain she endures during her extended death and the memory of that pain when she is reassembled in the cell. The last time, she was unable to move through it. She merely lay there as the time elapsed and the walls flattened her again. Now she has the hammer in her trembling hands and has found a hollow bit along the caustic wall. With numbed fingers she locates the thin edges of a plate. She circles woozily to her pack, selects the finest-edged of her chisels, and goes to work prying it up. Beneath the plate, she tells herself, there must be a lock. She pries off the plate. The time for the next death is nearly upon her. If she gets the plate off, will it still be off after she dies again? She hopes so. Logically, it will not be so. The place exists to torment her, does it not?

She rips the plate from the wall. Inset into the wall behind it is a sturdy-looking lock. Vitta reaches in to explore its outline with her fingers.

A blade slices through the join between the inset and the wall, severing her hand. She watches as the hand drops into a nest of gears. They whir together, grinding it into flecks of gore.

Clutching her stump, she slides to the floor.

So this is the next stage. Her Abyss has grown bored. It wishes to add variety to the equation. At least the part where the walls crush her is over with. Now it will dismantle her by inches. She will have to endure this, as she has endured the other. Grinning insanely through her pain, she crawls to her pack in search of bandages.

The walls slam shut, crushing her.

Gad registers a few coherent impressions of Yath's hall before the madness descends. They stand in a cavernous chamber. It extends up for hundreds of yards, and down for as many more. It offers no floor to stand on, aside from a lip of bone arrayed around the chamber's edges. It is so narrow that a single wrong step will send an occupant hurtling into the pit below. The chamber's dimensions shouldn't fit within the tower, yet here it is. He guesses that, in some way that would not make full sense to him even if Calliard carefully explained it, the cavern intrudes into the Abyss.

There are other details—cartilaginous breathing tubes, knifelike hairs, sideways pools of liquid—but they flash by at the periphery of Gad's awareness as he learns what everywhereness means.

The demon Yath pulses bends warps coruscates white shimmering milky purulent purling blinking insubstantial suppurating

formless yet formed

exploding and imploding

everywhere yet nowhere

It is like the chaos vault, but alive, malignant, perverse, and oh-so-much larger. A roiling contradiction of natural law. Its existence jolts and pummels Gad. Negation permeates him, drives him unbidden to the precarious walkway.

His overwhelmed senses cease to fully function. They fragment and detach.

He hears Fraton telling Yath who Gad is. Declaiming in a loud voice. In his most formal style, Fraton recounts their many run-ins, describes the threat Gad represents to the plans of demonkind. He is of disorder, yet not of evil, and so must be destroyed.

Gad shrinks against the wall, as far as he can get from the lip of the precipice. Someone is gibbering a string of high-pitched, meaningless vowels at him. No, wait—that's him gibbering. His bladder empties itself. There's a wetness on his cheeks. Without checking, he can tell his tears have, like Calliard's, turned to blood. He feels his mind disassemble, opening the floodgates of delirium.

He's Hendregan now. He's Calliard, with the shadowblood in him.

No, that's not correct.

He's Gad.

He is a man with one weapon. A weapon that can never be taken from him, even when he is searched, as the traitor paladins searched him.

His composure, his poise, his confidence—it is all he has and all he has ever had and all he will ever need.

The others. He brought them here. His plan got them thrown into the Abyss. This is his scheme. They are his team. They need him to get this right.

He straightens himself. Pushes away from the wall. Stands to face Yath.

Calliard throws him the bag. He catches it.

Fraton interrupts his speech.

Xaggalm flows toward him.

Gad pulls at a cord holding the bag together. It unfurls. Inside is the orb. He rolls it into his left hand.

"No!" Fraton yells.

Calliard draws his sword and stabs Xaggalm in the back of the head. The enchanted blade flashes as it digs deep into shadow-flesh.

"I stopped you!" Fraton cries. His stamping foot nearly slips from the lip of bone. He leaps back, pushing himself into the wall. "I stopped you from stealing that!"

"Correction:" says Gad, "You stopped us today. From stealing the fake orb we left behind yesterday. When we stole the real one."

With the pulling of the cord, the bag has fallen away into a single sheet of fabric. Occult sigils are woven throughout it in gilt thread. It is the fabric scroll woven for them on Maeru's loom.

Xaggalm wheels on Calliard, wrapping himself around the bard's leg, trying to pull him off the ledge. Calliard drives him back with a flurry of feints. The demon disperses and reforms.

"Fake orb?" Fraton mouths.

"From the monastery at Tala," Gad says, "You recall your history, yes? That they created many near-perfect orbs before making the one they thought would be a weapon against demonkind? But was in fact this orb here? Well, along the way, we stopped at Tala and liberated the closest of the prototypes. Which is now down in the vault, safely on its pedestal, serving as decoy. Now if you'll excuse me, I've a ritual to commence."

Yath comes at him, a white-black veil, a spiraling sharpness.

Gad pronounces the first syllable of the banishment.

Yath retreats, as a dark sea lashed by a hurricane. The impossibility of his physical form recedes. The Shimmering Putrescence turns into something bounded, describable. Yath becomes a funnel, pushed toward Fraton and Xaggalm. The spinning force creates a wake, pulling the shadow demon toward it, and away from Calliard.

Gad continues the ritual. As he reads the arcane words, the gilded threads vanish, replaced by a golden light.

Yath spins into ever tighter circles.

Fraton fumbles with his pack. "You wanted to be captured," he shrieks. "You needed to be captured, to gain admission to this place." He produces a crossbow. "And both of you had to be here, but why?" He seizes a bolt. "Because . . . because you were searched, but the bard was not." He places the bolt in the mechanism. "But he, contaminated with Xaggalm's blood, cannot perform the ritual, which is why you must also be present . . ." He pulls back the string, drawing tight the stirrup. "No, no, no. I am not a fool. I have not been fooled. You have not done this, Gad!" He places his finger on the triggering mechanism.

Calliard's thrown dagger pierces Fraton's hand. The shot arcs wide. The crossbow drops into the depths.

Yath thunders its fury.

Gad speaks the last of the syllables. The sewn letters of the final word disappear, sparking into the golden halo that has gathered around him. The halo attacks the orb. It pops, crumbling into a shower of glassy sand, and runs through Gad's fingers.

A black-white rent appears in the air.

Gad knows better than to look. On the other side lie the vastnesses of the Abyss.

The hole in space pulls at Yath. The diminishing entity snakes out shrinking tendrils. They encircle Xaggalm. They draw Fraton into the air. Yath speaks without words, cursing the stupidity of his generals. Tendrils rip through Xaggalm, lighting him from within, canceling his shadow with crimson Abyssal light. Calliard gasps with pain and relief.

The second tendril pulls Fraton into the hole in space. As Yath is drawn through it, Fraton hits its edge. The hole closes around him before he is fully through it. From the waist up, he disappears. His abdomen and legs tumble into the pit below.

The walls buckle. Calliard loses his footing, slipping from the walkway. Gad rushes to him as the floor wildly pitches. Calliard grabs the ledge with one hand. Gad braces himself and pulls him up.

"You good?" Gad asks.

"Been better," he says.

"Fine shot, though."

"Thank you."

They dive for the mouth-shaped arch. Calliard slams into its edge as the tower quakes.

There is no need for explanations. It is as they predicted. The tower is an impossibility in this world. Without Yath the entity to anchor it, its physical outgrowth will collapse and die.

Gad remembers what he told the others when he laid out the scheme: killing the tower is the easy part.

Getting out—now that will be hard.

They land in the midst of Fraton's ex-paladins. The crusaders skid across the tilting floor. One falls into an egg casing, popping it. A swarm of half-formed fetal demons disgorges from it. They descend on the fallen paladin. He bats at them with the flat of his blade. They screech under and over it. Rubbery arms tear the helmet from his head. They strip his face to the bone.

Gad leaps on one crusader from behind while plunging his dagger into another's throat. Calliard slides into a third, trapping him against a puckering wall, pinning his sword-arm.

Chapter Twenty-Six
The Hard Part

Hendregan wanders through a city of paper. It perfectly replicates a city from his youth—though the exact name of the place eludes him—with one exception. It is constructed entirely from parchment and papyrus. Words inscribe themselves on the paper cobblestones beneath his feet. When he first came here—how long ago was that, now?—he stopped to read them, but they were never interesting. Provision lists. Bureaucratic scribblings. Complaints from jilted lovers. Fragments of discarded poems. All trash.

Hendregan—a magician who was once able to burn things—tarries beneath a paper tower. The warm wind blows a cloud of confetti into his face. Paper people pass him. They tip their paper hats in jaunty greeting. Grin at him with paper teeth. Paper, paper, paper. They're mocking his impotence. Sometimes he wants to jump on them, to tear them to shreds with his hands. But that would violate a principle, albeit one he can scarcely bring to mind.

Famished, he shuffles to a paper stall and with pilfered paper coins buys a paper leg of mutton from a paper vendor. He puts the flavorless food in his mouth and wanders from the city into yet another forest of dead trees. How many of these brittle woods has he passed through now? He is long past counting.

Part of him knows that this is all a complicated trick. The other has concluded that it does not matter. The vexation is too great. It is better to forget who he used to be. That way he protects himself from madness. That is what this is all about, he tells himself. It's to drive him mad. But he was always mad. A paradox. Best not to dwell on it. If he really was a magician—and a nagging inkling says he was more than that—maybe he can learn a new magic, one that works here. Transform himself into a paper man. Then he might walk contentedly through parchment streets. Put that paper food to his lips and find the taste in it. He'll build a paper house, marry a paper wife, have paper children, settle into a paper happiness.

Dry trees encircle him. Desiccated leaves rise up to his ankles.

A jagged vent appears in the gray sky. A beam of faint yellow light drizzles down from the tear.

He remembers Gad. And then the mission, the others, the tower. Gad has done it. The scheme has worked. Every one of them a part in the scheme, each ready to play their part. They've wounded the tower. Killed it. Now comes Hendregan's task: to get out, and then to free the others, before they die inside it.

The spar of light strikes the leaves at his feet. For an instant, a red spot appears in the radial point of a curled, six-pronged leaf. A drift of diffuse smoke rises from it.

The hot wind snuffs the tiny red dot. Further tears appear in the sky.

Though real, the place is unreal, and so is Hendregan's place in it.

He knows who he is again. He is Hendregan. He is fire.

This place was made to destroy him.

It has wavered.

He was made to destroy it.

Flames sizzle from his palms and fingers. Orange, yellow, and blue, they wrap eagerly around him, delaying and extending the joy of their ecstatic release. He holds them to him until he can resist no longer. They fly from him. They strike the leaves. They explode. Pillars of flame roar up the trunks of the trees. Burning tendrils leap from branch to branch. The forest becomes a conflagration. The flames pick Hendregan up, hurl him into the air, throw him into the city of paper. He lands, sheathed in fire, in the dry flatness of the town square. The papyrus townsfolk flee from him, seeing their doom. The tiles of the square whoosh into an inferno. Flames caressing their shoulders, their necks, the backs of their heads, the paper people flee, taking the blaze with them like a contagion. Wherever they take shelter, whomever they embrace, they consign to ash.

"Take heart," Hendregan shouts, his words exhaling as a billowing flare. "You are only stuff of the Abyss!"

Igniting townsfolk wail their agony.

"You aren't real," Hendregan burns. Though secretly, he wishes they were.

A rainless storm rolls in, gathering up the flames and bearing them throughout the bounded kindling world. Hendregan feels through each flicker, each ember, as if they are extensions of his fundamental self. This is still unreal, still a trick, but now the trick is his. A foreshadowing—or is that fore-flaming?—of his final destiny.

As his advancing fire reaches the last untouched fringes of this paper world, Hendregan commands them to burn through the unreality to the greater truth beneath.

He makes an oval of flame in the wall of his prison, in the tower of Yath. He scorches Yath's vacated flesh, melts its imploding bone.

He steps through into swaying, bucking chaos.

"Wah-hah!" he exclaims, delighted.

A demonic guardian, all horns and insect parts, tries to carom past him. The mind-flame summoned in his doomed prison is still upon him. Its magnitude exceeds that of the common spells he would wield on any other day. He leaps at the demon, wreathed in a protective ball of fire. The demon disintegrates before the flames reach him, crisping it in rippling waves of heat.

"Wo-*hoh*!" Hendregan says.

Awareness filters though the haze of another death. Vitta groans to a sitting position. The iron chamber surrounds her once more. She'll have to do it all over again. Crawl to the spot on the wall. Remove the plate. Get at the lock, then try to find a way to disarm it. She suspects there isn't one. Not consistently, at any rate. The trap is chaos. It changes itself in reaction to her escape attempts. It's playing with her. The game is stacked. She can never win.

A change in circumstance has occurred, she senses. It takes her a moment to discern it: The chamber is hot. Hotter on one side than the others. The iron wall sweats. She stumbles over to it, burdened by the weight of her toolkit. The dripping substance condensing from the wall smells like the musk of some terrible beast. No matter what it may look like, she reminds herself, this place is alive. It is paradox, both mortal and demonic, both Abyss and Golarion, at the same time a structure and a creature. It hisses in muffled torment. The iron undergoes a metamorphosis. It loses its placeness, changing its state to flesh and blood. Pink veins spread across the metal surface. Rivets transform into infected buboes. Seams reveal themselves as lines of bone. The panel, so difficult to find and remove, shifts into a slab of jouncing meat. Smoke rises from its edges. It cooks, heated from the other side.

The wall mechanism shudders vengefully, as if preparing to shatter her prematurely.

Vitta wonders: if the link between the Abyss and world has been severed, if her prison has been pulled from a realm of the impossible to one of natural law, what happens if it kills her now?

Only one hypothesis compels: she dies for once and all, that's what.

She lunges for the meat-panel, rips it from the wall, finds a network of torpid veins and delicate, intertwined nerves. Vitta reaches in and grabs as much as she can in her compact halfling fist. She yanks it loose. A mixture of blood, bile and pulped viscera fountains over her. The lock, red with heat, has transformed into a moaning face of metal and bone. Reluctant to touch its sizzling surface with bare hands, she bashes it with her elbow. The face-lock crunches into pieces.

Flame jets through the opening. Vitta, ready for it, ducks.

"Hold up, Hendregan!" she calls.

Jittering laughter is her only reply. The fire sorcerer wades into the curtain of molten metal and searing flesh, unharmed, tearing it down, making a hole for her to step through.

"You found its weak point," he observes, with seeming lucidity, as she clears its sizzling edges. Then he says, "Woh, woh, woh."

"The same to you," Vitta replies. Her toolkit has vanished. It must have been Abyss-stuff, part of the trap. Her real gear will be outside, with that of the others, where the demon-ridden guardian let it drop. She runs to find it, and to take up her sword.

Vision blurred, eyelids clamped shut, Tiberio kills his way through a legion of foes. Gore slicking his limbs, he begs for their forbearance. He can't stop killing them. When he runs out of enemies to slaughter, they rise again, slit throats fusing shut, splintered bones loudly snapping back into place.

The fight ring grows hotter.

Tiberio's vengeful foes lose their impetus, confused by new arrivals into the chamber. They exist to torment only one soul. Their Abyss is meant to contain a solitary inmate. They look to one another, seeking guidance.

Hendregan blows into his hand. A ball of rippling heat forms there. He lofts it to the ceiling. There, the emanation splits apart. Like so many fireflies, its fragments seek out the false souls. The bloodied figures, caressed by the heat particles, disappear as puffs of steam. A gentle exhalation accompanies them as they fade away.

Tiberio backs himself into one of the fight ring's posts. The wooden platform wobbles beneath his feet. He hides his face.

Vitta bounds into the ring. Pieces of ceiling dislodge themselves and fall. They start their fall as pieces of stone and mortar. They land as chunks of decaying demon-meat.

"Time to go," Vitta says.

"Leave me here," Tiberio sobs.

"They weren't real."

"These weren't the real people I slew," Tiberio says, "but the real people, I slew them."

"Remember the plan. This place is coming down on our heads. We've got to get out before we're crushed."

"That's what I deserve."

"You've atoned already."

"Not enough."

She clambers onto the swaying chains to look him in the eye. She grabs onto his arms, steadying herself. "How are we supposed to feel about that? You know the rule. Everybody gets out."

"No."

"These people are on your conscience. You want you to be on ours?"

He stammers wordlessly.

"You going to get selfish on us now? Now, of all times?" She ducks, avoiding a steaming gobbet of plummeting flesh. "You want me to have to tell Gad?"

"Let's go," he says.

They run for the scorched hole to the corridor outside. Behind them, the portal to the Abyss winks out. A curtain of melting skin materializes to seal the hole between worlds.

Hendregan looses a column of flame at the last of the cell doors. Jerisa stumbles out. She falls into Tiberio's arms. He shakes himself from his own sorrows to hold her tight.

"Alone," she says.

"No, you're not," Vitta answers, thrusting Jerisa's gear into her hands: the pack, the crossbow, the belt of knives.

"We're all together," Tiberio manages.

A burning worm-demon drops from a hole in the ceiling to confront them, its masklike face hissing at them over a quartet of clacking mandibles.

The shock of its appearance triggers Jerisa's reflexes. A dagger, plucked from the still-dangling belt, is in her hand. Then it is buried deep in the demon's forehead. Tiberio rushes up to grab its mandibles. He uses them as handles to twist its neck. The demon's head nearly comes off in his arms. Green ichor spews.

"Demons I can kill," he announces.

The four of them hurtle through collapsing corridors and down bleeding stairs. They push their way through a tunnel as it tightens around them. They scuffle with cultists. They heave a spider demon into the pit of tar. Its eight flailing legs fold in on one another as the tar river is sucked away into the Abyss. They press on through a rain of acidic slime and into a maze of forking tunnels.

A white blur slips past a tunnel mouth as they pass by.

Jerisa stops. "The rest of you keep going," she says.

"Have you gone crazy?"

Jerisa bolts down the passageway toward the pale figure. "Business to finish," she calls, already inaudible to her comrades. Veins form a quivering V on her tightened forehead. She charges at Isilda, daggers out.

Gad and Calliard run a gauntlet of stinging tentacles. They reach out to grab at them even as they wither and melt. Ten yards after the last poison feeler swings uselessly in their wake, they slide into a knot of armored, helmeted cultists.

"The ones who did this—they're back there!" Gad exclaims, pointing behind them.

"Why are you fleeing them?" the biggest of the cultists demands.

"Reinforcements!" Gad cries, pushing past. Calliard follows.

The cultists run deeper into the dying tower.

Gad and Calliard press on. In a chamber lined with insect hairs, the two find themselves standing back to back, warily defending themselves from a trio of scorpion demons. Pincers and double sets of stingers rise from scaled, vaguely equine bodies. Wrinkled, half-formed faces slaver and groan between the pincers. Mushy, vestigial teeth gnash in pink and outraged mouths.

"Thieves!" they hiss, in eerie unison. With clacking pincers they emphasize their hate.

"You have robbed us! Robbed us of Yath's embrace!"

"I guess they know what we did," Calliard whispers.

As if in agreement with his statement, the scorpion creatures furiously bark and yelp. Venom oozes from the barbed tips of their bifurcated tails.

"At least the cultists don't," Gad replies.

A demon lunges at Calliard; he pushes it back with the tip of his sword. The point barely punctures the Abyss-spawn's carapace.

"Make a run for it," Calliard says.

Jerisa follows Isilda deeper into the tower. The structure lurches, throwing her against a collapsing wall. She falls through a stretch of deteriorating muscle, hitting her shoulder against a support strut of gleaming black bone.

Isilda's fly-creature herald, wings already crushed by some prior mishap in the collapsing tower, stumbles into view. Addled, it spins on his segmented heels.

Jerisa waits until its uncontrolled spinning leaves it facing Isilda and away from her. She plunges a dagger into its back. She twists, pushing deeper into the squishy mass beneath its external armor. When she withdraws the blade, ropy green gore arcs across the corridor. The demon drops to the floor, buzzing feebly.

The priestess reaches the threshold of her chambers. She fumbles her key into her lock. Jerisa looses a dagger at her head. Isilda drops, leaving a strand of white-gold hair pinned to her door under the vibrating blade. Green blood drips languidly from it.

Isilda utters an invocation to the demonic hosts. Ruby lips purse in frustration as it fails to take effect. Jerisa launches herself at her, a swinging blade in each hand. Isilda shrinks back. Jerisa presses into every inch her enemy gives her. Impact! A gash opens in the priestess's shoulder.

"Can't tell you much about demons," grunts Jerisa, "but I just heard you call on Yath. And my guess is, he's distracted right now." She smashes Isilda in the face. With a snap, the cult leader's porcelain nose breaks. The assassin clamps her hand across the priestess's mouth and jaw, pressing the broken nose flat.

Isilda kicks her in the leg, pushing her off. Jerisa looks down at the hole in her leggings. A white line on her thigh turns into a long red gash. Sodevina's description of Isilda flashes to mind:

Razors in the soles of her boots.

Isilda's boots are edged in metal, the soles honed to a sharp cutting edge. The priestess kicks at her head; Jerisa narrowly slips past the blow. She slashes at the retreating boot with her dagger. Isilda kicks it from her hand, leaving a red slash across her knuckles.

Jerisa drops low and punches her in the ribs. The priestess doubles over; the assassin grapples her. Isilda tries to get free. Jerisa hammers her with a repeat shot to the same spot, and another. Finally Isilda cuts her with her knifelike boot, forcing her back.

The two stand, panting and bleeding, as the tower comes apart around them.

"Why aren't you running?" Isilda gasps.

"Why aren't you?" retorts Jerisa.

"You're an idiot," the priestess says.

Jerisa plucks another blade from her assortment of sheaths. "He may not be mine, but he's certainly not for the likes of you."

Isilda's pitiless smile survives for only an instant, then Jerisa leaps at her. The priestess leaps away. Jerisa compensates. Her dagger-strike slices Isilda's ear, leaving behind a bloody notch.

"Enough of this, then," Isilda hisses. She adjusts her invocation, omitting her plea to the intercession of Yath. Instead she calls on the prevailing power of the Worldwound: "Deskari, Lord of the Locust Host, devour this carrion!"

A cycling buzz of crazed cicadas ricochets deafeningly from the buckling walls. Curls of Abyssal power wreathe Isilda's long-nailed fingers. She waits for Jerisa to stab her. Her enemy's blade punctures her forearm. She grabs Jerisa's weapon-hand. Demonic energy courses from her hand into Jerisa's. It flows through the assassin's forearm, up through her bicep, into her shoulder, up the side of her neck, and across the side of her face. Everywhere the demon force travels, Jerisa's flesh is scourged and contused. Her veins blacken; her pale skin becomes translucent. In shock, she rocks on her heels. The demon force surges through her muscles, devouring them. Her feet sail out from under her. She lands on her knees.

Isilda kicks her in the face.

"Make a run for it," Calliard repeats. Skittering scorpion-beasts hem them in.

"Not without you." Gad dodges an ill-placed tail-strike. The stinger lodges in the puckering muscle of the wall behind him. Gad lops off the demon's second stinger. It yowls out an imprecation.

"I'm not feeling self-sacrificial," says Calliard.

"Good," says Gad.

Calliard severs a front leg from his nearest opponent. It flops on the quaking floor. "But let's face facts."

"Facts aren't for facing, they're for getting around." Gad lets his scorpion catch his short sword in its pincers, then unexpectedly twists. With a snap, the claw wrenches and breaks. It dangles loosely from the demon's arm on a thread of chitin.

"I'm no good anymore," Calliard says. He grunts in pain as a pincer clamps itself onto his leg.

"Bullshit and you know it," Gad replies, stabbing his blade deep into his enemy's mouth parts. It scuttles back to gurgle and die. A third demon darts in to replace it.

"You're the one who won't see the truth. One, two . . . three!"

Calliard sidesteps his demon's lunge. Gad likewise leaps out of the way. In a tangle of arthropodal limbs, the bard's demon collides with Gad's. Struggling to reverse their entanglement, the scorpion-things worsen it, lashing each other with tails and claws.

"I can't be trusted," Calliard says, slashing down with his sword. A tail flies off. Calliard hops to avoid it as it bounces across the floor, leaking toxin. "With the shadowblood, it's worse than ever."

"You held out on Xaggalm."

"If you knew how close I came to ratting you . . ."

"But you didn't."

They take opportunistic blows at the tangled demon-scorpions. Calliard consults his demon sense to find their vitals. He drives an impaling blow into a gap between scaly plates.

"This is going to go bad. As soon as it wears off, I'll want more. And what I'll do to get it . . ."

Gad has an opening to run. He stays. "We'll burn that bridge when we come to it."

"This is one problem glibness doesn't fix."

"I reject your premise."

The scorpion beasts separate themselves. Rearing up, they come clacking at Gad and Calliard.

"Go, Gad."

"The rule, Calliard."

"It's too late for that."

As one, they plunge their swords into the demon's foolishly exposed underbellies.

"The rule," says Gad, pulling on his friend's arm. "Everyone gets out."

Jerisa feels her cheekbone gape as the priestess unlocks the door and slips into her chambers. The heir of Suma forces her ravaged muscles into action. She totters to her feet, uses her lack of balance to push herself forward, and drops into a shocked and graceless sprint. Pain rockets through her as she hits the door, preventing it from slamming shut.

The priestess retreats through the curtain separating her salon from her bedchamber. The floor shakes. A heavy candlestick slides down the polished surface of an upending side table. Jerisa catches it and hurls it at Isilda. It hits the priestess between the shoulder blades. She goes down, falling into the bedchamber. A cicatrix appears in the stoneflesh flooring. It opens into a bleeding fissure. Jerisa leaps over it as Isilda pulls herself to her feet, yanking on the dangling strands of curtain. The priestess lurches into the other room; Jerisa is on her, pulling her hair and punching her in the throat. Isilda elbows her in the chest. Jerisa falls away; Isilda keeps her at bay with a wide kick. The high cultist climbs, half-dazed, into her wardrobe, and through the open panel inside.

"You're here to retrieve your treasure, aren't you?" Jerisa's incredulous laugh spills a dark line of blood from the side of her mouth.

Rejecting the pain that wracks her, she lunges into the wardrobe. She plants a boot in the small of Isilda's back, kicking her the rest of the way through.

Tiberio, Vitta, and Hendregan tumble toward the tower's cavernous foyer. Its death throes toss them bodily from the passageway. They roll over the corpses of mangled cultists. A tick-demon the size of a plump housecat plops onto Hendregan's chest. Giggling, he hugs it tight until it bursts into flame.

The three land in a shallow pool of blood. Frantic cultists heave themselves toward the chamber's exit. Certain of their demon masters fly for the ruined gateway. Others prowl through the mass of panicking mortal worshipers, opportunistically slicing off heads or tearing open rib cages. The tower's juddering momentarily ceases. Sheets of skin fall from the chamber walls, revealing pumping veins and girders of glistening ebony bone. With a puff that is somehow audible beneath the screams of dying demon-worshipers, blue flame appears, wreathing the bone beams. The flames spread from the ground up.

"Are you doing that?" Vitta asks.

"No," says Hendregan.

"Good," says Vitta.

"Well, yes."

"What do you mean, *no well yes*?"

"I'm not doing it; I did it."

"Clarify, you barking—"

"When I set the fire that got me out of my cell, and you from yours—"

"—you set the tower aflame, and now it's spreading—"

"—in a nonlinear fashion, according to chaotic geometry—"

"—with half the team still inside!"

Hendregan nods tightly.

"Can you stop it?"

"Do I look like a water elemental?"

"You're not telling me that the entire tower is about to explode, are you?"

"I'm trying not to tell you that."

"But it is?"

Hendregan clenches his teeth in chagrined acknowledgment.

Isilda crawls on her stomach through her hall of preserved ex-lovers. Their resin-coated faces stare blankly ahead, indifferent to her plight. Jerisa, advancing, matches the inching speed of her crawl. She draws yet another knife.

"I came here to retrieve my jewels," Isilda rasps. "You came to murder me. Which of us is the greater fool?"

"Before I gut you," says Jerisa, "I have to thank you."

Contempt withers the priestess's words. "And you want to tell me why."

"For granting me perspective." With a convulsing shoulder, Jerisa indicates the stuffed men. "I thought I was one to hold uselessly onto a dead and petrified love."

Specks of red mar Isilda's mordant grin. "It's him, is it?"

Jerisa's face grows taut.

Isilda spits out a chuckle. "We are not the same, knife-wielder."

"I agree."

"I conquer my men," says Isilda. "Whereas you . . ."

Jerisa's hand whitens on her dagger hilt.

Isilda utters another invocation. Abyssal energies wail into being around her hand. She holds them, curling and crackling in the air, waiting for her enemy to come at her.

The skin walls sizzle. They fall from the bone girders as strips of charred, acrid-smelling meat. Hendregan's cerulean blaze roars up the tower's exposed, skeletal frame. Motes of flame spring from the skeleton. They land on the resin-covered lovers. Varnish crackles.

Jerisa dives through the hole that leads back to the wardrobe.

Isilda's slain lovers explode, blowing her to pieces.

Cultists squirm into the narrow corridor leading from the tower. Tumbling bodies spill into the chamber, vomited out from the shuddering passageways that lead into it. Like a dirty, noisome river they flood, a grunting, sweating flow of limbs and torsos, toward the single chokepoint. The weak and malnourished fall beneath the boots and sandals of their stronger colleagues. They punch and kick to force themselves closer to the bottleneck.

Tiberio and Vitta back away from the fatal scrum. The half-orc tugs on Hendregan's robes, dragging him from the ever-growing cultist horde.

"I should burn them out, yes?" offers Hendregan.

"No," says Tiberio.

"Not yet," says Vitta. Then she adds, "But we haven't much time."

Additional demons enter the chamber: shambling, crawling, flapping, skittering. There are frog-demons, cherub-demons, mantis-demons. All the demons of the tower appear, bearing the twisted features of scorpions, mantises, worms, and ants. There are the bony, tall demons dripping acid slime, the corpulent boar-faced beasts, the giants bristled in lizardlike horns. They fall on their mortal servants, biting, clawing, dismembering. Baffled, betrayed, the cultists bow down before their demon masters, only to be torn apart.

"Are they trying to get out?" Tiberio asks.

"No," says a voice behind them. It's Calliard.

Gad stands at his shoulder. Both are wet with ichor.

"The demons realize they're about to be called back to the Abyss," says Calliard.

"So they're having their fun before they go?"

A clamoring spasm shakes the tower. Chunks of meat and burning bone girder detach from the ceiling to drop on the struggling figures below. They crush mortal and demon alike.

"We have to find another way out of here," says Gad.

The base of the tower splits apart, opening holes in its wobbling sides. The five sprint for the nearest gap before fleeing cultists can fill it.

A group of armored men hie into view, disgorged by a set of upward-leading steps. The fleshy stairs melt as they charge up them. Their scorched and rotting tabards bear the mismatched blazons of various crusader orders.

"Aprian!" Tiberio exclaims, seeing the possessed soldiers from the guardpoint below. He counts them: Baatyr, Ergraf, and Pachko are there, too. He doesn't see Matesh.

· The corrupted knights carry crossbows, nocked and ready. They aim them at Tiberio and his gang. Tiberio ducks; the others follow suit.

Four crossbow bolts find their targets in the open maw of a bat-winged demon, caught in mid-swoop on its way for Tiberio. It crash-lands on the chamber floor, sliding into a corpse pile.

Aprian runs toward Tiberio. The five brace themselves for battle.

Aprian executes a quick bow before the half-orc, then springs back up, ready to defend him against any comers.

"Aprian?" Tiberio asks.

"We haven't met, my friend, and yet we have," says the knight. His pupils are clear and bright. The muscles of his face have lost their previous contortion.

"The banishment of Yath cast out the demons who possessed you," Calliard says.

The crusader nods. "Aye. And am I right in supposing the lot of you had much to do with that?"

"We'll take credit once we're out of here," says Gad.

The knights form a protective V around Gad and company. Crossbows slung over their backs, the crusaders unsheathe long greatswords. Aprian leads a charge toward the nearest rent in the tower base.

Their swinging swords cut down cultists and lop the appendages from approaching demons.

Tiberio shouts into Aprian's ear. "Where's Matesh?"

"Gone to Iomedae's hall!" the crusader hoarsely answers. "Acquitting himself courageously ere he fell!"

The escaping war party clambers through the rent to find themselves on a narrow ledge hugging the tower base. Boulders and clods of dirt jettison themselves from the edge in the rhythm of the tower's last seizures. Below them lies the moat of blood, steaming and churning, carpeted with the drowned. The drawbridge lies rattling across the moat, a hundred feet ahead. Aprian swaps his greatsword for his crossbow. His allies do the same.

Calliard's marrow freezes as a host of shadow demons emerges from the falling tower. They are ordinary specimens, none as large or malignantly numinous as Xaggalm. They swarm in formation at the impromptu war band. They slide into and out of one another, their forms interpenetrating as if they are all part of the same roiling storm front. Gad's company adds its own missile fire to the fusillade loosed by their newfound allies. Some shadow demons veer off. Others keep coming. They snatch Baatyr from the ledge and carry him into the sky. They rip Ergraf's arm off. In shock, he topples into the blood moat. Burdened by his armor, he sinks quickly beneath its awful surface. The escapees recoil in dismay as a round red missile bounces off the wall above them. It is Baatyr's severed head, returned to them as a projectile.

The assault's survivors make it to the drawbridge, where assorted demons await them. Aprian fires a crossbow bolt into the forehead of a shambling frog-demon. It lunges at him, dying before it reaches his feet. Aprian and Tiberio join together to roll the slain demon into the moat, clearing their path. The half-orc is first to reach the drawbridge. There stands the skeletal red demon who slew Vasilissa and her misguided crew of peasant demon-stalkers. Tiberio rushes it, hitting it sideways, enduring the burns its slimy coating causes. Grappling the rail-thin demon, Tiberio lifts it high in the air and breaks its back across his knee. The demon utters graveled obscenities as it expires. Its fellows scatter, diving into the bloodmoat or taking wing in search of easier prey.

With Aprian and Tiberio in the lead, the escapees bolt across the drawbridge. Pachko, his back to the others and his greatsword swinging, guards the rear. He is nearly across when a burning gobbet drops from the disintegrating tower, splintering the bridge into planks. The impact flings him into the air, back onto the ledge.

Aprian rushes to the other edge. Tiberio, arm slung around his breastplate, holds him back, stopping him from diving into the moat.

Frog-beasts shamble from both sides toward his trapped comrade.

"Swim for it, Pachko!" he shouts.

Pachko shakes his head; the moat will use his armor to pull him down, and there's no time to shed it. He throws his back against the increasingly gelatinous tower wall, swinging his enormous blade from side to side as the demons encroach.

"For Iomedae!" he yells.

Aprian stands rapt, watching his friend. "Iomedae!" he shouts.

"Better them than us," Vitta mutters.

Gad nods. He and Vitta turn and run. Calliard follows. Tiberio breaks away to run as well. Hendregan stands poised to conjure more fire. Nothing comes.

"Damn," he says. "Out of spells. No more flame. Damn." He shrugs and sprints to join the others, his wide, sandaled feet flying wide as he awkwardly dashes.

Numbed and light-headed, Jerisa wanders an unsteady corridor high in the dying tower. The black veins have faded, but the injuries from the demonic curse remain. She's losing blood from her cheek, her thigh, and gods know where else the priestess's razor-trimmed boots struck her. A meaty wall looms up before her. She either falls into it, or it falls into her. In her state, it's hard to tell.

In these last moments she feels a weird detachment from her circumstances. She ponders Gad, and wonders how he'll talk about her when she's gone. He'll speak of her little or not at all, she decides, after he puts her in her grave. Not that there will be anything to find that is specifically her, to lay in the Suma crypt.

But that's not the point.

The point is, she's breaking his rule. Spoiling his streak. The whole team is supposed to get out. And here she is, too deep in the tower to escape. All because her stupid homicidal temper got the better of her. Because she could not bear the thought that Isilda might still breathe after this. Or even that the priestess might be killed by accident, or any other's hand.

Stupid, stupid, stupid.

No, Gad will not speak of her. She will be the one who disobeyed. The one who doomed herself.

If he remembers her at all, it will be as an example to others. When laying out the scheme, during the talk before the job, Jerisa will become a veiled reference. Others have failed in the past, have gone off on their own, and look what happened. Maybe he'll say her name. More likely, a look of impassive annoyance will cross his features—one of the looks that still shivers her, damn the idiocy of it—and then Vitta or Calliard or one of the others will take the new recruits aside. And they'll tell the Story of Jerisa. The Story of the One Who Got Herself Killed Because She Was a Child, and Because Her Heart Was, In the End, Ungovernable.

Not as good as being a genuine lost love. Jerisa smiles, a fresh splash of blood falling from her curse-flayed lips. But it is something, maybe. Perhaps the new recruits, when they hear the story, will assume that Gad loved her. Even if he didn't. In a way, even if the wrong way, she'd be tied to him forever.

An ant-demon appears before her, its waggling antennae all but burnt off, its front legs twisted and warped. A dagger appears in her hand, then in its head. She stumbles past, the dagger back in her hand.

Inside the passageway wall, a burning bone snaps and bursts through charring tower-flesh, nearly impaling her. She dances back from it, insanely laughing. She's Hendregan now, she decides. Embracing madness, so as to shut out fear. Let it come, she tells the tower.

As if obeying her mental command, the floor drops away beneath her, breaking into a shower of noxious meat. She hears the level below it give way under the impact. The two falling floors land on a third, then a fourth. The reaction continues until all of the floors below her are gone, and the bottom half of the tower is nothing but an empty tube.

It occurs to her to wonder how she is still alive and able to observe this. She sees her right arm. It is outstretched above her, pulled to its full length. Her reflexes have accomplished what her conscious volition has shirked. Her fingers clamp tight around the hilt of her dagger. It digs firmly into the muscle of the tower's outer wall. Her grip, and the dagger, keep her suspended dozens of yards above the tower floor.

All right, Jerisa tells her body. If you're so determined to try, who am I to argue? She reaches her free arm around her back. Her fingers snake into her pack. Working only by feel, she hunts for the item she needs.

The pressure of her weight radiates from her shoulder socket through her injured body.

A jellied substance drips from the hilt into her face.

The wound created by her dagger widens. She drops a few more inches, then is brought up short as the blade meets resistance.

Her shoulder flashes white pain through her torso. It mingles sadistically with the wounds she's already endured. Her arm signals its imminent surrender.

She finds what she's rooting for. The grappling hook, the line of enchanted filament still attached to it. She threads the hook's terminal clip around her belt. It clicks into place. She tests it, ensuring that it is properly secured.

The walls around her whoosh into flame. The conflagration eats away at the tower's failing substance. Holes appear in the wall. They race for one another, joining up.

Jerisa places her feet on what remains of the rapidly immolating wall. She walks herself achingly up to the point of her knife. With her off-hand she sinks the hook into the burning wall. The flames lick her flesh. She lets go of the dagger. Drops on the line. Swings her body. Flies through one of the widening holes.

She is now on the outside of the tower, just as it collapses. It droops over. For an instant, it hangs over the rubbled landscape of the Worldwound, parallel to the ground. Jerisa, on her line, dangles down from it like a spider descending from its web. Hurt beyond the capacity to experience pain, she slides down the filament. It runs out twenty feet above the ground. It swings her on a crazy arc over slaughtered cultists and swarming demons. She drops into the blood moat.

Gad runs for her. He dodges through fleeing cultists, skids to avoid barrages of tower fragments as they pound to the earth. Debris pummels the ground, landing with wet, butcher-shop thumps. A burly, robed figure running from the scene stretches out a spiked club, aiming to catch Gad in the neck as he runs. Gad seizes a scrawny demon-worshiper by the shoulders and spins him into the blow. The big and small cultists tumble together in the dirt. The routing crowd thickens as Gad draws nearer to the moat. A bat-winged demon dives in with grasping talons, headed straight for Gad. He rolls between a pair of half-clad female congregants. The demon's claws rake their scalps and shoulders. It pulls them into the air as Gad darts past. The heavier of the two drops from its grip and is swiftly trampled. The bat-demon bears the other high into the mottled sky, until she and it are pinpricks, and then vanish.

Sooty clouds churn overhead. They darken and twist. Searing red flashes pulsate through them, casting weird light on the tumult of figures below.

The final pieces of tower debris fall, crashing into the stampede of cultists and demons. The impact sets off a wave, throwing men and monsters into the air. Bodies tumble up; gravity yanks them down. They land in a ripple of snapping thumps. Death-groans echo across the polluted plain.

The tower itself now lies flat, a deflated tube of burnt Abyssal matter. It resembles a snake's discarded skin.

A shock wave erupts from the tower's former base. It lifts Gad up; he lands on his back. Most of the trampling horde is likewise felled. Gad curls into a ball to avoid the kicks of the last few oncomers still on their feet. The mob loses its forward impetus as the fallen totter back up. Transfixed, they watch as a crevasse opens up beneath the tower. Beams of otherworldly red-black light stab from the widening fissure.

Gad pushes through them, keeps on going.

The crevasse pulls the tower remains—what is left of Yath's earthly manifestation—down into its unseen depths. Gad guesses what Calliard would say about this: it's a hole between planes, like the Worldwound itself. Drawing that which belongs to the Abyss back into the Abyss.

He reaches the lip of the moat. He scans its length. Three dozen yards from his position, he sees her. With her off-arm, Jerisa woozily clings to the edge of the moat. Her right dangles, spent, at her side.

Stabs of light reach out to catch hold of scrambling demons. They impale the sky, jab across the plain. Wherever they strike a demon, it is caught and inexorably pulled toward the crevasse. At speed they hurtle toward it, indignantly squalling. Gad hits the ground as a flying tick-demon tumbles his way.

He sees Jerisa's failing fingers slide from the moat's edge. Crouching and weaving to avoid the inundation of kicking, writhing demons, he slides to her side.

He grabs her wrist as the Abyssal vortex takes hold of the contents of the moat. It sucks away the demon blood, and with it, the bodies and debris that float within it.

The force subjects Jerisa's body to a powerful jerk. Her slicked arm nearly slides out of Gad's grip. He reaches down to wrap his arms around her. A second tug, mightier than the first, pulls at him too. Gad determines that it will not take him, and will not take her. Drawing on his depleting reserves of strength, he resists the pull. He drags her to safety. She lies like a damp rag on the gravelly ground. He presses himself flat to it as the last straggling demons zoom overhead and are sucked into the center of Abyssal light.

With an odd, anticlimactic expiration like the last breaths of air pushed from a bellows, the vortex winks from the face of the earth.

Save for stray, scattered chunks of already-decaying wall-meat, the tower is gone. The crevasse is gone. The moat yawns empty. The angry blisters that marred the sky have been replaced by the Worldwound's usual gloom. Gad looks for demons but sees none, not even as flocking dots on the far horizon. Only robed cultists remain, and of these, a quick estimation tells Gad that for each survivor there are four lifeless corpses.

He checks Jerisa: she's still breathing. He draws himself to a sitting position, then to his knees, then stands, his legs uncertain beneath him.

A helmeted cultist, his puce robes torn to ill-concealing shreds, sees Gad and makes his way toward him. The steaming figure is both obese and muscular. A huge gut jiggles over a tiny breechclout. Ashes and gore cover his unctuous skin. Hideous gashes mar his limbs. All of his body hair has been burned away. Gad braces himself for the man's arrival.

"You." The voice echoes from the helmet.

"Yes?" says Gad.

"You do not belong here."

"What tells you that?" Gad asks.

"I sense it."

"You are blessed with the second sight, then?"

"I was, poltroon. Until you stole Yath from us."

"You seem disoriented," Gad observes.

"He came to me in dreams. Lifted me from obscurity. Whispered of my greatness. Gave me the dark light of truth. Now my true sight is gone. But as it left me, I looked across this once-hallowed field and saw you. Saw that you have taken it all from us. Our glory. Our conquest. The blood we are due, owed by those who have mocked and disregarded us."

"You're not crying in there, are you?" Gad asks.

"Our dreams are slain. Now you shall be. With my bare hands, I shall murder you." The towering, all-but-naked cultist balls his hands into enormous fists. The bones of his fingers crack expectantly into place.

"Is that so?"

"Prepare to die."

"And here I thought I was going to get away with it," Gad shrugs.

The weeping cultist storms at him.

Gad kicks him in the nuts. The man gasps and thuds to the ground.

Gad picks up Jerisa's limp body and carries it to the others. He winces at the extent of her injuries. Calliard will have the party's healing potions on him, transferred from Tiberio's pack before the planned capture. Though not in the habit of bowing down before any particular god, he directs a mental prayer of gratitude for this fact to whoever will take it.

Jerisa flutters to bleary consciousness. "You came for me," she says.

"Everyone gets out," he says.

Chapter Twenty-Seven
The Toast

Gad interrogates Aprian carefully, charmingly, before inviting him to accompany the others on their journey out of the Worldwound. The knight provides a detailed accounting of his life, from his noble birth in an obscure Taldan holding, to his time as a young hostage in the household of his father's rival, to his acceptance of the call of Iomedae and investiture as a paladin. He speaks of his pilgrimage to Mendev, and his time in the Order of the Sunrise Sword. His possession he attributes to his rash seizure of an accursed ring which he falsely thought to have been cleansed of its demonic essence. The facts fit together. More to the point, Gad sizes him up and concludes that he is as he claims: a brave, straightforward man, perhaps too guileless, too hopeful, for his or anyone's good.

Gad tells him his own tale, false in nearly every particular. Aprian believes it.

At the knight's insistence, they detour on their way home. First, to the site of the battle, then to the encampment of the cultist army. The first location they find strewn with scavenged bones. Aprian pauses to pray, tearing himself away only when Gad and the others make to leave. The second is much the same: corpses burned to the bone and stacked in heaps.

The horror swells in Aprian's throat. "I don't understand . . . victors as well as vanquished, slaughtered."

"The great flame-whip demons," says Calliard. Since his departure from the tower, his demeanor has been drained, distant. "When they sensed the tower collapsing, they did what demons do. Knowing they no longer stood a chance of conquering Mendev immediately, they destroyed their own forces. Reveled in the slaughter, for slaughter's sake."

"What despicable foes we face," Aprian absently mutters. "Their threat is ended—for now, at any rate. Still, it is a sorrowful turn of events."

"How so?" Gad asks.

"These were innocents until those foul demon dreams led them astray."

"They had a choice."

"You don't mourn them, all the same?"

"I don't pretend to be a good man."

The paladin turns to him. "You pretend not to be."

Gad shrugs. "The Everbright Crusaders will be in need of a new commander," he says.

"As will my own order, the Sunrise Sword. Kenabres is saved, but will be short of defenders for some time. I'll make a proposal to you. I'll lead an amalgamation of the two orders, if you—all of you—agree to join."

They all laugh, except for Tiberio, who ruefully shakes his head.

"We're no paladins," says Gad.

"Perhaps we have too many paladins. Had we a few distrustful rogues among us, we'd not have fallen for

Fraton's ploy. We universally esteemed him as a man of peerless virtue."

"In part because he persecuted the likes of us," says Gad.

"I am more than ready to concede the point," answers the knight.

"Sentiment appreciated," says Gad. "But we'll go our own way all the same when we reach the border."

Aprian sees movement in the treeline. A band of ragged knights emerges, swords held ready. Behind them cower malnourished civilians. Their robes bear the mark of Yath. The group approaches hesitantly. They seem in no mood to fight.

"May I borrow Tiberio, to stand at my side as I parley with them?"

"That's up to him, crusader."

Without comment, Tiberio accompanies Aprian as he strides out to meet the wretched stragglers.

Gad catches Hendregan preparing a fireball. "Probably won't be necessary," he says.

After a discussion, Tiberio and Aprian return.

"I won't be going with you to Mendev after all," the paladin announces.

"No?"

"If these men survived, there are others, too. Several of the knights were as I was—demon-ridden, until the tower fell."

"And the cultists?"

"As you say, they had a choice, and took the wrong one. Now Iomedae has granted them the opportunity to repent. If they are capable of atonement, it is my duty to guide them."

"So you'll scour the place for survivors and penitents, and then bring them back home?"

"I too have atonement to make. For pride and blindness, if naught else."

"You'll understand if we don't stay for dinner," says Gad.

Aprian clasps his hand and then Tiberio's. "Farewell, my friend," he says.

"Goodbye," Tiberio answers.

"When the demons controlled our bodies," Aprian begins, "we were aware, but helpless. Trapped in our own minds as our forms became puppets for depravities unspeakable. The demons could not see it, blinded as they were by single-minded cruelty. But we could tell who you were, beneath your ruse. You felt our agonies, and we felt yours. I'll extend to you the same offer I made to your comrade here. Should you ever wish to join my crusader order, whatever that may be, I'll exalt you to the place of honor you deserve."

"Thank you, Aprian," Tiberio says, "but I'm with them."

They depart, hungry. They wait until they're several leagues from the encampment so as not to deplete the foraging there, before searching for food. With Tiberio's help, Vitta lays traps for birds. After several hours, she returns to their temporary camp with a bag full of well-fed crows.

"These are fatter than the ones we caught before. Let's try not to think why," she says, plucking glossy feathers.

"We weren't," says Jerisa, "until you mentioned it." It is nearly her first time speaking, and certainly her first attempt at banter, since her healing near the vanished tower.

Calliard, too, has been largely silent. His gaze is fixed on the middle distance. Despite the day's increasing heat, he shivers. With anxious hands he rubs the clammy goosebumps that dot the pale flesh of his forearms. Seeking distraction, he takes some of the crows from Vitta and joins in the plucking.

Gad watches the sky for airborne demons. His eyes track a few fluttering shapes that might be the spawn of the Abyss. They dart away and are gone. A day ago, he'd have seen dozens of them.

"Make no mistake," says Calliard. "We've staunched one leak from the demon realms, but the Worldwound itself remains. It won't be long until this place is as infested as ever."

"But they won't have so easy a time penetrating past the wardstones into Mendev," says Gad.

"That's right."

"Back to normal, then."

"Back to normal."

"I'll settle for that," says Gad. "Let no one say I'm a greedy man."

"Speaking of greed," says Vitta. She sets to work gutting the birds.

"Do I know what you're going to say?" asks Gad.

"I'm going to say it regardless," answers the halfling.

Gad sighs.

"It's a shame, that's all," Vitta continues, "that after all that trouble, us being thieves and so forth, and with all the planning we did, that we couldn't have arranged to put ourselves ahead. I'm speaking of the profit aspect, naturally."

"Naturally," says Gad.

Vitta passes the cleaned birds to Hendregan. He clutches them to his breast. They roast on contact, their skin crackling golden beneath his fingers. Forgotten hunger strikes the group as the aroma wafts around their camp.

"All I'm suggesting," Vitta says, "is that, should we attempt a gaffle of this magnitude again, we should expend more effort to wring some financial gain from it. Otherwise, almost by definition, it isn't a gaffle at all. It's a crusade. And as you told that paladin, crusading is not our business."

Gad lets his shoulders slump comically. "As I made clear . . . This was an investment. To make it safe to do business again."

"I prefer investments that make me richer," says Vitta.

"Calliard, look in your pack," says Jerisa.

With a quizzical look, the bard reaches for the pack. He thrusts his arm deep into it, rooting around, until his expression changes. He withdraws a ball of something that tinkles and clatters as it moves, wrapped in a fine silk scarf. Unrolling the scarf onto a clear, dry patch of forest floor, he scatters fistfuls of gems and jewels.

Jerisa stays nonchalantly in place. The others rise to lean appraisingly over the haul.

"Which of us wants to make a low, appreciative whistle?" Gad asks.

"It'll mean more, coming from Vitta," says Jerisa.

The lockbreaker bends down to run the jewels through her agile fingers. "This must be worth . . . must be . . ."

"A lot of money, even when divided six ways," says Jerisa. "Enough to live on for a couple of years. Or squander magnificently, as our various predilections dictate."

"You got it while out casing the tower," says Gad.

"From the priestess," says Jerisa.

"You stole this from Isilda?"

"Her taste for finery led me to think she'd have a little cache stored away."

"You were in her chambers?"

"You're not objecting, I hope."

"When were you in her chambers?" Gad asks.

"Let's not ruin the moment with details."

Gad stands over her. "That's what you were doing, when we'd banished Yath and you ran off from the others?"

"No, no, I got them earlier."

"Which brings up the question: what were you doing, when you ran off?"

"Learning a lesson," she says.

Their journey to the border of Mendev shows that Calliard is right. The Worldwound crawls with demons still. They hide from a frog-beast in a vale of flattened pines. Headless obscenities with mouths fore and aft harry them through the white canyons. In the depths of a fetid marsh, they fight and kill a shadow demon.

That night, Calliard sneaks back and is surprised to find the demon's dead, shifting form lingering on the earthly plane. He sticks his most highly magicked sword into the indistinct dark corpse. Shadowblood spurts out. He catches it in a bottle, and slinks back to the camp. When he arrives, the rashness of his act occurs to him. He was on watch, and left the others slumbering unawares, to go and do this.

A few minutes pass until he can bear it no longer. He drips a dribble of shadowblood onto his tongue. The substance burns through him. The dull, achy feeling subsides. Calm descends. He senses, not that he's seeking them or cares to know, where the nearest demons are. Luckily, they're at least a league away.

He suspected as much. It was hinted at in a fragmentary account he once read in the library of a Nerosyani chronicler of perversions. After ingesting true shadowblood, the body changes. The addict doesn't need his blood spiked with mesz before he consumes it. His altered organs produce their own mesz, unbidden. The unadulterated flow, straight from the vein of a shadow demon—or perhaps any other demon—does the trick.

From this moment onward, every time Calliard bloodies a demon, temptation will ride him.

Thirty-nine days after the fall of Yath, they reconvene at Krega.

Of the town's structures, the most completely rebuilt is the brothel. Raw new timbers cover its grand facade. A hunched servant, face scarred by a demon's slashing talon, teeters on a ladder to paint the beams red. Inside, in the mistress's inner salon, fresh boards cover the walls. Rolls of flocking, brought by Gad as a gift to the proprietor, lie neatly piled, waiting to be installed.

A feast has been set before them. Three fat river bass lie in pools of black sauce, dots of fat glistening on their surfaces. Crisp-skinned game hens heap upon one another on a porcelain serving plate. Medallions of honeyed ham ring a haunch of boiled mutton. Bowls of pickled white cabbage, garlic-covered beets, chive and tarragon dumplings, and peas with oil and pepper crowd the table. Wicker breadbaskets overflow with salty flat breads and round loaves dotted with crumbled walnuts. The house's whores, hired for an evening of untaxing duty, bustle in wedges of soft cheese and pots of stavisiberry sauce.

Gad pops the cork on a dark bottle of fine south Chelish brandy. Its sweet aroma rises into the air. Six pewter goblets stand before him, straight as sentries. He pours a splash into each. The whores pass them around.

"This is the room where Abotur died," says Gad, raising his goblet. The others raise theirs. "To Abotur." He pours the brandy on the floor. The others follow suit. Gad hands the bottle to a wide-hipped harlot. She refills each of the goblets, generously this time, ending with Gad.

He raises his goblet again. "To success," he says.

"To success," they chorus.

"Jerisa, what's the word from the border?"

"Father says that there have been a few testing feints against Suma's defenses, but nothing like before. Small sallies of flying demons, no more than a handful at a time."

"The wardstones are holding again?"

"A few get through, as before, but armies cannot pass."

"And it's the same to the north and south?"

"Father has been in communication with the other generals and commanders. They say the same is true at their positions."

"So then there are still enough demons getting through to cause disorder and lawlessness, which is good for business, but too few to wreak catastrophe, which is not."

"A fair assessment," says Calliard.

Gad hoists his brandy. "To success."

"To success," they answer.

"And to silence," Gad says.

"To silence?" Vitta asks.

"As we agreed at the border," he says.

"Oh yes," she nods. "Remind me again why we've sworn ourselves to secrecy. Why it's such a terrible secret that we saved this entire land? Having thought about it these last few weeks, I'm thinking there must be additional rewards to reap."

"From the glory of it?"

"Precisely."

"Another word for glory? *Attention*. We don't want that, do we?"

"I reckon not."

"Altruism is fine for crusaders and paladins. But for honest thieves . . . Do we want to ruin our reputations?"

"Point made," says Vitta. "Objection withdrawn."

"So noted," says Gad. He reaches for his pack, pulling from it five heavy leather purses, tied shut with a thick gilt cord. He tosses them beside the plates of each confederate. They clank satisfyingly against the wood when they land. Vitta, Calliard and Jerisa quickly snatch them up. Hendregan pokes his purse with his fork, as if unsure what it might contain. Tiberio, ignoring the money, rises to carve himself another chunk of mutton.

"As I reckoned," says Gad, "several of Isilda's pieces were antiques of great craftsmanship, worth more than the constituent value of their stones and metals. You'll find that, if anything, Jerisa underestimated their value."

"You've kept a leader's share, I trust," says Vitta.

"I've kept a sixth, neither more nor less."

"You're entitled to two shares," says Vitta. The others, except for an oblivious Hendregan, nod their agreement.

Gad colors slightly. "In my book, a real leader's share is the same as everyone else's." He sits down, spooning himself a hefty portion of dumplings. "However, if the rest of you aren't vigilant, I'll likely take more than a sixth of these." He passes the bowl to a grateful Tiberio. "Let's eat."

The wenches bring wine, a sugary local white, retrieved from cold basement depths. The talking gives way to eating. In a happy rhythm of chewing, slurping and lip-smacking, the thieves mount a formidable assault on the impregnable mountain of food.

"Now I've been thinking of the rip," says Vitta. "Reviewing it in my head . . ."

"Here it comes," groans Gad.

"I like to have matters straight in my mind, so as not to nag at me."

"I suppose you also tug at threads to see if your garments unravel."

"Answer a few questions and I can eat in peace." She gestures at him with her fork.

"What's the point?" Jerisa sighs. "We won, didn't we?"

"Yes, but there's the matter of not being included in the full details of the plan. Makes one feel like a dupe. A lackey."

"What are you on about?" Gad asks.

"Why didn't you tell us Calliard was going to go off and drink from the blood of Xaggalm? That might have been pleasant to know, instead of worrying constantly that he was on the verge of cracking."

"Your locksmith's mind hasn't tumbled that out?"

"Tell me, to confirm it," the halfling insists.

"I had to feel shame," Calliard says. "Xaggalm read not so much thoughts as feelings. The greater the shame, the smaller his suspicions. If the rest of you knew, if you did not spear me with your doubtful gazes, I'd have rested easier. And he would have sniffed out that ease, and never trusted me to take as a gift to Yath."

"Does that untrouble your mind?" Gad asks.

"On that point, yes."

Even Tiberio groans.

"Go on," prompts Gad.

"This I hate to ask," says Vitta. "But as I said, like a kit of tools, it is best after a rip to fit each moment in its proper compartment. For full understanding."

"Ask it."

"The letter from Jerisa. Spilling on your tryst with the priestess. That was also part of the plan, yes? Because I assume so. It makes sense. You needed Fraton blinded with anger and hatred, to drag you to meet Yath, not stopping to look for the gaffle in it . . ."

"But?"

"But when you butted her in the face, that seemed real even to me. I mean, yes, now that I say it out loud, I realize that of course it was all part of the rip. It was improvising, maybe. The detail of how you'd show your supposed betrayal. But Jerisa, the look on her face . . ."

Silence hangs in the air. Jerisa's cheeks lose their color.

Vitta blushes. "I'll stop now. Let's eat. Yes, obviously, you don't have to say it. I can see it. All part of the gaffle. Are there herring?"

Slowly they get back to eating, until the plates have emptied.

Gulping down the last of the dumplings, Gad says, "I don't have another rip lined up just yet, but there may be prospects . . ."

Tiberio shakes his head.

"Where will I look for you?" Gad asks.

"I may set up a shop in Nerosyan," says Vitta.

"You're going legitimate?" Jerisa asks.

Vitta makes the sign of the trickster goddess. "Calistria forfend!" she mutters. "I'll create a shop as a false front and establish a workshop for the study of exotic locks and mechanisms in the back. I'll find some well-connected, down-on-his-luck sort to run the place and act like he owns it."

"Thank heaven," Jerisa says. "For a moment there I thought you possessed."

"And you, Jerisa?" the halfling asks.

"Father wants me home, to ready myself for command."

"So that's where you'll be? Suma Castle?"

"Haven't decided yet," she says, studying Gad for hints of a reaction.

"Hendregan?" Gad prompts.

"Hrm," he says. "I am of three minds. One, return to my prison asylum at Bogilar fortress; I like the food there. Two, Jerisa's father has offered me a position as Suma's house wizard."

"Which is to say, sorcerer," Vitta interjects.

"He appreciates a man who can blast demons from the sky," Hendregan continues.

"That he does," says Jerisa.

"Third, there is a volcano in the savage lands of Belkzen that has long beckoned me. I may venture there to see what it has to say." He reaches for another round of ham. "Does anyone wish to come with?"

"I'd tell you you're mad," says Vitta, "but you already know that."

Hendregan smiles, raising his goblet to his lips.

"Calliard?" Gad asks.

"I'll be around, as usual. You'll find me."

"And you're good?"

"I'm good," he says. Gad doesn't mention the bulge of the demonblood vial in the man's pocket.

Calliard signals for the homeliest of the whores to refill his goblet. He downs its contents at once.

"You sure you're good?" Gad asks.

"Yes," says Calliard.

"And Tiberio, where will I look for you?"

The half-orc sets down his forkful of fish. "I'll be back in Dubrov, but don't look for me."

"No?"

Tiberio takes his time before speaking. "What you asked me to do, it was necessary. I see the reasons for it. We saved many lives, and that outweighs much. This purse will go far to help my village in the hard times ahead. Mendev has many fewer defenders than before. The demons will find another way to come at us. But what I do to help, I will not do by fighting. What we did reminded me how tired I am of blood and fear. I have done more than can be expected of any man. I'm out, Gad."

"I shouldn't even ask?"

"Come as a friend, when all is well. We'll have a meal together. Not as impressive as this one, but a good simple meal all the same."

"And if you're needed?"

"Find someone else. There's always someone else."

Gad reluctantly nods.

They pick silently at the remains of the feast.

"Should I belch flame to lighten the mood?" Hendregan asks.

"Maybe not," says Vitta.

When they can eat and drink no more, they stand and exchange embraces. Tiberio is first to leave, then

Hendregan. Vitta and Calliard go together, headed for the city.

Jerisa lingers.

"I'm sorry you found it difficult," Gad tells her.

"You knew I would."

"I needed you."

"For the rip."

"Yes, I needed you for the rip."

Jerisa sighs. "I gained insight, maybe."

"Maybe?"

"Employing the insight, that's another matter." She lets the statement hang in the air.

"So are we good, or not good?"

She steps out onto the brothel porch. She walks down the steps.

"And if I need you?" Gad asks.

"For another rip?"

"For another rip."

"What the hell, right?" Jerisa heads off, her black gear fading into the coming night.

From the indigo sky, Gad hears a flapping noise. A lone demon circles overhead, barely distinguishable against the twilight. Gad makes it for one of those bat-things.

It surveys the town, then, evidently deciding that it's too resistant a target, flies off.

Gad's eyes narrow. "To success," he says.

About the Author

Robin D. Laws is the author of six previous novels as well as various short stories, web serials, and comic books, plus a long list of roleplaying game products. His novels include *Pierced Heart*, *The Rough and the Smooth*, and the Angelika Fleischer series for the Black Library. Robin created the classic RPG *Feng Shui* and such recent titles as *Mutant City Blues*, *Skulduggery*, and the newly redesigned *HeroQuest 2*. His previous fiction for the Pathfinder campaign setting includes "Plague of Light" in the Serpent's Skull Adventure Path and "The Ironroot Deception," available free online at **paizo.com/pathfindertales** as part of Paizo's weekly web fiction. In his latest endeavor, Robin finds himself shepherding the launch of a new fiction line from Stone Skin Press. Those interested in learning more about Robin are advised to check out his blog, a cavalcade of hobby games, film, culture, narrative structure, and gun-toting avians.

Glossary

All Pathfinder Tales novels are set in the rich and vibrant world of the Pathfinder campaign setting. Below are explanations of a number of key terms used in this book. For more information on the world of Golarion and the strange monsters, people, and deities that make it their home, see the *Pathfinder Roleplaying Game Core Rulebook* or any of the books in the Pathfinder Campaign Setting series, or visit **paizo.com**.

Abyss: A plane of evil and chaos ruled by demons.

Abyssal: Of or pertaining to the Abyss.

Antipaladin: A holy warrior who crusades on behalf of evil gods.

Aroden: Last hero of the Azlanti and God of Humanity, who raised the Starstone from the depths of the Inner Sea and founded the city of Absalom, becoming a living god in the process. Died mysteriously a hundred years ago, causing widespread chaos, particularly in Cheliax (which viewed him as its patron deity).

Azlant: The first human empire, which sank beneath the waves long ago.

Azlanti: Of or pertaining to Azlant.

Bogilar Fortress: Frontier fortress in Mendev, originally built by the cursed Bogilar clan.

Brevic: Of or pertaining to Brevoy.

Brevoy: A northern nation famous for its swordsmen.

Cheliax: Devil-worshiping nation in southwest Avistan.

Chelish: Of or relating to the nation of Cheliax.

Chesed: Port city in Numeria.

Demon: Denizens of the Abyss who seek only to maim, ruin, and feed.

Demonblood: A powerful drug with demon blood as its primary ingredient.

Demon Lord: A particularly powerful demon capable of granting magical powers to its followers. One of the rulers of the Abyss.

Deskari: The principle demon lord responsible for the demonic invasion through the Worldwound. Also known as the Lord of the Locust Host.

Druma: Extremely mercantile nation.

Dubrov: Small farm town in Mendev.

Dwarf: Short, stocky humanoids who excel at physical labor, mining, and craftsmanship. Stalwart enemies of the orcs and other evil subterranean monsters.

Egede: Mendevian port city on the edge of the Lake of Mists and Veils.

Egelsee River: River flowing through southern Mendev.

Elemental: Being of pure elemental energy, such as air, earth, fire, or water.

Elf: Long-lived, beautiful humanoids who abandoned Golarion before the fall of the Starstone and have only recently returned.

Estrovian Forest: Large forest in Mendev.

Gaffle: Mendevian slang for a con or swindle.

Gnome: Race of fey humanoids known for their small size, quick wit, and bizarre obsessions.

Golarion: The planet containing the nation of Mendev and the primary focus of the Pathfinder campaign setting.

Half-elf: Of human and elven descent, half-elves are often regarded as having the best qualities of both races, yet still see a certain amount of prejudice, particularly from their pure elven relations.

Halfling: Race of humanoids known for their tiny stature, deft hands, and mischievous personalities.

Half-orc: Bred from a human and an orc, members of this race are known for their green-to-gray skin tone, brutish appearance, and short tempers. Highly marginalized by most civilized societies.

Inner Sea Region: Collection of nations around the Inner Sea that trade with each other. Mendev is one of the most northern nations of this region.

Invidiak: Another name for shadow demons.

Iobaria: Region east of Mendev, across the Lake of Mists and Veils.

Iomedae: Goddess of valor, rulership, justice, and honor, who was a holy crusader in life before passing the Test of the Starstone and attaining godhood.

Kellid: Traditionally uncivilized and violent human ethnicity from northern Avistan.

Kenabres: Fortified crusader city along Mendev's border with the Worldwound. Currently the center of a radical, witch-hunting faction of Iomedae's faith.

Krega: Small town in Mendev.

Lord of the Locust Host: See entry for Deskari.

Mendev: Cold, northern crusader nation that provides the primary force defending the rest of the Inner Sea region from the demonic infestation of the Worldwound.

Mendevian: Of or pertaining to Mendev.

Mesz: Alchemical agent involved in the creation of demonblood.

Monastery of Tala: Multi-faith crusader monastery in Mendev.

Mwangi: Of or pertaining to the hot, southern jungle region known as the Mwangi Expanse.

Nerosyan: Fortress city and capital of Mendev, situated along the nation's southwestern border. Also called the Diamond of the North, after its shining towers and diamond-shaped layout.

Nerosyani: Of or pertaining to Nerosyan.

Nirmathas: Fledgling forest nation constantly at war with its former rulers.

Nirmathi: Of or pertaining to Nirmathas.

Numeria: Land of barbarians and strange alien technology harvested from a crashed starship near the nation's capital. Borders Mendev and the Worldwound.

Paladin: A holy warrior in the service of a good and lawful god, granted special magical powers by his or her deity.

Rip: Mendevian slang for a con or swindle.

Sarkoris: Northern nation destroyed and overrun by the Worldwound.

Sczarni: Criminal gangs of ethnic Varisians who live via swindling others; the primary reason for prejudice against Varisians.

Sellen River: Major river that flows through Mendev.

Shadow Demon: Type of demon made of shadows and without a solid physical form; able to possess mortals and control their actions.

Shelyn: Goddess of love and beauty.

Shudderwood: Forest running through Ustalav and the Worldwound.

Sorcerer: Spellcaster who draws power from a supernatural ancestor or other mysterious source, and does not need to study to cast spells.

Starstone: A magical stone that fell from the sky and was later raised from the ocean floor by the god Aroden. Has the power to turn mortals into gods.

Suma Castle: Frontier fortress in Mendev.

Ulfen: A race of Vikinglike humans from the cold nations of the north, primarily Irrisen and the Lands of the Linnorm Kings.

Urannag: Dangerous, semi-sentient hazards from the Abyss, which lie concealed in the hope of trapping and slaughtering prey that moves across them.

Varisian: Race of northern wanderers, entertainers, and tinkerers who travel in caravans and have strong family ties.

Wardstone: Magically imbued obelisks that line the Worldwound's border and help hold back the tide of demons.

Wizard: Spellcaster who masters the art through years of studying arcane lore.

Worldwound: Constantly expanding region overrun by demons following the death of Aroden. Held at bay by the efforts of the Mendevian crusaders.

Xa Hoi: Far eastern nation, so distant that few in Mendev have even heard of it.

Yath: Strange demonic tower-entity recently arisen in the Worldwound.

Zharech: Rough-and-tumble town in Mendev with popular gladiatorial events.

For half-elven Pathfinder Varian Jeggare and his devil-blooded bodyguard Radovan, things are rarely as they seem. Yet not even the notorious crime-solving duo are prepared for what they find when a search for a missing Pathfinder takes them into the gothic and mist-shrouded mountains of Ustalav.

Beset on all sides by noble intrigue, curse-afflicted villagers, suspicious monks, and the deadly creatures of the night, Varian and Radovan must use sword and spell to track the strange rumors to their source and uncover a secret of unimaginable proportions, aided in their quest by a pack of sinister werewolves and a mysterious, mute priestess. But it'll take more than merely solving the mystery to finish this job. For shadowy figures have taken note of the pair's investigations, and the forces of darkness are set on making sure neither man gets out of Ustalav alive . . .

From fan-favorite author Dave Gross, author of *Black Wolf* and *Lord of Stormweather*, comes a new fantastical mystery set in the award-winning world of the Pathfinder Roleplaying Game.

print edition: $9.99
ISBN: 978-1-60125-287-6

ebook edition: $6.99
ISBN: 978-1-60125-331-6

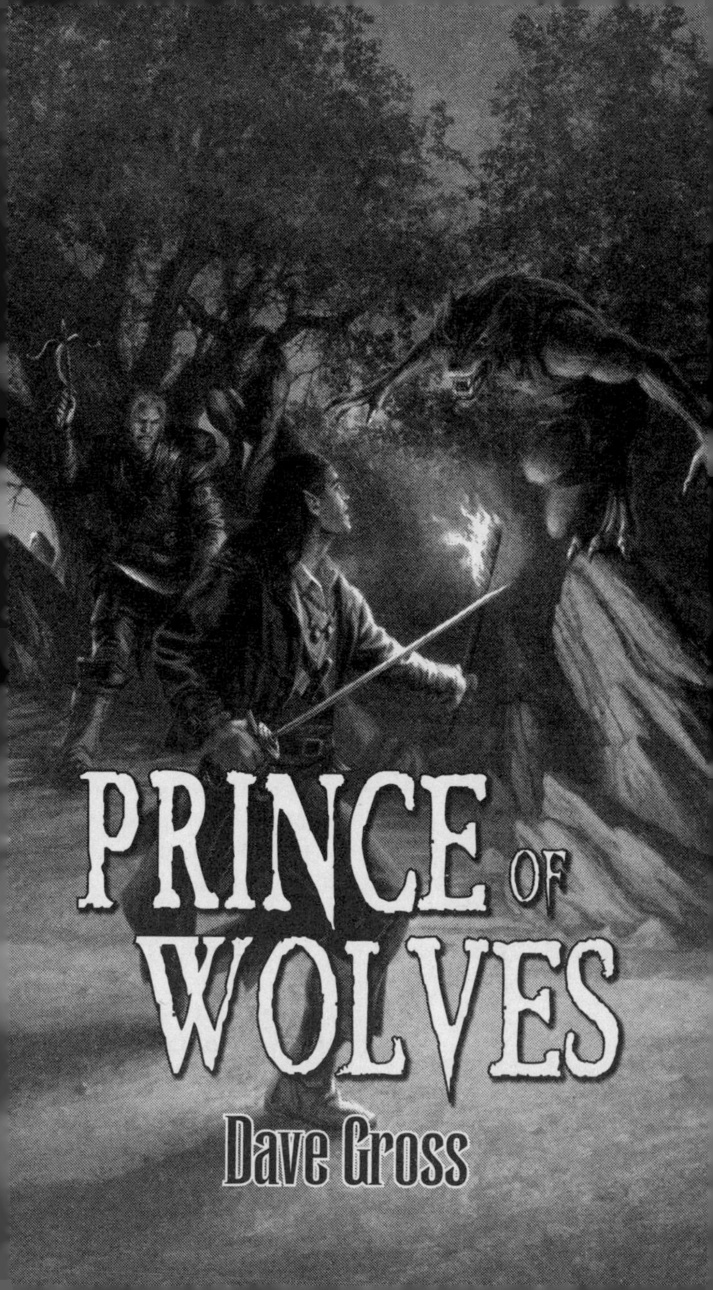
PRINCE OF WOLVES
Dave Gross

In a village of the frozen north, a child is born possessed by a strange and alien spirit, only to be cast out by her tribe and taken in by the mysterious winter witches of Irrisen, a land locked in permanent magical winter. Farther south, a young mapmaker with a penchant for forgery discovers that his sham treasure maps have begun striking gold.

This is the story of Ellasif, a barbarian shield maiden who will stop at nothing to recover her missing sister, and Declan, the ne'er-do-well young spellcaster-turned-forger who wants only to prove himself to the woman he loves. Together they'll face monsters, magic, and the fury of Ellasif's own cold-hearted warriors in their quest to rescue the lost child. Yet when they finally reach the ice-walled city of Whitethrone, where trolls hold court and wolves roam the streets in human guise, will it be too late to save the girl from the forces of darkness?

From *New York Times* best seller Elaine Cunningham comes a fantastic new adventure of swords and sorcery, set in the award-winning world of the Pathfinder Roleplaying Game.

print edition: $9.99
ISBN: 978-1-60125-286-9

ebook edition: $6.99
ISBN: 978-1-60125-332-3

Winter Witch

Elaine Cunningham

The race is on to free Lord Stelan from the grip of a wasting curse, and only his old mercenary companion, the Forsaken elf Elyana, has the wisdom—and the swordcraft—to uncover the identity of his tormenter and free her old friend before the illness takes its course.

When the villain turns out to be another of their former companions, Elyana sets out with a team of adventurers including Stelan's own son on a dangerous expedition across the revolution-wracked nation of Galt and the treacherous Five Kings Mountains. There, pursued by a bloodthirsty militia and beset by terrible nightmare beasts, they discover the key to Stelan's salvation in a lost valley warped by weird magical energies. Yet will they be able to retrieve the artifact the dying lord so desperately needs? Or will the shadowy face of betrayal rise up from within their own ranks?

From Howard Andrew Jones, managing editor of the acclaimed sword and sorcery magazine *Black Gate*, comes a classic quest of loyalty and magic set in the award-winning world of the Pathfinder Roleplaying Game.

print edition: $9.99
ISBN: 978-1-60125-291-3

ebook edition: $6.99
ISBN: 978-1-60125-333-0

Plague of Shadows

Howard Andrew Jones

On a mysterious errand for the Pathfinder Society, Count Varian Jeggare and his hellspawn bodyguard Radovan journey to the distant land of Tian Xia. When disaster forces him to take shelter in a warrior monastery, "Brother" Jeggare finds himself competing with the disciples of the Dragon Temple as he unravels a royal mystery. Meanwhile, Radovan—trapped in the body of a devil and held hostage by the legendary Quivering Palm attack—must serve a twisted master by defeating the land's deadliest champions and learning the secret of slaying an immortal foe. Together with an unlikely army of beasts and spirits, the two companions must take the lead in an ancient conflict that will carry them through an exotic land all the way to the Gates of Heaven and Hell and a final confrontation with the nefarious Master of Devils.

From fan-favorite author Dave Gross comes a new fantastical adventure set in the award-winning world of the Pathfinder Roleplaying Game.

print edition: $9.99
ISBN: 978-60125-357-6

ebook edition: $6.99
ISBN: 978-60125-358-3

Master of Devils

Dave Gross

NOVELS!

Tired of carting around a bag full of books? Take your e-reader or smart phone over to **paizo.com** to download all the Pathfinder Tales novels from authors like Dave Gross and *New York Times* best seller Elaine Cunningham in both ePub and PDF formats, thus saving valuable bookshelf space and 30% off the cover price!

PATHFINDER'S JOURNALS!

Love the fiction in the Adventure Paths, but don't want to haul six books with you on the subway? Download compiled versions of each fully illustrated journal and read it on whatever device you chose!

FREE WEB FICTION!

Tired of paying for fiction at all? Drop by **paizo.com** every week for your next installment of free weekly web fiction as Paizo serializes new Pathfinder short stories from your favorite high-profile fantasy authors. Read 'em for free, or download 'em for cheap and read them anytime, anywhere!

ALL AVAILABLE NOW AT PAIZO.COM!

PATHFINDER

CAMPAIGN SETTING

THE INNER SEA WORLD GUIDE

You've delved into the Pathfinder campaign setting with Pathfinder Tales novels—now take your adventures even further! *The Inner Sea World Guide* is a full-color, 320-page hardback guide featuring everything you need to know about the exciting world of Pathfinder: overviews of every major nation, religion, race, and adventure location around the Inner Sea, plus a giant poster map! Read it as a travelogue, or use it to flesh out your roleplaying game—it's your world now!

EXPLORE YOUR WORLD!

paizo.com

"AS YOU TURN AROUND, YOU SPOT SIX DARK SHAPES MOVING UP BEHIND YOU. AS THEY ENTER THE LIGHT, YOU CAN TELL THAT THEY'RE SKELETONS, WEARING RUSTING ARMOR AND WAVING ANCIENT SWORDS."

Lem: Guys, I think we have a problem.

GM: You do indeed. Can I get everyone to roll initiative?

To determine the order of combat, each player rolls a d20 and adds his or her initiative bonus. The GM rolls once for the skeletons.

GM: Seelah, you have the highest initiative. It's your turn.

Seelah: I'm going to attempt to destroy them using the power of my goddess, Iomedae. I channel positive energy.

Seelah rolls 2d6 and gets a 7.

GM: Two of the skeletons burst into flames and crumble as the power of your deity washes over them. The other four continue their advance. Harsk, it's your turn.

Harsk: Great. I'm going to fire my crossbow!

Harsk rolls a d20 and gets a 13. He adds that to his bonus on attack rolls with his crossbow and announces a total of 22. The GM checks the skeleton's Armor Class, which is only a 14.

GM: That's a hit. Roll for damage.

Harsk rolls a d10 and gets an 8. The skeleton's damage reduction reduces the damage from 8 to 3, but it's still enough.

GM: The hit was hard enough to cause that skeleton's ancient bones to break apart. Ezren, it's your turn.

Ezren: I'm going to cast *magic missile* at a skeleton.

Magic missile creates glowing darts that always hit their target. Ezren rolls 1d4+1 for each missile and gets a total of 6. It automatically bypasses the skeleton's DR, dropping another one.

GM: There are only two skeletons left, and it's their turn. One of them charges up to Seelah and takes a swing at her, while the other moves up to Harsk and attacks.

The GM rolls a d20 for each attack. The attack against Seelah is only an 8, which is less than her AC of 18. The attack against Harsk is a 17, which beats his AC of 16. The GM rolls damage.

GM: The skeleton hits you, Harsk, leaving a nasty cut on your upper arm. Take 7 points of damage.

Harsk: Ouch. I have 22 hit points left.

GM: That's not all. Charging out of the fog onto the bridge is a skeleton dressed like a knight, riding the bones of a long-dead horse, and with severed heads impaled on its deadly lance. Lem, it's your turn—what do you do?

Lem: Run!

NOW IT'S YOUR TURN . . .

CHART YOUR OWN ADVENTURE!

The PATHFINDER ROLEPLAYING GAME puts you in the role of a brave adventurer fighting to survive in a fantastic world beset by magic and evil!

Take on the role of a canny fighter hacking through enemies with an enchanted sword, a powerful sorceress with demon blood in her veins, a wise cleric of mysterious gods, a wily rogue ready to defuse even the deadliest of traps, or any of countless other heroes. The only limit is your imagination!

The massive 576-page *Pathfinder RPG Core Rulebook* provides all the tools you need to get your hero into the action! One player assumes the role of the Game Master, challenging players with dastardly dungeons or monstrous selections from the more than 350 beasts included in the *Pathfinder RPG Bestiary*!

The PATHFINDER ROLEPLAYING GAME is a fully supported tabletop roleplaying game, with regularly released adventure modules, sourcebooks on the fantastic world of Golarion, and complete campaigns in the form of Pathfinder Adventure Paths like Kingmaker and Serpent's Skull!

Begin your adventure today in the game section of quality bookstores or hobby game shops, or online at **paizo.com**!

Pathfinder RPG Core Rulebook • $49.99
ISBN 978-1-60125-150-3

PLANET

stories

HIDDEN WORLDS AND ANCIENT MYSTERIES

EXPLORE NEW WORLDS WITH

PLANET STORIES

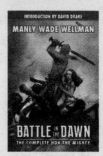

Strap on your jet pack and set out for unforgettable adventure with PLANET STORIES, Paizo Publishing's science fiction and fantasy imprint! Personally selected by Paizo's editorial staff, PLANET STORIES presents timeless classics from authors like Gary Gygax (Dungeons & Dragons), Robert E. Howard (Conan the Barbarian), Michael Moorcock (Elric), and Leigh Brackett (*The Empire Strikes Back*) alongside groundbreaking anthologies and fresh adventures from the best imaginations in the genre, all introduced by superstar authors such as China Miéville, George Lucas, and Ben Bova.

With new releases six times a year, PLANET STORIES promises the best two-fisted adventure this side of the galactic core! Find them at your local bookstore, or subscribe online at **paizo.com**!